INDESTRUCTIBLE

Book 3
Harmony Series

INDESTRUCTIBLE

Book 3
Harmony Series

Angela Graham

Copyright 2014, Angela Graham
Editor—Jen Juneau
Cover Design—Sommer Stein
Formatter—Joni Wilson

All Rights Reserved.
This book may not be reproduced in any form,
in whole or in part,
without written permission from the author.

Contents

Prologue 1
Chapter One—Reality 3
Chapter Two—Heat Wave 16
Chapter Three—Cleanse 28
Chapter Four—Nightmares 39
Chapter Five—Misconceptions 50
Chapter Six—Bliss 66
Chapter Seven—Loyalty 78
Chapter Eight—Surprises 89
Chapter Nine—Performance 101
Chapter Ten—Suspicious 114
Chapter Eleven—Regrets 130
Chapter Twelve—Enigmas 144
Chapter Thirteen—Calamities 161
Chapter Fourteen—Tension 170
Chapter Fifteen—Frozen 184
Chapter Sixteen—Downhill 196
Chapter Seventeen—Power 207
Chapter Eighteen—Running 220
Chapter Nineteen—Searching 231
Chapter Twenty—Priorities 247
Chapter Twenty-One—Frenemies 262
Chapter Twenty-Two—Truth 275
Chapter Twenty-Three—Control 287

Chapter Twenty-Four—Spurned 297
Chapter Twenty-Five—Collide 305
Chapter Twenty-Six—Dare... 316
Chapter Twenty-Seven—Hunger.. 329
Chapter Twenty-Eight—Progress...................................... 337
Chapter Twenty-Nine—Family.. 351
Chapter Thirty—Played.. 362
Chapter Thirty-One—Together 374
Chapter Thirty-Two—Bravery 385
Epilogue.. 395
The End.. 401
About the Author 402
Connect with the Author.. 403
Acknowledgments... 404
While You're Waiting.. 407
Chapter 3 Excerpt from *Pretty Instinct*................................ 408

Prologue

I was still a young girl when I learned that not every penny tossed in a fountain or plea with a shooting star would grant me a wish, and that not every story ends in a happily ever after. And as discouraging as that revelation was, it never deterred me from holding out hope.

Hope for the dream—for the fairytale. For the prince charming who'd storm into my life on a great white steed, pluck me from obscurity, and carry me away to his castle. Perhaps it was wishful thinking of an overactive imagination, but I still spent countless nights lying under the stars, fantasizing about a beautiful man who'd someday capture my heart. The prince who would adore me—a man strong enough to create the storybook-perfect world I longed for.

I'd read all about great loves and tragic romances, and knew that with every enchanted tale came challenges: those nasty hurdles in the road that delayed but rarely prevented the charmed finale. It was expected, and as I grew older, I saw the excitement in dreaming of what I'd do for the right man…what he'd do for me, and for my love.

And while there may not have been any swordfights or fiery dragons to slay, since the morning Logan West jogged into my life, I knew my world would never be the same again.

Logan was my prince; he found me, and was worth

everything I had to give—my love, my respect, and above all, my trust.

Epic ending or not, this was our story…and one I'd cherish until my final breath.

Chapter One

REALITY

My home, once my sanctuary, was now a chaotic scene of dedicated officers, continuous streams of monotone voices exchanging tedious facts, and the occasional snap of a camera. And then there was me, dazed, in the center of it all. Logan stepped into the hall, tucking me closer against his side, my hands clutching his bloodied shirt.

Mixed into the congested air were Kurt's agonized whimpers. They echoed around us as the paramedics rolled him past on a stretcher. I couldn't look at him; instead, I buried my face against Logan's chest, focusing solely on his soothing heartbeat and protective warmth that sheltered me.

The front door slammed shut and my entire body jerked, but Logan held me closer.

"It's okay," he murmured against my ear. "He's gone."

The paralyzing adrenaline buzzing through my veins began to settle, easing the tension in my shell-shocked muscles.

"Miss, I'm sorry, but we need to have the paramedic assess your injuries before we can do anything else. Is there a private room we can use?"

Miss?

I knew that voice. I lifted my head sluggishly and peered

up at the familiar uniformed man standing before me.

My brows pinched together, and all I could do was stare blankly at the officer who, as a boy, had mowed my grandparents' grass every summer. I was Cassie to him then, and so desperately wanted to be again—not 'miss'. I supposed a friendly greeting would be unprofessional considering the circumstances, but the lack of it only added to my wounds. I wanted to be me, not some victim.

My shoulders slumped as I peeled myself from Logan.

I blinked then swallowed, clearing the dryness from my throat as I swam back to the cruel reality awaiting me.

"Yeah, there's a guest room down the hall," I said finally. Speaking took some energy, but I even managed a small, albeit tight, smile as I gestured toward the room. I could do this.

He nodded, watching me for a moment with sympathy or perhaps pity before turning toward the room.

With my hand locked around Logan's, I took a step, then another, each one forcing me into the here and now. This was real life—*my* life—and there was no hiding, or denying what had happened. I had just been attacked. There was no dream or nightmare to blame—only the psychotic nature of another human being. *I'm lucky, thanks to Logan*, I reminded myself.

But as I took the third step, it hit me like a slug to the chest. Fear ripped at my gut, stopping me cold in my tracks. I tore myself from Logan's grip, feeling panic set in as I clutched his shirt and dragged my wide-eyed gaze up to meet his crinkled brow.

"Scout!" I all but cried. *Oh God, where is he?* "Have you seen him?" I asked, but I didn't wait for Logan's answer. His expression said it all.

"Scout!" I shouted more loudly, turning and running back toward the living room. "Scout! Come here, boy!"

"Cassandra…"

"Scout! Come here. Come on!" I weaved frantically and carelessly through the officers crowding the rooms, pushing them aside. I only had one goal: Find my pup.

I stopped abruptly at the back door, my pulse pounding at the sight. Shattered glass littered the floor, and the kicked-in bottom was completely demolished. A sharp intake of breath cleared my invading memory of Kurt. Then, with determined steps, I crossed the threshold.

Snow tumbled around me in a thick flurry, the temperature barely above freezing. With my arms wrapped around my middle, I scanned the snow blanket covering the backyard.

"Scout!"

"Cassandra." Logan's solid arms encircled my waist, lifting me from behind and carrying me back inside quickly.

I whipped around to face him, fiery tears in my eyes.

"Where is he? Did you see him?" I asked, shaking. *Please, please let him be okay.* I tried to remember if I'd seen him during the attack, but it was all still a blur.

Logan closed the door slowly, his expression heavy with contemplation.

"What!? Where is he!?" Tears streamed out as I clutched his arms for support. "Did that bastard hurt him? Oh, God!" I couldn't breathe. *No! No, no, no—not Scout!*

Logan cupped my cheeks gently, holding my attention.

"He must have gotten out, that's all. Wherever he is, he's safe now."

Logan's voice was calming—almost like a sedative. I eased into it as I felt tears drying against my skin. It was too painful to feel everything waiting under the surface, ready to explode. I had to push it away, had to stay strong.

"I'll call Jax. He'll find him," Logan added, stepping back and letting his fingers skim down to my forearms.

As numbness set in, I wiped my eyes and whispered, "Thank you."

He's safe. He's safe, I chanted in my head. It was all I could think about as Logan led me back through the crime scene inside. It felt like anything but home.

"Can you call him now?" I asked, stopping outside the guest-bedroom door, reluctant to go inside knowing Scout was out there somewhere alone and cold. "Please."

After a soft kiss to my forehead, Logan pulled his phone from his pocket and held the door open for me to enter. "Of course. I'll be just a moment."

With an appreciative nod, I entered the room alone. It was small and cramped, and held a chilly undercurrent despite the dry heat pumping through the floor vent.

I sat on the bed in silence as a woman in front of me opened her bag and began digging through it, pulling out multiple mystery items. I stared past her, allowing myself an escape into a foreign world of darkness. It held no pain or relief—only a vast, empty hole where my emotions should've been erupting but were instead eerily still.

I remained lost there, disconnecting myself from reality, until a sharp sting radiated through my cheek.

"Ah." I winced, jerking my head out of the paramedic's hold.

She finished applying a bandage below my left eye, then pulled back. "Sorry," she said, her voice devoid of emotion. The young paramedic—Tara, I believed she'd said—had been all business from the moment she'd entered the room seconds after me.

My knee bounced up and down, my agitation rising the longer I was forced to sit with a stranger touching me.

Seamlessly, she opened another tiny bandage and brought it closer until it disappeared from my line of sight, positioning it directly above the other. The sting was brief as the wound was covered efficiently, then she was back to rummaging through her bag.

Needing something to lean against, I tucked a pillow behind my back. My body was exhausted and preparing to shut down, yet my mind was restless.

"Try to relax, miss." Her gaze fixed on my fingers drumming against my thighs.

Miss. There it was again. I despised the term. And relax? *Right!*

I stilled my hands, stretching out my fingers.

Okay, maybe I was less composed than I'd realized, but considering the day's events it was as calm as I was capable of being. I'd been sitting there for far too long, or so it felt, and my body was buzzing in protest. I closed my eyes and inhaled through my nostrils, hoping time would offer its assistance and speed the hell up.

I tucked my bottom lip between my teeth. *Why is this taking so long?* It was only a few scrapes.

Unable to find any peace, I opened my eyes and watched as Tara examined my face closely before producing a smaller black kit. The overwhelming need to bolt shook my body. Not out of fear; no, I wasn't scared. Perhaps Kurt had drained all the fear from my system. Instead, I was worried.

The strangest thought came over me. I found myself wracked with anxiety over having a disfiguring scar on my face—a reminder I'd be confronted with every time I passed a mirror or took a simple photograph, just like the one on my leg. It was such a superficial thought in the grand scheme of things, yet it was still there in my mind, front and center.

Where were my pain, anger, the need to scream and cry…anything? I felt them for Scout, but for myself, these emotions were replaced simply by a numbing void in my chest.

Was that better than suffering through the emotions?

I clamped my eyes shut again and forced forward the memory of the branch slicing through my skin as I raced through the forest. The images came easy, but the traumatizing effect I expected to endure remained absent.

The muscles in my legs ached. I had run faster than I thought possible in those woods, sprinting as quickly as my feet could carry me, terrorized in the moment and severely aware of Kurt trailing behind. His menacing cackle and booming voice had ricocheted around me, reciting a horrific list of heinous acts he planned to inflict upon me if I slowed.

"I need you to stay still," Tara said, snapping me back to the present. She took my arm and began cleaning the scrapes. "Try some deep breaths; it will help calm you."

"I *am* calm!" The instant the words flew out, my head dropped and my cheeks flushed with embarrassment.

I couldn't breathe. This wasn't me. This wasn't fair. She had been nothing but lovely, and didn't deserve the brunt of my temper.

I straightened myself, searching for the right words. "I'm sorry, I just...need some fresh air," I explained.

She peeked up. "I'll try to hurry."

"The heater in here's been needing to be replaced," I explained, trying for a friendly conversation. Maybe that would help pass time, as well. "It's older than I am, and it gets to me after a while. Runs hotter than I set it."

"I just had mine repaired last winter. Expensive beast." She cracked a tiny smile, confirming there were no hard feelings. "Almost done."

I rose up just the slightest to slide my clammy palms under me, attempting to remain as still as possible for her.

"All right," she finally said, turning to toss something in the trash. "Now I need to get a better look at your stomach.

Mr. West explained you have some injuries there, as well."

I glanced up at the door and found him there, standing stoically quiet, watching with a tight frown frozen over his features. I hadn't even noticed he was there. His eyes were on me, his lips curled into a tender but sympathetic smile that eased a few of the nerves I felt at the thought of my stomach.

How could I forget? How was it that, until that very moment, I couldn't feel the pain of it?

"It's nothing," I choked out, lowering my gaze, unable to fully look at either of them.

My posture stiffened almost painfully and must have spoken more loudly than the words that had left my mouth, because Tara's stern approach softened. She tilted her head to catch my downward stare.

"Listen, I know you want this to be over with, but I can't leave until I confirm your injuries have been fully assessed and treated to the best of my ability."

"Cassandra," Logan spoke in a hard whisper.

With a relenting sigh and stiff hand, I held onto the end of the belt on the white robe Logan had covered me with earlier.

I knew from the pained expression on his striking face that he wanted to be closer instead of standing across the room, but the space was too narrow. I could clearly see anger written in his tense shoulders, and I honestly believed his pain for me outweighed my own. And even though I couldn't touch him, there was no denying the strength I drew from him being there for me.

"Do you mind giving us some privacy?" Tara asked, glancing over her shoulder at Logan.

My gaze caught his and never strayed as he answered her, his voice grave. "I'm not leaving her again."

"You can wait in the hall, sir."

Their conversation faded away when I blinked, breaking our connection, my mind focusing on the belt sliding between my fingers. I finally began to feel more than agitation. The blood rippling through my veins grew louder and louder as I allowed myself to feel the tenderness over my stomach. I knew it was sore, but for the first time I was really feeling it.

I felt the glass shattering over me as I wrestled to escape my vehicle. Kurt's vice-like grip locked around my ankle, hauling me toward him. I shuddered at the memory of the shards that covered the seat, digging into my skin.

"Cassandra." Logan's sweet breath brushed over my lips. "Look at me. Open your eyes."

Are they closed?

My lids fluttered open as I lifted my head listlessly and inhaled a shaky breath. He was so close and so perfect, squatting down in front of me.

"I'll be fine. Is Jax looking for Scout?" I asked, changing the subject while attempting a smile. But it couldn't cover the unexpected faintness in my voice.

"Yeah, he's on it."

"Thank you. And she's right, you can wait outside." My shoulders rose. "You know—privacy and all."

He leaned forward and placed a chaste kiss to my lips. "There's nothing about you I ever want hidden from me. Besides, I've already seen what you're trying to cover, and there's no reason for that. You're as beautiful now as you were this morning."

My smile grew.

"I'm staying. She'll get over it."

"Logan, you're so good to me." I placed another kiss on his lips. "Please just wait outside—for me." I gave his hand a squeeze.

A moment passed between us; silent words of comfort.

"If that's what you want, of course. I'll be on the other side of that door if you need me."

I nodded, grateful he was stowing away his tenacious personality for once.

"I love you," he mouthed before righting himself and walking out with hesitant steps.

Once the door was shut behind him, I lay back, stretching out my legs and resting my head on the pillow. Tara opened the robe fully to reveal my hidden injuries, and then, in the most unaffected tone possible, explained that there was some glass she needed to remove—remnants of the attack left behind inside me.

I closed my eyes to block it out, but it was becoming real. My defenses were cracking.

No, no, no. I'd rather be numb than a crying mess. Not again. I sucked in a deep breath, filling my lungs and chanting in my head, *I'm stronger than this. I'm stronger than this.*

The slivers she extracted were nothing compared to the assaulting images striving to burst through my chant and confront my defenses. I didn't want to deal, didn't want to understand. I just wanted the day to end.

But what I wanted didn't seem to matter. The memory of Kurt's grimy claws caused my gut to roll—his brutal hands forcing me onto the floor, his elbow shoved against my back.

I'm stronger than this. Stronger. So much stronger.

I shielded my face with my arms, stifling a sob—not from fear or trauma, but anger. For the first time since the attack, I felt a swelling ache between my shoulder blades that I was certain was the beginning of a nasty bruise. Worst of all was the touch of him, his bare skin pressed to mine. *He had no right!* My body had endured enough in the accident only two months earlier, and now it was happening again.

'Angry' wasn't the right word for what I was feeling in

that moment. I was pissed.

I wiped the tear prickling my eye before it could sneak out, then leapt up to a seated position. That bastard wouldn't reduce me to tears—not here, not yet.

"Cassandra, I need to finish."

My eyes met Tara's, and whatever she saw there caused her determination to waver. She pulled away, reached into her bag, and held out a tube of ointment.

"Here, put this over the wounds twice daily. You don't need stitches. All the glass is out, and it didn't embed deep. You can take Tylenol for the soreness and any aches you have, unless it becomes worse."

"Thank you."

Finally ready to really see, I looked down at my stomach. It was bright red, and covered with a few abrasions spread over what looked like a nasty case of rug burn.

Tara pulled off her gloves and tossed them in the trash. "You're all set. If you need anything else, don't hesitate to come into the ER or call your doctor."

I closed the robe and offered an appreciative smile.

She mimicked me and stood, crossing the room to the door where Logan, as promised, was standing on the other side. The instant she passed him he was beside me, his fingers interlocking with mine.

"Cassandra," he breathed, pulling me up and into his arms for an embrace. It was something we both needed.

"I want so badly to restart this day...anything to bring back the light in your eyes, the smile to those beautiful lips." He kissed the side of my head. "I should have been here. Should have known he was out. Should have..." His body began to stiffen.

Logan was the last person that should've felt guilt. I held him closer, locking my arms around his waist as I shook my head, silencing him. The scruff of his cheek drew me closer. I inhaled his heady scent and rested my head on his broad shoulder, his voice breaking through our heavy silence after a moment's pause.

"I want to take you away from here. Christ, if I could erase what happened—" He released a pained sigh then pulled back slowly, his eyes searching mine.

"You have to know by now I'd do anything, Cassandra. I can't bear the thought of you hurting and not being able to have you to myself right now—to comfort you the way you deserve. But I'm here...whatever you need, whatever you want. Say the words, and I'll take care of it. I'll take care of you. It's all I want to do...always."

"I know." I balanced up on my toes and placed my lips against his. "And I love you for that."

He kissed me back, but it was restrained and swift as a voice interrupted us.

"Miss Clarke, the—oh, I'm sorry. Excuse me."

Logan and I both turned toward the officer, who ducked out of the room as quickly as he'd strolled in.

"I think they're waiting on us," I said, staring back up into the brilliant depths of emotion in his eyes. It was paralyzing.

His free hand caressed my cheek, tucking a stray hair behind my ear. "They need your statement. If—"

"I'm ready," I interrupted, not wanting to overthink it. There was no way to avoid giving the report to the sheriff. It had to be done. Kurt had to be punished.

Logan watched me, gauging the emotions he was expecting to see, but I had nothing to offer him. It was time to recite all the facts out loud—to get it on paper and move on.

Logan cupped my face. "If you need time or..."

I shook my head. "No. I want to get it over with." *I need to get it over with.*

A faint smile touched his lips. "Always so strong." His thumbs traced the contours of my cheeks. I closed my eyes and leaned into his comforting touch.

Logan had become, in such a short time, the only person who was able to lift me up when I was down so low. It was a discovery I cherished.

"I'm here, sweetheart." He pressed a soft, tender kiss to my lips. "We'll get through this. I promise."

I knew we would. I believed in him—in us.

With his hand settled on the small of my back, he guided me out of the room. We proceeded down the hall toward the end, where my bedroom was located.

The door was destroyed, its remnants left still hanging from the hinges. As our steps grew closer, the voices and shadows of officers inside gripped my attention. The click of a camera rang through my ears and sent a shiver down my spine. It was like being in a horror movie.

We continued walking, turning the corner into the living room. As we did, I glanced into my room to catch sight of the blood stain on the floor—the floor Kurt had held me down against, his body pressed against mine. His erection...

I slammed my eyes shut to push the memory away and shook my head, quickening my steps.

"Hey, you don't have to do this yet," Logan whispered, stopping abruptly and moving in front of me. He lifted my chin. "They'll understand."

"I need to," I murmured.

"Cassandra," a familiar voice said. I looked past Logan to find the burly man with a receding hairline I'd known since childhood: the deputy sheriff and my mother's boss, Harry Mackwell.

He opened his arms and I walked straight into them. Harry had always smelled of warm spice, and today I sought comfort in it.

"How are you?" he asked when I stepped back.

"You know me," I replied coyly as Logan slipped his hand back in mine.

"I do." Harry gave a somber nod, then looked over to Logan. "I hate to jump right into it, but if you don't mind, I'd like to speak to this young man first."

"Of course." I peeked up at Logan.

"I'll be back," he assured me, his fingers slipping from mine as he followed Harry into the kitchen.

Unsure what to do, I sat on the sofa and watched as men and women in uniforms, some I knew, carried on around me. It was my house now and where I'd spent most of my childhood, yet I'd never felt more disconnected from it than I did in that moment.

Nothing felt real or whole. I was simply living, breathing, and waiting.

Chapter Two

Heat Wave

The longer I sat, the harder my eyes struggled to remain open. Logan and Harry had been in the other room for over thirty minutes. I knew that only because I'd watched every second tick by on the clock sitting on the table that once held photos, which were now scattered on the floor.

A kitchen chair squeaked, sliding against the linoleum. Heavy footsteps followed, and then Logan was there, sitting beside me. I sat up, snapping out of my trance and wiping my eyes to stay awake.

It's my turn.

With a slight tilt of my head in his direction, I forced a smile. He saw through me and lifted my hand, covering it with his before bringing it to his lips. Anticipating a peck to my knuckles, I relished the touch of his lips pressed to my skin. He closed his eyes and inhaled deeply, savoring it himself. The affectionate act soothed my tensions, and I believed his as well.

Harry sat across from us, his solemn gaze fixed on the notepad he held. When he raised his head, a commanding power emanated from him.

"I'm going to try and keep this as brief and straightforward as possible, Cassandra, but I need to know all the details for us to properly prosecute the case. I know how strong you are." A hint of a smile eased the heaviness of his words. "A lot like your mother. So let's get through this, and then I'll have my officers out of your home. All right?"

I bobbed my head awkwardly, unsure where to start. What *were* the details? My thoughts were a flurry of bits and pieces in no particular order. I needed to think back to the beginning, but all I saw was Kurt standing outside my car, reeking of resentment and hatred, and then his fist smashing the window. The snow I'd run through was deep and cold and the forest was viscous, wicked branches blocking my way as my feet trudged forward as fast as they could.

I recoiled, breathless, and stared at Harry. A sweltering, suffocating heat suddenly infiltrated my trembling limbs. I squirmed, suddenly uncomfortable in my own skin. *Is anyone else feeling this?*

Logan held our interlaced fingers protectively above his heart and gave mine a supportive squeeze. I peered his way and was met with cool, deep aqua eyes so soft and full of concern that I wanted desperately to relieve.

I traced my thumb over his knuckles absentmindedly and then looked back at Harry, who sat waiting patiently.

"I saw him in the grocery store—the one on Main Street." I shook my head. "Well, I guess there's only one grocery store, huh? So you know where it is already. At least…only one in town, only one I go to," I said, rambling like a fool. "I don't care much for the big-box store they built down the road. My mom does. I think it's too crowded…too many options, and honestly, I felt like I was cheating when I went—you know, like I'm not supposed to be there. I can't stand the thought of being responsible for closing down a local business that I've shopped at my entire life just to save a buck." I wiped my brow; Harry was just staring at me.

Crap, he probably shops there. What am I even talking about?

"Anyway, like I said, my mom shops there and loves it. Says it's worth the drive. She doesn't make much money, so she needs to save that buck. I mean, not that the station doesn't pay her well. You do. She loves her job, really—never has a bad word to say." I let out a short, broken chuckle. "Well, except for this one time at a Christmas party you threw. She said that—"

Logan's finger pressed to my lips, silencing me. *Thank God!*

"Breathe, then tell him about what happened with Kurt."

My head nodded for way too long. What the hell had I been about to tell him? My mom would've killed me.

"Right. Anyway, I...I s-saw him—I mean, h-he saw me," I stuttered. *Pull it together.* "I'm not sure who saw who first."

I wiped away the sweat that had begun beading at the back of my neck. Why was this so hard? I didn't even recognize myself.

Harry looked as confused as I felt. "You did or did not see him at the *local* grocery store?"

"I didn't." *God, I'm burning up.* I scrubbed my hand over my forehead, then it slid down between my throat and the fabric of the suffocating robe.

Okay, think. Stay focused.

Harry leaned forward, appraising me. "Would you like a glass of water?"

"Yes, please. I'm sorry, it's just so hot in here." I lifted my hair from my neck, twisting it over my shoulder. "The damn furnace." I huffed out an awkward laugh. *Not helping.*

Harry stood and walked into the kitchen. Did he know where the glasses were? I guessed he'd find them.

"Hey, you okay? You're shaking." Logan shifted to face me. He released my hand, his eyes growing wider as I tugged at my robe, needing airflow to calm the flames within.

"Just hot. Aren't you?"

Logan was still dressed in his work suit, but his jacket was missing and tie was loosened. He looked perfect, as usual, but there was no way he wasn't experiencing the same extreme heat.

"It's a little warm in here, but you're…you don't look well." His fingers brushed over my blazing cheeks. Closing his eyes with a poorly suppressed groan, he stood. His features hardened, and suddenly there was undeniable anger written across his face.

But why? I was fine—just severely overheated.

"That's it. I'm telling him you'll come to the station tomorrow. You need to rest—depressurize."

"No." I ran my hand down my chest, fanning the flames. "Can you just turn down the temperature?"

He shot me a crazed look. "Cassandra, that's not the furnace, that's you. You need to take some time. Get some sleep, and then you can give the statement."

"It's best if we take it now," Harry interjected as he reentered the room and offered me a glass of cold water.

Oh, thank God. I chugged a big gulp to douse my internal fire. Relief flooded my system.

"While it's still fresh in her mind," he continued. "I know this is difficult. There's no rush. Take all the time you need, but it has to be today." Harry sat back in his seat and pulled out a pen and notepad. His eyes were on me; they were full of kindness, and I knew he'd wait all night if he had to. "I'll be ready when you are."

I turned my gaze upward to Logan's, pleading silently for him to sit back down. Looking anywhere but at me, he raked his fingers through his hair and sucked in a breath so deep his nostrils flared. After a long pause, he conceded. The instant he sat, he folded his hand over mine and held it on his lap once again—exactly where it belonged.

I finished my water and set the empty glass on the coffee table.

"Okay, I'm ready."

Harry readied his pen.

"I felt someone watching me at the grocery store. I didn't see who it was, but Kurt told me he saw me there. He said it was a coincidence."

Harry jotted in his notepad and looked back up at me. "We can check security cameras. What happened next?"

I drew in a breath to fill my lungs and began reciting the events of the attack, my eyes cast down to the belt of my robe the entire time. The heat returned, searing my stiff body in place. I couldn't even lift my head to peek at Logan, but the fury radiating off him was evident.

"Kurt was mad at me. He blamed me for…" I stopped, remembering his words about Logan paying off guards.

"Blamed you for what?" Harry pressed.

I tucked that secret away and lifted my head. "For his arrest outside Haven."

Harry wrote it down, seemingly convinced, and continued with more questions that left me uncomfortable and fidgeting under the pressure to relive the events so soon.

"I'm sorry I have to ask this, Cassandra, but it's important." The sheriff's brows dipped as he glanced from me to Logan, then back at me. "Did he sexually assault you?"

I shook my head without thinking, not wanting to reveal those details, and bit down hard on my bottom lip. Logan's hand grasped mine tighter; I moved to pull it away, but his grip didn't falter.

My scalp prickled, my entire body scorching from the heat of what I wanted to avoid. My throat went dry; all attempts to swallow and clear it were in vain.

"No," I answered hoarsely. "He tried, but Logan arrived in time to…to intervene. He didn't rape—" My breath cut off.

"Yes, but was there sexual *assault?*" Harry asked, choosing his words carefully.

The shock of what I'd been trying to deny was setting in slowly. I wasn't raped, but I was terrified, threatened, and hurt by what Kurt had almost done—what had almost happened.

Almost. A pounding began in my temple, cruel emotions seeping through.

"I don't know." I shook my head again, willing the tears away. *No, I can't crack.* I didn't want to feel it yet. I preferred the numbness.

Logan dropped my hand and released an exasperated, drawn-out breath, startling me. I thought he was going to jump to his feet with how quickly he sat up vibrating with rage, but instead he pumped his hands into fists at his sides, his knuckles ghost white.

"Yes, he assaulted her. I told you already. He had her on the goddamned floor with his pants open. Her panties were…"

Logan pressed his lips together as though he was enduring physical pain before continuing through gritted teeth.

"He would have raped her! You're gonna charge him with sexual assault *on top of* attempted murder. His intent and threats were clear, so you better put together a list against that piece of shit long enough to keep him locked behind bars for the rest of his pitiful fucking existence, or I swear to God I'll…" Veins bulged in his neck.

I stared at him, unable to look away. Logan could never really scare me, but I still trembled at his intimidating tone and the excruciating hurt in his eyes.

"I understand this is difficult, Mr. West, but you need to remain calm," Harry said carefully, trying to defuse the ticking bomb beside me. "We will, of course, do everything in our power to ensure he remains off the streets."

"You're damn right you will. My family has a long-standing relationship with the district attorney. I won't let this case fall through the cracks of a backwoods buddy system."

Harry cleared his throat, his irritation evident, and sat up taller. *Shit, here it comes.* One thing I knew about Harry was he wasn't someone you wanted to cross.

"Mr. West, I can assure you that my office has no *buddy* system in place. We abide by the law—*backwoods* or not."

Logan's knee jolted, frustration seething from his features. "Really? Then how did Kurt get released?"

"The same way any inmate does: His bail was posted. He was out free while he awaited trial."

"Don't patronize me! I was to be notified if that happened, yet my guy knew nothing about it."

Harry cocked his head to the side, more interested in than annoyed by Logan's admission. "And who would your *guy* be?" Harry asked.

Logan said nothing, his expression frozen with fury. I'd never seen him like that before. He looked different—threatening and dangerous—but I knew it was because he cared about me and wanted to protect me. But still, the knowledge that he'd paid guards the first time Kurt was arrested didn't sit well with me. Was there a dangerous side to Logan I didn't know about?

I suddenly remembered my mother warning me about an arrest on his file.

Harry tapped his notepad against his leg. "It seems you have your own *buddy* system, Mr. West. As for the district attorney, I will make sure they have everything they need to properly prosecute this case."

Logan opened his mouth to respond but I spoke up,

ending the exchange before it got any more heated.

"Thank you, Harry."

Harry's smile was sweet and genuine as he looked to me. "Cassandra, I promise you we'll do everything we can. You're family to the station—to me."

Logan sighed when I placed my hand on his leg, but it did nothing to relax his set jaw and hard stare focused on the floor.

"All right." Harry closed his notepad and stood. "I think we have all we need for today. I'll be in touch."

He tipped his hat, then turned toward the officers pooled in the hall to leave the room just as my mother burst through the front door. I leapt up, wanting to cry at the fear in her bright-red eyes that glistened with unshed tears.

"Cassandra, thank God, Cassandra!"

I flew up and fell into her arms the second she reached me. My head dipped to her shoulder and her embrace tightened, just like it did when I was hurt as a child.

"I should have had George keep an eye on that scumbag. I should have known he was released. I didn't think he would—"

"It's okay. I'm fine."

"No! It's not okay, and don't give me that line. I know you. I know when my daughter is fine, and right now you are anything but."

"Mom…" I didn't know what to say. She was right, and deep down I knew it.

"I'm going to take care of this. George is working tonight, and I called him on the way over. He's got an eye on that fucker!"

"Mom!" I gasped, surprised at her language. She only cursed when she was extremely stressed. I pulled back, choking down burning tears.

She placed her fingertip delicately under the bandages on

my cheek and sighed. She closed then opened her eyes, a determined gleam emitting from them. "That's it—you're coming back home. You can move into your old room for at least the next few weeks."

I scoffed, wanting to laugh at how ridiculous it sounded. But I had to admit it also sounded comforting.

"No, I can't have anything else happen to you," Mom continued, her voice cracking. "You have no idea how it feels to hear your daughter's address over the radio. And after everything we went through on New Year's." She pulled me close again, smoothing my hair. "You're burning up. Are you feeling okay?"

I stepped back. "Yeah, it's just warm in here."

She wiped her eyes. "When I heard your address, I…I couldn't get here fast enough. I was in the middle of a traffic stop, and the guy had a warrant. I was going crazy not knowing if anyone was getting out here to you."

"I'm sorry," I rasped. "Logan got here, and…"

Her eyes shot past me to Logan, who was now standing. A tight, grateful smile grew over her lips, and her posture relaxed.

"Thank you." Her voice rose as she repeated, "Thank you, thank you, thank you."

Logan stepped beside me and placed his hand on the small of my back. "I won't let Cassandra out of my sight, Felicia. I'll keep her safe. She's going to be staying with me for a while, so there's no need to worry."

My head whipped to the side, and I found myself gaping at him. *I'm what?* That hadn't been discussed.

"I'm glad to hear it." My mother exhaled harshly, relieved. She stepped forward to hug Logan, and whispered something in his ear in the process.

"I will," was his only reply when he pulled away after a

brief moment.

My mother looked between him and me, then crossed the room to Harry. I watched as they exchanged a few hushed words, then walked out of the room together and into the kitchen.

"What did she say?"

"Just warned me I better take care of you." His hand reached around, ensnaring my waist and turning me to face him. "Are you feeling any better? Your cheeks are no longer cherry red."

Cherry red? Nope, only molten lava coursed through my veins—and there was no way he was going to change the subject.

"Logan, I don't think it's a good idea that I—"

"Don't," he interjected, rubbing his thumbs over the thick fabric of the robe covering my hips. "Don't think about anything except how much I love you and that I want you safe with me. Just a few weeks."

"Weeks!?" I gasped, trying not to appear as freaked out as I felt. We were not ready to live together for any period of time. It had only been two days since Valentine's—two days since I let him in and confessed I loved him. I didn't want to rush things and risk ruining what we had.

"All right, Cassandra, like I said, we have everything for now." Harry reentered the room and stopped in front of the door. "The report will be processed, and you'll be notified as soon as a court date is scheduled."

"Okay." *Court date*. The flames were back. It had to be the furnace.

"Take care of yourself." He gave me a brief hug, and when he pulled back, I caught the hard stare he shot Logan.

My mother spent the next twenty minutes scouring the house for anything missed as the last few officers cleared out. My constant attempts to sway her to leave and return to work were received on deaf ears; she was determined something was still amiss. She even checked the furnace, which both she and Logan insisted was fine but lowered the temperature on anyway.

I stood alone in the living room while my mother attempted to sweep up some of the glass from the back door. With each passing minute, the frantic sobs climbing from her grew louder, resonating off the walls around me. I didn't know how to comfort her. She had seen the damage to the house, and I knew she was afraid to leave me.

Logan stepped out from the hall where he'd disappeared to for a short time and snaked his arms around me from behind. He saw the same scene I did, and without a word stepped around me and walked toward her.

He kneeled down beside my mother and explained how he'd have everything cleaned up and new, sturdier doors installed immediately. She almost clung to him in a hug, speaking in a whisper I couldn't hear.

Was this really the man I'd met months ago? How had I gone so long without seeing exactly how thoughtful Logan really was? He'd done an expert job keeping it hidden.

"You're right." My mother's words broke through my thoughts. Then I couldn't hear anything else they were saying.

I watched as they both looked to me. Then she took his hand as he helped her to her feet. She handed him the dustpan she'd been clutching and, with anxiety etched over her brow, left hesitantly after numerous hugs and promises from me that

I'd take it easy and call her daily.

I stood at the door, watching her squad car drive down the road as reality hit me. It was over…for now.

Chapter Three

CLEANSE

The weight of dark clouds shadowing my thoughts was becoming unbearable. Outside, the sunset was more a thing to dread instead of behold, and there was no relief in having an empty house after watching everyone but Logan leave.

But life still moved forward. Minutes rushed by, the day continuing into night while I was stuck in my own weird limbo. I needed to find my place back in step with it, but I remained emotionally and physically stagnant. How do you move on from something your subconscious can't comprehend—something too painful to digest, with the haunting *what if* lurking outside your mind's door?

With a blink, I pulled myself back to the present, staring blankly out at my empty driveway. The tracks from multiple vehicles were mixed with deep footprints still evident in the snow. My car hadn't been returned, which meant it was either still parked on the side of the road or had been taken to a garage.

My eyes closed and shoulders slumped in exhaustion as I sagged against the doorway, wishing for a redo of the day.

"I'll call and check on the car tomorrow—make sure it ends up with a reliable mechanic," Logan said from somewhere behind me. How could he always read my thoughts? Was I that transparent, or was our connection deeper than I realized?

"Thanks, but I can call. You should go home and check on Oliver." I turned to face him, shutting the door. "You've been here all day. He's probably worried sick."

"I'm not leaving you."

"I don't want Oliver to worry, that's all." I shrugged, suddenly nervous. Did I really want him to leave?

Logan stepped toward me. "He's not. Both Julia and Jax are looking out for him."

"Did they find Scout?" I interrupted. Hope tinged my voice, raising it an octave.

Logan skimmed his fingers up my arms. "They will, and Oliver will shower that pup with more affection than any dog can handle."

I believed it, and when Logan's hands traveled up over my jaw, my lips curled into a smile just for him. "He's such a sweet kid. I don't want him wondering where you are, or out looking for Scout with Jax."

He grasped my chin gently, lifting my head. "He's not. Oliver has too much fun with Jax and Julia to worry about anything. He's probably getting ready for bed as we speak, anyhow." He tucked a piece of hair behind my ear, knuckles caressing my cheek, eyes locked on mine. "If he mentions my absence, I'll make it up to him."

"Thank you." My heart beat louder as I lost myself in his crystal-blue orbs.

"Now, as much as I adore your concern for my son, I want to talk about *you*—worry about what *you* need."

I blinked twice, then released a breath as I dropped my gaze. What *did* I need? I could use a shower and some clean clothes, for sure—not to mention I needed to get the blood off the floor before it set into the wood. Logan had dutifully kept my mom from trying to clean up in my bedroom. I didn't want to clean it either, truth be told.

I placed my fingers on the bridge of my nose and closed my eyes. "I need to wash it all away," I murmured, with so much meaning behind the words.

He didn't say a word as he scooped me up into his arms, his scent calming me with every step he took. I buried my head in his neck, welcoming his warmth. When he stopped and flicked on a light, I peered over his shoulder just enough to see we were in the bathroom.

Ever so gently, he sat on the edge of the tub with me resting on his lap and reached down to plug the drain. Never wanting to leave his hold, I didn't move a muscle when he leaned back to turn the faucet on. After finding the perfect temperature, he placed a warming kiss to the top of my head, then slid his hands up and tugged at the belt of my robe.

My eyes held his as he slipped the robe over my shoulders and let it fall around me. I lifted myself slightly and allowed him to pull the fluffy material away and drop it to the floor, leaving me in the pink cotton panties I'd pulled on in a rush earlier. The ones I'd been wearing during the attack had been mutilated.

We sat silently as the tub filled; words were unnecessary. His fingers trailed up and down my back as I rested there, watching the ripples of water filling the tub. Once the water level neared the top, Logan arched back and turned off the valve. I climbed off his lap and stood before him, wordlessly giving him the permission his eyes sought.

With a smoldering look reserved strictly for me, he hooked his fingers into my panties and slid them down my legs. I placed my hands on his shoulders and stepped out when they reached my ankles. He held them in his hand a moment before balling them up and tossing them into the hamper across the room.

I stood unabashedly. His eyes that once held nothing more than lust now spoke volumes of the love there. A smile pulled at my lips as he stood and, without warning, his easiness fell away and a pained frown stretched over his expression. Unsure why, I followed his gaze, pivoting just enough to catch the reflection of an enormous bruise forming between my shoulder blades. Another mark—this time courtesy of Kurt's elbow.

"I'm so sorry." His voice was hard. "This never should have happened."

"Stop." My hands reached out and cupped his cheeks, pulling his focus back to me. "A bruise is nothing compared to what could have happened had you not arrived when you did. You saved me, Logan. Don't apologize."

His finger outlined the bandages on my cheek. His jaw clenched.

"He's going to pay for this," he whispered.

"Shhh, please. I don't want to talk about it. Not now." I lifted his head, running my hands through his hair to calm him. The crease on his brow smoothed.

"I love you, Cassandra. Do you hear me?" I smiled, listening to him continue. "Never in my life have I felt this, and I swear I won't let anyone ever hurt you again."

Believing every word he spoke, I caressed the scruff of his cheeks with my thumbs. "You can't promise that, but I know you mean it. I love you too." I balanced up on my tiptoes, brushed my lips over his, and murmured, "Join me in the bath."

He smiled into the kiss. "It's a small tub."

"All the better."

Logan's tongue darted out, moistening his lips before he

pressed them against mine in a soft-yet-demanding kiss. His arms snaked up my back, taking hold at the base of my neck.

"You're still hot."

It was a statement and not a question, which meant he must've felt sweat lingering there. *Yuck*. But instead of pulling away from embarrassment, I kissed him again, harder—deeper.

When I finally stepped out of his reach, my lips were tingling. "You tell me." I fought for confidence, denial fueling me to erase the events of the day with a distraction. "Am I still hot?"

His eyes raked down my nude body, never once halting at the redness on my stomach. He made me feel beautiful with that tender look in his eyes. A repressed growl rumbled in his chest.

"I'm trying to be a gentleman here…get my beauty cleaned up and help her relax. So you best put away that look right now."

My bottom lip tugged out from my teeth that had been holding it as I stalked back to him.

"Help me relax? I like the sound of that."

Logan stepped forward, closing the gap between us, and I wasted no time pulling his tie free and tossing it to the floor. His head tilted slightly, eyes watching me as I unbuttoned his shirt, pulled it off, and let it meet the same fate as his tie. He didn't say a word, but when I tugged on the waist of his trousers, opening his belt and popping the button of his fly, his body tensed and eyes slammed shut.

I watched the fabric of his pants tighten around his growing erection. I sucked in my lips, holding back a grin. I loved how his body reacted so easily to me.

I took a moment to fully appreciate the man in front of me. Logan was by far the epitome of a flawless, virile male, with narrow hips highlighted by tight abs and a powerful chest.

With a glint in his eye that told me he enjoyed my unashamed stare, he smirked. It was nice to see after the day we'd had.

With a teasing slowness, I lowered his zipper and pulled down his pants. He stepped out of them and I reached for his black boxer briefs, but his hand encircled my wrist to stop me.

"I'd say that's enough teasing for tonight. Let's get you in the tub."

He made quick work of removing his briefs and socks, allowing me more time to study him in the process. Logan was, without a doubt, the most beautiful man I'd ever laid eyes on, and he loved me—wanted me.

He stepped into the tub with his hands on the edges. I watched his biceps flex as he lowered himself, then held out his hand. Smiling softly, I took it and stepped between his legs, snuggling down with my back to his front. My head found the perfect pillow against the peaceful thumping of his heart and rise and fall of his chest.

After submerging a washcloth in the water, he rubbed it down my arms and slid it over the lesions on my stomach. His gentle hand against my skin left a trail of goose bumps in its wake. His other hand took mine, entwining our fingers and resting our hands under my breasts.

"I was serious about you staying with me," he said after a few minutes of soothing silence.

"I know you were." I smiled to myself, my eyes closed. The washcloth made its way over my thighs, sending a quiver up from my toes. "You're always serious," I added.

"Stay at least a week." His voice rang through my ear, tickling my insides. Feathery strokes caressed my inner thighs that spread for him as though his hands spoke the only language my body knew.

"What about Oliver? I don't want to confuse him," I reasoned.

His fingers didn't skip a beat, sliding the washcloth up and down my skin, further awakening the desires I was surprised to feel so soon. I closed my eyes.

"There's nothing to confuse him about. We'll tell him you're staying while your house is being repaired. It's not a lie—you'll need a new back door and work done on your bedroom."

"Yeah," I whispered to myself, mentally falling away from where I was with Logan and back to reality.

"Cassandra, listen to me." Logan's hand took my chin, tipping my head back to meet his stare. "I'll take care of everything. Don't worry about all that. But please, I want…" His brows creased. "I *need* you with me right now. For a few days, at least. I won't be able to sleep knowing you're here alone."

My mouth opened, and I spoke before I could process what I was agreeing to. I needed to be with him as much as he needed me.

"Okay. Two days."

"Five," he countered.

"Two."

"Three, my stubborn sweetheart." His hand slipped back down, his palms covering my breasts.

Twisting back against his chest, savoring the feeling of being safe in his arms, I conceded. "Fine, you win." I took the washcloth from his hand and dropped it in the water, then placed a kiss on the pad of his thumb. "Three days, but on one condition." I held his pointer finger to my mouth and ran it across my lips.

"Anything."

"I'm sleeping in a guest room."

He cocked a brow. "Will I be sleeping in that guest room, as well?"

I shifted my body further, water splashing over the sides as I swatted his chest playfully. "I'm serious. I don't want Oliver to see us together like that. Not yet, anyway."

Logan scoffed and tugged me closer, his lips lingering over mine. "I've never met anyone as persistent as you."

"Get used to it." I pressed a kiss above his left nipple.

"I plan on it." He lifted my chin with his index finger and nipped my lips. "Now let me finish soaping you up, and then you need to rest that pretty little head of yours."

Rest? Not what I was thinking at all, especially with the growing hardness pressing into my side.

With a frisky smile, I placed leisurely kisses on his neck. "I was thinking of something a little more intimate." I turned to face him fully and straddled his lap as best I could in the tight space. My knees pressed between his thighs and the side of the cast-iron tub as I lifted myself up and sat over him, his cock situated under my ass.

Logan closed his eyes and sucked in a tortured breath, stifling a grunt when I slid over him again, grinding down against his hardness.

His hands landed on my hips and lifted me up quickly, but before I could land back down, he was standing and grabbing a towel.

My lip jutted out in a pout. I felt suddenly rejected—especially considering the trials of the day.

I stood, ripped the towel from his hands, and stepped out of the tub, wrapping the soft cotton around my body. Too hurt to speak, I'd opened the door to leave when he snatched me around the hips and tugged me back against his strong, wet body.

"Cassandra, all I want right now is to see you sleeping peacefully. You need it."

As though I could ignore his rock-hard erection pressed

against my stomach? My heart pounded, arousal soaring through me.

"I know what I need." I pressed a kiss to his neck, then down to his shoulder. Each bit of contact with his skin wiped away, albeit temporarily, the memory of Kurt. I needed more.

"Cassandra, I think we should wait. You had a traumatic day, and—"

"And I need you more than ever because of that. Please." I met his wary gaze, wanting him to overwrite the bad. "Help me forget. You want me as much as I want you." I pulled back enough to gaze down at his hardness, then peeked back up at him. "So take me."

"I was in a tub with a goddess, who's now in my arms." A sweet smile touched his lips. "You can't expect my body not to react."

Heat rose to my cheeks and I murmured, "So then what's the problem?"

Logan released me, stepped away, and ran both his hands through his hair. He didn't say another word, instead grabbing a second towel and wrapping it around his waist.

I waited quietly until he looked up and stepped around me out of the small room. I could see conflicted worry lines marring his handsome face. He stood in front of my bedroom door, looking in at the blood stain and miscellaneous items scattered around from the nightstand drawer I'd dumped out.

After following him, I leaned against his back, burying my head between his shoulder blades. I didn't want to look in the room again.

"We need to pack you a bag," he said, stepping forward toward my closet. With his towel tucked around his waist, he pulled my duffle bag from the floor and took it to my dresser.

His words penetrated something I'd kept buried deep while in the bathroom, but now it was bubbling back to the surface.

"I can do it," I said, defeated, taking the duffle from his hands. "Let me just get dressed first."

Not looking me in the eyes, his only response was "Okay" in a mere whisper before he left the room.

There was nothing to do but stare at the bag, unsure whether I should fill it with three days' worth of clothes or throw it at him when he returned. Why was he acting like this? I didn't want the day to define the start of our relationship. I just wanted to suck it up and press on.

I dropped the bag and pulled on the first pair of panties I grabbed, not even caring what they looked like, followed by a pair of sweatpants and an oversized sweatshirt. I didn't even bother with a bra. I was starting to crash already. If I couldn't have Logan loving me the way only he could, then I wanted sleep.

As I walked to the door, the full-sized mirror on the back of it reflected my tired, puffy eyes with the tiny bandages underneath. My hair was a mess of curls that was still dirty, since we hadn't got around to washing it in the tub.

I winced, closing my eyes. I looked hideous.

"I'm ready," I said as I walked into the living room. Logan stood fully dressed, staring darkly out the front door.

He turned. "Where's your bag?"

"I'm not in the mood to pack it. I'll come back tomorrow or something. Let's just go."

With anguish displayed on his face, he didn't speak, but finally held out his hand. I couldn't resist; I needed to feel him close. It was the only thing that felt safe.

The short walk over was dark, brutally cold, and filled with a viscous silence; the crunch of snow under our feet was the only sound. I noticed the lights were out at his house just before we entered. To say I was relieved was an understatement; there was no way I could face Oliver in that state. I was lost, and completely unsure what I was feeling.

Logan led me up the stairs and down the hall before opening the door to his room. It was everything I'd imagined, with grand, large-scale furniture and a few paintings on the wall. I went straight to the bed, kicked off my boots, and climbed in.

The bed dipped behind me a few moments later. Warm arms encased me, pulling me into their safety.

"I love you, Cassandra." His voice was conflicted and strained.

Still facing away, I placed my hand on his arm, my thumb caressing his wrist. "I know. Me too."

There was nothing else to say. The tension was too thick, drowning us both. He didn't know what to say and I didn't know what I needed, so I closed my weary lids and allowed myself to drift away from it all.

Chapter Four

NIGHTMARES

My feet were painfully heavy and blisteringly cold. The bitter crunch of snow mixed with a breathless, hard panting blared around me, refueling my adrenaline. Panic swept through my veins. Was it me running out of steam in my steps, or...him?

I raced faster, not willing to slow down, stumble, or trip, but it still wasn't enough. Heavy hands shoved against my back, ripping the air from my lungs and sending me face down.

I whipped around, heart racing, blood crashing in my ears. I crawled backward on my hands and feet, staring wide-eyed up at the dark figure looming over me. Panic hit hard when the figure barreled forward, and a face met mine.

Kurt.

I woke with a start, my head pounding, skin buzzing. Once calm enough to process my surroundings, I found Logan asleep against my back. It took everything I had to sneak out from under his arms and slide down the bed without waking him. As I stood over him, the anguish consuming me grew thicker. He looked so peaceful. I didn't want him to lose that—didn't want us to fall apart before we'd even had a real beginning.

I needed to work all fragments of Kurt from my system—

prove to Logan and to myself that I could move forward, and that I was still the woman I was before. No more nightmares.

Convinced it was now or never, I threw on my coat, grabbed my boots, and tiptoed out of the room.

Once over the threshold of Logan's front door, no longer protected by the safety inside, I closed it all behind me quietly. Fumbling with my boots, I shoved my feet in and stared across to my dark house next door.

What am I doing? What's the plan—my goal?

I didn't have answers. The only thing I knew for sure was that Kurt was in my head and needed to get the hell out.

I shuffled forward warily over the sugaring of snow covering Logan's front porch. My senses were hyperaware of every noise, movement, and shadow around to mock me.

Get it together! Nobody's out here! I'd been alone outside in these parts my entire life, never fearing a single thing, and I wouldn't let that change now.

Still, when the harsh security light from Logan's porch flashed on, my body betrayed my spirit. My spine stiffened and stomach lurched; as hard as I fought through the unwarranted fear, my fingers clutched my coat against my chest, palms sweaty and hands trembling.

I stared out at the floodlit path, cutting through the night from his yard to mine. Inhaling a rapid breath of cool winter air, I released the hold on my coat and rubbed my hands together briskly, determined it was time to tackle this beast head on. And I did, jogging down the porch stairs, my courage returning with each step until my feet crunched into that deep wicked snow on the earth—a trigger I couldn't avoid.

The texture under my boots was the same as in the dream. Everything in me froze as it all rushed back: the nightmare, the terror, and the anxiety, but mostly the anger. It hid deep inside my gut, building under the surface.

My head shook. Rage boiled through my veins, but I wouldn't let it spill out. I'd never let anyone see or know. I'd bury it in a subterranean hole behind my heart, where my pain and sorrow were locked away in a place I never had to deal with them again.

I needed at least enough closure on Kurt to satisfy the scared, tiny girl inside that required it. *His actions won't define me.* I ached to scream it so loudly that it would ricochet through the forest, letting everyone to know I wasn't some fragile child. I was stronger than the fear, and my will was stronger than any pain Kurt could cause me.

Prepared to storm over to my house and remove all signs of him, I felt Logan's gentle voice jerk me back to the now.

"Cassandra."

My shoulders were the only part of me that moved out of my body's rigid state, but I didn't look back, staring with fixed purpose at my house.

I heard him move closer, descending the first step before standing behind me. He didn't touch me. "Come back to bed, sweetheart."

I opened my mouth and a low, heated whisper crawled out. "I can't."

His hand appeared beside me, folding lightly around my arm. "Okay. Tell me what I can do."

I didn't know, and I hated myself for it. We'd been through so much, been pushed to the brink, and he'd proven he was there for me and cared for me again and again. I knew with every fiber of my being that he loved me. I never wanted him worrying about me again.

I leaned backward into his chest, absorbing his scent. "Nothing. I'm fine." An awkward bubble of a bitter chuckle leapt from my throat. Was every relationship tackled at every turn, or was it just mine?

His hands circled my waist, and he turned me around slowly. I stared down at his black boots, unable to look into his eyes.

Strong fingers captured my chin and lifted my head up until his penetrating gaze locked on mine. "No, you're not. Don't ever hide from me, Cassandra. Let me be here for you." His voice was stern but tender. "Please."

Unsure what to say, I simply nodded. Together, we stood there, neither breaking the connection our eyes held.

"I'm not a victim. I never will be," I finally confessed, staring past him, emotions too high to control. "I don't want to feel this." My chest tightened, forcing myself to go deeper—to purge. "He would have won. He would have—"

I folded my bottom lip between my teeth, unable to say it as I felt tears well up in my eyes. Logan's hand caressed my cheek, and I drew from his strength to continue.

"After everything the past few months, it's like I've lost myself. I… I don't know what I've become. This brittle girl that people look at with pity? I hate it. It was why I was so headstrong with you…" My eyes met his again. "…because you…you had that same look in the hospital when Julia and Oliver came by. You saw through me, and I couldn't bear it."

He sat on the top step, taking me in his arms and setting me on his lap. His powerful gaze demanded my attention.

"I saw a strong, powerful woman lying in a bed, covered in injuries I was responsible for," he began. "I let you go that night—let you drive away, fully aware that you weren't fit to be behind the wheel. I was selfish, only thinking about myself.

"And then it hit me, the moment your taillights disappeared: the enormity of how much I fucked up something so beautiful, so pure. The look you saw on my face that day in the hospital was not pity—it was pain, guilt, and regret. But it was also love. I loved you, and more than anything I wanted to protect you...take care of you any way you'd allow."

His head fell and he blew out a breath.

"I love you," I said. "I did then, and I do now. I just want to feel like myself again."

"I promise you, Cassandra, I will fight with everything I have to make you happy. You're still the same girl I watched leap over that puddle, so carefree. You've dealt with more than your fair share, we both know that, but I'll make things right. And you have my word: You'll never have to fear that monster again." His voice hardened. "*Nobody* will ever hurt you again."

Maybe it was the protectiveness that radiated off him or the love his words cocooned me in, but in that moment I was through talking. Soothing warmth flooded my chest. There was only one thing I wanted: to be lost in him. I was safe and happy there.

"Make love to me," I murmured.

He pulled back the slightest bit. Had I not been so attuned to his every move, I may not have noticed.

"We don't have to, Cassandra," he said softly, his hands smoothing down my back. "We can just sit here. I'll hold you as long as you need. I'm not going anywhere—ever. I want to love you in every way imaginable, but I want you to be ready to move on from today in your own time."

"Logan," I sighed, framing his face in my hands. "I *am* moving on, and right now I need to be reminded of what I have—what we share. I need you not to make me forget, but to remind me that it's over." Unshed tears beckoned, blurring my vision. "My body needs your touch to..." My voice lowered; I was suddenly nervous. "...to remove the feel of his. I need to feel you—need for you to make me whole and safe again."

The pad of his thumb slid over my cheek, wiping away a traitorous tear. I sucked in a cleansing breath, ceasing further tears as I watched him swallow. Almost instantly, I was enveloped in his strong embrace: the one place I belonged. He tipped my head back, his lips massaging mine, soft and gentle.

"How can I ever deny you? Anything you need, it's yours. Let's go inside. I want you warm in my bed first."

"No. Here." My voice cracked, but I didn't think. I only moved from his lap and tugged at the waistband of my sweatpants.

He grabbed my hand, stopping me. "It's freezing. You'll catch a cold—"

"Logan, please…I don't want to be afraid out here. I want to be free—safe." I nearly yelled it, expressing my need to the wind, then pulled on a coaxing hint of a smile to prove I was ready. "Besides, I know you'll keep me warm."

Logan stood wearing only his unbuttoned dark wool coat, grey pajama pants, and unlaced boots. He regarded me with an intense stare, reading me, until his lips began curling up. His hesitance lifted into determination when I whispered the challenge.

"I'm waiting."

"Come here," he replied hoarsely, kissing me hard before taking my hand and leading me back up the steps to his front door. "Don't move."

I waited as he disappeared inside. Alone outside, I felt no fear—only anticipation.

When Logan emerged a moment later, it was with the grey throw from his living-room sofa. He placed it over the railing, then turned his attention back to me. He pulled me into his arms, his stubble warming my cheek as his lips ran over my ear.

"I love you," he whispered.

There was no time to reply. I gripped his shoulders for support as he grasped the waist of my sweats and lowered them down my legs. I'd bent quickly to remove my boots when his hand grabbed mine.

"Keep them on," he rasped.

"What? No!" I replied, conscious of how ridiculous they'd look. I attempted to kick them off again, but he wasn't having it.

"I want those cute toes of yours nice and warm."

He removed one pant leg over the boot, then lifted my other to do the same. I didn't fight him. His expression lightened when he glanced up, feasting on my nearly nude state, and hooked his fingers in my panties. The look wasn't one of lust, but pure adoration. With the slowest movement I'd ever seen him make, he dragged the pants down my legs and over the boots.

The security light flickered off, and his aqua eyes glistened in the darkness surrounding us. Ever so slowly, he unzipped my coat, pulled it down over my shoulders, and let it fall. The freezing temperatures didn't have time to attack as he directed my arms up over my head, freeing me of my sweater before immediately wrapping the blanket around my shoulders. There I stood on his porch, in only my brown UGGs and a fleece throw.

Logan's hands slipped inside the blanket, encasing me as he stepped closer. Without warning, his lips collided with mine, loving and tender. I lost myself in the moment, which was over too soon when he stepped back to release me, then slowly worked his lips down my neck before dropping to his knees.

I watched my beautiful man, staring up at me, take my ankle and place his mouth just above my boot. His lips trailed up over my leg, then paused at a small cut on my shin, where he placed a lingering open-mouthed kiss.

"I'll always keep you safe," he murmured, slinking up to the next cut just above my knee. "Always."

My body woke with vigor, trembling as I braced myself against the front door. He placed my leg back down and took the other, repeating the movements. His hands began kneading the backs of my thighs, holding me in place as his tongue ran up over my knee. The heat of my arousal melted away the anxiety our setting had brought. My fingers weaved through his messy short hair, my body relaxing, legs widening to welcome him.

He lifted my foot and rested my calf over his shoulder, then maneuvered his head to trace the dip below my knee with his tongue. "You're mine. My angel."

A moan sang out as I moistened my bottom lip, my stomach buzzing with eagerness.

Logan's tongue swirled, working its way up until his nose brushed below my sex. "Every part of you. Only *my* hands are allowed here. I'll kill any other man that thinks otherwise."

His words soothed me, refueling the power that had drained from my soul. It felt amazing; his body against mine, his lips trailing around my sex, was everything I could want. My body would only ever answer to him. Kurt was becoming a distant, foggy memory.

"I love you," I managed, my eyes focused solely on Logan.

His only reply was the raise of his head, showcasing the familiar glowing smile that consumed my heart. He slipped my leg back down, then opened the afghan to reveal my raw stomach and placed a warm kiss over my belly button.

"I'm the luckiest man alive…an undeserving beast, but I'm too greedy to care," he spoke against my skin. "I finally have you—all of you—and I'll guard you with my life."

I whimpered when his left hand slipped up and intertwined with mine, holding me there with him. His lips placed one last kiss over my stomach, and the pain from the wounds disappeared. "These hands belong to a man that could never bring you harm," he said, running his fingers up over my breasts.

He rose up and took my nipple into his mouth, suckling. My gaze never strayed from him. The overwhelming desire to feel him pressed inside me, connected to me in every way, grew unbearable.

A reverberating snap sounded around us and my entire body shuttered, nearly jolting me from his arms. Logan held me tightly while he surveyed the area carefully. Together, we watched a small raccoon sneak from around the corner of the house.

"Sorry." I covered my face with me hand, relaxing, embarrassed at my overreaction.

Logan stood and peeled my hands away. "Shhh, don't be. I've told you never to be sorry. I'm the only person out here with you. It's only ever going to be me this close to you. I promise." He reached under my ass and lifted me up. I wrapped my legs around his waist instantly, locking my ankles together. "God, how I wish I could help you forget," he said in barely a whisper.

"You do more than that," I replied, holding him close and crushing my lips to his.

My foremost need for him was stronger than ever. I reached between us, slipped my hand into his pajama pants, and freed his erection. Not waiting for his response, I lifted up slightly in his arms and plunged down, filling myself with his thickness.

He sucked in a hiss through gritted teeth, his face tight, eyes closing as I took all of him.

"Cassandra," he growled as I began to rock against him.

"Yes." I rode him harder, faster, my mouth on his neck, tongue tracing his jaw. I was wedged in place between him and the door, and I used them both to support me as I took what I needed—what he gave me.

I parted his lips with my tongue and delved in. The kiss was fierce, hungry, and alive with passion. It was as though everything was right in my world. Our bond, our connection, diminished everything else.

My moans were lurid and uninhibited as I ground myself harder down onto him. He filled me with everything I was seeking. His mouth broke our kiss and lowered down to claim my breast that ached for his caress. A thick, desperate whimper rang out from somewhere deep inside me.

Biting down on his shoulder, I felt the first heavy tear fall. Then another. His sweet lips pressed to the dampness on my cheek. My eyes squeezed shut as I lost myself fully in him. My right hand slid from his neck, covering his on my breast. He closed his fingers around mine.

"Slow...no rush." He bit back a hard grunt. "Too good—" His lips ensnared mine, kissing me with ferocious tenacity.

I couldn't slow—couldn't do anything except lift up, and with each plunge down the remnants of Kurt's touch were wiped away.

Logan was panting, a thin sheen of sweat covering his strong body. He lifted me up higher, holding me in place, and grabbed his cock in his hand. I wasn't sure what he was doing until he tucked himself back in his pants, not yet enjoying his release. Neither of us had.

I was still locked around him when he rested his forehead against mine. He'd seen what I'd been avoiding: the endless tears spilling out in a vast wave of vulnerability.

It must've had a sobering effect on him. His eyes were soft, and filled with not pity or sympathy, but love.

No longer hard and wanting, Logan cradled me in his arms selflessly and carried me back inside. He didn't stop until we were in his room. He maneuvered us over the bed, resting down on a pillow with me sprawled across him. My sobs finally broke out of the tomb they'd been locked inside. They came fast and painfully, showing no mercy. He stroked my hair as I trembled and shook.

My sobs grew into heavy cries as I clutched the sheet under us. An ungodly roar sneaked up from somewhere deep in my soul and danced off the walls. Logan didn't try to silence me, even as I looked back and wondered if Oliver had heard. He allowed me to release it all.

It felt incredible, freeing, and, above all, needed. And Logan was there, holding me the entire time, keeping me safe while my mind replayed the events of the day. Each tear that fell washed it away. It wouldn't destroy me, and the only mark it would leave was the power I found in overcoming it. I wouldn't let it control my life.

By the time my body was numb with both physical and emotional exhaustion, Kurt was nothing but a name I never wanted to speak again. It was up to the courts now to handle him.

Logan held me in silence, but I knew he was awake. I wasn't sure when I fell asleep, but his warmth never ceased to comfort me throughout the night. The hazy memory of him reminding me how perfect I was infiltrated my dreams.

I was safe there with him, and nothing else mattered.

Chapter Five

MISCONCEPTIONS

I woke from what felt like a winter's hibernation to the sound of hushed voices. Lying on my stomach, buried in a heap of cozy blankets saturated in Logan's natural scent, I smiled at the familiar laugh that greeted me.

"Please, Daddy, can we wake her up now?"

The moment of panic happened instantly, my eyes popping wide open. Shit, was I dressed? *Oh God!*

My hands slid to my sides, running stealthily over the feeling of expensive cotton. I breathed a sigh of relief, ignoring the fact that I had no recollection of dressing. I'd been in his bed for more than 24 hours, and he'd let me sleep the entire time.

"I think she heard us," Logan said, chuckling.

I rolled over and faced the two handsome faces standing in the doorway, watching me.

"Yay! She's up!" Oliver stumbled forward with glee and Logan's hand shot out to his shoulder, stabilizing him.

"Careful," Logan said.

Oliver walked over with precise steps, slow and determined, careful not to spill the tall glass of orange juice in his hands.

I sat up, smiling. The precious view of his cheerful face first thing in the morning was the perfect start to any day—especially when paired with Logan's.

"This is for you. I made it all myself," Oliver boasted, wearing a proud grin and holding the glass out to me.

"I'd like to think I helped a little," Logan added, with a playful smile aimed at me.

I took the glass carefully and brought it to my lips. As I swallowed, my brows rose. I was impressed.

"Delicious!" I praised. It wasn't an exaggeration, either—the juice was freshly squeezed and ice cold. I took another drink.

"She likes it!" Oliver looked over to Logan, then back at me. "I do too. I picked the biggest oranges. Aunt Katie says those are the best."

I couldn't remember the last time I'd felt so relaxed. His smile was infectious. "It's perfect. Thank you." I set the glass down on the bedside table and noticed the clock. It was close to nine. "Ah, I'm sorry. I was exhausted and overslept. You better get going so you're not late for school."

"I will. But promise to drink lots of juice, 'kay?"

I giggled at the persistence that rivaled his father's. "You got it."

Logan stepped forward just inside the door. "I'm going to drop him off at school, then I'll be back. You sleep, and if you need anything, I'll be here."

"Don't you have work?"

He shrugged. "I can take a few days."

I sat up straighter. "Logan, you need to work. I don't want to be a burden. Plus, we both know I won't be getting much resting done if you're close by."

He cocked a brow, that playful smirk creeping over his enticing lips.

"How come?" Oliver asked suddenly, reminding us we weren't alone. "You bot'er her, Daddy?"

I bit my lip to stifle a laugh, my cheeks flushing.

"Never. I give you my word: I'm always *very nice* to her," Logan told him, eyes still on me. My insides melted at those seductive baby blues.

"Good," Oliver said, watching me lift the glass and finish the last of the juice. "More?"

I shook my head, sobering as I tore my gaze from Logan's. "No thanks. We can have a glass together when you get home, though. With some cookies, maybe?"

"I love cookies. But I love them with milk, not juice." He scrunched his nose.

Makes sense.

"You're right. Milk is better with cookies." I smiled, then glanced back over to Logan with a cocked brow. "So you're going to work then."

"If you insist. I'm sure I have plenty to do at the office to distract me from the fact that you're here, in my bed." His tongue peeked out, wetting not only his bottom lip but my entire sex. "But you best stay in that bed and *sleep*. You need it."

His eyes spoke volumes over his words. *Yeah yeah. Sleep—got it.*

"Yes, sir." I saluted, and Oliver giggled. My laughter joined his, and I reached out for a hug. He was too adorable to resist. He hugged me back tightly. "You have a fun day at school, and when you get home you can tell me everything you learned. Deal?"

"Deal." Oliver stepped back, staring at me—or, more accurately, at the small bandages on my face, hesitant to inquire about something clearly on his mind.

"Hey, what's wrong?" I asked softly.

Oliver glanced from my eyes to the bandages and back, then bent down and whispered in my ear, "Daddy said that you're not sick, but...you have more Band-Aids. I don't want you to get hurt no more. 'kay?"

I struggled to hold my smile for him. Logan stepped closer, watching with a hint of wariness on his set features.

"Your daddy is right," I replied. "I'm fine, and I'll try really hard not to need any more Band-Aids."

Oliver smiled softly, satisfied with my response, then walked toward the door.

"Thank you for looking out for me, Oliver. Your daddy's raising a perfect little gentleman."

His smile grew when he looked back at me. "Yeah, I know. Uncle Jax says Daddy raises hell, too, in his bedroom. Weird, huh?"

My uncontrollable laughter spit out, and I watched as Logan ushered a confused Oliver out of the room.

"Cassandra needs to get some more sleep. Go put on your coat and shoes. I'll be down in a minute."

Oliver waved goodbye from the hall before disappearing. I slouched back into the bed, a grin covering my face as Logan sat beside me.

"So," I drawled, "what else does Uncle Jax have to say?"

Logan rolled his eyes—literally. I wanted to ask him to do it again, because it was one of the funniest things I'd ever seen.

"My brother has trouble censoring himself even around children."

"Mm-hmm. I'm sure that was as clean as he could have put it."

He grabbed my arms and slid me further down the mattress, his weight hovering over me. I giggled until I saw that look of his: the one I'd never be able to resist again.

"You're gonna sleep, my sweetheart, and tonight..." His

lips placed a feather-light kiss to my chin, his body pressing down over mine. "...I'll show you exactly what I can do in the bedroom."

"Ah. I'm intrigued." My leg rubbed up his thigh, forcing him completely atop me, where I folded it over his body.

He rose up and nipped my lips. "You should be. But first, tell me, how are you feeling? You sleep harder than anyone I've ever met."

I laughed. "I'm better. I should say thank you for sharing your bed with me."

"No need. I enjoyed it, myself."

"I can't believe I slept the whole day yesterday." I couldn't hide my embarrassment. "And I'm even more surprised you didn't try to wake me to get me to eat or bathe."

"You looked too peaceful."

I kissed his lips with one short peck. "So now you're gonna tell me what I can expect tonight. I wouldn't mind seeing what hell you have to raise in the bedroom."

Without warning, his head dipped low, mouth clamping over the sensitive peak of my breast hidden under my T-shirt.

"Soon. I like to keep you on your toes." His words ignited a spark that needed fanning now, not later.

"Is that so? Not even a hint?" I ran my finger down his stubbly cheek as his teeth grazed my pebbled nipple. "Ow." I writhed under him, and his nip softened to a gentle suck. My flames grew hotter and wilder, my sex grinding in urgent fervor against his swelling cock.

He released my finger. "I was thinking of something extra special—something that will have you holding on for dear life."

"Mmm." I liked the sound of that. It was what we needed: normal relationship sex. Nothing sounded better.

He breathed his thick, husky voice into my ear. I closed

my eyes, my skin buzzing in anticipation. "How about...a horror flick? I remember fondly how handsy those make you."

"What!?" I pushed him away, although I had to admit I had enjoyed cuddling close to him on the sofa. Still, I feigned a pout. "You're joking, right?"

Logan chuckled, running his thumb over my bottom lip. "Depends on how good you are today."

"Meaning?"

"Meaning you better not leave this house. Promise me."

"Will I be rewarded?" I bit my bottom lip, hopeful.

"Oh, yeah. You'll be rewarded."

Exactly what I wanted to hear. *Smart man!*

I pulled him back down to me and pressed my lips against his, my tongue intruding inside his mouth and dancing with his. He tasted of melon and mint, and it was heavenly.

Logan moaned into the kiss, his arms sliding under me as I dug my hands into his damp hair. Damn. He'd already showered, and I'd missed it.

"Daddy!" Oliver called, his voice echoing around us. "I can't find my book bag!"

Logan's lips fell away and his forehead dropped against mine, his breathing rapid.

"Better go. I'll see you tonight," I said with a knowing smile.

"Yes, you will." After one more kiss, this time to the tip of my nose, he was up and crossing the room. "And help yourself to anything in the kitchen. We have plenty, but I can have groceries picked up if you need anything specific."

With that, he walked out, shutting the door behind him.

I knew the moment I stepped out of Logan's bedroom

that I should've gone back to sleep. Being alone in his house was unsettling. Loneliness hit me in an unexpected wave; I missed him. Still, I showered, found the duffle bag full of my clothes, and pulled on a grey track suit. After skittering down the hall and descending the stairs, uncomfortable being all alone in such a big house, I came to a stop at the sound of a guy's voice.

Seemed I wasn't alone after all.

"This is stellar! I can't wait to tell all my buddies how good you are. Never thought I'd leave another dude's bedroom so satisfied."

I cringed, not wanting a run-in with Jax to ruin my perfect morning. I wanted to hide, but it was too late. When I peeked back, I realized I'd been seen—and judging by the look on Jax's solemn face as he followed behind the young frat boy wearing an enormous grin, I could sense he wasn't thrilled about my presence. He seemed almost nervous, which was unlike him.

After giving them both a friendly smile, I continued to the kitchen while Jax showed the guy out. I needed something to eat before I could sleep any longer.

"Cassandra. I heard you were here," Jax said a few moments later as he strolled into the kitchen.

"I'm just staying a few days. Having some repairs done on my house."

He huffed out a chuckle. "Relax—I heard about Kurt. Most of the town knows about it…or at least think they do."

Fabulous. Just freaking great.

"I'm, uh, sorry," Jax added, watching me.

I attempted to blow it off with a flip of my hand. "It's fine."

Of course the town knew. I inhaled a breath and released it slowly, reminding myself it didn't matter.

I stood next to the stove, my muscles tight, as Jax opened the fridge and ducked inside.

"Don't you worry about the douchebags. Logan will set it right. Trust me," Jax said, still hidden by the fridge door for another moment. As he stood up straight, he brought the pitcher of orange juice to his lips and finished it off.

There goes my after-school glass with Oliver.

"Have you had any luck finding Scout?" I asked, desperate for his answer but knowing it wasn't going to be the one I wanted. If he'd found him, the little pup would be running around.

He set the empty pitcher on the counter and smiled over at me. "Not yet, but no worries. He probably found himself some stray bitch to hook up with out in the forest. I bet he's having a hell of a time with some freedom."

"Right," I mumbled, shuffling my feet. Despite how crudely he'd put it, I hoped that was the case.

Jax interrupted my silent pleas.

"So I got the rundown this morning—you know, all the things I can and cannot say to you if you break free of his sex den."

"Gross! And I'm only here a few days. I'm sure you can control yourself that long."

"No promises, baby, but I'll try my best." He threw me a salacious wink.

"Thanks…I guess."

"Don't thank me, thank my big brother. His threats were extreme this morning. Shit! You must have some magic in those panties of yours, huh?" He grinned. "Good for you."

Maybe I wasn't that hungry. Logan was right: Sleep was what I needed.

"Hey, don't go. I didn't mean to offend you, I swear. It was a compliment."

"Relax. I won't rat you out to Logan," I called back as I left the kitchen.

"No, seriously, come back. Have you had any breakfast? I make some killer omelets, no joke!"

I stopped and inhaled deeply. I was going to regret this.

"Okay, but they better be amazing."

"You got it." A satisfied grin curled his lips. "So, what you want?" He strolled back to the fridge and started pulling items out. "We got turkey, ham, a few kinds of cheese, every vegetable you could possibly want. Logan's always pushing for the little man to eat the greens."

"You decide. I'm not picky."

"Obviously—you wound up with Logan."

"Ha ha."

"Kidding." He held up his hands, chuckling. "So how are you doing? I mean, after yesterday..."

"I don't really know, to be honest. It all feels like a bad dream."

What was I saying? It just came out. He was way too easy to talk to. I blamed the charm that he exuded off him as easily as it did Logan. Oliver was going to have it easy when he grew up.

"I get that." Jax pulled out a bowl and began cracking eggs into it. "You know, Logan's crazy about you. He won't let that ass fuck get away with what he did."

I didn't say anything. I just sat at the table watching him whisk the eggs, then take down a skillet from a rack hanging over the island.

I was afraid to ask what exactly Logan was capable of. Would Jax even know? The thought of Kurt getting roughed up in prison at that point didn't sound so bad.

I recoiled. *I'm a horrible person for thinking that.* What was wrong with me?

"Can I help with anything?" I asked after a long pause.

"Nah, I got this. You just sit back and prepare your pretty mouth for what it's about to devour."

"Funny."

He chuckled. "You say that now, but one taste and you'll be begging for more." He cocked a brow while chopping a green pepper with a swift hand.

"Begging for what, exactly?" Natasha asked, startling me when she rounded the corner and stopped in the doorway.

Ugh, I knew I should've stayed in bed—the king-sized, comfy, Logan-scented bed. I twisted in my seat and pretended to be distracted by something out the window as I blew out a breath.

"Natasha." Jax's smile was all ice.

"Jax," Natasha replied with a grin as she strode forward. "Would you mind losing the death ray, little boy? You know you love me."

"Nope, really don't," he fired back before refocusing on breakfast, pouring some egg mixture into the searing skillet.

"Mmm, now I know what you two were talking about. Smells divine." She turned to me, offering a smile I wished I could believe was genuine. "Jax here is almost as good in the kitchen as Logan. Not *quite* up to par, though."

Jax's back was to us as he sprinkled in the fillings, but he took her insult in stride and didn't miss a beat. "So, how was your trip, Natasha? Hope you didn't get too *lonely* up there in the mountains." He peered back over his shoulder, a smirk on his lips. "I can assure you, Logan sure as hell wasn't."

Natasha held his gaze, unspoken threats flowing between them until his head snapped back to the pan and hers shot to me.

I held her gaze, not batting a lash. *Bring it on.*

The smile returned to her lips. "It was eye-opening, and turned out to be quite beneficial for me, actually." She walked over and pulled out a chair beside me. "Jax has a way of annoying me like only a kid brother can, and it brings out the bitch in me at times. Sorry."

I raised my shoulders. "Not my business."

Her smile grew, and I mimicked it with my own. Both were fake and strained.

"Look, I think—" She sighed. "All right, I *know* you and I got off on the wrong foot. I'm sorry if I had anything to do with that."

"Honestly, I don't know you, so we haven't really had a start," I replied, trying to keep it light.

"Right, but I'm sure you know I came to Harmony with every intention of repairing my family."

I remained silent. *Yeah, I'm aware.*

"I know you probably have questions: Why am I back now? What might I still want? And I've seen you and Logan obviously getting…close." The words didn't come out easily.

The predator in me needed her to understand 'close' didn't accurately describe Logan and me. It was time to mark my territory. If that made me a bitch, so be it, but I didn't trust her.

"He loves me," I stated with easy confidence.

"He sure does," Jax chimed in, setting a perfectly folded omelet in front of me. "Enjoy."

"Well, I'm happy for Logan," Natasha said after a brief pause, watching me slice through the dense, gooey mini feast. "He's a good guy. You're a lucky girl."

"Yes, I am."

Slowly, I pulled my gaze from hers down to my plate. That thing had everything in it, sending my stomach into a pleading fit. I took a small bite. *Oh, good God, yes!* After another bite, I could see that the West men had a lot more than charm and good looks on their side.

"Wow, Jax, it's..." I had no words. "Wow," I repeated.

"See? Tomorrow morning you'll be begging for another."

I smiled at him. "We'll see."

He sat on the other side of the table across from me, took a big bite of his equally perfect-looking omelet, then leaned back in his chair, watching Natasha and me.

Silence hung over us until he swallowed, waving his hand in the air. "Oh, go on. Don't let me intrude," he said before shoveling in another bite, clearly entertained.

Natasha rolled her eyes, and I couldn't help but want to laugh. But that impulse disappeared with Natasha's next words.

"I still want my family, Cassandra."

I set my fork down and readied myself as she continued.

"It may be too late with Logan, but not Oliver. He's my son, and even if Logan and I are not married or together as a couple, we're still his mom and dad. That's all I want. I love them both dearly, and I'm not giving up on a chance with my son."

"Good," I replied instantly. Oliver deserved a family—deserved a mother.

She seemed surprised by my response, and her smile relaxed. What Logan and I had was strong, and she wasn't a threat to it. I wouldn't let her be.

"Fabulous. Well, if it's not too much to ask, I'd like to have lunch sometime. I know it may be awkward, but—"

The clang of Jax's fork hitting his plate drew our attention his way. With a loud scoff, he threw up his hands. "Only Logan would have the ex bitch and new pussy sitting at a table together without slaps being thrown. Lucky son of a bitch." He muttered the last part.

"Anyway, you were saying?" I looked back to Natasha, disgusted at his reference to me.

"I just want you to know that I don't expect us to become

fast friends, but I'd really like to try. I've made so many mistakes with this family, and I'm here now to right those. I'm sure you have put together some nasty conclusions about me, but I'm asking for you to give me a chance to show you that I'm here as a mother—nothing more."

I nodded, wanting desperately to believe her, but it didn't matter. Whether it was a game or not, I'd play along…for now.

"I care about Oliver, and because of him, I'd like to get to know you better." It was true—the best way I could make sure she was really there for him was to find out more about her. "This week is no good, but next week maybe. I'll let you know a day then."

"Sounds good."

"Un-fucking-believable," Jax spit out, slamming his glass down on the table and standing with his empty plate.

Oliver was right: Jax could eat a lot—and fast.

Natasha and I shared a smile. "I don't want any issues or unnecessary drama, Natasha. Getting to know each other better is for the best, I agree, but let me make myself clear on one thing: I won't ever let you hurt my boys again."

She appeared taken aback, but altered her expression quickly to cover it. "I'm glad they have someone that cares for them."

"More than you know," I replied easily, holding her stare.

She looked away first, standing as I turned my focus back to finishing my meal. The sooner I was back in bed, the better.

"Well, I need to go find some boxes and start packing. I'll look forward to hearing from you," Natasha said as she crossed the room.

"Please, for the love of God, tell me that means you're moving out of the guest house," Jax said, halting his steps out of the room.

"If I'm going to prove to your brother that I am here for

Oliver and done pursuing him, it's what I need to do." She looked at me. "I found a place a block away from that bar you all hang out at, Haven. Paid the first six months and can move in today."

Jax's easy grin was back in place. "Still doesn't make up for the lack of catfight this morning." He chuckled and continued out of the room, calling back, "Time to throw a party! The bitch is moving out!"

The annoyance Natasha was feeling was written all over her face as she called back to him. "Party away, little boy! It's one of the few things you're any good at!"

Unable to avoid the tension between them, I finished the last two bites of my breakfast and stood with my plate. After walking it to the sink, I said, "Well, congratulations on the apartment. I'm going to lie down for a while," and headed toward the doorway.

"Thanks, and I'm sorry to hear what happened yesterday. It's not my place, but there was a lot of gossip I couldn't help overhearing last night when I got back in town. I'm sure Logan will take care of that quickly enough, though. Like you said, he loves you, and I know better than anyone how strong that man loves."

My fists clenched at my sides. And things had been going so smoothly. *Jax might want to come back in, because a catfight sounds just about right.*

I ground my teeth, then muttered, "I'll see you around." I was making a beeline toward the door when I heard her call my name.

"Cassandra—one more thing. Could you not tell Logan about me moving? I want to wait till I'm settled in at the new place so I can show him myself."

I looked back, a tight smile firmly in place. "I'll try to remember." I doubted that was going to happen.

When I reached the top of the stairs, Jax was there with an impish grin.

"She's a bitch, right?" he said, laughing.

The front door slammed downstairs, and I released an aggravated breath.

"I'll take your word for it. I'm going to bed. Thanks again for breakfast."

He followed beside me as I started toward Logan's bedroom. "Sure, no problem. So how long you staying again?"

"A few more days."

He snorted, unconvinced. "I guess it doesn't matter. Logan will have you here permanently soon enough." He shook his head and ran a hand through his unruly dark locks. "Christ, I never thought Logan would end up pussy-whipped. I owe Lawrence a grand, damn it."

"He's not." I rolled my eyes, not bothering to defend that statement.

"Sorry, I can't help it." His shoulders rose, his expression feigning innocence. "It's just so easy to get a rise out of you. You get all flustered, and it's fucking cute as hell."

"Cute?" My brows shot up.

There was that wicked grin of his again. "Relax, you're not my type."

I stopped outside Logan's door and puffed out a short laugh. "Is that so?"

"It sure is. I'm not into blondes, although the whole schoolteacher thing is pretty hot."

Time to change the subject—fast.

"So, what were you up to in your room earlier?"

His brow creased. "What? When?"

"When I came down, you had that frat boy with you. He was saying how *stellar* it was?" I reminded him.

"Right, yeah, that was uh…just, you know, hanging out."

"Okay." No, I didn't know. Why the hell was he being so weird?

"We were just chilling out. Video games and guy shit."

"You don't strike me as the gamer type."

A slight smirk curved his lips. The resemblance to Logan was striking. "And what type of guy do I strike you as?"

"The type that thinks a bit too much of himself."

He cocked one brow as he rocked back on his heels. "Well, you're right. I'm not much of a gamer, but I have plenty of other activities to keep me occupied, as you may recall." His eyes brightened. Ah, of course. How could I forget catching him with the redhead?

"Aren't you proud?" I drawled out as I opened the door to Logan's room and stepped inside. "And Jax? Refer to me as a vagina again, and you'll find out Logan isn't the only one to be afraid of."

And with that, I shut the door and left him in the hall. I shook my head to myself, grinning. I never thought I'd actually be there, ready to climb into Logan West's bed to sleep. Yeah, it wasn't a thought I'd had before, but now, it was paradise.

The giant bed in the center of the room beckoned me, and I wasn't stopping until I was back under those blankets, saturated in Logan's scent.

Chapter Six

BLISS

The tingling sensation of warm, firm fingertips brushing across my ankle rattled me from my dream. It was a sweet one, too, in which my feet dangled from my treehouse, my body wrapped in the strong arms of the man I adored.

My breath caught and body stilled, paralyzed until I heard a sweet voice.

"My love."

I released the breath but remained absolutely still. *I'm safe.* It was Logan's voice, soft but clear.

I forced myself to remain on my stomach, where I always slept. I bathed in his touch, exposed and cherished under his tantalizing stare that I could feel upon me even without peeking.

His fingers continued deftly under the blanket from the end of the bed and up my leg on a devious adventure. They trailed over my ass, which was shielded in nothing but a string of lace. His palms pushed deep into my flesh, the pressure of his short nails awakening the skin as they dug in. It was an exhilarating albeit brief sensory delight before they traveled back down the other leg. I smiled into the pillow, feigning sleep.

The security of his touch was like a soothing balm taking control of my senses. A zing of electric current nipped the left side of my body, and I knew he was close. He was silent, and no longer touching me.

It was nearly impossible to remain still, but I was resolute. How far would he take his little *exploration?* He wouldn't give up so easily. I knew better.

The tug of the blanket was slow, unwrapping me just to the waist, keeping my bottom half covered. I forced the giggle bubbling up to cease, sucking my lips in tightly so there was no signal I was awake. It felt good there, at his will. I didn't want it to end.

"So lucky," he murmured, slipping his hand under my shirt again and outlining the contours of my spine with his thumb.

Unable to resist the scent of him, I wore one of his shirts. I'd spent time lying in bed earlier seriously debating whether he'd mind if I snatched a couple before I returned home.

He stopped at my bra and slipped his fingers underneath, where he unhinged the clasp expertly. I lay there while his fingers stroked down and back up again. I wanted the shirt gone. His warm lips were pressed right above the fabric on my bare shoulder. There was no stopping the building shiver he produced. The bed dipped beside me with his weight, his other hand brushing down my ass as he lowered the blankets to my knees.

There was no denying the low growl deep in his throat. My smile was back, swirling with pure satisfaction. Who would've thought I could affect him as much as he did me?

He tucked the comforter snugly around my bare legs, keeping them warm but giving him access to the rest of me.

My caring, stealthy pervert.

The sun was setting through the sheer curtains, and I

realized I'd slept most of the day away yet again. It wasn't a bad thing; I could use it to my advantage—I'd have more energy to spend a night with Logan.

His hands stole my full attention again as they traveled back down over my ass and caressed teasing circles, massaging out the tension they found. Over and over again, he kneaded and soothed my stressed muscles. But he wasn't taking it further, and I was in need of much more than just a good masseur.

With a soft yawn, my eyes still closed and face planted in my pillow, I arched my back and dug my upper chest down into the mattress. His hands left me.

No, no! Not what I was asking for. Teasing him back, I pushed my ass off the bed.

His chest rumbled, that irresistible growl of his keeping me blissfully distracted as his palms slapped down over both my ass cheeks, strong and demanding. The sound echoed off the walls surrounding us.

"You know what happens to a woman that teases her man, right sweetheart?"

"Mmm," I moaned sleepily, enjoying him bathing my sting with his caressing touch. Oh, I hoped I knew.

When he gripped the hem of my panties, my breath shuddered. All too slowly, he dragged them down just under my ass, and then there was nothing. Where were his hands?

I wiggled my hips just the slightest bit; my silent plea for more. The anticipation was building, stirring my arousal.

"So damn beautiful." His words vibrated across my skin, causing goose bumps to swell over my backside.

There he was—watching me again. To be fair, I'd have been doing the same thing if the tables were turned.

My enjoyment of his words amplified when his lips swept over my ass, followed by his teeth nibbling my flesh. *Oh my*...that was new. And I wasn't complaining—not at all.

With each kiss and lap of his tongue gliding over my skin, my arousal grew, eliciting a strangled moan. I couldn't take anymore, and my body must have sent out the signals because his hands moved down the cleft of my ass and found their way under me, sliding into my wetness.

I bucked against him with the first thrust. Again and again, his fingers worked over me. My body cowered to his actions. Another finger slipped inside while his thumb played skillfully with my pressure point until I was on my knees, panting his name and grinding against his hand.

"Logan," I moaned, "don't stop."

My fingers curled desperately into the sheets. I wanted to cry out louder but silenced myself, aware we weren't home alone.

"Never." His other hand splayed over my hip, holding me in place while he seized full control of the pace. My shirt was halfway up my back and begging to be removed.

His warm breath sizzled on the back of my neck. He collected my hair in his fist and let it fall down over one side of my shoulder before returning to his grip on my hip. My desire swelled when he lifted my shirt further up my back and kissed between my shoulder blades.

I arched my back further and whimpered, unable to resist the feeling of his lips on such a sensitive area that had never experienced such treatment. I wanted more and he gave it, running his tongue up my back, sending a tremor through me. The scruff on his cheeks prickled against my tingling flesh until he reached the nape of my neck.

Thrusting harder, he held me closer, his other hand wrapped under my waist. His fingers never ceased as he added a third, filling me, stretching me. My mind was drunk with desire.

"All mine," he murmured.

Yes, all his. Always his. The man knew exactly what I needed…exactly where to touch me….exactly how to clear the sludge from my head.

I was losing control. Fierce sparks of my impending orgasm wracked my limbs, and with another buck of my hips, I exploded around him. My arms gave out, and Logan followed me down as I sank into the mattress. As I inhaled a few times to catch my breath, his hand slid gradually from my body.

I winced at the separation, never wanting him apart from me. He must have felt it too, because suddenly I was being hauled up in his arms, where he held me against his hard body.

Ah, to be spooned by Logan. There was nothing better. When he traced the shell of my ear with his tongue, I nearly came undone a second time.

"Good evening, beautiful." His breath tickled my neck.

As much as I loved being in his arms, I needed to see him. I rolled over to face him, weaving one of my legs between his.

His glistening eyes studied me.

"Hi," was all I could manage before my lips crashed into his and I lost myself in the sensations still fluttering deep inside me.

I clung to the perfectly tailored suit he was still wearing. My head rested in the nook of his neck as I ran my fingers up and down the silkiness of his tie. Our kiss ended in a beautiful show of light nips.

Everyone else be damned. Life was good.

"I missed you today," he confessed in a whisper. "Couldn't think of anything else."

"Ditto."

He took my hand and nuzzled my palm. "You slept well, I hope?"

"I did." The room was dark. I wondered if Oliver was already asleep, which would mean I'd missed dinner. It wasn't the worst thing; I wouldn't mind eating in bed. I just hoped Oliver hadn't worried about me. "And all day, it appears. Looks like I earned that reward."

"*That* was just a friendly hello."

"Mmm." The thrill of *more* sounded like heaven.

"What were you dreaming about? You looked stunningly peaceful when I came in. I almost hated disturbing you."

"Almost?" I lifted my head, a playful grin on my lips.

"What can I say? You're a temptation I can't resist." He threw me a smirk and I giggled, dropping my head back to his shoulder.

"The massage felt good. Feel free to give them often."

He shuffled us up, lying back on his pillow. My chin was propped over my arm that was splayed across his chest. I stared up at his easy smile.

"You can count on it," he said, then took my chin and leaned down to nip my mouth. "But I am far from done with you tonight. I have some hell to raise, remember?"

"How could I forget?" I kissed him more deeply, never wanting to leave that bed.

Sunrise was upon us before either of us was ready. We'd only just fallen asleep when Logan was kissing my forehead, explaining he needed to wake Oliver for school.

I grumbled, not wanting to move, my limbs sprawled lifelessly across the mattress. I was deliciously exhausted and fully satisfied.

His body shook with a soft laugh as he attempted to shimmy up to escape from under me. I pressed my body harder against him, pinning him in place.

"Don't worry, sweetheart. You can go back to sleep, but you'll need to release me first."

"Mmm."

"I adore you sleepy." His hands knotted through my hair, shifting my head gently to face him. Despite the heaviness of sleep, my eyelids fluttered open. The room was dim, barely lit by the sunlight filtering in.

"Stay longer," I protested, my voice hoarse. "You're my pillow." His body was the finest place I'd ever laid my head.

"I wish I could." He managed to climb out of bed, and started across the room in all his naked glory.

God, he's gorgeous. I couldn't pull my eyes away.

"I set a meeting for this morning under the pretense you'd be kicking me out like you did yesterday."

I pulled his pillow closer and crushed it under my weighty head, my hair wild around me. "I didn't kick you out. I just thought it was best you return to work."

"And now…"

"And now I am fully aware of how good it is to keep you barricaded in this room with me. Consider it a win for you." My lips curled.

He walked back to me and leaned down, lowering the blanket and ensnaring my nipple. His mouth gave a pop when he released it after a rough suckle. "I do." He straightened, staring down at me with a tilt to his head. "As long as you're here when I return, I'll help you barricade that door after dinner. I'll be your prisoner all night."

"Sounds like paradise," I said, swooning.

"Yes, it does."

"I guess I better be awake when you get home this time."

That familiar devilish smirk I secretly cherished crept over his lips. "I have no issue waking you myself."

A primitive thrill shot through me. "I'm sure."

Logan climbed back on the bed, hovering over me and caging me within his arms. I rose up and kissed him, ignoring the nag of what I hoped wasn't terrible morning breath. I wouldn't focus on the mood killer, though. I was too happy.

"Wake up, you dirty lovebirds!" came the booming voice of Jax as he pounded on the door. "I have to go, and the little prince is being a terror about getting out of bed."

Logan's head dropped down for a moment. Then slowly, with a tired groan, he sat up on the edge of the bed.

"I have to say, I think I have the wrong impression of your brother. Is he always up so early?" I asked, wrapping my arms and legs around him from behind.

He shrugged. "Sometimes, yes. He can be helpful with Oliver, but I'm not foolish enough to count on him due to his lack of consistency. Honestly, I haven't really been paying much attention to Jax lately." He held my ankles on his lap.

I stroked his hard length with my foot. "And why is that? You have other things distracting you?"

His head dipped back, landing on my shoulder, his eyes closed. He looked so peaceful; sated. "Many things. Wonderful, sweet things that keep me in my bed longer than I should be."

"Oh, well. I'm sure no one minds," I teased.

He chuckled. "I do consider that one of the perks of owning my own business."

"Employees may ignore it. Oliver, however, I'm sure will insist on you leaving this bed at some point. That kid is too adorable to disappoint, so you better be getting up."

"Maybe. But from the sounds of it, he too is looking to sleep in today, so…"

In a wildly dexterous move, Logan whipped around and snatched me up, tossing me under him. There was no time to react before he slid inside me, thrusting as my body stretched to accommodate his thickness. My throat singed as lurid, continuous moans spilled out. The benefit of having a gorgeous man in my sleeping place was that my body was always ready for him.

Logan's lips covered my taut breast, his tongue torturous. My back arched off the bed and his arms slipped under me, pressing me to his chest. With each plunge, his groans morphed further into feverish grunts.

A hammering fist roared against the door. "Fuck her later!" Jax bellowed. "He's going to be late!"

Logan never ceased, thrusting faster and harder, sweat beading over his forehead. I gripped his arms, holding on as he did just that: fucked me. His body began to quiver, and when he pulled out, careful not to unload inside me, he was grinning.

I burst out laughing, my arm shielding the heat flooding my cheeks.

"You still need yours," he said, eyes glistening with mischief.

I couldn't say a word once my laughter faded, my chest heaving. Yes, I needed more.

After a fierce kiss, he pulled back and stood from the bed, disappearing into the en suite. I listened to the sound of running water until he emerged, holding a wet washcloth. Running the hot damp cloth over my stomach, he leaned down above my ear and murmured, "You'll have to wait till I return tonight."

"Who's the tease now?" I pushed at his chest to shove him away, a smoldering ache already present in my body.

He chuckled. "Consider it my way of keeping you here waiting for me…waiting for more."

His devilish voice spoke to the most feminine place hidden deep in my loins.

"You know I'm not going anywhere."

"It's best to have assurances in place."

His cockiness only added to my need for him.

Logan helped me up, and I'd padded halfway across the room to take a shower when he whirled me around, my back colliding against his chest. His hot breath caressed my ear.

"Tonight, I'll have you unraveled and spread over my bed for hours and hours once again."

"Looking forward to it." I pivoted back, landed a quick kiss to his chin, then slipped out of his arms and retreated into the bathroom.

Logan and an adorably grumpy, sleepy-eyed Oliver sat at the table while I carried over a tall stack of pancakes with strawberries sprinkled around the platter. They were from a quick-batter recipe I'd learned from my grandmother.

"Pancakes!" Oliver squealed, his tired eyes flashing bright.

Logan chuckled under his breath as Oliver shoveled a piece into his mouth the second I'd poured syrup over the top. I sat across from them both with a glass of orange juice in hand, smiling.

"Hope they're good. I haven't made them in a while."

"I love 'em." Oliver swallowed, smiling widely. "Daddy never makes 'em when I have school."

Oh crap! I hadn't even thought to ask what Oliver could eat. Logan had showered in another room—I'd guessed to avoid another sexcapade—and then had been helping Oliver get ready. I'd used my free time to make breakfast, since I knew they were behind schedule, and it was my fault. Not that I regretted my morning...at all.

I chanced a glance at Logan, who was placing a bite in his

mouth, staring at me with amusement written over his relaxed features.

"Sorry," I mouthed, my face scrunched with worry.

His eyes sparkled with delight, his smile relieving my anxiety. "They're delicious. Thanks for making them—especially in a rush."

"More syrup, pleeeease," Oliver drawled, stretching his arm out, but the bottle sat on the other side of Logan. I had a feeling that was for a reason.

"You have enough," Logan told him. "Let's finish and get you to school."

I felt worse. God knew how Oliver would act at school after loading up with sugar. *Great, Cassandra.*

Oliver's shoulders fell, a pout forming as he forked another bite into his mouth. Perhaps as a method of distraction, Logan reminded Oliver to give his teacher a paper in his book bag he'd signed. Soon, Oliver started going on and on about the new class pet: a lizard named Zed.

Logan was amazing with Oliver. I already knew that, but watching their interactions at the table swelled my heart. They were totally in sync and completely natural together. The bond between them was undeniable, and Logan made being a hands-on father look easy and effortless. I knew that probably wasn't the case, but he never seemed annoyed or bothered by Oliver.

"If the teacher picks me, I get to bring 'im home!" Oliver exclaimed.

"For the weekend *only*," Logan clarified.

That didn't faze Oliver. Whether it was for a weekend or forever didn't matter—he was simply excited about the opportunity to take care of Zed at his house.

Logan wiped Oliver's hands when he held them up, complaining they were sticky from the syrup but with the most natural smile. He loved his boy, and I loved them both. I couldn't remember the last time I'd felt so at home. It was a family morning—and one that I couldn't help wanting to experience every day.

As they carried their cleared plates to the sink, I made a mental note to ask Logan for a list of foods Oliver could and couldn't eat. It was for while I was staying there, but I also knew I'd need it for much longer than that.

Chapter Seven

Loyalty

After a bear hug around my waist, Oliver rushed out the door, calling back for his daddy to hurry.

"Breakfast was perfect," Logan crooned against my lips, his voice decadent. "You're perfect."

"You're not too bad yourself," I teased, my mouth brushing his.

With a low growl, he claimed my lips, his strong hands sliding through my hair. He cupped my head as he drew me closer, deepening the kiss. Passion and heat swirled within me when his tongue parted my lips and stroked my own. I ached to wrap myself around him, holding him there indefinitely. Our lips finally parted, albeit reluctantly, leaving me breathless and greedy for more.

"Drive safe," I said in a panting whisper, my pulse racing.

"I always do," he answered, hands still cradling my head. He pulled me in for one final kiss: a single, delicious peck that left a lasting tingle over my swollen lips. With that, he was walking away, heading out into the frosty morning.

I stood in the foyer, my skin buzzing and panties soaked, unsure what to do with the rest of my day. A run was the first thing that came to mind. It had been three days since my last one, and I needed the fresh air as badly as I needed more of Logan's touch.

By the time I was halfway up the stairs to dress in warmer clothes, the doorbell was ringing. I halted my step and waited to see if Jax would answer it, but another ring of the bell told me that wasn't happening. It appeared I was alone, though I hadn't heard him leave.

The bell continued almost incessantly until I reached the door and yanked it open in a huff of annoyance, expecting to find some punk friend of Jax's.

Instead, there stood Hilary. Redness rimmed her fury-filled eyes, dark bags underneath them. She looked exhausted, but I knew that wasn't all she was feeling when she stormed past me and blew out a sigh.

"Well, *hello*!" she bit out, unwrapping the thick black scarf from her neck.

I scrunched my brow, ignoring the barb in her tone. "Why aren't you at school? It starts in, like…" I scanned the room for a clock.

Her eyes bulged. "Are you serious right now?"

To say I'd been avoiding her wasn't entirely true—I was simply unconsciously avoiding everyone outside the West household. I'd seen Logan pack my phone before he brought me to his house, but I'd never felt like charging it. Instead, it sat in the small pocket inside my duffle. I knew there'd be consequences, but the peace I'd experienced the previous day was worth it.

So worth it.

Slowly, I brought my attention back to her, watching as she paced. A pang of guilt hit me when I took in the paleness of her usually bright complexion. Now I was the one at a loss of what to say, so it was best to settle in and let her get it out. I knew her well enough to know I was in for it, but was somewhat surprised to see she looked almost unsure of where to start her rant.

Hilary stalked toward me with slow, determined steps. "Do you know how many times I called you, huh? It's been *three* days, and I haven't heard a word from you!"

Yeah, I'm in trouble. "I'm sorry. I figured you'd know I was here, or—"

"Or what—assume you decided to skip town? Or worse, were hiding out somewhere alone, needing me?" Her voice and head both dropped with the last two words. She was hurting, and had the tables been turned I would've been going out of my mind as well.

"Damn it, Cassandra." She looked up, glossy-eyed. "I've been so worried."

"I'm sorry, really. I guess I figured you'd call Logan. Caleb has his number."

She rolled her eyes. "That's not the point. But yes, Caleb called Logan. I damn well insisted."

Relieved I hadn't caused too much anxiety for a pregnant woman, I replied, "So you knew I was safe."

"I knew you were *alive*." She threw her hands in the air, getting worked up again. "If not for Logan forcing Caleb to keep me away for a couple days, I'd have come busting through that door the second I heard."

I smiled to myself. "Logan just wanted me to rest."

"I know." She relaxed, her shoulders sagging as she stood in front of me. "I was just hoping you'd do so after calling your best friend and telling her you're all right."

Before I could reply, her arms were around me. She dragged me in for a hug, her anger a thing of the past.

She pulled back, tears glistening in her eyes. "I'm sorry for freaking out. I can't even imagine what you're going through. Tell me what I can do—anything."

"Honestly?"

She nodded.

"You can go to school. The last thing you need to be doing is missing a day of work—you'll be missing plenty I'm sure once the morning sickness hits. You've never been good at handling yourself sick." I smiled, relieved to see her shoulders deflate further.

"I can handle myself just fine," she retorted, holding back a smile. "And I wouldn't be late if I didn't have to wait forever for Logan to leave. He'll be lucky if Oliver makes it on time."

"You waited for him to leave?"

"Yeah, I sat in your driveway next door. Didn't want him standing over us, trying to convince me to leave."

Where did that come from? "He wouldn't. He knows I'm feeling better—and don't try to change the subject. How are you feeling? You're already such a baby when you're sick, and now you're having one." I laughed wholeheartedly, basking in the comfort I felt from teasing her. "It's a good thing I got plenty of rest. It's going to be a long nine months."

"Funny." Hilary turned her attention to the foyer, surveying the area before walking toward the living room. "Your man has some good taste." She stared up at the massive painting of Oliver as a toddler playing with wooden blocks, which hung in the center of the room. "And a seriously cute kid." She turned back to me. "You make the perfect addition."

Addition? "Meaning?"

She slouched down in the leather chair. "I'm just saying—you fit in here."

"Hardly," I scoffed. "This house is not me."

"Maybe not yet, but I know you, and I was the one getting an earful the other day from a man crazy in love—a man that wasn't going to let anything happen to you. It's inevitable—before you know it, your painting will hang on one of these walls." An abrupt giggle caught in her throat. "I'm guessing the first will be hanging in the bedroom: a scandalous nude."

I rolled my eyes and sat across from her. Was this my future? My relationship with Logan was technically new, but with everything we'd been through, it felt like I'd known him forever. I couldn't recall a time when he wasn't in my life, and I didn't want to. And Oliver...I didn't want to confuse him.

My thoughts were interrupted.

"So has he...you know..." Her brows rose suggestively.

"No, I *don't* know." *What is she getting at now?*

She released a disappointed breath. "Has he painted you? Caleb said models hire him. I mean, I think....I don't know." Her brows pinched together, her features sympathetic and her words rushed as she tried to back pedal the subject. "Forget I said anything."

"No, he hasn't painted me," I said, ignoring the burn of jealousy. A grin covered my lips as I added, "Yet."

She relaxed. "I don't know why I even brought it up." Crossing her leg over her knee, she tried to grab my attention again, which was fighting the pull to drown in thoughts of Logan surrounded by beautiful supermodels. He'd better not have kept those paintings.

Logan loves me, supermodel or not, I reminded myself, brushing off my silliness.

"So how long are you staying here?"

I sat up in my seat. "Going home tomorrow. Do you want something to drink?"

"No, you're right, I better get to school. I just needed to know you were okay." She stood and fastened the top button of her coat—one she'd hidden in the back of her closet when her mother bought it a few years earlier, claiming it was too bulky. It was too early for her to have a bump, so why was she trying to cover up?

"Have you told Caleb yet?"

She shook her head. "I've only known a week. I need more time." She pulled her gloves out of her pocket and focused on them instead of my inquisitive stare. "Call me when you get settled back home and I'll come over. We can do a girls' night."

Oh no, she isn't going to avoid this. "You need time to what?"

She sighed, dropping her head. "I don't know...to think. Let's not worry about it right now. After everything you've been through, we shouldn't even be talking about my issues."

"No, I want to talk about it. Tell me, what is there to thin—"

My words fell away at the sudden, somber drop of her expression.

"I better go." She tightened her scarf back around her neck and headed toward the door.

"Wait! Hilary, I'm serious, we need to talk about this. I know you're nervous, but making a rash decision isn't—"

"I can't be a mom, all right!? Not yet, anyway. That's what *you* always wanted." Her shoulders fell as she blew out a breath of air. "Damn it, Cass, let's not do this right now."

"Sit down," I ordered curtly. "If you want to know what you can do to help me, you can talk to me, because right now you're all I'm concerned about."

Slowly, she moved back to the sofa and sat. "There's the Cassandra I've been missing," she mumbled with a small smile.

"Talk," I prompted, sitting beside her.

"You know I love Caleb and I always dreamed one day I'd make him mine, but beyond that...I never gave it any thought. Dumb, I know, but I just want to have some fun with him before we settle down with kids and responsibility."

"You're going to make a wonderful mother." I placed my

hands on hers and squeezed gently. "Look at me. I'll be here—anything you need, I'll be here to help, so please don't do what you're thinking of doing."

"I would never. I thought about it, but I can't." Her gaze fell to her stomach, where she placed her hand. "It's a little Caleb in there." A smile touched her lips as she looked up, but it was brief. Her next words flew out in one rapid breath. "Adoption is the only way. I have to wait till I'm beginning to show, then leave. I have family up north I can visit till the birth, then—"

"Whoa whoa whoa! Hold up!" I shot out. Was she serious? "You can't just disappear for six months and expect no one to ask questions—for Caleb not to ask. This isn't 1950! Are you insane? This is the real world. You have a job, and..." I shook my head, flabbergasted we were having such an outlandish conversation. She couldn't leave. She couldn't just give up the baby without telling Caleb. That wasn't even legal.

I stood, needing space to comprehend.

"You're my friend, Cassandra—my best friend. I need you to keep this secret."

"What?" I breathed out. She was serious. *Holy crap! How do I talk her out of this?*

"I talked to my aunt in Toronto. She said she knows the landlord of a small loft apartment on her block, and the rent is cheap. I'll get a job there, and before you know it I'll be back. Everything will be normal again."

My head was spinning, tears burning my eyes. "Hilary." I had so many words to say, but no way to get them out. I was shocked silent. All I could muster was a lifeless, "Don't."

"I have to."

"No, you *have* to talk to Caleb. Let him be there for you."

"Right, like you let Logan be there for you?"

That hit low and hard.

"That was different."

"Really? 'Cause I remember seeing you hurt and scared, a guy who loved you and wanted nothing but to work his ass off for your forgiveness, and you treating him like shit!"

My mouth fell open. "What? That was...he hurt me."

"And he apologized again and again! Do you know how many nights he showed up at Caleb's drunk out of his mind, with worry and regret over what he did to you? He would just sit there on Caleb's couch staring at nothing in the dark until he passed out."

Logan. I wanted to hold him and comfort him more than ever, even though we'd already moved on from the past together.

"Why didn't you tell me?" I whispered, sadness overwhelming me.

"I couldn't. You were so angry, and I understood that. You had a right to be. But Logan...he took everything you threw at him, and I stood by you each and every time. All I want is for you to do the same."

"But Caleb hasn't done a thing wrong."

"I know, but I'm terrified of losing him, and of being a shit mother. I don't want this. Not now. So please, either stand beside me and help, or stay out of it and keep your mouth shut. You owe me at least that much."

The door was slamming behind her before I was able to speak. *What the hell just happened?*

"I believe you just got put in your place."

I turned and glared at Jax, who was wearing a smug grin.

"Didn't think you were still here," I said, irritated at too many things.

"Well, I am, and your friend...is she always that bitchy, or is it a pregnant thing?"

"She's not... wait, you heard? Jax, you can't tell anyone.

Do you understand? Not even Logan."

His eyes gleamed. "So you're saying this is a secret?"

"Obviously."

"A secret you're keeping from my dear big brother." He clicked his tongue in mock disapproval. "I'm not sure he'd appreciate me lying to him. I mean, he's given me a place to stay, money in my pocket..." He let his words hang.

"What do you want?" I sighed, gathering my hair and twisting it in the back out of my way.

"Your help."

"With?"

"Natasha."

"Why? You hate her."

"I do, but for the moment I need to appease her."

"So let me see if I understand correctly: She has something on you, so you're attempting to blackmail me?" I wanted to laugh at the ridiculousness.

"That about sums it up. I knew there was more than one reason Logan fell for you."

With a disgusted grunt, I crossed my arms. "I'm not helping you with anything." I brushed past him to exit the room, making my way toward the stairs.

"Just ask Logan to be nicer to her. That's all I'm asking."

"No. Why don't *you* be nice to her?"

"I am!"

I reared back, gaping at him. "That was you being *nice* yesterday?"

"Sure was." He flashed a cocky grin that spurred my irritation and had me moving again—faster.

"I'm not helping you with anything that is ordered and not asked for politely. Find some manners, already." Yeah, bitchy Cassandra was in the house.

"Then I'll just make a quick call to Caleb to let him know

his girlfriend is planning to give away his child. Caleb has a temper—especially where family's concerned. You ever see it?"

I exhaled a long-winded breath and halted my steps. "Tell me why you're helping Natasha to begin with. What does she have on you?"

His smugness disappeared, and was replaced with irritation. "She just wants a chance to prove herself, that's all. What she has on me means shit compared to my nephew having a chance with his mother. We need to give her a chance to try. Ask Logan to at least acknowledge her, and I won't speak a word about Miss Preggo."

Holding his stare, I felt a smile creep onto my expression. "No. If I want to help Natasha, it will be on my own terms, and because I believe she deserves it—not because of you or anyone else. If you want to call Caleb, I can't stop you. But if you do, you and me?" I pointed back and forth between us. "You can kiss any chance of us ever being friendly again goodbye."

I'd begun climbing the stairs when he called out, "All right, damn, can't blame me for trying. Honestly, I'm impressed. Thought you'd do anything to protect her secret."

"Like I said, it's not my secret. And I'll never lie to Logan."

That seemed to please him. "Well, it's safe with me. I won't tell a soul."

Smiling to myself, I continued walking. "Thank you."

"You should know, though, Logan hates secrets. Just a little fact to remember."

I nodded as he appeared beside me. "Good to know, but I told you, I won't lie to Logan...*ever.*"

We walked up in silence a few steps before I asked, "So, where were you?"

"When?"

"When the doorbell rang. I waited for you to answer it. Wait, let me guess—chilling in your room for some guy time?'

He chuckled. "Nope. Shower."

"Ah." We reached the top. "I'm about to go running. Want to join?"

Suddenly, he was laughing. "I attempted to blackmail you minutes ago, and now you're asking me to go jogging with you?"

"I am. No reason we can't be friends."

"I'm intrigued. Most chicks would've either folded and accepted defeat or threatened to tell Logan."

"Well, I'm not doing either. So what do you say? Are you a runner?"

"Sounds fun, but I have plans."

The doorbell rang a moment later, and his brows rose. "Now *that* is someone I'll be spending time with in my room—and I'll be greatly enjoying myself."

Jax headed down the stairs and opened the door to reveal a beautiful brunette with a short pixie cut and not even a trace of makeup on. She looked sweet, friendly, and so not Jax's type, but what did I know about what he looked for in a girl?

He held out his hand, telling her to enter, and led her up the stairs past me. "Cassandra, this is my tutor. We have some studying to do."

"Studying?" He wasn't in school.

She said a quick hello as Jax threw a sly wink my way behind her. "Lots of studying," he mouthed, grinning.

Shaking my head, I laughed. Yep, it was in the genes. Poor Oliver.

Chapter Eight

SURPRISES

The instant I stepped outside, frigid air filled my lungs and my feet sprinted forward, searching for warmth. Logan's driveway was recently plowed, but the road was covered in drifted snow. I jogged steadily until I reached my usual turnaround, then began my trek back.

My mind was jumbled with thoughts of Hilary, her unborn child, and the opportunity she was robbing Caleb of. It was surreal to think of how much her life was changing, and I knew it was her body and her decision. But I also knew Hilary better than anyone. She was obviously scared, and I needed to figure out a way to break through that fear and convince her that she had the support surrounding her to raise a child. Regardless of whether Caleb was one of those people, she'd be taken care of. That baby would be loved—I'd make sure of it.

My eyes closed briefly as I attempted to clear my head of everything, including the image that fought to break through as I passed the place where I'd parked my car innocently behind Kurt's a few short days ago: the spot where I'd started my race through the forest.

I shook the thoughts from my head, increased my speed, and cranked up the music on the iPod I'd found on Logan's dresser. His preference in music was different from my own, which created a sense of safety around me. I felt as though he was there looking out for me.

When I reached Logan's driveway, I gazed over to my house, where two white trucks with construction logos on the side doors sat. Strangers were in my home. I knew they were there to repair the damage, but it still left me unsettled.

I switched off the blast of Pearl Jam and entered Logan's house, ready to shower and begin my mission to find Scout. Whatever 'studying' Jax was up to in his room didn't involve looking for my pup, and I couldn't sit around and wait any longer.

Dressed in a pair of jeans and white snug-fitting sweater after my shower, I made my way to Jax's room. It wasn't hard to find, considering the sounds leaking out. *So much for asking him to print flyers.* I made my way farther down the hall to Logan's office and opened the door. A massive flat computer screen sat on top of his desk, with a printer off to the side atop a hutch.

My internal debate to use it ended quickly. It felt wrong without Logan's permission—not to mention, knowing him, it was probably password protected. Going to my house wasn't an option, which left only one alternative.

I waited patiently, playing solitaire on my fully charged phone until Jax's door cracked open and the surprisingly gracefully composed tutor slipped out. The second she saw me, she flushed.

Relax, I wasn't listening.

"Jax is a great guy," she said, as if words were necessary, slipping into her coat. With one sleeve on, she winced, lowering her head.

"You okay?" I moved toward her.

"Yeah, thanks. I'm a bit of a wuss. It was my first time."

What! First time? And a wuss? What the hell? I was seething. *This poor girl.*

"Hey, don't say that about yourself. I'm sorry...I know it's not my place, but..." I couldn't hold back. "...Jax doesn't seem like the type of guy to get serious with a girl. You should be careful."

Her brows knit together. "I have no interest in dating Jax. I mean, he's hot..." She smiled. "But he's screwed both of my roommates."

"Oh."

"In the last week," she added.

"Ew, okay then." I was officially confused and grossed out.

"See you around," she said, looking a bit too satisfied for my taste. How was it that the West men brought even the strong women of Harmony to their knees? I was *not* impressed.

Holding back my frown, I waited until she turned out of the hall. The second she was out of sight, my fists began pounding.

"No need to knock."

I opened the door slowly and warily, especially at his next words.

"Forget something, or did you change your mind about wanting more?"

Yuck. I made a face with my head downcast, not wanting to see anything I wouldn't be able to block out. "Nope, just need a favor."

"Shit!"

Jax's legs were all I saw leaping across the room. I peeked up, catching sight of a white sheet floating down from his hands, covering something in front of the wall. Cautiously, I raised my head, relieved to find him standing there fully dressed and looking surprisingly nervous.

"What do you want?" his voice grated.

"What's that?" I nudged my head toward the sheet.

"Nothing. You said you needed a favor?"

He was definitely hiding something, but considering he wanted me gone, now was the perfect time to ask. "I need to borrow your car."

He blew out a rapid snicker. "No, seriously, what's up?"

"Come on. Mine's not back yet, and I wanted to make some flyers to post around town."

"Flyers for what?"

My eyes widened. "For *what*? For Scout!"

"Oh, right, yeah." He at least attempted a sympathetic shrug, but I wasn't convinced. He'd forgotten all about my dog.

"I take it you grew bored of looking for him."

"Not at all. I got everyone I know out there searching. So, did you make the posters?"

"Not yet. I need a computer."

"Here, use mine." He grabbed his laptop from the desk and unplugged it. "It will print in Logan's office. I'd give you my car, but nobody drives it except me, so how about a compromise? I'll give you a ride downtown, drop you off, and when you're done with your…business, I'll pick you up and bring you back."

"So that would make you my…personal driver?" My lip quirked up.

"Yeah, yeah, go make the flyers. I need a shower." His hands raked through his hair.

"I'm sure you do!"

He grabbed a towel hanging over his desk chair and snapped it at me. "Out! I'll be ready in ten."

Carrying his laptop, I laughed at his persistence as he guided me back to the door and ushered me out into the hall. I turned back to throw a clever retort for his briskness, but was faced with a slamming door and the telltale sound of a lock clicking. He was definitely hiding something, and if need be, I'd find out. But for now, I was pleased I had a computer and a ride.

"Call me when you're ready, but not before three," Jax said, pulling into a fire lane in front of *The Harmony Tribune*.

I unbuckled my seat belt. "Why three?" It wasn't even noon yet.

"'Cause I have things to do, too. So if you want a ride, hit me up after then."

"Fine." I climbed out, my hands full of a massive stack of flyers. "Thanks," I said, my smile genuine.

"No problem. Oh, and uh, no need to tell Logan I helped with those." He glanced at my hands.

My brow scrunched. "Okay," I replied.

With that, I closed the door and watched as he merged back into traffic, heading toward the college. When I turned back, I couldn't help but want to pay a little surprise visit to Logan.

The newspaper was housed in one of the oldest buildings in town. It was also one of the largest, which wasn't saying much; if you plucked it up and situated it in the middle of a real city, it'd probably be one of the smallest there. But to us in Harmony, it was grand. The architecture alone had caught my attention even as a young child, and although I'd been curious, I'd never entered; for some reason, the mystery held more appeal. But now I'd finally get a glimpse inside.

I wondered if Logan would give me a tour. The thought had me way too giddy.

Inside, the design was as breathtaking to behold as the exterior's. Massive columns and domed ceilings highlighted the mural on the front wall: an image of the building during its construction over a hundred years prior.

"Cassie?"

I turned to find Mrs. Welsh, my high-school librarian and the widow of the previous owner, walking out from behind the front desk. I'd only seen her in occasional passing over the last few years.

"Mrs. Welsh, hi! How are you?" I asked, surprised to see her there. I figured she'd retired for good after her husband's death and selling the paper.

"I'm doing great, as always," she said, though the concern etched over her brow told me she wasn't immune to the town gossip. "How are you, dear?"

"Good, as always." I smiled brightly. She didn't need to worry about me.

She sighed thoughtfully. "Still the spitting image of your mother at your age. A hellion, she was."

I laughed. Every time I saw her, she told me the same thing. And she wasn't the only one—I'd heard it from others, but never once could I picture it. The mother I knew was the epiphany of moral standards.

"I didn't know you were working here."

"I know. Everyone thinks I need to retire, but to do what—sit in my house till death comes a-calling? No thank you." She looked around as if remembering another time. "This was his home, his life. It's the one place I still feel connected to him. I'm not leaving."

That was the ultimate dream for me: a powerful love that consumed you, even when you were separated by death.

"I'd do the same thing."

"Yes, well, maybe one day you will. I've heard through the

town cesspool that you've nabbed the affections of our mysterious new owner."

"Mysterious?" My amusement couldn't be contained.

"Yes, all the young ladies here are stepping over themselves for a chance at his attention, but he's all business the entire day."

I doubted that. My joy vanished. There were probably a few employees he'd dabbled with before me.

"I'm glad he kept you on board," I said, swallowing down the acidic burn of jealousy.

"He had no choice. I gave this paper to him because he had a dream for it—a passion for what needed to be done to get it rolling again—and he agreed to keep me on until my death, no matter how old or senile I became."

I grinned, laughing softly. "Sounds like you." *And him.*

"He said he'd never let me go, even if I changed my mind, and I said, 'Sold!'"

"He's persistent, so you better watch out."

"I'm counting on it." She looked pleased.

"It was good to see you again." I gave her a quick hug.

"You too. Don't be a stranger around here."

I waved goodbye and made my way further through the building. At desk after desk sat employees hard at work. I gave a few head-nod greetings, and a wave to an old friend from high school who was typing away, her baby bump pressed to her desk. She'd married her high-school boyfriend, and every time I saw them together they still seemed just as into each other as they were back then.

Smiling to myself, I continued until I reached the door at the end bearing a gold name plate inscribed with 'Logan West'.

"Can I help you?" the woman who sat at a desk directly across from his door asked. She was in her late thirties, with a PTA-mom vibe—exactly what I wanted to see in his secretary.

"Yes, I'm here to see Lo—uh, Mr. West." I smoothed my hand down over my coat and shuffled the stack of papers in my hands.

"Do you have an appointment?"

Did I need one? "No, but..."

"One minute." She lifted the receiver to her ear, then quickly set it back down. "His line's busy. Have a seat."

I nodded, suddenly uncomfortable. What if I was interrupting his day?

I'd placed the stack of flyers on my lap and was wondering if I should come back later when the door to his office opened. Mackenzie, the bitch who'd screwed Mark and flirted with Logan on more than one occasion, moseyed out.

What the hell *is she doing here? And in his office!?*

The poor flyers were rolled tightly in my grasp as rage simmered just below my surface. I fought the urge to jump up, grab her cheap extensions, and pound her face against the wall.

I blinked, holding my composure, and bit the inside of my cheek—hard. I hissed from the pain it triggered.

Mackenzie's gaze shot my way, and an instant fake grin appeared across her mouth.

"Cassie, hi! I haven't seen you in forever. How are you?" Her face screwed up and her voice lowered. "I heard about your streak of bad luck lately. Sucks."

I would've bitten my cheek again if it wasn't still throbbing, so instead, I stood up.

"I'm doing just fine. And how about you? Oh, wait, I don't care," I sneered.

She brushed off my rudeness, her smile unwavering. "Well, I'm perfect." She glanced back at Logan's door. "And so is he...*now*." She adjusted her shirt, as though anything she did would hide the obvious fact that she was trying to use her body in whatever she was scheming.

Keep my hands to myself. Hands to myself, hands to myself.

The mantra bounced around my head, along with so many other things I'd rather say or do. But not there—not at Logan's office. I wouldn't embarrass him. So, ever the classy one between us, I straightened my posture gracefully and stepped close to her.

"Always a pleasure," I hissed, shoving my shoulder into hers as I strolled to Logan's door and pushed it open.

"Miss!" the secretary called out, but I was in no mood. She should've been happy I was only barging into his office and not cat fighting in front of her desk. I shut the door slowly the instant I was inside, not giving Mackenzie the satisfaction of seeing me flustered.

Logan looked up from behind his desk, phone to his ear and confusion obvious.

"Fine, yes…listen, I have to call you back. Something important just walked in." He hung up a second later, his eyes never leaving mine. "Cassandra, sweetheart, how did you get here?"

"Jax." I strode toward his desk, where he regarded me carefully. He was right to do so—he had some questions to answer.

I set the flyers upside down on one of the chairs in front of his desk, then stepped around to him. He stood.

"How is your day going?" I asked, running my fingers over his tie.

"Much better now." His lips curled up.

"Yeah?" I balanced on the balls of my feet and kissed his neck. He smelled like my Logan—not a hint of Mackenzie on him.

What is wrong with me? He wouldn't. I knew deep in my soul that he would never hurt me, but still, I needed to show him that I was every bit a woman as any other that threw herself at him. I'd keep him overly satisfied to prevent him from even thinking about another.

"How are you feeling? Jax didn't give you a hard time, did he?" He cupped my cheeks, and I leaned into the gesture.

"I can handle him. The question is…can you handle me?" My brows rose suggestively.

His thumb traced my bottom lip. "I'm not always so sure of that," he confessed, his voice low.

I pushed against his chest and my eyes lit, demanding he sit. He obliged quickly. His tongue darted out, running over his lips, moistening them for my kiss that fell instead to his chin. The stubble there awakened my need for him.

"So, what were you up to before I came in?" I asked, bent down. My mouth ran down his jaw and began kissing his neck.

"Nothing important," he replied. His hands reached out to pull me onto his lap. I stepped back, out of reach.

"You sure about that?" I asked, swaying my hips as I sauntered back to his door and turned the lock. When I peered back at him, his eyes were blazing.

"Positive."

I bit my lip and undid the top button of my coat, then the next.

"What about the girl in here?" I prompted.

"Who?" he asked, his eyes drinking me in. With another open button, he was lost to my actions. "You're gorgeous. Come here," he demanded.

I shook my head, smiling coyly. "Not yet. First tell me what she was doing in here."

He blinked away his lust and stared at me, bemused. "What girl? Nobody's been in here all day besides a couple couriers."

"Couriers?" Mackenzie wasn't his employee. I felt the urge to break out in a happy dance, but instead undid the last button and let my coat fall to the floor. My hands moved to the hem of my sweater.

"Yeah, some papers were delivered. I was on the phone putting together a meeting. Didn't have time to pay attention, just signed off on them. Why?"

"Call me curious," I said in my best seductive voice.

"I'll call you whatever you like, just bring that gorgeous ass over here."

"Patience," I cooed.

"I have none where you're concerned."

I strolled back to him, stopping between his parted legs. When he reached for me, I stepped back again.

"No touching."

He frowned. "I don't think that's possible. You're too luscious."

"Then I'll have to do something about that."

His smile grew, and I knew he was intrigued. I pulled at his tie to loosen it, then slid it free. "Hands at your sides, or I'll restrain them."

His lip twitched. "*Restrain* me? Hm, that might not be so bad." He leaned back, getting comfortable. "Do your worst."

I placed the tie around my own neck, then dropped to my knees. "So, that last courier...did she do this to you?" His confusion at my question faded when I untucked his shirt and placed a wet kiss over his tight abs.

"No, nothing like that." His voice was thick and husky.

"Mmm. What about this?" I took his belt in my hands and opened it slowly, popping his fly with ease while my tongue ran down his happy trail.

"Ah, Christ...no, no, only you."

I smiled. "Good. Then that means she never had her hands in here?" I slid his zipper down, reached inside, and gripped my hand tightly around his cock.

"Never…ohhh…" He was panting, his head dipped back in pleasure as the pad of my finger caressed the tip of his head.

He raised his hips when I tugged at his pants and pulled them down just enough to free him. Shooting him a playful, crooked grin, I leaned down and pressed a kiss at the base.

"Only me?" My tongue ran down his shaft, and I noticed his hands clutching the arms of his chair. He was losing the battle of keeping his hands to himself, and it was obvious it was one hell of a fight.

"Yes, only you. I swear it."

"Good." I took him in my mouth fully, bobbing my head up and down, swirling my tongue. His groans filled the room, encouraging me to let go of any last inhibitions and show him just how crazy I was for him.

"I can't… Cassandra…yes…I'm going to…"

His hands flew out and fingers threaded through my hair; the battle was lost from his end. I continued harder and faster, and with another grunt, he let go.

Chapter Nine

PERFORMANCE

Logan dragged me up onto his lap and covered my lips with his. "I adore that hot mouth of yours."

"Mmm, ditto." My voice was silky and smooth. Every bit of woman I had hidden within me was raw on the surface.

"Now before you seduce me any further, my little vixen, tell me..." He tilted my chin up so my eyes met his inquisitive stare. "Why the questions about the couriers?"

"Nothing. Like I said, just curious." I was too relaxed to think about the she-devil run in.

"Try again."

Uh oh. The last thing I wanted was for him to think I was insecure in our relationship. I wasn't—not after all we'd been through.

I gazed past him, my eyes trained on the brick wall covered in paintings behind him. I wondered how many were his. "You look good in this office," I said. "It suits you."

His fingers stroked my knee delicately. "You look good in here with me, but don't try to change the subject." He cupped my cheeks gently, forcing me to acknowledge any fear I might have left over from Mark. "You were jealous? Worried?"

"No!" I pulled back, my hands bracing my body on the

arms of the chair. Logan was not Mark, and that little reminder ignited my spirit. "You're lucky to have me. Doubt you'd find anyone better in this town."

My feet hit the ground, but Logan swooped me back into his arms.

"Aren't you a confident one?"

"What can I say? My boyfriend brings it out in me. He just goes on and on about how perfect I am. It was bound to go to my head eventually."

"He sounds like a smart man." His eyes brightened.

"He has his moments…and what he lacks he makes up for with his deliciously perfect kiss."

"You don't say." Our noses brushed.

"Mm-hmm. Every single night I spend dreaming of his smooth lips running all…" I bent forward and kissed the side of his temple. "…over…" I placed a kiss to the corner of his mouth, then slid to his ear and purred, "…me."

His eyes sizzled. "Perhaps I could try, just this once."

"I should also mention he's pretty possessive and strong. I'd hate to see you get your ass kicked."

Logan released a full, hearty laugh, then curved his hands behind my neck. "It'd be worth it. I'd take a thousand beatings to spend the next hour with you."

"I like the sound of that." I wiggled on his lap.

There was a short beep, followed instantly by his secretary's voice.

"Mr. West? Sorry to interrupt, but it's a quarter till noon and you asked that I remind you of your meeting."

He released a breath of annoyance. It filled me with joy to see how much he wanted me.

"Seems that hour with you will have to wait until tonight," he said with a frown, leaning forward and pressing the intercom. "Thank you, Laura."

I rested back in his arms, nuzzling his neck. "Shame. I guess that means you can't join me for lunch?"

"I would love nothing else, but I have a meeting with an investor for a project my brother Lawrence and I have been trying to get off the ground for the past couple months. I can't miss it." His fingers stroked the area behind my knee.

"Okay," I replied easily.

He smiled. "How did I get so lucky?"

Giggling, I kissed him again. "I was wondering the same thing."

After I climbed off his lap, I grabbed my purse and began searching for my compact. "By the way, I like Laura," I admitted. She was the perfect secretary: attractive but not flashing it, and appeared extremely professional.

Logan stood, tucking himself back in. "Is that so?" he asked, zipping his fly and closing his belt.

"It is." I swiped on a streak of ChapStick while glancing at his reflection in the background of the tiny mirror. "But she should try harder to keep out the riffraff."

Humor filled his expression as he spun me around and grabbed both ends of his tie that was still around my neck, gently drawing me closer. "Anyone in particular?"

My shoulders rose innocently. "No one you need to worry about. I'll be sure to take care of it myself."

He pulled on the tie again, bringing my lips to his. "Anything you say."

"Anything?" I challenged.

The dirty path his mind was taking was evident in his eyes. "Anything."

"Could you hand out some flyers for me?" I ducked under his arm, the tie sliding over my head. He slid it back around his neck, watching me as I picked up a handful of papers from the stack and held them out to him.

"Flyers? For what?" He took the smaller stack, and when he looked down at it, his entire mood shifted.

My expression melted into a somber one. "I know you said Jax was on it, but it's been days and I can assure you Jax has been too occupied to properly search."

"Cassandra…" His gaze lifted slowly from the photo of Scout up to me, his features softening.

"If you could just put some up around the office, or…maybe I could buy an ad! Isn't that what clients do—buy a spot in the paper? How much is it for a small section?"

"Cassandra."

Something was wrong. It was written all over his face and deep in his tone.

"What is it?"

"Sit down," he said.

I shook my head. "No, just tell me. Did you already find him? Is he…"

Oh, God. I slumped down onto the seat. No—I was overreacting. I had to be.

"Logan?"

He set the papers on his desk and kneeled down in front of me, his hands taking mine. "Forgive me. I was only trying to protect you."

I fought back the sting of tears. "Protect me from what?" My breathing grew harsher. *Scout.*

"You were so overwhelmed that day, and I didn't want to add more stress to it."

My pup, my Scout. What did Kurt do!? I trembled as I waited for him to continue.

"One of the officers found Scout by the back door. I didn't know how to tell you. We were in the hall together when I saw the officer carrying him over. I directed him to go out front so you wouldn't see."

"He's dead!" I shrieked, my hands flying up to cover my mouth as tears obliterated the dam.

"No, he's going to be okay. Shit, I should have said that first, I'm sorry." He cupped my face, his thumbs wiping away the wetness there. "He's still at the vet, and should be able to go home soon."

I released a breath. "You *should* have told me that first!" I slugged him lightly in the chest for causing me to panic. "You should have told me that day!"

His hands traveled down my arms, reclaiming mine. "I know. I struggled with it. When you told me to call Jax, I did. I went to check on Scout. He was in the back of a squad car, barely able to breathe. Jax came right over and took him to the animal hospital. I was told Kurt has a vicious bite on his ankle; Scout attacked him—probably when he first entered your home." Logan's slight smile was a proud one. "He's a good dog. He was protecting you."

"What did Kurt do to him?"

"We believe he kicked him. He has a couple broken ribs and a ruptured spleen, but he's a fighter, just like you. Jax has been checking on him."

I sighed, willing further tears away. "That's why he didn't want you to know he helped me make the flyers."

Logan ran a hand down his face. "He made it clear he wasn't going to be the one to tell you. My brother doesn't do well with emotions."

"Not surprising." I rolled my eyes. "When can I see him? Scout, I mean."

Logan stood, pulling me up. "Whenever you like. He's at the vet around the corner. I'm sure he'd love to see you."

I wrapped my arms around him, holding him close. "Thank you—for taking care of him, and me. You're right...it probably wouldn't have helped if I knew then."

"Does that mean I'm forgiven?" he whispered.

"That means I understand and didn't have enough time to get mad at you," I clarified.

Laura's voice rang through the intercom. "Mr. West? Lawrence West is on line one."

"I'll leave you to it," I told him. "Good luck with the investor."

"If you can wait to see him, I'll take you first thing after work," Logan offered.

"Thanks, but I want to go now. I need to see he's really okay."

"I understand."

The kiss we shared when he snuggled me close in his arms left me breathless and swooning. But then again, his kisses always did.

"I'll see you this afternoon," he said, releasing me to return to his desk. I grabbed my coat and dumped the flyers in the recycling bin by his door. With his eyes on me, he lifted the phone.

"Lawrence, did you receive the fax yet?" he said into the receiver.

I blew him a kiss and walked out at a brisk pace, heading for Scout.

My visit with Scout was an emotional one. There was a bandage around his middle. The vet explained all the care he'd need to heal properly, and that I could take him home in the morning. After holding him on my lap for over an hour, thanking him for protecting me while simultaneously chastising him for not hiding from Kurt, I kissed the top of his head and promised to see him in the morning.

My walk from the vet to Haven was complete with damp eyes and shivering bones, but that wasn't what gripped my attention.

It was the keen sense that I was being watched—followed. I'd felt it since I'd left the vet's office, but didn't focus on it until I'd walked over a block and still couldn't shake it.

Stopping abruptly, I shot my gaze back, looking to see if it was paranoia or actual fear to confront only to find no one. I was alone on the sidewalk.

Pull it together! I reprimanded myself internally as I turned back and continued on.

Outside the front doors, I pulled off one glove and took out my phone, sending a text to Luke.

You busy for lunch? I'm outside Haven.

It took only a minute before he replied.

Can u deliver it to the office? I'm stuck here going over a case.

I can be there in twenty. What u want?

A break!

I chuckled. His father worked him harder than any other associate.

I meant food wise.

Surprise me!

Just a heads up I have a favor to ask.

I hoped he'd help me with Scout. I couldn't bring him home until he was healed at least enough to withstand one of Oliver's bear hugs.

U got it. I have one as well. C u shortly.

I sent a little happy face his way then tucked my phone back in my pocket, curious what his favor entailed. I wondered if he and Julia had hung out again since Valentine's Day.

When I walked into Haven, Caleb spotted me instantly.

"Hey, Cassie! How are you feeling?" he asked, stepping around the bar to wrap me in a hug. He pulled back, his brows scrunched. "You been crying? No way. Not in my place. Dry it up and show me that dazzling smile of yours."

It worked. He had a way about him that could pull a smile from even the most pessimistic fool.

I rubbed the corner of my eye. "Sorry. I just saw Scout. He's at the vet."

A slight frown appeared on his face. "Yeah, I heard about that. Sorry. But I gotta say, that's a damn good dog, protecting his pretty lady. Although I know Logan is more than happy to relieve him of that duty while he heals."

My smile grew. "I'm starving, and I promised to bring your brother lunch. Tell me you have something special back there."

"No grilled cheese today?" His brow shot up teasingly.

"Nah, I was thinking something different."

"Come on. I got a new chef who's been whipping up these unbelievable little sandwiches. Hilary can't get enough of them." He chuckled, passing through the swinging doors that led to the kitchen.

"Jacob, we need about eight of the deli delights," he told the guy standing in front of the massive oven. "A variety."

"You got it!" Jacob called back.

"Eight?" I questioned. That sounded like a lot. How small were they?

"I know Luke. He'll have half of them gone before you get a single bite." He looked back to Jacob. "Make that ten."

I laughed, following Caleb to a room farther in the back, where he sat. I hopped up on a long counter littered with paperwork, next to a tall beer. Caleb took a swig.

"So how are you, really?" he asked.

I swung my feet in the air. "Besides finding out about

Scout, I'm doing pretty good. Logan knows how to keep me distracted."

"I'm sure." He peeked up from the paperwork and snorted.

"So how are you and Hilary doing?" I asked, changing the subject, my blush fiery.

He jotted numbers down on one of the sheets in front of him. "She's been on edge lately." After writing a few more things down, he looked up at me. "Obviously she's been worried about you."

"Yeah, she stopped by Logan's this morning."

He chuckled, setting the top sheet aside and writing on the next. "She promised me she'd give you some space till today. I had a feeling she'd be there first thing this morning, since she disappeared while I was in the shower."

"She wasn't too happy I hadn't called her. She's like my sister," I told him, which was true. And right then, she was mad at me like one.

"I know. She's lucky to have you."

I changed the subject as sadness began settling in. "So, did you hear Luke spent Valentine's with Julia?"

"I did. She's a good girl, he'd be lucky to land her."

"Logan told me she was the reason you and him met."

"That's right. Logan knows I had no idea she was jailbait. The moment I realized, I stood there and took the hit. You know I never had a sister, but I can imagine if I did I'd be damn well protective of her. Logan was in the right, and next thing you know, we're poker buddies."

"Poker buddies?" I loved learning anything new about Logan I could.

"Yeah, Logan's my wingman. Damn, he'd take the shirt off someone's back; he's ruthless. I'm good, don't get me wrong, but Logan plays dirty when he has to. When he wants something—"

"He takes it," I finished for him. Oh, how I knew that. "Yeah, I know. I'll have to play him sometime. You taught me, remember? I was like twelve, and you were on the picnic tables at the park with Luke."

He looked ahead, almost thoughtfully. "Ah, right, I forgot about that."

"Hilary and I play sometimes. We suck, which means you weren't a very good teacher."

That broke through his musings. He shook his head once and looked over at me. "Hey now, I've been teaching Hilary a few tricks, so you best watch out for her."

His love for her was spelled out clearly in his crooked smile. I wished it was enough for her to see that he'd support her—that she could trust him enough to tell him about the baby.

"So are you and Jax friends?" I asked, searching desperately for an in to read him better.

"We're not enemies." He released a clipped laugh. "Jax has some growing up left to do, but he's a good kid."

"Yeah," I nodded, debating my words internally. "He reminds me of Logan when we first met: a bit of a whore."

"Hey now, you don't want Logan to know you thought so low of him."

"Believe me, he knew." I cracked a smile.

Caleb grinned. "Yeah, he did." He took another swig of his beer and added, "For the record, I tried to steer him away from you—at least, until I saw he was genuine."

"And when was that?" I was on pins and needles with curiosity.

"Shortly after you guys went to the farm. He said you were adorable." Caleb shook his head in amusement. "Logan never tells me anyone is adorable—not even Oliver. But you…you were adorable to him. Not sexy, or a superficial prospect—"

I scrunched my nose in disapproval of his choice of words and held up my hand to interrupt. "I got it. Adorable. That's me."

I wasn't sure how to feel about that. Logan saw me, *really* saw me, for more than just sex even then. Maybe it was relief I felt warming me to my toes, but still…I wouldn't mind if he found me sexy as well.

"Don't worry. He still checked out your ass more often than not."

I swatted his arm, another blush creeping over my cheeks as I swung my feet higher.

After a brief pause to build up courage, I took a stab. "Can I ask you a question?" My head was down, teeth gnawing at my lip.

"Of course."

Here goes.

"You ever think about the future? I mean, you turned this place into something amazing, you make a killer drink." I laughed, trying to relax my suddenly stiff shoulders. "You're obviously talented. And let's face it: You and Logan don't really fit in around here."

"You kicking us out of your town already?" He mocked a dramatic, stunned look.

I laughed more loudly, nervous hesitation in my next words. "No, I'm just curious what you want—in life and all."

He set his pen down slowly and turned to face me with his full attention. "That's a pretty deep question. Hilary send you down here?"

"What? No!" *Crap, not good! Abort! Abort!* "I was just thinking about *my* future and what I wanted, and…and thought I'd compare notes."

And I'm done. Blown! Stealth does not *work for me.* My palm itched to smack my face.

"Well, for now I want exactly what I have. You can tell Hilary I'm not interested in walking away from her." He leaned in and, with a mischievous crooked smile, whispered, "She and I have too much fun yet to be had."

And with that, he turned back to his paperwork.

"Seriously, she didn't send me down here. I came for the food and was just curious."

He nodded, unconvinced. *Great!*

"Food's up!" Jacob called, sliding a bag down the line. Caleb grabbed it and handed it to me.

"Take care of yourself. And tell Hilary I'll be waiting for her tonight."

With a sigh, I jumped down and opened my purse. "Right, so what do I owe you?"

"I won't tell you again—your money's no good here."

"Thank you." After a peck to his cheek, I headed toward the front. I glanced at the kitchen clock, and was surprised to see it was almost two. No wonder I was so hungry.

As I stepped through the swinging doors, I stopped, my gaze falling on Logan sitting at the bar with two men wearing uniforms from the prison. Guards.

Why is he here? I just saw him not even two hours ago. Did his meeting go well?

I decided to get out of my head, and had begun walking over when I heard the guard closest to him speak.

"Don't worry about it. He's scum, and will be dealt with as such."

Scum? They were talking about Kurt—had to be. My mind flew back to his words, remembering how Logan had paid off the guards last time.

"Another round on me, gentlemen," Logan said, his face

lit with a pleased grin.

Chapter Ten

SUSPICIONS

I stepped toward them with slow, precise steps, my entire body stiff. I was unsure how to interpret what they were saying.

No! I'm overthinking things—jumping to conclusions. I had to be.

I released a rapid breath and bounced my shoulders to break apart the heavy burden of unwarranted suspicion settling there.

"Hey. Thought you had a meeting," I said, surprising Logan when I rested my hand on his shoulders.

His barstool swiveled toward me. His relaxed features and easy smile sent my stomach into a full somersault.

"I did. Finished a while ago." He took my hand and pressed a kiss to my palm, his eyes never straying from mine. They spoke on their own—told me he was pleased to see me—and right there, with that single look, I was at ease.

He'd always had a way about him, but since Valentine's, I could no longer deny or fight the pull of his charm. I hadn't figured out whether that was a good thing.

I smiled back, forcing myself to ignore the two guards watching us.

"I didn't know you were still in town, or I'd have called

you to join me," Logan continued, patting his lap for me to sit.

I lifted the bag in my hand. "Can't stay. Bringing lunch to Luke at his office."

He pulled my hand to bring me closer, dragging me down until I collided with his chest. "Your office call to him better not be anything like mine," he whispered roughly, then placed a gentle kiss to my ear.

Ah, so Logan still had a hint of jealousy where Luke was concerned. It was ridiculous, yet it left me with a cheeky grin.

I straightened, adjusting my coat, and casually replied, "Doubtful, but you never know."

"Is that so?" he questioned, his eyes glistening.

I raised my brows playfully. Slowly, I tore my gaze from his and redirected it to the guard beside him, who was chewing on a toothpick.

"Sorry to interrupt your lunch. I'll let you get back to it," I said, suddenly uneasy, not wanting them to get back to anything involving Kurt.

"No problem, doll," the guard replied. "You're Felicia's daughter, right?"

I nodded, a tight smile in place. "That's me."

His smile grew. "She's got our pal George falling all over himself."

The other guard snickered, popping a fry in his mouth. "Sure does. The poor bastards that work the graveyard shift with him say he's writing poetry now."

"Really?" I made a mental note to get to know George better.

All three men looked at me and laughed. I narrowed my eyes at Logan and scowled playfully. "You'd be surprised what some poetry will get a man."

"Sorry, sweetheart, you're right. I need to give that some more thought," Logan said, his laughter still rumbling around us.

I bent to give him a kiss goodbye and he murmured, "I can't even imagine it getting any better, but if poetry does it for you…"

He left his words hanging between us.

"Enjoy your lunch—and don't be so hard on George. He seems like a good guy," I said, giving a slight wave as I turned to leave.

Halfway to the door, I felt an unsettling tingle that raised the tiny hairs on the back of my neck. On instinct, I jerked my head back and spun on my heel, ready to attack at the feeling of hands wrapping around my middle. Logan was there, his hands shooting into the air in defense.

"Just wanted to give you a proper goodbye," he explained, and I relaxed.

"Well, if that's all…" A soft laugh bubbled up from within me.

A mischievous gleam crossed his steely blue eyes, and instantly his hand encircled my waist, drawing me into his chest.

"People are staring." I scanned the room, but surprisingly enough, the patrons were too engrossed with their meals to notice us. Biting back my smile, I bathed in that wicked gleam in his eye. "Never mind, carry on."

And he did. His mouth demanded mine, tongue dipping inside, caressing and teasing. "I missed you," he confessed across my lips.

"I just saw you," I giggled.

"I always miss you."

I tugged on his bottom lip as we separated. "Good."

"Stay with me tonight."

It was a strange feeling, suddenly remembering the four days were up already. His eyes darkened as he watched the deliberation in my expression.

"Okay," I said softly. How could I say no? "One more night."

I blew him one last kiss and headed out the door, ignoring the troublesome thoughts about guards being bribed. Logan and I were happy, and nothing was going to ruin that.

During my lunch with Luke, he agreed to keep Scout for a couple weeks. In exchange for the favor, I agreed to find out why Julia had been not-so-subtly hinting that she had no interest in dating. If it had anything to do with Mark, I understood completely—a girl needs a break after dating a scumbag. I still didn't know the story about their breakup, but I had plenty of ideas.

After lunch, I met Jax, who was waiting outside the building to give me a ride as promised. I opened the passenger door and stepped back, surprised to find his car occupied not only by him, but the redhead I'd met once before who'd been bent over Logan's kitchen counter. I preferred her fully clothed and with the innocent smile she wore as she sat there, watching me.

"In the back, babe," Jax said, and the girl lifted her seat for me to climb in. But before I could duck into the back, Jax said, "No, not you—her."

The girl's head snapped his way, but he was unaffected.

"It's fine, I can take the back," I said, embarrassed for her.

He ducked his head, looking past her to me. "I said *her*, not you." His hand moved from the gear shift to her knee. "Now get that fine ass back there."

I crossed my arms over my chest, blocking her exit as she

attempted to step out.

"No! I said *I'd* sit in the backseat!" I yelled, revealing the depth of my annoyance. "Don't be a dick!"

Furious, I gestured for her to sit up out of the way, then lifted the seat forward and climbed in the back. The front seat slammed back into place, and timidly, the girl shifted back and shut the door. I met his glare in the rearview mirror with a firm one of my own.

"Calm down, Cassie. She doesn't mind," he grumbled. I heard him curse under his breath as we pulled away from the curb.

"Sorry," she whispered to him.

"Don't apologize. He was rude." I sighed, buckling my seatbelt. "Honestly, you can do better."

My statement was out of line, but watching her sit there satisfied to be just a toy for him left me irritated. My annoyance boiled over when she placed her hand tenderly over his on the gear shift and he shot her a mocking smile, then moved her hand to his lap.

Yuck!

My eyes rolled and I turned to stare—or, more accurately, glare—out the window. I hadn't figured out what made Jax tick, but I wondered if Logan's past lifestyle had rubbed off a little too much on his brother. If that was the case, I'd need to figure out how to intervene before he broke too many hearts in my town. Logan, I understood—Natasha had left him jaded. But Jax was too young to be that cynical. There was no way I'd sit back and bite my tongue.

But what was I supposed to say—'Learn some manners'? It was tempting, but it wasn't really my place.

"So I got a call from Logan," Jax said, his voice slicing through the awkward silence. "He said he told you about Scout."

"When did he call you?"

"About an hour or so ago."

Probably after his meeting with Lawrence and before the guards. My stomach sank, wondering once again why he was there with them, buying them drinks.

"Thanks for taking him to the vet," I said, ignoring the pang of worry I couldn't seem to shake. "I can't even imagine how scared he must have been."

"I'll admit I was a little nervous myself, but he curled up right here on my lap the whole drive and went to the doc with no problem."

Seemed Jax had a heart in there after all.

"Good. He can go home tomorrow."

"You need a ride to pick him up?" he asked in what appeared to be a sincere, no-strings-attached offer.

"Yeah, that would be great. I'm going to take him to Luke's in the evening. He's gonna watch him till he's feeling better—or at least until he's able to withstand some roughhousing with Oliver."

"Good idea," Jax replied with a chuckle. He glanced at me in the mirror and I nudged my head to the girl, who was picking her nails silently. His forehead crinkled in confusion.

I kicked the back of his seat and he shot me an irritated scowl in the mirror. I nudged my head to the girl again and raised my brows expectantly.

"What?" he mouthed, oblivious.

Men. I sat up in my seat as far as possible within the restraint of the belt, willing myself to hold in another eye roll.

"Hi, I'm Cassandra. We've never been properly introduced, and I don't think Jax has the manners to do so any time soon."

"Yeah, didn't cross my mind," Jax said, eyes on the road.

"No biggie. Jax and I aren't that close anyway," she

replied, peeking over at him with pursed lips.

Uh oh, somebody was in trouble. I'd put good money on him not getting what he wanted from her—at least not without some serious sweet-talking.

"Close enough to enjoy, but not close enough to get on my nerves," Jax explained. "Perfect acquaintance."

The girl rolled her eyes, forgetting I was waiting for her introduction. I slinked back in my seat, deciding it best to stay out of Jax's love—no, sex—life until I figured him out.

The instant we pulled into Logan's driveway, the redhead was out of the car and marching up to the front door, hands on hips.

"Good luck," I teased, climbing out.

"Right," Jax laughed, shoving his keys in his pocket. "She'll get over it the moment I take off my shirt and whisper a few sweet words in her ear."

"You sure are a cocky one. Logan teach you that act?" It was I who now had my hands settled on my hips.

"I don't need lessons on how to seduce a woman. How much you want to bet she'll be under me within ten minutes?"

"Ew, nothing." My face screwed up.

He laughed again, harder. "See you around, Cassie. I'm glad Scout's gonna be all right."

There he went, being all nice again. That made it really difficult to stay repulsed with him. In spite of myself, the corner of my lip curled up the slightest bit. It was all it took to show him we were good. With a knowing nod, he headed up the porch steps.

Deciding I didn't want to be in the house with them regardless of whether they were arguing or making up, I looked over at my place. It'd been only four days, but it felt like weeks.

I pulled my phone from my coat, checking the time. It was nearing four o'clock, and I knew Logan and Oliver would be home shortly. If I was going to stay another night, I needed a fresh change of clothes. And if I was being completely honest, it felt like the right time to face any lingering fears and go home for a little while.

Smiling, I adjusted my shoulders and crossed the lawn to my front door. My hands trembled as I dug out my keys. I stopped to inhale the cold air, allowing it to clear my nerves.

The lock turned easily, and I pushed open the door.

Once inside, I surveyed the living room slowly. Everything was in its place, as if the day Kurt had broken in was nothing more than a distant nightmare. I dropped my keys on the foyer stand and took a few steps farther into the living room, my hands buried deep in my pockets, fingers gripping my cell phone in the right pocket just in case I needed it.

With hesitant steps, I made my way to the kitchen. The only sign that anything out of the ordinary had happened was the new back door. It was constructed of a sturdy metal, with a glass window at the top. The deadbolt above the doorknob eased a fraction of my tension. I double checked it was locked, smiling when I saw it was.

Next was the bedroom, which was easier to take in than I'd thought it'd be. The blood stain was gone—not a hint of it remained. My new bedroom door was exactly the same as the previous one aside from the extra lock at the top.

My smile broadened as I pictured Logan with his three-piece suit and stern expression, rattling off his list of demands to keep me safe. He was too good to be true. That single thought warmed me to my very core.

My bed was made perfectly, but the comforter was new. I ignored the pesky memories of why it was replaced; it didn't matter. The new one was beautiful: pure white with a flower pattern just visible enough, stitched in white thread. I wondered if Logan had picked it out himself. It was too girly for his taste, but it was obviously something I'd love. I wanted to believe he knew me that well.

I sat on the bed and ran my hands over the soft material. When my eyes fluttered shut, it wasn't Kurt I saw storming into the room. Instead, I saw Logan. He was there on my bed, making love to me as he had on Valentine's Day. The mere thought of him erased the wickedness clawing to get back in.

I was home, and I was safe. The stiffness melted from my muscles and seeped through my pores as I lay back and closed my eyes, smiling.

"Cassandra!"

I shifted in my sleep, rolling my head to the side.

"Cassandra!"

"Mmm," I moaned, Logan's voice heavy in my dreams.

"Cassandra?"

It was now a soft whisper of a sigh calling out to me. I opened one eye slightly, peeking through a haze to find Logan standing over me, his hand scrubbing down his face.

"I couldn't find you. I was…" He closed his eyes and shook his head. "It doesn't matter. What are you doing here?"

With a hollow yawn, I stretched my arms above my head. His uneasy expression softened when I grabbed his arm and tugged. He complied instantly, shrugging out of his coat and pulling me into his arms as he lay down beside me.

"I fell asleep," I whispered groggily. "Sorry. What time is it?"

"Sixish. How are you feeling?" he asked, looking around the room.

I followed his gaze, ignoring the question. "They did a good job. I wish you'd let me pay you back," I said, running my fingers over his abs. My head rested in the nook of his neck.

"You already know the answer to that."

My eyes drifted skyward, and I knew he could hear the slight growl in my throat. "Can I at least make it up to you?" I shifted my head to see his face.

His lip quirked up. "As much as I like the sound of that, Oliver's waiting."

"I wasn't implying sex, perv boy! Something...better." Was that possible? I'd need time to think of something extraordinary.

"I'm intrigued." A full-blown grin spread over his lips. "But unfortunately, for now, we should go. We made you dinner. I thought you were up in my room resting."

"Okay, just let me grab some clean clothes." I looked back down at our entangled legs. "I wanted to come here alone first."

Logan encased me more tightly in his arms and pressed a kiss to the side of my head. "Understandable. So just one change of clothes?"

I smiled, pushing myself up to capture his mouth with a swift kiss. "Play your cards right and I might give you a bonus day," I murmured.

"Now you're talking."

He grabbed my hips and flung me on top of him, setting off a fit of giggles I couldn't control when his fingers worked painfully slowly up my sides.

"I thought Oliver was waiting!" I panted between squeals.

"He is, but you seem to be holding me captive," he teased, a wicked grin in place.

"Me!?" I yelped, gasping for air when he sat up, one hand locked around my waist and the other tickling me torturously.

"Stop!" I cackled. It was a horrible sound, yet his fingers

refused to relent. Swatting didn't help, and as much as I tried to roll off him, he blocked my every move. My heaving gasps and his boyish laughter were all I could hear.

Realizing I needed to gain control, I lunged forward and ensnared his bottom lip, then bit down gently.

His gaze darkened in surprise and his hands fell from my stomach, moving up to cup my cheeks. I opened my mouth to free his lips and placed a soft kiss over them.

"I forgot you play dirty."

"We need to go over your definition of 'playing dirty'. You know—pot, kettle, and all." I climbed off the bed and crossed the room to my dresser, pulling out a few items. "Come on, let me get some clothes packed before dinner gets cold."

"How about this?" Logan asked, appearing beside me. He grabbed the silk nightie I'd worn in his pool months ago, when he'd been watching me. My skin seared with goose bumps.

His breath was on my neck. "I want this framed on my wall to remind me of a night I'll never forget."

I grimaced, glancing over at him continuing to rifle through my drawer. "Not sure how that would look next to your artwork."

Logan held up the thin fabric, admiring it. "True. Then how about I paint you wearing it?"

My rummaging through the drawer ceased instantly at his suggestion. Slowly, my gaze moved back to his. "You want to paint me?"

"Since the day I met you, I've wanted you in my studio posing for me."

I blushed. The intensity in his eyes was thunderous.

"Okay," I said, nodding. His hands traveled up my stomach, and I winced at the burn from the scrapes still marring the area. I didn't want to be painted until my body was fully healed. "But not this weekend."

There was pure pleasure in his smile. "There's no rush. I'll always want to paint you."

I stepped back, loading my arms with a couple blouses and pairs of jeans.

"So, have you painted a lot of women?" I asked softly. *Why did I go there?* I knew the answer from Hilary, yet the question still came out. "Not that it matters. I was just curious, I guess. Never mind—don't even answer. Not my business." *Shut up!*

"Yes," Logan answered instantly.

"Right," I breathed out, my gut churning. *I should've known better than to go there.*

His hands encircled my waist, twisting me to face him. His finger took my chin, lifting my head. "I greatly enjoy painting, and there are many people who enjoy sitting to have someone capture them on canvas."

That's good enough for me. I swallowed, not needing to hear more.

"Any woman I painted outside of a paying job was faceless to me."

Seriously, you can stop now. Should I say something, or will it show insecurity? Maybe he needed to tell me. If he did, then I'd listen. I wanted to know everything about him, but the women...I'd seen enough to know I didn't really want to go there.

"Cassandra, they never meant anything," he explained.

I nodded, a tight smile in place. *Time to change the subject.* "I think I've got everything. You ready?"

"I want to show you," he offered, and I could've sworn I felt my jaw drop.

"What?" I stepped out of his hold, my face scrunched. "No! I don't need to see...anything. I'm good, really."

"That came out wrong." He sighed. "I meant I want to

show you my work. I never kept the paintings I did of women—only the ones I'm related to. And I promise they're fully clothed."

"I would hope so!" I laughed, knocking down the walls of tension that had been building.

Logan's thumb traced my chin, his eyes locked on mine. "You know I love you, and my past is just that—the past. I can only tell you that before you entered my life, I was a very lonely man. Oliver was my only reason to smile. To have you pose for me...." A smile curved his lips. "It would be an honor. A privilege."

I kissed his thumb, no longer caring about the women of his past. I already knew they were there, and that they meant nothing to him.

"I look forward to it," I said, then turned back to close the drawer. "Can you grab my bag from the hall closet?"

Logan left the room, and the excitement of imagining him behind the easel painting me sent my arousal into overdrive. He reentered a moment later and opened my closet.

"So, just out of curiosity...Natasha's painting, the one Oliver showed me..." My voice lowered, unsure of its next words. "Are there others you have of her? I mean, that are up in your studio?"

"No. I only have that one because..." He seemed to think it through as if he didn't already know the answer. But that look was cleared from his expression within seconds, and his confidence returned. "I thought one day Oliver might want to have it. It's the only image of her that I held onto for him."

"She found an apartment in town," I blurted out.

"And?"

"She wanted to tell you herself, but I figured you might want to know sooner rather than later. I'm sure you're relieved she'll be moving out."

"Yes, I am."

I'd been expecting a different reaction—surprise, at least. But he didn't seem surprised at all as he opened my closet door casually and flipped through the hangers.

He already knew.

"She already told you," I guessed.

He peered back. "No, I believe she wanted to wait till her apartment was ready—a reason for her to show me she was capable of responsibility."

It was true, but how did he know that? "Jax told you?'

"Sweetheart, nothing happens in my home that I'm not aware of—nothing." His thick voice was smooth with resolve.

My brows pinched together at his assured tone. As I thought over how he could've known without Natasha or Jax telling him, I realized he wasn't just looking through my closet—he was full-on inspecting my clothes.

"What are you doing?" I asked, bewildered, watching with wide eyes as he continued.

"You need something warm for this weekend," he said matter-of-factly.

What was this weekend? Did he have something planned? "Warm for…?"

With a beige turtleneck I'd never worn in one hand, he turned to show me a heavy wool sweater in the other. Both items had been tucked into the furthest depths of my closet.

"These will do," he said, removing them from their hangers.

"Um, no." My attempt to grab them from his hands was botched when he jerked them back.

"Why not? They're very…" He looked them over appraisingly before adding, "Cute."

"Great, but that's not exactly what I'm going for around you."

He smiled. "You're cute now," he said, watching me stuff the sweater in the bag but toss the turtleneck back into my closet, where it would remain.

"I guess that will do." He moved behind me, brushing against my back. "I'll be there to keep you warm if you catch a chill."

My breath caught at his words—a living, breathing entity full of promise.

Oliver is waiting with dinner! Stay on task!

"So where exactly will I be wearing this?" I prayed it was somewhere deep in the forest with no other humans around—only animals that could appreciate warm layers.

"That's a surprise." He glanced at his watch, then to me. "Come on. Oliver will be complaining if I don't get you home."

Get me home? The sound of that brought a smile to my lips. "I *am* home," I said, sauntering over to him. I dropped the final handful of clothes into the bag and zipped it shut.

"You know what I meant," he said, placing the duffle strap on his shoulder and taking my hand.

"I do." I smiled to myself.

The very second the front door to Logan's house shut behind us, Oliver came stomping out from the kitchen.

"It's cold now!" he pouted.

Logan placed my bag on the floor, chuckling lightly. "Blame Cassandra. She kept me distracted."

I feigned innocence. "I did not. Your father got lost."

"Lost?" Oliver questioned, his brows knitting together.

I approached him, nodding. "He sure did. Couldn't find his way back from my house."

Oliver debated what I was telling him for a moment, then slowly, a smile curved his lips. "Daddy needs a map! It's not far. I know how to get there all the time."

I followed him into the dining room, throwing a quick wink to Logan. "I think a map is exactly what he needs."

Chapter Eleven

REGRETS

Growing up an only child, I'd often dreamt of what it'd be like to have a brother, sister, and real family meal. Delighted smiles and pleasant streams of conversation about our days was how I'd painted the image, but for the first time I realized that might've been a skewed vision.

Dinner at Logan's that evening was the perfect domestic image I'd craved, with Oliver reciting events from his school day and Logan's easy smiles cast continuously my way alongside an occasional wink. Life in the West home was everything I could ever want.

That was, until lurid giggles burst into the room, followed by the piercing slap of what I assumed to be someone's ass. The chair beside me pulled out and the redhead sat, plate in hand.

I glanced her way, annoyed that she hadn't bothered to fix her matted hair or wipe away the mascara smeared under her eyes. Jax sat across from her beside Oliver, and the room became eerily quiet aside from Oliver's exclamation of, "Uncle Jax!"

They filled their plates and Jax stole Oliver's attention, telling him about some new dinosaur movie he'd picked up for them to watch. More silence followed, producing the first of many pointed scowls between Logan and Jax and awkward squirms for me.

The redhead never spoke a word. She simply ate quietly, sending flirty looks over to Jax and shifting occasionally in her seat. At one point, that shifting was followed by a disturbing smirk that spread across Jax's face.

There is no way they're playing just footsie under the table. I focused back on my food, occupying my mind before it wandered to what exactly they *were* playing.

Oliver brought a welcome distraction in the form of a discussion about whether he could have glasses like his best friend in class. Our family meal was heading back on course; my relief eased the tension that had been building in my shoulders.

Just when I thought we were in the clear, the front door slammed. We all looked up to see Julia rounding the corner into the dining room, her hands full of textbooks.

"What's for dinner? I've been studying *all* day and skipped lunch." She dumped the books on the counter and peeled off her gloves, coat, and hat.

"Stew," Oliver told her, his spoon in his mouth. "I made it!"

I smiled over at him.

"Is that so?" she asked, strolling over and leaning down to kiss the top of his head. "Did anyone help you?"

"Daddy did, but he said *I* made it. Right, Daddy?" Oliver looked to Logan.

"You did most of the work," Logan assured him, eyes full of pride. "I simply cut a few vegetables."

"See? Told ya." Oliver lifted his glass of juice and took a sip.

Julia sat at the end of the table, across from Logan.

"Smells great, and looks just like Grandma makes it." She peered up at me while spooning some stew into her bowl. "How are you feeling, Cassandra?"

"I'm good. How's school going?" I went to grab a roll at the same time as Miss Redhead. I withdrew my hand, allowing her to take the last one.

Logan let out an irritated sigh. It wasn't a big deal—the girl could have it—all that mattered was that my man was on edge.

One way to fix that.

I placed my hand under the table and settled it on his thigh, drawing his focus off the girl and over to me, where his irritation melted away.

"School's school. It keeps me busy, but it's impossible to get much studying done at the dorm." She swallowed a spoonful, then turned to Oliver. "Perfect, buddy!"

Oliver raised his shoulders proudly as he continued his meal.

"There's a library for that, you know," Jax said.

"What do you know about libraries?" Julia cracked.

"Plenty." The wicked grin he boasted said enough.

"Gross." Julia puffed out her cheeks and let out a mock gagging sound.

"You okay?" Oliver asked, looking unsure if he should laugh at her expression or be concerned.

"That's enough! She's fine. Aren't you, Julia?" Logan said, the mature voice in the room.

Julia only nodded with a grin, wriggling her nose at Oliver. He laughed, happy in his own little world. Lucky kid.

"And I'm sure you can find plenty of places to study," Logan continued. "There's more than enough room here anytime you need." He threw a quick glance at me out of the corner of his eye, but I still caught it before he looked back at her, his expression as serious as before.

"During the day, anyway," he said.

I slid my spoon back into my mouth, fighting the blush stinging my cheeks.

"Thanks, but I'm still holding out hope that my dear, sweet, *generous* brother will look into getting me my own apartment for next semester." She was all innocence and puppy-dog eyes when she finally lifted her head from her food and gazed at Logan.

That's *where Oliver gets it from!*

"We'll see," was Logan's only response, and it had me wondering how far into the furnishing he was at the house he was going to surprise her with over spring break. I hadn't asked, as I'd honestly forgotten about it over the past week. I made a mental note to ask about it the next time we were alone.

Julia appeared placated by his reply. I watched her subtly, my hand tensing on Logan's leg as she took another bite of stew before slowly training her sight on Jax's date. I wasn't sure 'date' was the correct term to use, but anything else seemed too crude even in my own head.

"So, I'm guessing you're a *friend* of Jax's?" Julia asked, disdain heavy in her words.

The girl nodded, nibbling on the bread.

"Do you have a name?" Julia prompted.

"Leave her alone," Jax chimed in.

I hid my smile, relieved to see him defending the girl but just as surprised as Julia appeared. Her jaw actually dropped.

"Courtney," the girl answered after a pause. She turned her head, looking back at Julia.

"Lovely name." Julia took a drink, then lowered her glass. "So, how long have you and Jax been..." She glanced warily at Oliver, who was happily in his own world, humming to himself. "...seeing each other?"

Oh, here we go. That question could lead nowhere good.

I fidgeted in my seat, uncomfortable with the tension building around the table. I lifted my glass and chugged a mouthful of water to settle my flittering nerves, painfully aware that Courtney was sitting on the wrong side of the table at this family dinner.

"We're just friends, nothing more," Courtney explained, and the liquid in my mouth caught in my throat, causing me to choke.

Just friends? My hands flew to my mouth as I attempted to swallow, my lips closed tightly to keep from spitting water all over the table. All eyes were on me, which didn't help.

"You 'kay?" Oliver asked, sitting up taller.

I nodded and offered a tight smile, unable to seize control over my awkward cough. I took one glance at Logan, and the concern in his eyes erased my embarrassment instantly.

Logan spoke up for me, explaining away my reaction. "Jax rarely has *friends* for dinner."

"He never has anyone for dinner," Julia muttered.

"What? Logan can have friends over..." Jax looked to me. "...but I can't?"

Julia's face contorted into an *Uh oh* expression that I knew reflected what she was seeing from Logan's. I chose to focus my narrow eyes on Jax. Obviously, his flippant statement wouldn't sit well with Logan.

With my nerves on fire, I'd fixed my attention down on my food when I heard a low growl in the back of Logan's throat, followed by him barking, "Cassandra is *much* more than a friend, and this is *my* house. Watch it!"

An uncomfortable silence hung over us for several minutes. It wasn't until the tickling vibration from my phone in my pocket that I was reminded life outside the cloud over us still existed.

I pulled it out discreetly, hiding it under the table, and saw a text from Hilary.

I'm sorry about how I left. I'm just confused & scared. I'll call u soon.

"Everything all right?" Logan asked, staring down at my phone.

I tucked it back in my pocket, nodding. My heart clenched. I needed to talk to her. With what she was going through, I knew she needed me.

Julia's scornful voice shattered my worry with her next snide remark to Jax.

"What happened to the twins?"

I rolled my eyes. Was every meal they shared like this, or was today special because of Courtney?

"I have twins in my class," Oliver boasted, always the ray of light in the room. The tightening of Logan's grip on his glass, however, caught the corner of my eye. A natural need to protect Oliver from Jax's scandalous reputation consumed me.

"So you and Caleb play a lot of poker, huh?" I blurted out. "He says you're ruthless."

"At one time, perhaps," Logan replied dryly.

I chuckled. In fact, it was less a chuckle and more a cackling of air forced from my lungs. Still, I expected to see an appreciative smile for the subject change growing on Logan's perfect lips instead of the deep frown that had materialized there.

"I'm sure you have at least *one* fun story to share?" I prompted, desperate to shift the conversation from his siblings. It wasn't a stretch for me to imagine him controlling a game.

"Logan, Caleb, and poker? You kidding? He has *plenty* of fun stories to share," Jax said with a snicker.

Logan shot him a sidelong glare while I sat nervously, unaware of what Jax was implying. Did I *want* to know? Probably not.

"Is that a game?" Oliver asked, curious.

"Yes, one with cards," Logan told him. "I'll teach you when you get a little older."

"I remember the one game you had where you came in late carrying an entire bag of clothes." Jax chuckled, looking from Logan to me. "He'd literally taken them off the guy's back! Ruthless, and I'm sure Caleb was no better."

"You ever play with them?" I asked Jax.

Logan sighed quietly, and I became overly aware of his stiff shoulders and locked jaw. He definitely didn't want to talk about it.

What was there? Whatever story he had, he wasn't ready to share. Or maybe it wasn't me he was worried about hearing, but his son.

"Nah, Logan wouldn't allow it. Said I was too young." He made a face. "I think he just didn't want me to see how he lived it up—the cash he and Caleb made, and all the girls."

I placed my hand over Logan's in an attempt to soothe his unease. "Understandable. Caleb seems pretty happy now, between Hilary and Haven keeping him occupied," I said, trying subtly to steer the conversation from poker.

It seemed to work. Logan's expression softened, and he gave my hand a gentle squeeze.

"Yeah, Caleb's happy…for now. He sure has a thing for your friend. I hope she doesn't screw with him. Poor guy never even talked about settling down before her, huh Logan?"

Logan looked to me with a secret smile. "The right woman can change a man."

Jax snorted. "Or ruin him. Caleb's a tricky guy to pin down, but I do remember him once saying he wanted a little boy like Oliver here. Hope he gets that someday."

My entire body stiffened. *Where's he going with this?*

"Caleb's nice," Oliver threw out before shoving a giant piece of bread into his mouth. My giggle couldn't be contained, but the anxiety from how far Jax would go still had me on edge.

"A family would do him good—settle him down in one place, finally," Logan said.

One place. "You don't think Caleb will stay in Harmony?" I asked casually, relieved I sounded unaffected by his statement since I was anything but. He couldn't leave—ever.

Logan shrugged as he took a drink. "Hard to say, but I doubt it. He always gets bored eventually. Haven's been good to him, though, so we'll see."

"Hilary's worth sticking around for," I reasoned. "He knows that."

"Is she?" Jax prompted.

I lifted my chin slowly and held his amused gaze. He was toying with me.

"Absolutely," I defended.

"She looked a little green around the gills when she was over this morning. And a little...what is it you girls call it...bloated?"

Game on!

"She looked beautiful, as always. The girl you had up in your room today, however...she looked—"

"You're right, she looked beautiful!" Jax blew out, waving a figurative white flag.

A triumphant grin curled my lips as I raised my brows at him. *Just try me*, they said clearly.

"You had a girl over today?" Courtney asked, her voice low and hard.

My smile fell away. I felt bad for her, but it was for the

best that she knew exactly what she was getting with Jax. I honestly thought she'd already known until I heard the abrupt screech of her chair as she jerked up and marched out. It was clear she wouldn't be back.

"See ya later!" Julia called after her, her voice riddled with amusement.

"Don't be a cow. You're just jealous you got dumped," Jax spat at his sister.

Dumped? Mark left her? No way!

She was the next one to fly up. "Screw you!" With a quick kiss to Oliver's cheek, she grabbed her stack of books and headed out of the room.

I rested my elbow on the table, two fingers rubbing slow circles into my temples. I'd never again dream of what having siblings was like.

"Aunt Julia's mad," Oliver pointed out.

Logan explained to Oliver that she was fine. Their conversation bled into the background as my thoughts ran wild. Why would Mark dump her? He was lucky to land a girl like Julia to begin with. I'd figured she'd caught him cheating, but apparently I was wrong.

I leaned over to Logan. "Mark left *her*?" I asked softly.

Jax chuckled, eavesdropping. "I take it Logan didn't fill you in on that, huh?"

"On what?" I asked, eyeing Logan for an explanation. He gave nothing away.

"Mark made his choice," Logan said smoothly. "Julia will get over it."

Get over what? Did Logan do something?

Before I could ask what that meant, an impish spark appeared in Jax's eye. "Ah, yes, just like Hilary's going to make a choi—"

"Drop it!" I snapped, slamming my palm down on the

table.

I reared back, stunned at my own actions. A gasp from Oliver seized my attention, and when I looked to him, I winced at his wide doe eyes.

"I'm sorry," I said breathlessly, ashamed. "I didn't mean to yell."

Oliver nodded, but looked to his father for reassurance. I shrank further into my seat. Where the hell had that come from? I never yelled like that.

"Dinner was delicious, little man. Thanks," Jax said to Oliver as he stood, rueful eyes on me, before strolling out.

He was smart to duck for cover. I'd be having a very long, very loud conversation with him shortly.

Logan said nothing, the silence unbearable until his chair scooted away from the table. I couldn't even look at him; all I felt was shame. Was he angry?

"Are you finished?"

I peered hesitantly up at cool eyes shielding profound emotions behind them. Did he mean with my dinner, or my out-of-line outburst?

"Yeah," I mumbled, lifting my bowl. He stacked it on top of his own before standing and disappearing from the room with Oliver.

I sat sulking in my chair, my head in my hands. Logan didn't return, and finally I realized I couldn't sit there all night, as much as I felt rooted in place.

With a heavy head and slow strides, I passed through the foyer just as Julia was heading upstairs with her books. "Is Logan up there?" I asked.

She gave me a sympathetic smile and nodded. "Yeah, he's giving Oliver a bath and getting him ready for bed."

"Okay." My head dropped again. He was mad, Oliver was scared, and I was ashamed—perfect ending to my first real

West family meal. *Did I just put the kibosh on the honeymoon phase of our relationship?*

I slumped down in the armchair in his living room, refusing to leave before I'd apologized properly.

I waited for almost an hour, debating between going upstairs to apologize again to Oliver before he went to bed or going home. My head shook; leaving wouldn't help matters. I'd messed up, I'd screamed at the dining-room table, and I needed to deal with the consequences.

When Logan came down with a frown on his face, I felt worse. How that was possible, I wasn't sure, but it was the truth. He stood in the doorway, which felt miles away both physically and emotionally. Looked like our first fight as a couple was about to hit.

I stood nervously, my clammy hands clutched behind my back.

"I'm so sorry. Jax just had me rattled, and…" I sighed, composing myself. "I don't know what happened. I swear I just snapped. That's not like me. Is Oliver all right? Did I scare him?"

Logan nodded once. "He's fine. Worried about you is all. I'd hoped you'd come up to see him to bed."

My heart dropped. "Oh, I wanted to, but I thought…I didn't want to make it worse. Is he still awake?" I moved forward.

He shook his head, and I stopped. I'd speak with him first thing in the morning and I wanted Logan to know that, but he surprised me with a sudden change of topic.

"What's going on with you and Jax?"

"What? Nothing. He was just pressing my buttons." I fell

down onto the sofa.

"What buttons exactly? Is something going on with Hilary?"

This was it—now was the time to tell him—but I could never betray Hilary like that. It would also put Logan in an uncomfortable position. Would he tell Caleb? I could plead with him not to. No, in time he'd learn the truth and would have to understand how important loyalty was to me.

"She was over this morning, and we had a fight. She was mad I didn't call her earlier this week."

"That's all?" he asked, unconvinced.

I was a horrible liar—even I knew that—but still, I nodded. "That's all."

He didn't move as he considered me carefully. Would he call me out on what we both knew wasn't the full truth, or let me keep my promise of secrecy to Hilary?

"Look, I know you're angry over my outburst, and you have every right to be."

Logan walked over, and my mouth closed. He stopped directly in front of me, his knees nudging my legs apart before he stepped between them. His heated stare bored into me.

"I don't tolerate anyone except me raising their voice around my son. However, it was obvious Jax had provoked you. He'll be dealt with tomorrow. As for you, if you don't want me angry, then come upstairs next time. Oliver told me to tell you goodnight, and that he loves you."

He loves me?

I bit my bottom lip as my smile grew, but the fact that I hadn't been there to hear those words myself twisted my gut. I loved him, too.

Logan towered over me. "And for the record, I was more confused than anything else. I refuse to be in the dark with those I care about."

I swallowed. "I'm sorry."

"Don't apologize." He bent down, brushed aside the wisps of hair blocking my eyes, and curled his finger under my chin. His kiss landed on my cheek, easing me out of my own anguish. "We all snap at times. Had Oliver not been there, I'd have kicked Jax out of the room and bent you over that damn table. Few people can shut my little brother up."

My head reared back in shock. "What?" *My outburst had turned him on?*

"It took all the strength I had to keep my hands to myself."

My smile grew. "Really?"

His fingers slid under my legs, gripping my ass and pulling me into him. "You have no idea how hot you are when you get angry, do you?"

I giggled under my breath. "Hot?"

Apparently, I'd been completely off base with my expectations for the conversation. I'd spent an hour worrying for nothing.

"Sexiest thing I've ever seen." My legs wrapped around his waist, his erection digging into my center. "I could have devoured you whole right where you sat."

"Nothing stopping you now," I murmured as his lips nipped my neck.

He leaned back enough to meet my lustful gaze, taking me by surprise when he grabbed my shirt and ripped it open. I shrieked and his mouth crashed over mine, silencing me.

I giggled against his ravishing lips. "I want to try that tub of yours upstairs." He kissed me harder, his lips trailing down to my breasts where his palms cradled and teased the sensitive flesh. "It's bigger than mine. You ever use it?"

He shook his head, humor in his tone when he released my captive mouth and replied, "Never—I prefer the shower.

But with you, always the tub."

Before I could respond, I was in his arms, being hauled up the stairs as wild anticipation filled me. His tub was built for making love, and I was more than ready for a long night in it.

Chapter Twelve

ENIGMAS

Passion, pleasure, love—the previous night had it all. This included lavender-scented bubbles that had splashed over the marble floor in Logan's bathroom, which was exactly where we found ourselves when the sun came up.

Wrapped in his arms, I was wonderfully and utterly satisfied. My limbs were wracked with beautiful exhaustion, but I was still on my feet the moment his alarm buzzed from his bedroom. With a low chuckle, Logan opened his eyes. His stare was all I felt as I skittered around, throwing my hair in a messy high ponytail and hopping into a pair of jeans from my bag.

To say I was anxious to be the one to wake Oliver would've been an understatement; I *needed* to be the first person he saw when those little blue eyes peeked open. I tugged on a shirt and decided to forgo socks—or anything else, for that matter. Oliver wouldn't notice, and I couldn't bear the thought of Jax getting there first.

"Might want to try again," Logan said, rising to his feet.

"Huh?" I asked, nearly tripping over myself in my rush to the door. I stopped and twisted back, sucking in a rapid breath at the close proximity Logan had acquired so quickly.

His finger dipped inside the neck of my shirt and pulled up the tag that was supposed to be in the back.

"Backwards," was all he said, but his hands were already taking care of the issue. I lifted my arms and he reached down, gripped the fabric, and dragged it over my head.

He held my shirt in his hands, his held tilting just the slightest, eyes filling with a deep-rooted desire. He had that look again, and now was so not the time.

"No, no more!" I snatched the shirt, made sure the tag was in the back, and pulled it back on.

"Not even a kiss?" he teased, a soft pout on his lips.

Lord help me, I'm doomed. As I was about to lean in to give him the best damn kiss he'd ever experienced, I heard a door creak open, followed by heavy footsteps.

Jax!

Spinning around with not so much as another glance at Logan, I yanked the door open and flew out into the hall, sprinting to Oliver's room.

Jax stood a few feet away. He was stopped mid-step, his tired eyes wide, gaping at me.

"In a hurry to get somewhere?" he asked, stretching his arms out at his sides.

"I've got Oliver this morning. You can go back to bed."

"I was just heading out. Unless Logan's running late, I'm not one to wake the little prince. He can be a terror in the mornings."

"I doubt that."

"Uh-huh. See you around, doll face." He tugged a strand of my hair as he walked past.

Turned out Jax was right: Oliver wasn't much of a morning person. After I weaved through landmines of dinosaurs covering the floor, it took multiple wakeup announcements and a few minutes of rubbing his back before those little baby blues finally peeled open.

"Cassie!"

"Hey, little man! Or should I call you little prince?" I sat beside him on the bed.

"Uncle Jax says I'm the prince of the house." He looked extremely pleased by that.

"You sure are. Now, what would the prince like for breakfast?" I scooted over as he sat up, wiping his eyes. His blonde curls were adorably wild.

"Pancakes!" His words were a high-pitched squeal, abolishing any last hold of sleep that clung to him.

"How about oatmeal? I can see what fruit we have lying around to add to it."

"Um, no, I want pancakes."

So here it was: the moment I had to be the bad guy. I could either cater to his every whim, which would only end badly in the long run, or make it clear that as much as I adored him, I wasn't a pushover.

"How about scrambled eggs and toast?" I suggested, hoping he'd make it easy for me.

"Pancakes! I like your pancakes."

"Oliver."

It was Logan's voice that interrupted, but I who took Oliver's hand and, with nothing but kind sincerity, told him, "I'm not making pancakes. This weekend we can have them, but not on a school day. The other day was a special treat. So what do you normally eat before school?"

He understood and even smiled, despite a small twitch to his lips. It was more of an 'Oh well, I tried' expression than an actual frown.

"I like oatmeal. With apples cut real tiny."

"I can do that." I drew him in for a quick hug and whispered, "Sorry I didn't say goodnight last night."

"It's okay." He leaned back and swung his legs off the bed, knocking over a giant T-rex in the process.

"You gonna introduce me to these dinosaur friends of yours this weekend?" I asked, standing.

Oliver jumped up, excitement bright in his eyes. "Will you play with me?"

"Of course, but right now you need to get ready for school."

He leapt up, grabbed a stack of clothing sitting on his dresser, and headed into the bathroom.

"Brush your teeth," Logan called out to him just before he shut the door.

When I finally looked his way, Logan was leaning against the doorframe, his arms crossed. It wasn't a smile that greeted me—more a thoughtful stare.

I walked over to him. "I'll go start chopping apples." I lifted myself up on my toes and kissed the corner of his mouth.

"Thank you." He took my hand and brought it to his lips. "You're too good to be true." After a kiss to my knuckles, he walked past me toward Oliver's bathroom door.

I left them to their morning routine, a peaceful calm settling into a place in my heart I never knew existed before that moment.

I couldn't have asked for a more perfect morning. Once my boys were out the front door, all smiles, I crawled into Logan's bed that had been neglected overnight and fell quickly into a slumber. With no alarm set to wake me since I was still out of work for a while longer, I could've napped the day away if not for the piercing scream that bounced off every wall in the house and smacked me square in the head.

My body shot up, and on pure instinct I whipped the blanket off and leapt up. There was no time to think or process—only to react. Adrenaline roared through my system, fueling my movements as I scurried out the bedroom door in nothing but a long button-up of Logan's.

Once in the hall, I followed the sobs and curdling blubbers until I found myself outside Jax's bedroom door. The cries quieted and I took a moment to catch my breath. After I took a fretful look at the knob, my brain fired to life, processing that something was very wrong on the other side of that door.

My pulse quickened as realization sank in. I knew opening the door could lead me to see something I'd rather not if on the other side of it lay some sordid roleplaying episode, but the next words that rang through the door left me no choice.

"Stop! Please stop!"

My head spun as I flung open the door to find a gangly teen boy broken down in tears, laid out on a folding massage table. Jax sat over him, a tattoo needle in his hand.

It wasn't what I'd expected—at all. *Guess Jax isn't playing for both teams after all.*

"Ah, shit!" Jax grumbled, switching off the needle and placing it on a tray beside him.

The boy sat up with a wince. "I'm sorry. You're gonna finish, right? You can't leave it like this!" he bellowed, staring down at his side where the word 'Jam' was etched.

"'Jam'?" I asked, more so reading it aloud than asking. I poked my head closer, tilting it to the side for a better look. The script was perfect—Jax had talent—but 'Jam'?

"Jamie! It's Jamie. I just...I need a break, okay?" the kid explained, breathing hard.

Jax looked annoyed and unimpressed. "I'll give you ten minutes. Then either pull it together or I'm rescheduling you to finish it. Last thing I need is you passing out." Jax stood, pulled off his gloves and threw them in the trash, then stalked toward me. A dipped brow framed his heavy scowl.

On instinct, I stepped back into the hall, my eyes on him. I waited as he closed the door, giving the kid some privacy.

As soon as the latch sounded, I screeched, "How old is he!?"

"Eighteen," Jax replied with easy confidence.

"Are you sure? Did you see his ID?" My face screwed up as I began pacing the hall, questions firing rapidly through my mind. *Is this legal? Could the kid's parents sue Logan, since it was his house? How many times has Jax done tattoos here? Is it even hygienic?*

Jax chuckled. "Calm down. I check every ID. Caleb even taught me how to spot a fake. The kid in there's a freshman on campus—just a pussy, that's all. I get them from time to time."

I wrenched to a halt and snapped my head his way. "*Time to time?* Meaning you do this often?" I gaped at him. "And Caleb knows? Does Logan?" My chest burned with my held breath as I waited for his answers.

"Yes, Caleb knows—and he agrees Logan doesn't need to know."

"What!? It's *his* house, Jax!"

I was stunned to hear Caleb was okay with keeping a secret from Logan. But then again, I had hidden my own secret from him.

After a pause, my head dropped and I released a sigh. "That's what you were hiding the other day—your tattoo equipment?" Shaking my head slowly, I smiled to myself, remembering the pixie-haired girl who'd left his room the previous day. She hadn't slept with him after all, which was a relief considering he'd screwed her roommates.

"Let's just say Logan wouldn't be pleased to know I'm doing this, whether here or elsewhere—which is why I need you to keep your yap shut." His voice was rough, but his eyes were pleading.

With a huff of annoyance at the situation, I balked. "I won't lie if he asks."

"Fair enough. Just don't bring it up. I'm doing it here to save money to open my own shop. If Logan shuts me down—or worse, kicks me out—there's no place left for me to go. I'm enjoying my reprieve from the city, and not looking to return just yet."

"Why not explain to Logan about your goal to open a shop? Maybe he'd help. I mean, he could partner with you or something. Isn't that what he does—owns businesses and all?"

His face fell and his voice grew hard. "Not tattoo shops. Logan's like my father: wants me to pay my dues and all and thinks tattoos won't earn me a living. He won't see that it's the only thing that I want. It's what I love to do."

I felt for him. He was following his dream. How could Logan try to shut that down?

Jax continued, his eyes lighting up. "Caleb gets it, though. He knows Logan will eventually see that I can earn my way and open my own place without his help. So, seriously, can we keep this between us?"

"I guess," I answered after a long pause.

"Good. Just like your friend's bun in the oven." He shot me a smirk. Playful Jax had returned, and was about to meet the angry bitch from the previous night.

I pointed my finger at him, a tight scowl in place on my face. "If you ever try to mess with me again like you did last night, I'll not only tell Logan about this little venture of yours, but I'll also make sure Caleb finds out you knew about the baby and didn't tell him."

He held up his hands. "Fine, you win. Last night I was more irritated about Courtney insisting we eat dinner with you guys than anything. I knew Logan would be pissed, and when Julia stopped over, I was screwed. My sister's a protective one—twins and all. So, yeah, it was a dick move to take it out on you. I'm sorry. Friends?"

Did I just receive a sincere apology from Jax West? My smile was huge. "Apology accepted. And yes, friends."

He moved to reenter the room as I asked, "So, *friend*, how about I borrow your car today?"

He looked back. "I thought I could taxi you again."

"Nope. I'd rather drive."

He rolled his eyes. "You know Logan has other vehicles in the garage, right? He'd gladly loan—"

I shook my head. "Nope." I held out my hand.

He dug into his pocket. "Fine. But if I have to go anywhere, I'll be taking one of Logan's."

"Works for me," I said excitedly as he placed the keys in my hand.

"Be gentle with her."

Now I was the one rolling my eyes. *Men and their cars.* He and Luke would get along well. "You got it. And be gentle with that kid in there."

He chuckled. "Not my fault he can't stand a little pain."

"Right. I'm sure it's more than a little."

I'd started walking away when he asked, "You don't have any, I take it?"

"Tattoos?" My brows shot up.

"Yeah." He grinned.

I shook my head. "No, not my thing."

"Well, if you change your mind, let me know. It's on me."

"I'll keep that in mind," I said, turning back away toward Logan's room.

Once I was dressed and climbing into Jax's Mustang, I sent a text to Luke.

What time can I bring Scout by?

His reply came when I was halfway to Main Street.

Anytime. I took a sick day.

A sick day? He'd seemed fine twenty-four hours earlier.

Are u sick?

Who's asking lol

I smiled as I replied.

I take that as a skip day then.

Whatever u want to call it. I'm home so bring him by any time. Apt 20A

K be there in an hour.

I arrived at Logan's office after shooting him a text saying I'd bring lunch by if he didn't have plans. To my pleasure, he didn't. We ate tucked away in his office with clothes strewn about, the door locked and blinds shut.

"I better go." I stood, grabbing my bra that had been tossed over his desk chair.

"Why?" he asked. His eyes were closed peacefully.

"Because you need to work," I replied, giggling.

His eyes shot open, and he dragged me back down. "I could use another break."

"As tempting as that is, I have to pick up Scout." Reluctantly, I pulled away and straightened myself, scanning the room for my shirt.

"Now? I thought that was this evening."

"It was, but Luke took the day off so I told him I'd bring him by..." I checked the clock. "...twenty-five minutes ago."

With a groan, he sat up. "Too bad. I haven't had my fill."

"You rarely do." I smiled.

"Very true."

"I'll see you tonight—unless you have some wild Friday-night plans out on the town." I hopped into my pants.

He thought it over, a wicked gleam in his eyes. "I could take you out. Anywhere you want to go."

Standing over him, I watched as he buried his head in my navel. "How about a movie night with Oliver, and after his bedtime..."

He looked up at me with a soft smile. "I love that you care for my son...that you truly care for him."

"Always," I told him before stepping out of his hold to find my blouse.

Logan stood gloriously naked. "He's excited about our surprise for you tomorrow."

"Right, the one where I have to wear an old turtleneck and ratty sweater. How could I forget?"

His smile grew as he gazed at me with a look that seared my soul. "Stay with me through the weekend," he murmured.

"I can't."

"Why not?" he asked, sliding on his shirt.

I stepped back to him and placed my hands on his biceps, which bulged against the silky fabric. "Because on the way here, I called the school to confirm I return next Monday and they said I could return this Monday instead if I was up for it."

A frown settled over his lips. "Were you talking on your cell while driving?"

"What?" My brows furrowed.

"You said it was on your way here, which implies that you

were talking while driving."

I snorted. "*That's* what you took from what I just said?"

He was deadly serious. "My girl putting herself at risk is the only thing that struck a chord."

His concern for me warmed me to my toes. "Your girl, hm?" I whispered across his lips.

"My girl, my angel, my lover. So many descriptions, but only one question remains." His head moved back slightly so he could read my eyes. "Were you talking while driving on snow-covered roads?"

My shoulders sagged. "Yes, okay, but I was at a light for most of that time. And for the record, I can look out for myself. I've been doing it for quite a while now."

His lip quirked, his arms encircling me. "I know, but now you have help. So tell me about this parked-at-a-light explanation. Are you lying?"

"Maybe," I muttered, my eyes cast downward.

He chuckled, and I jumped when his hand swatted my ass. He kissed the tip of my nose and murmured, "You're so damn adorable."

"I thought I was hot," I teased, kissing his jaw.

"You're everything I could want and more." He kissed me softly, then moved away to grab his pants. "So, are you sure you're ready to return to school?"

"More than ready, which is why I can't stay through the weekend. But I will till Saturday night. I need Sunday to get organized."

"Spend Saturday night with me, and I'll release you bright and early Sunday."

"Release me?" My brow cocked.

"What would you call it—set you free to return every evening?"

My teeth dug into my bottom lip to catch the laughter

that was bubbling inside me. "You might want to skip the poetry."

Finally fully dressed, I grabbed my coat and purse and placed a kiss to his lips as he stepped into his trousers.

"See you later, lover," I purred.

"Looking forward to it." His eyes glistened with adoration, and I sauntered out his door with an intoxicating high.

Scout slept soundly in the passenger seat, his head resting on my bag. The vet had explained everything I needed to know to help him heal quickly and safely, and had even given me a printout for Luke.

I stroked his back, wishing I could take him home. It wasn't an option, though. I wouldn't do that to Oliver—or Scout.

Once I'd parked at Luke's apartment building, I scooped up Scout, swaddled him in a thick blanket, and made my way upstairs, cradling him like a baby.

The apartment wasn't hard to find; it was the first one on the second floor. After I knocked once, Luke opened the door looking anything but sick. He stepped aside, allowing me to enter, and there sitting on his futon was Julia.

"Hey Cassandra," she said cheerfully, standing and approaching me.

I should've felt surprised to see her, but instead I was simply happy for them. There was a natural vibe between them that spoke more loudly than anything else. They'd be good together.

Julia cupped Scout's face. "Hey there, buddy. How you feeling?"

"He's still a little sore, but he seems happy to be out of that place," I explained. My gaze was on Luke, however. He was standing slightly behind Julia, admiring her kindness for Scout.

She looked up to me. "I bet. They don't like to be out of their comfort zone for too long. We had a dog growing up, and he hated whenever we were away or he'd have to go to the vet." She looked away thoughtfully. "Miss him. He was family."

"What was his name?" Luke asked sweetly.

"Larry." She looked back at Scout, a cautious grin tugging at her lips.

"Larry?" I laughed.

"Did you name him?" Luke asked.

She released a breath, obviously debating whether she wanted to answer. My curiosity was piqued.

"No, I would have preferred something stylish for him. Larry, however…" Her body suddenly shook with laughter. "You don't want to know."

"Oh, no you don't! Now you *have* to tell us," Luke teased.

"Maybe you should ask Logan," she suggested.

I slouched down on the futon and petted Scout, who was on my lap. "No, no, I'd rather hear this now." I chuckled, readying myself for what could have Julia of all people chewing her perfect nails.

"All right. Larry was the name of Logan's imaginary friend," she confessed.

Luke spit out his laughter and I sat there staring, my eyes wide, jaw dropped. Logan had an imaginary friend?

"*Shut. Up!*" I gasped.

Julia sat beside me, stroking Scout's tail. "Swear to God. Drove my dad nuts, or so I was told. I wasn't born yet, but Lawrence still cracks on him about it. Dad bought the dog *supposedly* so there was a real Larry for Logan to talk to."

I was laughing so hard my chest ached, and my breath was all but lost. "Now *that's* adorable! How old was he?"

She raised her shoulders. "Don't know. I think six or seven? Larry was already there when I was born."

"I can't picture a little Logan having an imaginary friend," I said, sitting back.

"Me either, but good to know," Luke said, his expression revealing obvious amusement.

"He'll kick your ass if you tease him," Julia warned with a smile. "Lawrence is the only one that gets away with it, and even still, Logan hates it."

"Wow, the things I learn about your brother," I said, my smile still locked in place.

"Oliver had one too," she explained.

"Seriously? An imaginary friend?"

"Yeah, which means when you and Logan have a child—which will be named after me, FYI, in case you forgot—I'd keep an eye on that."

Julia and Luke were both snickering, but my laugh had ended abruptly.

"Lovely," I grumbled. Logan and me, with a child? I wasn't ready for all that just yet.

Scout limped out of my lap and collapsed down on the couch against Julia.

"He likes you," Luke said, leaning against the wall and watching her.

"I'm glad. I like you too," she cooed, petting his ears.

I pulled the paper bag from the vet out of my purse and stood, holding it out to Luke. "Here's everything you need to know, and some meds they gave him."

He nodded and walked the bag to the kitchen table. I followed.

"You don't feel good, huh? Well, I'll come by every day until you do," we heard Julia promise Scout.

Once Luke and I were in the space designated as the kitchen but still in the same room as Julia, he spoke. "Don't worry about him. We got it. How long you thinking he'll be here?" The look he shot me told me the longer, the better.

I smiled. "At least a week. The vet said dogs heal quickly, but until he's at full strength it's best he stay here."

"No problem. I don't mind at all." He leaned in and whispered, "I need you to feel her out for me."

"What? When?" I blew out in a hushed voice, staring nervously back at the living room only a few feet away. Could she hear us?

"I'll go get some blankets to make him a bed," Luke said more loudly than necessary, eyeing me for my understanding.

Okay, I guess now *is when*. I gave a slight nod and watched him leave, disappearing into his bedroom. Reluctantly, I turned to Julia, considering my words carefully.

"Thanks for helping him with Scout," I started.

"Of course. I'm more than happy to." She glanced at the bedroom door Luke had disappeared behind, then back at me. "He's a good guy," she said softly.

I stepped closer, my hands kneading together. "He is—which is why I'm curious if you're, you know, interested in him…I mean, as *more* than friends."

Her gaze dropped back to Scout as she released a heavy sigh. "There's no point to it."

I sat back down beside her. "No point in dating someone you like who likes you back?"

She perked up, but only slightly. "He told you that?"

"He did, but he didn't need to. It's obvious. You have to see that."

"Maybe in time we can be more, but for now I don't want

to ruin things," she said, looking completely miserable.

"Ruin things how? Did something happen?"

Her hand stilled on Scout's back. "Yeah, Logan happened. I'm not going to let him get to Luke like he did Mark."

My spine straightened painfully. "Get to him?" I breathed.

She looked right at me, fury written all over her face. "Logan thinks he can control my life, but eventually it will backfire on him," she spit out. "Wait and see."

"Okay, so this is the most comfortable blanket I could find," Luke announced, strolling back out of his room.

Still processing Julia's words, I was surprised she'd already cleared away her irritation and replaced it with a polished smile directed at Luke. Everyone needed a calming force in their lives, and it seemed Luke provided that for her.

I, however, was unsure what to say. What had Logan done to Mark? Seemed Jax and I weren't the only ones with secrets in Harmony.

Luke placed the neatly folded blanket on the floor, then sat on the other side of Julia, Scout between them.

"Well, looks like he's in good hands," I said, standing and grabbing my bag. "I better get going. Thanks again."

Luke leapt up. "I'll walk you out."

I nodded and gave Julia a tight smile. She deserved to be happy, and Luke was the right guy for that. I was determined to help that happen.

"So, do I have a shot?" he whispered, holding the door for me.

"Yeah, you do. Just give her some time." *And give me time to talk to Logan. I'll set this straight.*

"I owe you one." Luke's grin was optimistic, and I was pretty sure I was his new favorite person.

"Consider us even for you taking care of Scout." It was a

win-win in my book.

Chapter Thirteen

CALAMITIES

After calling out a quick goodbye to Scout and Julia, I made my way downstairs to the parking lot. My thoughts were lost on possibilities of what Logan could've done to Mark that had Julia so put off. The last time I'd seen my ex was at Haven, where Logan was detained in the kitchen, nearly destroying the place trying to get to Mark. It was clear he didn't like the guy. I didn't mind, but whatever had happened between Logan and Julia needed to be worked out.

"Shit!"

A loud shattering noise followed the curse, and I spotted Natasha standing beside her car. The box in her hands had broken open at the bottom, and shards of glass surrounded her feet.

I had two choices: continue to my car and pretend I never saw, or...

"You need some help?" I asked, walking over. Typical. It'd always been in my nature to be the nice one.

She peered up at me, her eyes squinting in the bright sunlight. "Uh, yeah actually. But I'm sure you're busy. I got it." She shoved the empty box in the passenger seat and shut the door.

My lips pulled up, my smile tight but friendly. "I don't mind, really. I've got some time, and I just moved last year so I know how much *fun* it can be." I stopped at her trunk, eyeing the massive box waiting to be hauled out. There was no way she should carry it by herself. Even if it was filled with pillows, it looked too large to be handled by one person. "Grab the other side?"

"Thanks, but I say we take these first." She handed me a smaller box from the backseat that was more my size. "That one is gonna be a pain." Natasha gestured toward the trunk. "Feel free to walk away now."

She laughed, and I relaxed.

"Nope. I said I'd help, so let's do this."

Natasha grabbed a vase from the backseat, shut the door, and led the way.

Surprisingly, she lived only three apartments down from Luke. I blanched internally at the thought of her and Julia running into each other regularly. I could only hope it wouldn't put a damper on Julia's visits with Luke.

Natasha's apartment was standard but a slightly different design than Luke's, with a small combined kitchen and dining room, tiny living room, and hall with three doors. That was the difference—his had only two doors. I assumed one was a bathroom, and the others…

"Two bedrooms?"

She nodded, placing the vase on the counter. "Yeah. I know Logan isn't going to let Oliver stay the night anytime soon, but I hope that will change eventually. I want him to feel at home here, and it wouldn't feel right if he didn't have his own room."

A smile broke out on my face.

"You want to see?" she asked, excitement in her tone.

"Sure." I wasn't sure there would be anything *to* see, since she was just moving in and boxes lined the walls, but I was proven wrong as soon as she opened Oliver's door.

You'd never guess a room so perfect was situated in a small-town apartment. It was fully furnished and decorated, complete with a wallpaper border of dinosaurs running along the center of the walls. There was a twin-sized bed against the wall, with a maple side table that held a lamp boasting a giant T-rex surrounded by miniature dinosaur figurines. On the other side of the room were a dresser and bookshelf loaded with a mix of children's novels and toys. And above the bed, wooden letters hung, spelling out OLIVER.

I was in awe. It rivaled his room at Logan's house.

"It's...perfect. He'll love it."

"I know. I spent all day yesterday shopping, and then stayed up till two this morning decorating. He said he and Logan like to play dinosaurs."

I turned away from the Pottery Barn-styled showroom and looked to her. "They do. I think it's their little thing."

"Well, now we'll share that."

Maybe it was just me, but the way her lips pinched together when she'd said those words bordered on disturbing.

"We should get that box from the trunk," I said, leaving the room.

I didn't want to dislike her, despite having every reason in the world to be cautious. She was Oliver's mother, and at the end of the day he needed to have one other person who could at least stand to have her around. For him, I would be that person—or at least try to be.

"Can I ask you a question?" Natasha asked as we walked through the living room.

"Sure." I stopped and turned back, my routine smile in place.

"I volunteered to help out in the PTA last month when I

moved here and haven't heard anything back. How does that usually work?"

PTA? I'd have been slightly impressed had there been no nagging wonder if it was all for appearances.

"Did you do it in person?"

"Yeah. The lady was…a little rude." Her face screwed up. She looked almost embarrassed.

I shook my head, eyes rolling back. "Tall, a little gut, with too-short greying hair?"

"Sounds like her."

I laughed. "She has, like…10 children, and thinks she has all the power in that school. Did you attend the meeting last month?"

"Yeah, I saw it in the newsletter in Oliver's book bag and thought it would be something good to check out, but the ladies were…"

"Bitches," I finished for her.

She laughed, relaxing. "A little bit."

"You're an outsider to them, that's all. It's one massive clique there. Give it time and keep up with the newsletters to show them you aren't going away."

"Thanks."

I nodded, feeling a little lighter, as well as proud that we could be amicable.

As I turned back and began walking across the room and through the kitchen, my gaze fell on a table that held stacks of framed photos. From where I stood, they all appeared to be of Oliver. I couldn't understand how she had so many photos of him. They weren't all recent, and there was a mixture of shots from every age.

Natasha walked forward. Noticing me staring, she lifted one of the photos from the far end of the table.

"He's grown so fast," she said, her eyes on the frame in

her hand.

Sadness was heavy in her voice. Or was it regret? I wasn't sure what to think as her head rose and her gaze shot over to me, a tear glistening in her dark grey eyes.

She set the frame back down, and for the first time I saw it: not a photo of just Oliver, but a family portrait, with Logan standing behind her and a newborn Oliver in her arms. Logan's face held pride and love. He looked so young, so gentle. And Natasha looked…sad. Her smile was limp and forced as she looked down at the small bundle in her arms.

"I don't know how to do this, Cassandra." Her voice startled me, and my head jerked up from the photo. "I want my son to look at me the way he does his father. And Logan…" Her voice dropped.

Did I want to hear more? I didn't really have a choice as she found her words again.

"I've accepted that he's moved on—I swear I have. But for him to continue to push me away while another woman steps in as the role of mother to my son when I'm finally ready…" She closed her eyes tightly.

"Natasha, I'm not trying to—"

Her eyes flew open, a strained smile on her face. "I get it. I do. Logan has every right to hate me. But I was young, Cassandra—too young to be engaged, and way too immature to have a child. Logan…he was the perfect father. God, he was so amazing, and I…" Her voice shook. "He loved Oliver from the moment I told him I was pregnant. He worked incredibly hard to buy us a home, signed us up for every birthing and first-aid class he could find…" She huffed out a laugh, nostalgia heavy in her tone. "He never missed a single doctor's appointment, no matter how busy his schedule got. He was always there."

Her head and voice both lowered, tugging at my

heartstrings.

"I couldn't even stand to shop for my unborn child. Logan was so happy, and I was miserable. Once he was born, it only got worse. I couldn't even stomach changing a diaper. I couldn't breastfeed like Logan wanted, or stand to hear Oliver cry. His screams just...irritated me to no end," she confessed, holding my wary gaze, trying to explain and justify her actions.

"I wasn't good for him. Logan had this idea in his head that we'd be the perfect family, but I couldn't do it. It was too hard."

Her fingers dabbed under her eyes as she sniffled. I stood silently, stunned at everything she'd revealed.

Her features softened on a heavy sigh. "I know you're being nice to me because you're just a sweet person. I've heard it from everyone. You and I being friends is probably the last thing you really want, but... I can't stand for another person close to my son to hate me."

"I don't hate you," I said quickly. It was true: With every emotion I felt toward this woman I hardly knew, hate was not one of them. Great dislike, perhaps, but not hate.

"Maybe not yet, but you will. Logan and Julia will fill your head. With Logan, I broke his heart—for that alone you should hate me, not to mention what I've done to Oliver. I want so badly to make things right. I love my son, and I'm finally able to be the mother he wants."

I couldn't hear anymore.

"Natasha, I'll be honest: Us being friends is a little awkward, but mainly because I know when you came back, you still wanted Logan. And that was only a couple months ago."

She nodded, running her fingers through her long hair. "Part of me still does, and probably always will."

My jaw clenched.

"We share a child, Cassandra, and he will always be my

first love. But I know, I really do know, that I've lost him, and my focus now is only on my son. He needs me, and I need him. This last month with him has opened my eyes. I want to be his mother, his mommy...but I also hope that, in time, Logan will be my friend again."

What could I say to that? It was honest—or, at least, it *felt* that way.

"He will. Just give him time and show him. Prove to him that he can trust you."

"See, you're too sweet. I tell you I'll always care for your man, and not only do you not attack me, but you...you give me advice."

My shoulders shrugged, a reluctant smile growing on my face. "That's just me. I'm not looking to make an enemy out of you, Natasha."

"I get why he fell for you. You're good...everything I wasn't."

"Nata—" I started to interrupt, but she cut me off.

"When I realized Logan had played me, sending me alone to Aspen for Valentine's, I was furious. I planned on coming back here and telling you to back off, begging you to let me have another chance at putting my family together again. But I realized that's not going to happen. Logan will only hate me more if I try to force you to leave him. I want Oliver, plain and simple—and he adores you."

The apprehension in her voice broke my last thread of suspicion. My eyes closed for a moment, and I collected my thoughts before staring back at her, appraising her emotions. I couldn't help but feel for her. For Oliver. For Logan.

"Jax said I could talk to you...that you'd understand," she said, hopeful.

And then it happened: Something clicked inside me, and it all became clear. One single memory was triggered, and a greater understanding suddenly sat at my feet.

She was blackmailing Jax. He wanted me to be nice to her, which meant she was desperate for a way back into the West household—into the hearts of those I loved.

A performance was exactly what it felt like when I looked at it with eyes wide open. Whether I was right or wrong, I went with my gut. If she was being genuine, she'd prove it to me in time. If not, I had to give it to her—she was good.

But for Oliver, I could be better.

"I'll try to help in any way I can." The lie came out smoothly for the first time in my life. Hilary would be proud.

I started toward the door again. "I'm sure things will get easier. Now let's go get that box."

The walk down to the car was a quiet one, with me on edge. I wanted so much to believe her words, but had to assume I could never trust her.

"Muffins," I said, breaking the silence. "Preferably chocolate ones."

Her brows knit together as we stopped at the trunk.

"That's the key to the PTA. You can pick them up at the grocery store, put them on a fancy platter, and bring them next month. It will get you the in you need."

She looked thoughtful, and her smile fell. "In the papers I was given, it said no snacks were to be brought to meetings."

I reached into the trunk and grabbed a side. "They just say that, but they secretly love it."

It was true—most of the women would be thanking her. But the key player she needed to impress? Not so much. But I wasn't about to feel bad. She was blackmailing Jax, and she deserved it.

But still, it nipped at me. I wasn't an evil person, but I wouldn't be manipulated. And if she thought of me as the weakest link in the West chain, she was in for a surprise.

"Oh, and also try wearing something a little frumpier. And *no* red lipstick."

She looked down at her low-cut sweater, skintight jeans, and mile-high heeled boots.

"Just being honest. You don't want them jealous or thinking of you as a threat, since a lot of husbands help on some projects."

"Maybe they should." Her smile curved into a wicked grin. "Kidding. I like my men unmarried." She laughed.

"Right." I chuckled, all fake and uncomfortable, not missing the fact that she'd said 'unmarried' and not 'single'.

The game was officially on.

Together, we lifted the box out of the trunk—and it was *not* filled with pillows. If anything, it felt more like lead weights.

"What's *in* here?" I asked, turning around when we stopped at the bottom of the stairs. They looked steeper than before. Cautiously, I started up backwards, placing my feet carefully. The higher we climbed, the more my grasp slipped from the corners, but I kept a firm grip.

"Logan's sex swing."

My steps halted and jaw dropped in shock, and before I could stop it, the box was slipping out of my hands.

"AHHH!" was all I heard as Natasha bore the weight of the box, attempted to keep her balance, then flew backward. She landed with a hard thud on the concrete and I raced down, trying to stop the box that was tumbling after her.

I was too late, grabbing hold of it just as it landed hard on her stomach. Panic gripped me as she lay there sobbing. I pushed the box over, and its contents spilled out.

To my relief and mortification, they weren't a sex swing at all, but a collection of hardcover books.

Chapter Fourteen

TENSION

There are some things in life we can't take back, with no possible way to rewind time and do them differently. Instead, we're forced to endure the crushing blow of regret while anxiously awaiting a chance to apologize in some vain attempt to make things right.

For me, the ripples of remorse I stomached for letting that box slip from my hands grew more unbearable the longer I waited for Natasha to speak to me. I'd ridden in the ambulance with her—not that I'd asked to, but the paramedic suggested it, and with no possible reason not to I'd climbed in.

It was over an hour later that I was sitting in a small cubicle next to an empty spot where her bed had been before they'd rolled her off to have X-rays taken.

The doctor believed something might be broken or sprained, which wasn't surprising considering she couldn't sit up. And as worried as I was for her, it ate at me that even though I'd repeatedly tried to explain how the box had slipped purely on accident, she was too doped up by the time we were alone in the ER to even acknowledge it. Or perhaps she was making me sweat a little by withholding the 'It's okay, accidents happen' I desperately needed to hear. My guilt was unfathomable; nothing could make me feel worse.

"Holy shit!"

Jax strode through the curtain, a wide grin covering his face. "Down the stairs, huh? Gotta say, Cassandra—didn't think you had it in you."

I sat up in my chair, my eyes narrowed in his direction. "What are you doing here?"

He didn't seem to notice as he glanced around the room, amused. "Word travels fast in this town of yours."

My heart nosedived into the furthest depths of the shame pool. "Does...does Oliver know?" My words were a broken whisper.

Jax cackled, his head actually thrown back at my despair. "Doubtful, but seriously, when you push someone down a flight of stairs—especially someone that deserves it—you don't hang your head. Fucking own it! Now where is she? I'm gonna need to capture this moment." He dug into his pocket and retrieved his cell.

"Out!" I stood, pointing to the curtain he'd entered through.

"Come on, just one pic when she gets back."

Smug as ever. "Now!" My voice dripped with unspoken threats.

"Damn, you're cute when you're pissed." He tucked his phone away and held up his hands in surrender. "I'll go, but I can stick around a little if you want—in the waiting room, of course. I heard you hopped a ride over with her, so I guess you'll need a ride to go get my car you left there."

My scowl lessened, but only by a fragment. "Fine, but stay away from Natasha."

"Sure, of course." He began to turn then stopped and glanced back, a wicked gleam in his eyes. "But at least tell me her ass took a few licks from the pavement?"

"She's a woman, you pig!" I spat.

"If you say so."

"*Get. Out!*"

"Shit, all right, let's go then."

"What? I can't leave her here." My expression twisted up.

"Why not? You think she'd sit here waiting for you?"

"I don't care what she'd do. I won't leave her here alone unless she asks."

"Your call. I'll be around. Just text me when you're ready." Looking bored already, he turned and walked out.

I slouched back in the chair, my fingers massaging my temples as I waited for Natasha to return. I checked my phone, aware Logan would be looking for me and probably blowing up my inbox, but there was only one text.

At home waiting for u sweetheart

I didn't know what to say—at least, not over text—so I slipped the phone back in my jacket pocket just as the nurse rolled Natasha's bed back into the room. Natasha lay there half asleep, facing the other way.

I stood, concern my only emotion.

"Is everything okay?" I asked the nurse, choking on my words.

"The doctor will look over the X-rays soon and then come talk to her."

"Thank you," I said, then watched her begin to leave as quickly as she'd come. Feeling suddenly uneasy, I asked before she disappeared, "Did she have an in-case-of-emergency contact, or someone else that you guys notified?"

The nurse nodded. "Yes, he should be here."

I shook my head, knowing in my gut exactly whom she'd have them call. I stopped the nurse's steps once more.

"What's his name?"

"Sorry, I'm not sure. I was just told someone was coming

in for her."

The nurse left, and then it was just Natasha and me in the tiny room. I paced the room, wondering if Logan and Oliver would materialize behind the curtain at any moment.

Logan, I could handle. Not that I was thrilled about explaining it to him, but Oliver…just the thought of the worry he'd hold in his bright blue eyes was too much to bear.

I never spoke a word, feeling it best to leave Natasha to sleep. After a few more strides, I sat back down and waited. I rested my head on the wall behind me and closed my eyes.

The doctor's voice pierced the air as he walked in. "All right, well, I looked over the images."

Natasha peeked up. "And?" she shot back, unable to control her irritation.

"Nothing's broken, but there is quite a bruise on your tailbone. We'll give you a prescription to alleviate some of the pain, as well as a doughnut cushion to relieve some pressure when you sit. You should be feeling good as new within about a week."

Exasperated, Natasha let her head fall back on the pillow. "That's it? Drugs and an ass pillow?"

"That's all we can do." Chart in hand, he wrote something down, then looked up and smiled. "Follow up with your doctor, and if you need anything else, we're here. The nurse will be in shortly with some instructions, and then you can go home."

"Right. Thanks," Natasha said with a sigh.

After he left, the silence returned. Internally, I debated different ways to speak to her naturally. But when nothing sounded good enough in my head, I finally just blurted it out.

"I'm so sorry, Natasha. Truly, it wasn't on purpose. The box was so heavy, and it slipped. You have to know I'd never do that intentionally."

With an awkward squirm, she rolled to her other side to face me, her expression hard.

I swallowed. If she wanted to, she could try and twist things around to make me look guilty. I wouldn't let her tell lies, but even if she did, I knew Logan wouldn't believe her over me. That small piece of knowledge was enough to keep me calm.

My eyes widened as a small, brittle smile appeared on her face.

"I know, Cassandra. Accidents happen, and I'm partly to blame. You do know I was just kidding about the sex swing, right?"

Finally, I could breathe. The tension began to fade, and her smile grew as she continued.

"When I left Logan, I only took a few things. A sex swing wasn't one of them."

"I know. I mean, it just shocked me, I guess, but the box...I should've held it better."

As soon as she opened her mouth to speak, the curtain flew open. His back was all I saw as a man rushed past me and dropped down on his haunches beside the bed, taking Natasha's face in his hands.

"What happened, baby? I told you I'd help you move. Why didn't you wait?"

Natasha was unable to sit up, but she did lean forward and press her forehead to his. I stood, feeling suddenly awkward. They didn't seem to notice me, so as I backed toward the curtain, I cleared my throat. The guy's head snapped in my direction.

I knew him. Not well, but he was a buddy of Mark's. All I knew was that he used to own what was now Haven, and that his name was Josh.

"Cassie, hey. What happened?" he asked.

"Um, she—" I started, but Natasha tugged on his arm, snaring his attention back.

"I'll explain later, but it could have been worse," she said before looking to me. "No hard feelings, Cassandra. I'll see you around."

I nodded, thankful she was going to be all right and appeared to be letting me off the hook. With an apologetic hint of a smile, I stepped out of the room and inhaled a full, deep breath. Feeling a little lighter, I headed to the waiting room, but was stopped dead in my tracks at the sight of Jax leaning against the nurse's desk.

His smooth charm was evident from across the hall—not to mention how easily he seemed to have put the on-duty nurse under his spell. Her blush was bright, her expression almost as awkward as the doughnut-shaped pillow in her hand.

"Let's go—now!" I snapped through his laughter, storming over and snatching his arm. I tugged him toward the double doors that led to the outside.

Jax's teasing was the playlist of the ride as he drove me back to the apartments to retrieve his car. He was driving a flashy black Porsche I'd never even known Logan owned. Ignoring him had turned out to be the best defense.

"Good luck, Buffy the Bitch Slayer," he snickered as I climbed out. "I'd love to be there to watch you explain all this to my brother, but unfortunately I've got plans tonight."

I glanced back. "Logan will believe me that it wasn't on purpose. He knows me."

"Oh, I have no doubt about that. I just know that you'll look hilarious, all nervous as you try to explain it."

He had no idea what he was talking about. I could tell

Logan without freaking out. It was Oliver I was worried about, and that was what had me wracked with anxiety.

My eyes narrowed to slits. "We'll see. And you watched Buffy? A little before your time, wasn't it kiddo?" I taunted.

Jax's grin grew wider. "Ever heard of reruns? I grew up with a sister who watched anything with a so-called tough girl, and Buffy was smokin' hot. Filled my spank bank with screen shots of that chick!"

I slammed the door, feeling how I always did when I left Jax: disgusted and irritated.

When I arrived back at Logan's around seven, I still hadn't found the right words to explain to Oliver what'd happened. The air was thick and sweet with the aroma of Italian food. I followed it to the kitchen, where Oliver sat at the table and Logan stood in front of the stove.

"There you are." Logan turned around.

"Hi, Cassie!" Oliver called out, hard at work on a paper in front of him.

"How was your day?" Logan asked, pulling me into him.

"Good."

His brows knit together at my hesitance. Yeah, I was nervous—embarrassingly so.

"Jax said you borrowed his car. I thought you'd have taken one of mine. They're much safer. He always has his buddies working on his, and I don't trust them." Logan brought me in closer and placed his lips over mine for a quick kiss.

"Hopefully my car will be back soon," I said, brushing our mouths together again. He smelled like home and everything else I loved.

"It will," he murmured.

With my lips parted slightly, I stroked my tongue over his bottom lip before stepping out of his hold, earning me a wicked smirk at my tease.

With a smile, I walked over to Oliver, who was writing his numbers. I ruffled his soft curls as I sat beside him at the table.

"You have lovely handwriting," I praised, watching his concentration on the number '8'.

"Thanks! Daddy says so too."

I smiled over at Logan, who was busy at the stove once again but wearing a much larger grin than he'd had on when I walked in.

"Dinner's almost ready," Logan said a few moments later as I watched Oliver focus on the number '9'. "Why don't you go wash your hands, Oliver?"

"Not done yet." Oliver drew an almost-perfect circle for the number '10', then dropped his pencil. "I'll be back. Don't write on that, 'kay?" he said, pointing to his paper.

I held up my hands, smiling. "Promise."

Once he was out of the room, I almost shrieked as Logan lifted me from my chair and backed me up until I hit the refrigerator. His mouth covered mine, ravishing it while his hands slid under my ass and yanked me upward. His tongue caressed my own while my legs wrapped around his waist, my ankles locking at his back.

As his lips trailed down my jaw and away from my lips, I panted, "I missed you, too."

A growl was his only reply. His teeth seized my breast through the fabric of my shirt and lightly bit my nipple, which peaked at his demanding touch. Just as I became lost in my desire to have him right then and there, he dropped me to my feet abruptly and turned back to the stove. Oliver reentered not even a second later, rubbing his hands together.

"All clean!"

I stood there, struggling to catch my breath as Logan moved back over with a wicked smirk. "Excuse me, sweetheart. I need to get the milk."

"Huh?"

A twinkle gleamed in his eye, and suddenly he was pulling me toward him—not for another go, but to gain access to the refrigerator.

"Oh, milk, right," I said, composing myself.

He pulled it out and placed a kiss to my cheek. "You smell delicious. Promise me you're mine the rest of the night," he whispered.

"All yours," I mouthed. The man had impeccable hearing. Maybe it was a parent thing.

Feeling giddy, I sat back at the table with Oliver. A few minutes later, Logan appeared with plates full of steaming-hot pasta and placed them in front of us. We ate together, enjoying each other too much for me to think of dampening the mood with details of my afternoon. I decided that as soon as Oliver went to bed, I'd tell Logan what happened with Natasha.

Despite multiple protests, I managed to load the dishwasher after dinner. The doorbell rang just as I finished, and my heart sank at the thought of Natasha showing up.

I stepped out of the kitchen to find Logan helping Oliver with his coat and Hilary and Caleb standing in front of the door.

"Hey," I said. "What are you guys up to tonight?"

"Taking the little man out to see a movie," Caleb explained. Logan shimmied Oliver's hat down over his ears.

I stood staring at Hilary, willing her to look at me. It didn't work.

"How's Scout doing?" Caleb asked, glancing at Hilary then to me. It was obvious he knew something was up—

especially given the sidelong glance he shot Logan. The tension in the foyer was thick, and there was no way they didn't feel it.

"He's in good hands with your brother," I said, my voice monotone.

"Right." Caleb and Logan exchanged another look.

"I'm ready!" Oliver squealed, rushing to the door.

Hilary followed him without a single word to me.

"Well, I guess we'll see you in a couple hours." Caleb looked at Logan, and I could've sworn the words he spoke didn't match the silent discussion between them.

"No candy!" Logan's voice boomed with warning.

"I know. We got this." Caleb placed his hand on Hilary's back. "We can handle a little tot, can't we, baby?"

She paled, and I hoped I was the only one who noticed. She nodded her head in an awkward haste while pulling on an almost-painful smile. I wanted to run over and hug her, sit her and Caleb down, and force her to confess and tell him the truth. But instead, I watched as she opened the door and led Oliver outside in a rush.

"Have fun, you two." Caleb threw me a wink then shut the door, leaving Logan and me alone in the house.

It was in that moment I realized we were really alone in his home for the first time all week—which meant Logan had plans for us. And I knew they'd be in his bedroom.

But first, I needed to tell him about Natasha.

He moved toward me with smooth, determined steps and took my hands. "Alone at last."

"Lucky us." I balanced up on my tiptoes to kiss him, but his head moved back.

My brows raised in surprise. *Did he just dodge my kiss?*

"First, you have a few things to tell me."

Oh, crap.

"Logan, I was going to tell you the moment I got here. I

just didn't want to say anything in front of Oliver."

He said nothing. He knew, and was waiting for my explanation, so I gave it. And Jax was right—I did look ridiculous.

My hands flew about as I rattled it all off. "I was helping her with boxes, but one was really heavy, and I—I tried to hold it, but then she said...well, she—she made a joke, and the box slipped." My voice rose. "I swear it was an accident. I tried to grab it, but it was too late. She went down the stairs. But the doctor says she'll be fine, that it's just a bruise."

I blew out a stream of breath. My shoulders deflated as I waited for him to speak.

It felt like eternity before his mouth twisted up. "I knew all that already. I was talking about what's going on with you and Hilary."

"Oh." *Double crap!* "So you're not mad at me?"

His finger trailed down my chest to my stomach. "It was an accident. Why would I be mad?"

How could he be so cool about it? "How did you find out?"

His lips pressed to my cheek and he whispered, "Nothing happens that I don't know about. I've told you already."

"Jax." I sighed. *Of course.*

He took my hand and led me to the living room, where he sat on the sofa and pulled me onto his lap to straddle him. With both his hands sprawled against my back, he held me close, my breasts to his cheek.

"Actually, Natasha had given the hospital my information as her emergency contact."

I wrenched back. "You were there?"

He shook his head, his face impossible to read. "No. I told them not to call me again and gave them Jax's number."

"And he told you what happened?"

"No. That I discovered from Caleb. Luke heard the commotion when the ambulance came, and one of his neighbors said he saw it happen."

I wondered if that was when he asked Caleb to watch Oliver for a few hours—his reason to get me alone to hear my side of the story.

"Does Oliver know?"

One hand moved to my chin while the other pressed the small of my back as he drew me in and placed his lips over mine. The kiss was gentle and quick.

"No, and he won't ever find out."

I tugged away. "What? Either she'll tell him, or he'll see her like that."

"She knows better. He will find out she fell and got hurt, but not that you had any part of it."

"Logan—"

"Tell me, what did she say to you? What so-called joke was it?"

I squirmed in his lap, gnawing at my bottom lip as I muttered, "Your sex swing."

"What?" His forehead creased.

"I asked why the box was so heavy, and she said it had your sex swing in it." Mortified, I dropped my head against his chest, unable to look at him while I waited for his laughter.

But it never came. Instead, he lifted my chin, his eyes holding not a shred of amusement.

"You believed her?"

"No! I mean, I don't know…it just shocked me," I admitted.

"Well, a bruised ass was deserved then. So tell me, what else did you two discuss while you were there?"

"It doesn't matter."

"It does to me." His voice lowered. "She'll use you,

Cassandra—your kindness. She's not like you."

"I'm not an idiot!"

"No, but it was foolish of you to let her talk you into helping her."

Now I'm pissed. "She didn't talk me into anything! I went to her and offered to help."

His lip quirked up, but it wasn't in a smile. "Don't you get it? Natasha living in the same building as Luke, one of my closest friends' brothers? Her *happening* to need help the same moment you were there? That's not a coincidence."

"You're paranoid!" I attempted to move off his lap, but he locked his hands around my wrists.

"No, I see clearly what she's trying to do, but I won't allow it."

"And what's that?" I spat, angry that he'd think me meek enough to be controlled by her.

"She's using you."

"She can't. I'm not blind, Logan, but I'm also not a bitch, and I won't let her turn me into one. I'm sorry she hurt you, and it kills me that she walked out on Oliver, but I won't treat her like trash. Oliver deserves better—and she deserves a chance to make it right with him."

"What?" Logan pushed himself up to his feet, all but tossing me aside. "Deserves a *chance*?" His scowl was hard and set on me.

"She's his mother. You can't ever change that."

"Maybe not, but I sure as hell won't make it easy for her. If she really wants to prove herself, then she'll do it by finding a job, accepting she and I are never going to be together, and spending time to get to know her son—not trying to manipulate the girl I love."

I stepped into him and placed my hands on the scruff of his cheeks, forcing his sneer to soften.

"And I love you, and I love Oliver—more than I ever thought I could love anyone. You're both…"

Words failed me. A soft sigh escaped as the depth of my emotions and our connection settled in. "You're part of me, and I'll never let anyone hurt either of you ever again. I'll protect your son with my life. But for him, I'll also try to understand his mother—try to give her a chance, because *he* deserves to have a mother in his life. Don't punish him for her mistakes."

Silence hung between us. He closed his eyes slowly as my hands slipped down and wrapped around him. He held me flush against him and buried his face in my hair.

"You really are an angel."

"No, I'm just a woman in love. And nothing will change that."

Chapter Fifteen

FROZEN

Logan and I lay on the sofa, utterly satisfied. Our naked limbs were tangled together, bodies covered in sweat, clothes strewn across the room. His fingers stroked my hair, my back against his front. I was thankful for his oversized furniture that accommodated us perfectly.

"Before I forget, your car is parked safely in your driveway," Logan said, surprising me.

I smiled to myself. "Thank you."

We lay in silence a while longer before he spoke again.

"How was Scout?" he asked, kissing the shell of my ear.

"Good. He likes Julia," I said in a tranquil whisper.

He tensed. "Julia? I thought Luke was watching him."

I perked up at the subject at hand, remembering the inquiry Logan had coming and relieved he'd seemed to forget his own about Hilary. "He is, and Julia's helping."

"So their Valentine's date went well, I take it."

"She didn't say anything to you?" That didn't surprise me.

"Not a word, but she rarely does." His hands added relaxing pressure to my scalp. "I wish she'd focus more on school than boys."

I relished the massage, but needed to hold my wits. "He

likes her—a lot."

"What's not to like? My sister's a doll."

Before I could say anything, he added with a snicker, "Most of the time."

A smile curved my lips as I rolled onto my stomach. Half resting over him, I placed my chin in my hands, my elbows against his chest. "She told me about Larry."

His hands stilled just as they found my back, and after a moment's pause, he replied, "Our dog?"

"Of course. Is there another Larry?" I teased.

"I was a child, and I hardly remember half the stuff Lawrence goes on about. That's the only reason Julia even knows about the so-called imaginary friend, which I'm sure she told you about given your tone."

"I think it's charming." I traced my finger over his nipple.

"Liar."

My giggle couldn't be contained. "You had an imaginary friend! What's not cute about that?"

"Can we change the subject, please?"

"No." I dipped my head and ran my tongue over the ripples of his abs.

"You're impossible." He moaned as I continued my ministrations.

"And *you* are adorable. So what was he like?"

"I don't remember, but our dog was awesome. He was a Great Dane, and terrified everyone that came by—kid *or* adult."

I lay there enjoying the sound of his husky voice washing over me. The moment was too tender to disrupt it with a firing squad of questions about Mark and Julia, but my curiosity got the best of me.

"So did anything else happen today that I should know about?" Logan asked.

"Actually, your sister said something I wanted to ask you about."

"Did she now?"

"What did you do to Mark?"

His carefree expression dropped. "*Do?*" He laughed, but it was humorless.

"You forced him to break up with her?" I knew he wouldn't lie to me, but I was on edge with disappointment.

"No, I did nothing but help the guy."

My eyes squinted in confusion. "And how did you do that?"

"I pulled a few strings and got him a job in his field that pays triple what he was making before and could lead to a lot of new doors opening for him in the future."

That wasn't what I was expecting.

"I don't understand. Why would that—"

"The job is in Africa," he added, looking bored.

"Oh."

"So you can see why my sister wasn't happy. But nobody forced him to accept the offer. He made his choice."

"You dangled gold in his face. Of course he took it. Who wouldn't?" I scooted down and sat at the end of the couch.

"I wouldn't." He sat up, gripping my shoulder and turning me to face him. "If given the choice between money and you, I'd choose you without a second thought."

"Because you *have* money! Mark doesn't. You can't even compare the two. And you only did this because he hurt me. It had nothing to do with Julia."

"Believe it or not, I'd rather be poor with you in my arms than the richest man alive without you."

Damn it. How could I hold on to my anger when he said things like that?

He pressed his lips to my shoulder.

"You don't know...Mark might have felt that for Julia if given the time."

"They dated for months. He made his choice, and one day Julia will see I was looking out for her best interest. Mark is a douchebag. My sister deserves a man that will adore her."

In spite of myself, I laughed. "Did you just use the word 'douchebag'?"

He raised a brow. "It seems I did."

"Wow, you really don't like him, huh?"

"You already know that answer."

I did, but I still hated that Julia was suffering because Logan's perception of Mark was skewed due to my past with him.

"Would you have done this if Mark and I had never dated—if he'd never hurt me?"

"Yes." His reply was quick, and his next words were genuine. "I met Mark the first time I came to Harmony a few months before I moved here. I know the type of guy he is, and *that's* why I did it. But because he hurt you, Caleb and I settled something a while ago."

I winced. "What does that mean?"

"It means Mark knew better than to speak to you at Haven the night you and Hilary came in, and he paid for his mistake."

"What did you do?"

"Nothing for you to worry about. Just know I gave him a chance to fight for my sister, to prove me wrong, and he left her with only a text-message goodbye, dropping blame on me. Not that I mind, as long as he's out of her life."

"Maybe he'll come back for her—save up and return to make things right." It was doubtful, but I'd always been a hopeless romantic underneath it all.

"And if he does, then he may earn a *crumb* of my respect."

The whole conversation was exhausting. I didn't disagree with Logan—Julia *was* better off without Mark. But of course I'd feel that way.

I lay back, resting against his solid form, and tucked my head into the nook of his shoulder. "What about Luke? Will you run him off, too?"

"Should I?"

"He likes her, genuinely, and I know he'll never hurt her if he can help it. But she's scared you'll do something to ruin it if she gives him a chance. That's not fair, Logan."

"Her new place is almost ready. I don't want him spending the night there."

I smiled, excited to see how the house turned out and whether she loved it. If she did, Logan would lose our bet and become my little whipping boy for a weekend. I still needed to decide what I'd have him do for me.

"So that means you like Luke? You don't still think he wants in my panties?"

"Caleb speaks highly of him, even as his brother, and Luke's been a friend to you. So yes, I guess that means I don't mind him. And I won't interfere with him dating my sister. As for your panties, he'd be a fool not to want to peek in there but a bigger fool to try."

Logan's hand slid between our bodies, cupping my sex. A moan rang from my mouth, and before he could show me all that hand could do, the doorbell rang. Oliver was home.

I searched frantically for my pants, finally finding them and rushing to put them on. Logan was at ease with his, buttoning them casually and handing me my bra.

"Thanks," I said, my head down, zipping my pants. The bell rang again, but we didn't move. I dragged my gaze slowly up his smooth, bare chest to meet his soft, hooded eyes.

"We'll finish this later."

"Promises, promises."

Despite the frigid air early Saturday morning, I was outside, wrapped in my bulky sweater Logan had packed. I couldn't help not minding, though, since it was hidden under a supple red coat he'd surprised me with before we'd left his house. It was made to ski in, and he assured me that by the end of the year he'd have me at his place in Aspen learning to do just that.

Logan helped Oliver out of the car as I stared, blissfully happy. It was our first official date as a couple, and the thought warmed me. We'd been through so much, and there we were, together and in love. Who'd have thought?

"How did you find out about this place?" I asked as I tightened my thick scarf, ready to tackle the winter weather. I headed toward the massive hill before us, carrying a small round sled. The last time I was on a sled, I could barely call myself a teenager, and it was with Hilary on a small hill in her backyard. But this seemed so much better. How I'd lived in Harmony my entire life and never known about the impressive mountain five minutes outside its town limits was both a mystery and a shame.

Logan was beside me, holding Oliver's hand and dragging two larger sleds behind them.

"I have my connections," he answered, throwing me a flirty smile and the sexiest wink.

I laughed. "Ah. Caleb told you, huh?"

"Actually, an employee at the paper. Said he brings his kids here every year, so I figured it was worth checking out. Impressed?"

"Very."

After we reached the top of the hill, Logan placed the long two-rider sled on the ground and held it in place for Oliver and me to climb on. Oliver could hardly sit still waiting for his father to release us. I had to admit that, as I stared down the vast snow-covered hill that felt more like a rollercoaster from my angle, my nerves were buzzing with anticipation.

"You ready?" Logan asked, adjusting his son's hat to cover his ears fully.

Oliver and I shouted a loud affirmation. Logan leaned in behind me and whispered, "Hold tight, beautiful."

His lips nipped the back of my ear, but there was no time to reward his sweetness. I had one hand around Oliver's waist and the other gripping the rope of the sled. We flew down the steep hill, giggling at the unexpected velocity.

My adrenaline spiked as the sled skidded gently to the side and slid to a stop at the bottom of the hill. My laughter was bordering on hysterical.

"That was fun! Again, again!" Oliver gushed, running to the side of the hill and marching back up.

I waited at the bottom, dusting myself off and collecting our sled. The ride was not only exhilarating, but something I already knew I'd be coming back to experience yearly.

My hand blocked the sun from my eyes as I peered up to see Oliver standing at the top of the hill, high-fiving his father. *Wow, he climbed fast!*

"Here we come!" Oliver yelled down, his hands circling his mouth to act as a speaker.

I stood to the side, smiling as Oliver climbed onto the other sled with Logan.

It was a picture to behold, which reminded me of the camera I'd brought. I pulled it from my pocket and took picture after picture as they flew down and wiped out at the bottom, laughing madly. The sled landed on top of them, but they didn't seem even a bit fazed.

Boys.

I walked over just as Oliver jumped up, snow plastered to his snowsuit, and grabbed the rope to the sled. I watched as he struggled to tow it back up with slow trudges, extending my arm down to Logan.

"Need a hand there?" I teased.

"I could use more than that." He reached up and hauled me down on top of him, ensnaring my lips with his.

"Kids are watching," I gasped against his warm, relentless mouth.

"And?"

"And your son is waiting. Come on." I pushed off from his chest, giggling when he dragged me back down for one last peck and rolled me over in a wrestling move before leaping to his feet.

I glared up at him from the cold snow he'd abandoned me in, feigning a pout.

"Well come on, sweetheart. Oliver's waiting and all."

I chucked a handful of snow at his boyish grin, which he only laughed at before reaching down and scooping me up.

"What a gentleman," I purred as he placed me upright on my feet.

"Hurry!" Oliver yelled.

Logan laughed, kissed my hand that was wrapped in his, and grabbed the sled I'd used. He jogged after Oliver with me at his side, relieving his son of dragging the other sled so his little feet could carry him faster back up the hill, where he waited for us at the top.

"I wanna race!" Oliver squealed, hopping down on the round single-seat sled the moment Logan dropped it.

"You're on." Logan sat on the other sled, his grip tight on

Oliver's sled beside him. His feet were planted in the snow on either side, holding him in place. "Come on, Cassandra. We have a race to win."

Until that moment, I hadn't realized just how much I'd missed the fun-spirited Logan I'd gotten to know during the few months we were friends. His eyes twinkled up at me as an impish grin sharpened his features.

The man was everything I would ever want, and the feeling settling into my heart at that little revelation caused my entire body to relax.

Logan patted the spot in front of him, wiggling his brows at me. With a soft giggle, I sat between his legs and grabbed the rope.

I leaned back and whispered, "Clever. Was this why you suggested sledding—another ploy to get me between your legs?"

"It's *your* legs I enjoy spending time between, but not while sledding." His low, hushed voice rumbled through me and wrapped me in adoration, warming me. "Unless you'd like to come back for a midnight ride."

Tempting.

"Ready!" Oliver shouted, holding the handles on each side of his sled and beaming.

"Three, two, ONE!" I bellowed, and Logan released his hold on Oliver's sled, giving him a head start before sending us shooting down.

Logan's lips were on my neck, his hands on my thighs as his thumbs traced lines back and forth over my jeans. Mixed with the adrenaline of the lightning speed, his touch had me bustling with life.

"This is perfect," he said, kissing up my ear when I leaned into him.

I caught sight of Oliver sliding off to the side, hearing his animated laughter upon beating us to the bottom.

"I won! I won!" he cheered, bouncing up and down just as we came to a stop a few feet away.

"Congratulations, baby."

My stomach dropped at the sound of her voice, my body going painfully rigid. I wanted the day to include just me and my boys—she was the last person I wanted on our date. Still, I shook it off.

"Mommy!" Oliver ran past us as Logan stood, brushing the snow from his jeans.

I couldn't look up at him or even blink; my entire body screamed at me not to turn around. My movements to stand were deliberately slow as Logan held out his hand to me. *Why is she here? Will she tell Oliver what happened?*

It was obvious Logan could see it written all over my face.

Taking my time, I wiped the snow from my legs, coat, and gloves—anything to stall the moment.

"*That's* what you call a sled?"

My head shot back at the sound of Caleb's voice. So it wasn't only Natasha high-jacking my date—she was with Caleb and Hilary.

My day was crashing fast. There was far too much drama wrapped in that group for me to have a fun sledding day.

Caleb bent down and was laughing with Oliver. Hilary stared at the hill, pretending to watch the other sledders.

Logan stepped into me when I finally stood, ran his hands up and down my arms to warm me, then leaned into my ear.

"I invited Caleb last night, since it's obvious you and Hilary have something to work out. But I swear I have no idea why Natasha is here."

My gaze met his, and I knew instantly that he spoke the truth.

"I'm sorry," he whispered. "I'll tell her to leave."

Yes, please! my internal bitch screamed. However, as I watched Natasha climb the hill hand in hand with Oliver—with an awkward gait, no doubt from the accident, slowing her steps—my shoulders deflated with a sigh.

"It's all right." I pulled on a wide, albeit thin smile. "Oliver's happy, and that's what matters."

I began to walk away, ready to climb the hill with heavy legs and a troubled conscience. I wanted Oliver to have his mother, but it still stung—though I'd never admit it aloud.

Logan slipped his hand in mine and brought it to his lips, kissing the pads of my fingers one at a time.

"Thank you." His voice was so sincere, yet filled with nerves. "Now, do you plan on saying hello to Hilary or continuing to ignore her? It's quite uncomfortable."

"Sure is!" Caleb said, standing closer now to eavesdrop.

Glancing his way, I noticed Hilary was halfway across the field, heading to the restroom.

"We're fine, just—"

"Just not speaking?" Caleb finished.

What could I say? I stood there with two gorgeous yet irritated men in front of me, looking for answers.

"Look, whatever you two are fighting about, go make up. My girl has been crying every night and she won't say why, but I know it has to be about you. Hell, standing in that damn foyer to pick Oliver up last night made that clear."

"We just had a disagreement; it's nothing serious. We're fine, really."

"Bullshit!" Caleb took a step toward me, but Logan's hand shot out to make sure he kept his distance. Caleb ignored it, his eyes hard on mine. "She's hurting, Cassie, so whatever is going on, fix it!"

Without another word or allowing me to speak, he turned on his heel and headed up the mountain. I hadn't seen Caleb's temper since I was younger, and even then it was only on display when he fought with bullies at school.

I glanced back at the restroom Hilary was now entering. Her crying every night wasn't about me, but it *was* time for us to talk.

"I'll be back," I said to Logan, my nerves frayed.

His lip curled up and I leaned forward, pressing a kiss to the corner of his mouth.

"Take your time, sweetheart."

Chapter Sixteen

DOWNHILL

If I knew one thing about Hilary, it was that she didn't do well with confrontation. She'd always been one to jump into defensive mode before hearing someone out. But as many times as I'd witnessed it, I somehow forgot that little fact when I creaked opened the door to the small brick building. An unpleasant stench of sewage assaulted my senses as I entered.

It was dark and dreary, and likely housed a few critters from the looks of it. My steps were cautious as I surveyed the small sink and three stalls. All the doors were open except one.

"Hilary?" I moved toward the back stall quickly.

"G-go away." Her stutter broke into unmistakable grunts of vomiting.

I waited for her to finish. "Hilary, are you—"

The retching started again almost the same second it'd ceased, cutting off my words. A few seconds later, a loud, disgusted gasp of breath filtered through the door.

I stood on the other side, uneasy at the fact that there was little I could do for her.

"You want me to see if I can find you a bottle of water? There was a vendor—"

The stall door flew open and I leapt back, nearly catching

it in the face. Hilary ambled out, wiping her mouth with the back of her hand.

"No, I'll be okay."

"You sure?" I asked, unconvinced. Her face was pale, and beads of sweat glistened above her brow.

"Positive. There isn't anything left in me, so unless the dry heaves hit I should be good to go for a few more hours." She stood at the sink, splashing water on her face.

"Morning sickness?" My lips twisted up in a sympathetic smile.

The faucet handle squeaked as she turned it off. She peered up at me, glaring. "Wow, you must be a genius considering its 9 a.m. and I'm knocked up!"

A scowl scrunched my face. This was my date time with Logan, and there was no way I was going to sit there and take her attitude—especially when I had Natasha waiting on that hill.

"You know what? I came in here to check on my best friend, not a mean bitch! So now you're either gonna hear me out," I stepped into her, "or I'll march back outside and up that damn hill to let Caleb know *exactly* why you've been crying every night!"

"You wouldn't!" she sneered.

"I would." Those two simple words rolled out with an unyielding strength. I was done trying to be nice to everyone. Regardless of whether she wanted to hear it, I wasn't holding back this time. "Now let me ask you: Do you *really* think he'll never find out—that you can disappear for a few months and come back like everything is fine, knowing that you *stole* his child?"

"It's *my* choice!"

"Really? All yours, huh?" I shook my head, dropping my gaze. "He'll never forgive you."

"He's never gonna find out!" Despite the hardness in her voice, it still cracked with rattled nerves.

I looked at her, demanding her full attention. "Listen to me: You *will* regret this. Caleb wants kids someday; he told me himself. He also adores you, Hilary."

Her features began to soften as I continued with a gentler voice.

"And maybe he *will* break your heart and leave you a single mother. But if that happens, you won't ever have to raise this child alone. You know that. And at the end of the day, you'll have a clear conscience. Please, just tell him the truth. Give him a chance."

The bathroom door swung open abruptly. Both our heads whipped in its direction as a woman sauntered in, typing away on her phone. When she looked up, her body jerked back, startled.

"Oh, Miss Clarke! Hi, how have you been? We heard you're coming back on Monday."

Her name failed me, but I recognized her as one of my students' mothers.

"Yeah, I am, and I can't wait," I replied.

"Excuse me," Hilary muttered, slipping out the door with her head down.

I gave a look of apology to the woman. "I'm sorry, I have to go. I'll see you in a couple days. Take care!" I threw out hastily as I rushed out.

"Hilary, stop!"

She turned back quickly. "Cassandra, I love you—I do, and I know why you're pushing me. Honestly, I'd be trying to convince you to do the same thing, but please…I can't be a mother."

She started walking away again.

"But you'll steal away Caleb's chance at being a father?" I

said, not bothering to whisper.

She spun back and stormed at me. "Stop! Come on—please. Don't do this to me."

I stood my ground, despite her shaking hands and trembling lip. When she saw I wasn't going to back down, her shoulders slumped on the rush of her drained exhale. Tears welled in her eyes.

"I tried. I almost told him last night. Seeing him with Oliver broke my heart because he's so good with him. So…natural. Like, it just came so easy to him. But after we dropped Oliver off and got back in the car, Caleb was kissing me and said he was glad it was just us…that as much as he loved Oliver, he couldn't imagine doing that every night."

"Hilary, he was probably just tired. Logan said Caleb rarely babysits. Don't do something so extreme based off one stupid statement he made. Tell him what's going on, and let *him* decide how he feels about it."

Slowly, she sank down onto the snow, looking defeated, cradling her knees to her chest. I sat beside her, staring ahead at Logan and Oliver squaring off against Caleb in a snowball fight. Natasha stood to the side, watching them. Not wanting to think about her, I shook my head and turned my focus back to Hilary, but she'd seen the same picture as me.

"Sorry about Natasha," Hilary said with a frown. "Caleb's fault."

"What? Why?" Did Caleb and Natasha even know each other? She was long gone from Logan's life before he met Caleb.

Not the time. "You know what? Doesn't matter. I'm not letting you change the subject. You always do that."

She smiled and lay back with a thud, slipping her hands under her head. "We ran into her and Jax at Haven when we stopped in for a drink last night."

Subject change, it was...for now. I lay back beside her.

"They overheard Caleb telling me we were going to meet you guys here in the morning. Jax insisted Caleb invite her, going on and on with some sob story about her always wanting to take Oliver sledding. I tried to talk him out of it."

"I don't get Jax," I confessed, squinting my eyes in the morning sunlight.

"What's to get? He's a perv! Every time I run into him, he's checking out my tits." Her head fell my way, and she revealed a secret smile. "But he's hot, so it's not the *worst* thing."

I narrowed my eyes playfully. "Caleb doesn't strike me as one to share."

She blew out a laugh. "You kidding? He almost knocked the shit out of him for just staring at me!"

We both laughed, relaxing into the earth as we lay there. The distant chuckles from the sledders mixed blissfully with the chirps from the birds overhead. It was surprisingly peaceful.

"He loves you," I said after a few moments.

"I know." She rubbed her stomach.

We lay there a while longer until the sight of Logan and Caleb heading our way caught my eye. Time was up.

"You can do this, Hilary. You're one of the strongest people I know. " I wrapped my hand around hers and held it there in the snow.

"It's so unfair."

I sat up and turned to her, holding her hand more tightly. "I know, but give him a chance. He deserves that—and so does the baby."

"Hey, you beauties looking for company?" Caleb asked as they drew closer.

Hilary sat up and drew me in for a hug. "I'll tell him. First thing tomorrow, I'll tell him everything," she whispered, then pulled back and held up her hand for Caleb. "I'm looking for a gentleman to help me up."

Caleb pulled her to her feet. "Since when do you prefer a gentleman?" He snickered, nipping her neck. She giggled, falling against him so naturally I couldn't imagine her with anyone else.

"A hand, sweetheart?"

I looked up at Logan and smiled. "I'm sure you have more than just that to offer."

Before I could reach out, he leaned down and scooped me up, shifting me around to straddle him as he straightened. "Oh, I've plenty to offer you." The thickness in his voice seeped through my skin, planting seeds of sensual promises.

There was no denying my need for him when he cupped my ass, pressing my center along the ridges of his abs. My fingers threaded together behind his neck, my needy eyes on his. I trailed my tongue over my suddenly dry lips, preparing to show him what *I* had to offer.

"Hey, now, this is a PG park!" Caleb teased.

Logan set me back down, but not before capturing my lips for a quick but memorable moment. Damn…he always tasted so perfect.

We made our way back to Oliver and Natasha, who were now at the top of the hill.

"Mommy, race me!" Oliver called out, plopping down on his sled.

With a hesitant smile, Natasha glanced my way, then back at her son. "Sorry, baby, I can't. My back's a little sore."

The guilt that crept through me at the somber drop of his cheerful expression bit me.

"You can use your pillow," Hilary suggested, pointing to the tote Natasha had set off to the side that had her butt cushion peeking out.

Natasha said nothing as Caleb grabbed it and tossed it onto a sled. "No shame. You wanted to come sledding with him, didn't you?"

"Yeah, of course," Natasha replied, her features devoid of any irritation. "Logan, can you help me?" She held out her hand, but Hilary stepped forward to take it.

"I can help you," Hilary said, her expression bright and tone overly friendly.

Natasha stared at Logan, who didn't move to help. And I knew he wouldn't—not with Hilary standing there, willing and ready.

"Never mind, I got it," Natasha said, then slowly lowered herself down onto the pillow.

"You gonna snap a pic of that?" Caleb whispered from beside me.

I swatted him. "Be nice. She's genuinely hurt."

"Right," was all he said as he took Hilary's hand and moved back to where they'd been sitting a few feet behind us, talking amongst themselves. Turned out sledding and morning sickness didn't mix, and luckily, telling Caleb her stomach was upset was enough to get Hilary off the hook.

Logan remained stoically quiet beside Oliver, watching his son who stared up at Natasha. Logan looked lost in his head. Not upset or happy—just thoughtful.

"You ready?" Logan finally called out, moving behind them. "Three—"

"No, get on with Mommy too!"

My stomach roiled and my head dropped as an unexpected gasp of air flew from my lungs. No, I wouldn't be jealous. As a child, I would've wanted the same thing Oliver did. But that thought didn't seem to help soothe the ache inside my heart.

"Better not make him wait," I laughed, hoping it'd come out more smoothly than it felt. I peered over to find Logan regarding me with a creased brow.

His lips curled up, as did mine when he lifted Oliver and sat behind him on the sled.

"How about I ride with you and we race boys against girl?" Logan told him.

Oliver nodded eagerly, gripping the rope.

"Cassie, count down!" Oliver called out to me.

"All right: three, two..." My smile grew as I watched Oliver bopping from side to side, unable to still his excitement and taunting his mother about boys being faster.

"ONE!"

In a flash, they were off.

Once they hit the bottom, I watched with a tight gut as Logan and Oliver helped Natasha up. Out of nowhere, I was suddenly hit with sadness. Part of me compared Oliver's situation to mine as a child. My father had left and never come back...but if he *would* have...

I shook it from my head. I hated that I knew I'd have welcomed him back as easily as Oliver did Natasha. Seeing what appeared to be a happy family sledding together consumed me with jealously. Did that make me a bad person? I wanted Oliver and Logan to be happy, but I knew I was being selfish considering I was a part of that happiness already. I felt like crap for even going there in my own head.

When they came back up—Oliver on Logan's shoulders, the sleds dragging behind them—I bit the inside of my cheek at the picture of Natasha at his side, laughing. They looked like a picture-perfect family. For Oliver and Oliver only, I pulled out my camera and, with shaky hands, snapped a photo. They didn't seem to notice through their laughter and talk about how good it felt to be out there in the fresh country air.

Logan stopped in front of me, smiling.

"Nat, hey baby!" Josh appeared, running up the hill behind them.

They all turned, and I watched Logan's expression darken when Natasha flung herself into Josh's arms.

"There you are! Always so late," she said, then kissed him. It was quick, but definitely involved a bit too much tongue.

"How the hell do you know him, *Nat?*" Logan all but growled the nickname.

Caleb moved beside me.

"Hello Logan," Josh said, then looked past him. "Caleb. How you guys been? Haven sure looks like a success."

"Answer my question, Natasha—now!" Logan demanded, ignoring Josh's words. His tone was hard and fierce—so much so that Caleb took Oliver's hand and helped him onto a sled.

"Don't you dare talk to my girl like that," Josh seethed, stepping closer to Logan until they were almost toe to toe.

What the hell was going on?

"Logan, let's sled," I said softly, attempting to ease the tension that had materialized in his jaw and everywhere else.

"Ride Oliver down, babe," Caleb said to Hilary, who was just as focused on Josh and Logan's standoff as I was. He tugged Hilary's hand, and she went over to climb behind Oliver.

As they flew down the hill, I slid my hand into Logan's, prying his fingers open to weave mine through. "Whatever is going on, this isn't the place," I whispered.

I wasn't even sure he'd heard me. He just stared at Josh, who was more relaxed then he should've been considering both Logan and Caleb were now in front of him. Josh placed his arm around Natasha and pulled her into him.

"What's the problem here, guys, huh? You got my restaurant, you both had your way with a friend of mine right outside my own door, but still I hold no grudges. So unless you want to start something in front of half the town, I say we move on."

"Logan, Josh is a sweet guy," Natasha offered.

Did she really like him? I mean, he was cute and had been popular in school, but he was more of a jock that never grew up rather than the man in front of her wearing a frown so deep I wondered if it would ever disappear.

"Sweet? You think this putz is *sweet*? He's a fucking kid, Natasha!" Logan growled.

And then it hit me: He was jealous.

Those three little words knocked the wind from my chest and the warmth from my soul. It wasn't possible. He despised her.

Caleb spoke at the same time Hilary and Oliver appeared. "Not here, Logan."

Logan finally took notice. "You're right. I came here to have some fun," he said, picking Oliver up and plopping him back on the sled.

I was going to be sick—of that, I was certain—and after watching the satisfaction on Natasha's expression as she pulled Josh flush against her for a full display of their lust, I knew I needed to take a walk.

"I'm going to get us some hot chocolate. I'll be right back," I said, avoiding eye contact with anyone as I headed for the vendor in the parking lot. I wasn't sure why I felt the way I did, but I needed a second to clear my head before my entire mood was ruined.

"Don't f'get marshmallows!" Oliver called out to me, and I smiled to myself at how happy he sounded. "Come on, Daddy, let's go again."

"You go with Hilary again. I'll help Cassandra," I heard Logan say, and I quickened my pace.

What was my problem? Did I really think he was jealous? I wasn't sure of anything right then, and it wasn't the time to ask him. But I would soon.

"No—again, Daddy, again!"

"Cassandra?" Hilary was beside me out of nowhere. "You okay?"

"Perfect. You guys want marshmallows in yours, too?" I asked, a forced smile in place.

"No, I want to watch Natasha on her ass pillow again!" She laughed, and I knew she was only trying to lift the sour mood.

"Don't. It's my fault she even got hurt."

"Seriously? She wants your man—it's so obvious—and I get the evil eye for laughing at the bitch?"

I sighed. "I'm just trying to play nice."

"Well, let's play then. We should get to know her a little better, don't you think?" Hilary stopped and turned back. "Hey, Natasha!" she yelled.

"Wait, what are you doing?" I whispered, my anxiety spiking.

The smile on Hilary's face was overly wide.

"Yeah?" Natasha called back, still attached to Josh. I dropped my gaze, shifting uncomfortably.

"You want to go out with Cassandra and me tonight? We haven't been dancing for too long."

"I hate you," I said under my breath, attempting to keep my lips still and in a seamless line.

"Sure, that sounds fun, thanks!" Natasha answered, looking surprised but thrilled at the offer.

"Fabulous!" Hilary called out, then turned back and continued walking down the hill. I followed, but my steps were anything but light. A night out with Natasha? 'Fabulous' was the last word I'd use to describe it.

Chapter Seventeen

POWER

The drive home was awkward, to say the least—especially with Oliver lying in the backseat, awake but too exhausted to distract us from our own thoughts. Logan was clearly on edge from Josh's unexpected arrival, and I was biding my time until Oliver was out of earshot so I could start the interrogation.

Deep down, I knew he couldn't be jealous of Josh, but still...there was that little nagging voice that kept reminding me they had a lot of history, including but not limited to the adorable little boy in the backseat.

We pulled into Logan's driveway right around noon. As I moved to open the passenger door, Logan's hand covered my knee.

"Wait."

"Huh?" I glanced his way.

Oliver's back door opened suddenly, and Julia was there helping him out.

"Five minutes, got it?" she said quickly. "I have plans." She shut the door.

"What's going on?" I asked, my expression tight.

"I just wanted to talk to you alone for a moment." Logan's hand was molded around the gearshift, his eyes forward.

My nerves sparked at his seriousness "Okay. Actually, there was something I wanted to ask you—"

"Stay away from Josh and Natasha." His harsh demand cut through me.

I narrowed my eyes. "Wait, what?"

He turned his head to face me, his expression dark. "You heard me. She's up to something. There's no possible way she'd freely date someone like him."

"*Someone like him?*" My tone was mocking, but not amused. "What the hell does that mean—she's too good for the locals?"

He shook his head, scowling. "He's nothing but an idiot, and will use anyone he can to hurt Caleb and me. In case Josh is there tonight, you're not going out."

"*Excuse* me? Since when do you dictate who I hang out with or where I go?"

His eyes cut to mine. "Josh has every reason not to like me, and I won't let you get dragged into something—"

"Why?" I interrupted harshly. "Because you and Caleb stole the diner from him?"

His entire body stiffened, eyes blazing. "Josh bet it, and Caleb won. That's all that matters. Josh is clearly bitter at the success of Haven, since it was a shithole when he ran it."

There had to be something more. As Logan lowered the heat blasting through the vents, Josh's words slammed into me. "What did he mean about you having your way with his *friend?*"

Logan's head tilted, his lips parting slowly as his anger swam away. "Doesn't matter." It was almost a whisper.

"It does to me. If he has an issue with you, there must be a reason—and not just Haven."

"You know about my past, Cassandra. There's no need to rehash it." He sighed, then turned away.

"You screwed around with someone he cared about." I didn't need to ask it—it was obvious in the way he shut me out. The one thing from his past he didn't like to discuss was liaisons.

When he didn't deny my accusation, I continued, my stomach churning. "And outside his place? Both you *and* Caleb?" It was too much to process, but I couldn't stop one final question from coming out as the realization beat against me. "You shared women?"

"Sweetheart..." Quickly, he turned back and reached for my hand. I pulled away, unable to ignore the disgust crawling over me. I couldn't even look at him. "Before you, I was a different man. You know this. Please, just look at me."

"I should go." My voice was flat; numb. "I need a shower, and maybe some rest before tonight."

"Listen to me: No one else has ever meant anything to me. Caleb and I..." He exhaled deeply, running his hands through his hair. "We were bored most of the time."

"I'm sure," I murmured.

Logan lifted my chin, forcing me to meet his rueful gaze. "I love you, Cassandra. I can't stand you looking at me like this. Tell me you love me. Tell me my past doesn't matter. 'Cause if that fucks up what you and I have...I can't bear it."

"I do love you—more than anything. But you have to admit, that's a lot to take in—at least, for me it is. You're right, though...it's in the past."

He stroked my cheek and drew me closer, his mouth skimming mine.

"Stay with me tonight." His words brushed across my lips.

I pushed off from his chest. "No, I'm going out."

"You can't honestly tell me you want to spend time with my ex."

Hearing those words—'my ex'—cause something to snap within me: a reminder of what I'd been waiting to talk to him about.

"Just because you're jealous she's obviously moving on doesn't mean you can make demands on me! Understand?"

"Jealous?" His laughter was raucous. "*That's* what you think?"

"Don't you dare laugh at me!"

Logan held up his hand as though he was trying to contain the chuckle, but his grin only grew wider as his chest continued to rumble. He cupped my cheeks, and was twisting me to face him when I grabbed the door handle.

"Christ, woman, what the hell would make you think I'd be jealous of someone I don't even care about?"

"Then why were you so upset about her and Josh being together? You nearly took his head off. If it was a simple case of you and him not getting along, you wouldn't have been that upset. It was that they were together that got to you."

"Not because of Natasha." His thumb traced my lip and, like a masochist, I closed my eyes and relished his touch. *Damn it.* "I don't want anyone I don't trust around those I love. I wasn't trying to protect Natasha—I was trying to protect you and Oliver."

Oh. "Right. Look, I'm sorry for thinking—"

"Don't. I understand why you did. But please, Cassandra, what do I have to do to prove that it's only you?"

I leaned across the center console and slid my leg over his, maneuvering slowly to straddle him. He clicked a button, and the seat went back.

"Just kiss me," I said, enjoying making my own demands.

"My pleasure."

"I can't believe you talked me into this!" I groaned, walking into Haven with Hilary at my side.

Logan was right: I should've stayed in and cuddled with him. It was Saturday night and barely five degrees out, and the place was packed. Only for Hilary would I be out.

"Oh, come on, it'll be fun. We can dance, and *you* can drink real liquor while I nurse a virgin. You got me to DD, so let loose a little. And all the while, we can pick that cow's brain."

"Hilary..." I warned.

"Relax. Tonight we're gonna kill her with kindness till she either leaves or adores you too much to ever lay a skanky finger on your man."

I handed my coat over in exchange for a ticket. "Right. I'm gonna need a drink for sure."

Fighting my way through the dense crowd was worth it, because at the end of the bar were three stools sectioned off for us—one of the perks of dating the owners.

"What you having tonight, ladies?" the bartender, Matt, asked, leaning across the bar the instant I sat down.

"Nothing for me. She'll have her regular—and keep them coming!" Hilary yelled over the music, a twisted smile on her face.

"Am I gonna need to be drunk to endure tonight?" I asked.

"Probably," Hilary laughed.

"I sure hope not."

Both our heads shot to the side as Natasha slid onto the stool beside me. "Hey, girls, hope you haven't been waiting for me." She held up her hand to wave Matt over, then looked back at us. "Josh kept me busy this afternoon." Innuendo seeped from her words.

"I'm sure," Hilary said, her smile too wide to be genuine.

"How are you feeling?" I asked.

"Better, with these." She held up her clutch, shaking it to reveal the sound of pills rattling around.

Matt brought our drinks and smiled at Natasha. "Your regular as well, doll face?"

"You got it, babe."

He threw her a wink. From the look of it, she knew Matt better than we did.

I grabbed my drink, swiveled around, and stood as the DJ blended Flo Rida seamlessly into his mix.

"Let's dance!" I shouted. In two more gulps, my drink was finished, and I placed the empty glass on the bar. I snatched Hilary's hand and led her to the floor. "You coming?" I called back to Natasha.

She held up a finger, signaling me to wait, then pointed at the drink Matt was setting in front of her. I smiled and gave her a thumbs up.

As Hilary and I pushed our way farther onto the dance floor, I threw my hands above my head and let my body follow the rhythm. The dance floor was crowded, but I hardly noticed. The music was loud and energetic, and I was feeling good as the tension trickled slowly from every inch of me.

Kat Graham's "Power" slid on next, and Hilary and I sang along. Hilary had some outrageous moves, and was just getting into them when a tall, slender guy behind her who looked barely twenty-one slithered flush against her back, sliding his hands down her arms and hooking them onto her waist.

Hilary's head snapped back and she moved forward at the same time one of the bouncers was on the creep, pulling him away. She flew at me, stunned as we watched the large bouncer lay into him.

"What was that about?" I asked when the guy was finally able to walk away, heading straight to the bar with his head down. The bouncer eyed Hilary once, then spoke a couple words to no one. We couldn't hear what he said—and then I noticed his discreet headpiece.

"Caleb," her voice grated, nostrils flaring. "I made him stay home tonight, and he wasn't thrilled about it. Should have known he'd have eyes on me."

"He loves you."

Her frown lifted. "How about you have another drink for me? I need to live vicariously through someone tonight."

I slipped my arm around her. "I'll do my best, though Natasha might be better for you than me," I said, watching Natasha shimmy between two frat guys who wore the biggest grins I'd ever seen. Their hands were everywhere, and she didn't seem to mind.

"Looks like Josh doesn't mind sharing!" Hilary shouted into my ear.

"Or he's a fool and doesn't know. Either way, not our business."

Back at the bar, I ordered a shot. I tipped it back, then slammed the glass down on the bar. My lips puckered at the burn. It was rare for me to drink alone, but I went with it.

"Another?" Matt chuckled.

"Why not?" I shrugged, a lazy, quenched smile emerging across my lips.

He refilled the shot glass, but this time I took it with me to a booth in the back. Hilary and I sat, and a moment later Natasha was there sitting beside me.

"You looked like you were enjoying yourself," Hilary said, staring at Natasha. Judgment darkened her expression.

Natasha didn't seem to notice or care. "I was."

I slammed back my shot the moment the waitress arrived, then ordered a vodka tonic.

"Sounds good. Make that two," Natasha said.

The waitress looked to Hilary, who was staring past all of us. "I'll be right back."

She was up instantly and heading across the bar, where Caleb stood, his eyes on her. I scanned the room, my nerves spiking. *Did Logan come with him?*

"I don't see him," Natasha said.

"What?"

"Logan. I don't think he's here."

"Right. Doesn't matter. He knows it's a girls' night." I peeked again in the direction of Caleb to find him and Hilary gone.

"Caleb seems like a friendly guy. Good to Oliver, from what I hear," Natasha said, turning to face me.

The waitress appeared with our drinks, stunning me at how quick she was. "Anything else?" she asked.

"No, thanks." I lifted my glass and took a sip before turning my attention back to Natasha. "Caleb loves Oliver. He considers him family."

"I want Oliver to have a lot of good role models in his life, Cassandra. I don't know much about Caleb, but I do know if he's close to my son, I'll be getting to know him better as well."

I said nothing and took another sip—a bigger one this time, draining nearly half the glass. Hilary would have a real problem with Natasha cozying up to Caleb, even in the interest of Oliver. Hilary wasn't one to trust easily, and Natasha wasn't exactly easily trusted.

"I've known him most of my life," I told her. "He's a good guy. No need to worry."

"That possessive, irritating, gorgeous man is gonna drive me crazy!" Hilary growled, slipping back into her side of the booth. "Seriously, can you believe him?"

"Is he still here?" I followed her penetrating stare and spotted Caleb watching us as he maneuvered toward the door.

"He's leaving. Said he only stopped in to pick up some paperwork. I call bullshit! That bouncer called him, and he just *had* to come and check on me."

"I think it's sweet." I smiled. "And it's not like he's standing here hounding you. He left, didn't he?"

A slow smile brightened her face. "Yeah. Damn it, he *is* sweet."

"Or has a guilty conscience. You know, those that cheat worry others will too," Natasha blurted out.

My head snapped her way, my jaw dropping. I started as she continued as if she hadn't just slapped Hilary in the face.

"I'm just saying—he's hot and he's been around the scene. I'd be careful."

I shifted my gaze to Hilary, aware she was struggling to keep her claws sheathed.

"Caleb isn't cheating on me, I assure you."

Natasha frowned. "I'm sorry. That was a shitty thing for me to say. I didn't mean it to come out that way."

"Right." Hilary sipped the juice in front of her.

"So how long have you and Josh been dating?" I asked, offering a reprieve from the tension.

"A couple weeks. It's still new."

That surprised me. As of last week, she still wanted Logan, as far as I knew.

"He still throwing all those parties at his place?" Hilary asked, an edge to her voice.

"A few. They're fun. I've never spent much time in the country. It's a different crowd than I'm used to. Josh was the first person to get me on a quad. I knew then he was what I needed…someone different than who I'm usually attracted to." She looked back at Hilary. "What about you and Caleb? How long you two been together?"

"Long enough to know he doesn't want anyone else," she said defensively, then threw up her hand to flag the waitress. The young woman appeared almost instantly.

"A water. Thanks," Hilary told her, then she was gone again.

"Water? Where's the fun in that?" Natasha laughed.

Hilary's eyes narrowed. I sighed under my breath, then finished off my drink and grabbed the next one.

"I'm DD tonight," Hilary explained. "I also don't need to drink to have a good time."

"Right. You sure you're not knocked up?"

Hilary paled for all of a second before composing herself, straightening her shoulders and lifting her chin. "Why? Were you hoping to go a round with Caleb after you blew through the frat boys? 'Cause I promise you, he's not interested."

Natasha blew out a sharp laugh. "Relax, I was joking." She took a sip of her drink, then added, "Although it's a shame Caleb wasn't around when Logan and I were still together. Logan's always had some *fun* friends. We all had a lot of memorable nights together."

My stomach lurched. Had Logan shared Natasha with his friends? Would he want to share *me*—pass *me* around? No, I wasn't even gonna go there.

"Yeah, well, Caleb doesn't need Logan to share anything. I take care of him just fine."

"Yet he's still here every night, charming and eager to please. I bet your bed gets quite lonely."

"Hey, stop it!" I snapped. The sneers they exchanged were fierce.

"No problem. So what was your mom doing at Logan's tonight?" Hilary asked, changing the subject completely.

My body stiffened. *My mom?* "What? When?"

"Her squad car was pulling out of his driveway when I got to your place. Everything all right? Wasn't sure if it had to do with…about…you know, Kurt." Her eyes flickered to Natasha, then back to me.

I blinked, relieved when the waitress returned to take the focus off me.

"I don't know why she'd be there," I finally muttered between swallows, finishing off my drink before asking for another.

Kurt. I couldn't think about him. Would my mom go to Logan with information before me? Probably—especially if she thought it'd protect me.

I pushed it from my mind. I'd ask Logan first thing in the morning.

"I'm sure it's nothing," Hilary offered. To my surprise, Natasha spoke up as well.

"Yeah, I wouldn't worry about it. I'm sure if something's going on, Logan would have told you," she said with a small but sincere-looking smile.

"Thanks." I took another drink and rested back against the booth.

Thankfully, the conversation took a lighter turn when a few frat guys took over the center of the dance floor. They had wild moves, and pulled girls into the routine with them one by one, tossing them around while the patrons cheered in a circle around them. I laughed with Natasha while Hilary stood on her seat hollering, enjoying the show as the young women tried to keep up with the guys' smooth moves.

By the end of the night, I was mindlessly buzzed and barely able to keep myself upright on the dance floor. It wasn't like me to get drunk when I was out, but between all the heated exchanges and the raucous crowd, I lost myself in it.

"You okay!?" Hilary shouted over the music.

I swayed to the music, keeping close to a brick column for support just in case.

"Yeah! Ready to go?"

She nodded. "Gonna use the restroom first. Stay here."

I wasn't going anywhere. A passing waitress handed me a bottle of water. Where she came from, I had no clue, but I gave her a grateful smile before taking a drink.

Hilary was back by the time the next song ended, and despite my drunkenness I knew something was wrong. I moved toward her, worried at her rattled state. She was trembling.

"What happened?" I asked, sobering instantly.

"Nothing, let's go." Anger edged her tone.

"What about Natasha? We can't let her drive. She's been drinking."

"Fine. I'll meet you both in the parking lot." And with that, she was gone.

I turned around to find Natasha. My breath caught when I saw her exit the ladies' room, looking more than a little pleased. Had they been in there together? *Did something happen?*

"Natasha!" I yelled, but the music was louder. I started toward her, yelling again until she finally looked my way, her smile growing.

"Hey, let's dance!" she shouted, rolling her shoulders and rotating her hips to the beat.

"We should go. Hilary's waiting outside. She can drop you at home."

Natasha waved her hand dismissively. "No worries, I'll catch a ride later," she said, shamelessly turning her hungry gaze on a tall, built guy leaning against the wall next to her.

"You sure?"

"Positive."

I nodded and had begun to move away when she grabbed my arm.

"Thanks for tonight, Cassandra. I don't have a lot of girlfriends, so I appreciate you giving me a chance."

I nodded once more with a tight smile, then headed to the coat check. I was exhausted and ready to climb into bed—Logan's bed.

Chapter Eighteen

Running

I woke up in Logan's arms, inhaling his masculine scent and trying to ignore the pounding present both in my temple and at his front door.

"Shit," Logan grumbled, then flung the blanket from his side of the bed and stood.

The doorbell rang not just once, but twice in a row. My head dug further into my pillow, blocking it out.

"Stay here," he said, crossing the room. "I'm going to kick someone's ass."

The banging continued between the constant rings of the bell. Someone *has no patience*. One of Jax's friends, I assumed.

I rolled my head slightly, enjoying the view of Logan slipping into his white pajama pants. I smiled, memorizing the magnificent sight.

After he'd thrown the bedroom door open and stormed into the hall, I snatched my phone from the night table. My head protested the movement, so I kept it down on the pillow. I'd drunk too much the previous night, and barely recalled the drive home. Hilary had been quiet the entire time. She'd dropped me at Logan's, and he was there in the doorway to welcome me in. The rest was a blur of pleasure.

Focusing back on my phone, I sighed. It was a little after eight o'clock, and I had twelve missed calls from Caleb and one text from Hilary.

Panic set in, and I instantly regretted turning my ringer off at Haven. Despite my assailing hangover pain, I sat up straight.

Nervously, I touched the screen to open the text.

I'm sorry. Don't hate me.

As soon as I read it, I heard Caleb's voice, loud and angry, echoing up through the floorboards.

"Where the hell is she!? Tell Cassandra I want to talk to her—NOW!"

I couldn't hear what followed next. Logan must've been speaking to him, and in an appropriate indoor voice. Trembling with uncertainties, I texted Hilary back, my fingers sprinting over the keys.

Where r u? Call me asap! Caleb is here!

Something crashed downstairs and I jerked up further, sweeping my legs off the bed. My pulse raced.

"Cassandra, get your ass down here!" I heard Caleb shout, which was followed immediately by another loud boom.

Like a child heading in for punishment, I slipped on my robe, tightened its belt, and made my way down the hall. I stood at the top of the stairs, my jaw dropping at the scene below me.

A vase from the foyer was shattered across the marble floor, picture frames scattered around it. Caleb charged toward the stairs, dangerous eyes pinned on me. I froze, panic surging, ready to bolt just as Logan intervened, throwing him back.

"Don't!" Logan threatened, blocking the first step. Then he called out over his shoulder, "You know where Hilary is, sweetheart?"

Blood rushed to my ears, loud and spiteful. *She really did it—she left him.* My stomach churned, hands slipping inside the pockets of my robe as I shifted from foot to foot.

"Um, I—"

"For fuck's sake, WHERE IS SHE!?" Caleb roared. "Something's wrong—don't you dare lie to me! What is it, huh!? TELL ME!"

"Watch your fucking tone, or I'll throw you out and you can find her yourself," Logan warned him, in a voice so hard and intimidating my skin flushed with goose bumps.

Caleb was panting with rage, fists pumping at his sides. "My girl up and takes off before dawn leaving only a note, and I'm supposed to be okay with that!?"

Logan moved closer to Caleb and placed a hand on his shoulder. "I get that you're angry and worried, but you *will* back off Cassandra or you're gone."

Caleb shoved Logan's hand away and stormed backward. It wasn't just anger radiating off him, though—he looked lost, confused, and worst of all sad. I couldn't stand it.

"I'm sorry," I managed finally, barely above a shamed whisper. "She was fine last night. What did you say when she told you? You must have done something to provoke her to leave."

"*Told* me? She didn't say a word. I woke up to a Dear John letter explaining she had a sick aunt she was going to take care of and that she'd be back in a few months. Months! Who the hell leaves in the middle of the night for *months*? Something is up, and I want to know what!"

I stood there, baffled. "Wait, but then..." She hadn't told him. *What the hell did I miss last night?* As far as I knew, she was planning to tell him about the baby that morning.

A door in the hall opened, and Oliver's head peeked out. I started toward him, stopping when I saw Jax leaning against the opposite wall. He'd been listening. The moment he saw Oliver, he went to him, lifting him up and carrying him toward me.

"Look who's up!" Jax broadcasted for everyone to hear.

"Morning, Cassie," Oliver squeaked after finishing a yawn.

"Morning, sunshine."

"It's loud," he complained, scrunching his nose.

"Don't worry, Daddy's gonna make it quiet," Jax told him as he carried Oliver past me and down the steps.

Caleb shoved his hands in his pockets and dropped his head.

"It's all right. Caleb accidentally knocked a few things over," Logan explained, not taking his gaze off Caleb. "You want some scrambled eggs for breakfast?"

"Yeah, and chocolate milk!" Oliver looked down at the mess on the floor. "You 'kay, Caleb?"

"Yeah, I'm fine, buddy. Just clumsy." Caleb managed a semblance of a smile for him. "My bad."

"Come on, let's get you fed," Jax said through the unbearable tension, carrying Oliver into the kitchen.

I descended the steps with wobbly movements. My throat was parched and my head throbbed worse than before, but all I could see was the grim display on Caleb's face. It wasn't my place to tell him, but how could I not?

I stopped midway down, closed my eyes, and drew in a shaky breath, unsure where to start. *Damn you, Hilary!*

"Why don't you come have some breakfast, let Cassandra wake up, and then we can talk," Logan said calmly. It was a statement, not a question.

"Please, Cassandra, just tell me where she is." Caleb moved toward me as I reached the foyer, but Logan was there in front of me again, his protectiveness tangible.

"Is she leaving me? Did I do something?" Caleb's brows pulled down as if he was scouring his mind for an answer—a spark of memory to mollify his fears.

"Come on! Breakfast time!" Oliver's voice rang out.

Logan took my hand and led me away to the kitchen. Once there, he pulled me in close, our eyes connecting as his hands settled on my hips. He leaned in and whispered, "Whatever is going on, I want to know everything. I don't do secrets, Cassandra."

He was angry—or was it disappointment I saw flash in his eyes? There was no time to decipher it before he pulled away and went to the fridge, grabbing a carton of eggs.

I sat across from Jax at the table, scanning my brain numbly for the best way to tell Caleb the truth. He had followed us into the room and was leaning against the wall, typing on his phone. To Hilary, I presumed.

"How many eggs?" Oliver asked, then counted the fingers we all held up. Even Caleb held up two and shot Oliver a wink when he added them all up correctly.

Shit. Hit. Fan, Jax mouthed in my direction. I narrowed my eyes but didn't reply.

We all ate together with Oliver as the conversationalist of the group; no one else spoke. We were just finishing when the doorbell rang.

Logan cursed under his breath, then went to stand.

"I'll grab it," Jax said, dropping his plate in the sink on the way out.

I glanced at Logan beside me. He was staring blankly down at his empty plate. I'd never seen him so quiet.

Under the table, I reached over and placed my hand on his thigh. He didn't move—didn't even look my way to relieve some of my anxiety. He wasn't making it easy, which pissed me off. I needed him to trust me and give me a sign of comfort, but instead he was blocking me out. Did he really think I had secrets from him? This was the only one—and it wasn't mine to tell.

Irritated, I removed my hand and stood. As I walked to the sink with my plate, Jax reappeared.

But he wasn't alone.

"Morning."

"Mom!" Oliver flew from his seat and raced to her, his arms wide. She dropped down on her haunches and giggled when he reached her, squeezing tightly.

"Looks like I was too late. I'd been hoping to take Oliver to breakfast," she explained.

"Then you should have asked yesterday." Logan's voice was harsh as he stood.

"Sorry, you're right. Maybe I can take him to dinner tomorrow after school?" she asked, releasing Oliver and straightening.

"I'll let you know," was all Logan said.

"Well, maybe I can hang out now for a little while and play with him?"

"Fine, but he stays in the house," Logan said. He turned to Oliver, his features softening. "Go get dressed, and make sure to brush your teeth."

"'Kay! Be right back. Don't leave—promise?" Oliver's eyes were big and bright as he stared at Natasha.

She smiled. "Promise."

Appeased, he ran out of the room.

Caleb was on his feet crossing the room in the same instant. He stopped in front of me.

"Now—let's talk."

I nodded, chewing my bottom lip. I had to tell him—and as scared as I was of how he'd react, he deserved the truth.

"Living room?" I suggested for privacy's sake.

He headed in that direction without a word.

"Everything all right?" Natasha asked.

"Yeah," I answered as I left the kitchen.

Natasha followed, but I didn't realize it until we were standing in the entryway to the grand room and I heard her sharp intake of breath.

So much for privacy.

I'd turned to ask her to give us a moment when I caught the look of horror darkening her expression. Confused, I followed her gaze over my shoulder, my mouth open and heart swelling at the sight it beheld.

There, above the mantel in the center of the room, hung a new painting I'd never seen before. The canvas was massive, frame elegant and bold. And there in the center were Oliver and me, sitting in the dirt below my treehouse. Logan's brush had perfectly captured the relaxed feeling and instant connection of that afternoon, as well as the cheerfulness in Oliver's smile and adoration in mine. I was in awe.

I was in awe. When had he painted it? It wasn't there the previous day, which meant he'd hung it while I was out at night.

One look back to Logan—who was now standing in the doorway, his head cast down in thought—reminded me it wasn't the time to gush, or overanalyze what it meant that I was hanging on his wall as though we'd been together for years.

I blinked and refocused my attention on Caleb, who stood in front of me, waiting impatiently for answers.

"Can you guys just give us a minute?" I asked, peeking back at Natasha.

She tore her gaze from the painting to look at me, a tight smile twisting her lips.

"Sure. Oh, and Caleb, can you tell Hilary I had a great time last night?" Natasha asked. "She's a sweet girl. It was great getting to talk to her."

"Did she say anything to you?" Caleb moved quickly, sweeping past me straight to her, hopeful. "Anything at all?"

Natasha's brows drew together, but her smile never wavered. "Like what?"

"Anything. She left this morning, and I'm trying to find her. I know you two aren't close, but if she said something, I need to know."

Her shoulders slumped, face puckering with fake sympathy. "Ah, I'm so sorry. She didn't say anything. I can't believe she'd leave. Especially considering...never mind."

She knew; I'd seen it the moment she cut her gaze to me after seeing the painting. Natasha knew, and seeing me take up half a wall with her son in her ex-fiancé's house meant she was pissed enough to spill the beans.

I shot forward and grabbed Caleb's arm as I opened my mouth to speak, but his broken voice stopped me.

"Considering what?" His voice dropped dangerously low. "Tell me."

"Look, I know I don't have the best track record, but I could never have taken my child away from his father. It's just not okay. I'm sorry, Caleb. It's your baby, too—you have rights."

My lungs stung; I hadn't realized I'd been holding my breath. I blew it out in a giant puff, balling my hands into tight fists, wishing I was wearing actual clothing and not a robe as I struggled to watch the scene unfold. Caleb's eyes went wide as he processed her words, the air thickening around him and igniting his rage.

One moment, Caleb was near Natasha, and the next, he was pounding his fist into the wall across the room. His words were incoherent growls that continued until Jax and Logan flanked him, yanking him back and trying to calm his rage.

It was useless. Natasha moved to leave the room, but I

stepped around her.

"You know what's not *okay*? Playing off someone else's pain to weasel your way back into this family. I should have known better than to think we could ever be friends. You haven't the first clue about what friendship means." I stepped closer, but she stood impassive, my words ricocheting off her frozen heart. "Who told you?"

Her lips curled up. "*Told* me? I figured it out myself, and she all but confessed in the restroom last night. A shame, really—like you said, Caleb's a good guy. I'm sure he'll find someone he deserves."

She moved around me, but I sideswiped her. "What did you say to her?"

"Nothing but the truth: That fatherhood changes a man—changes a relationship. But I didn't know she'd up and leave after our conversation. That's on her. Now, if you'll excuse me, my son's waiting." Natasha shouldered past me out of the room.

I stood there watching Logan and Jax restrain Caleb, attempting to talk him down.

"I didn't know she'd leave," I said, walking toward them.

"Stay back, damn it, Cassandra!" Logan shouted.

I flinched at his cruel tone, but halted my steps. Caleb wouldn't hurt me, would he? The look on his face frightened something inside me, though, and I moved back. If he was like this with me, what was Hilary in for? I needed to talk to her.

"She was going to tell you—today, actually. She was scared before—thought about leaving, but we talked it out. She wanted you to know. Something must have changed last night, but I can bring her back. I know I can."

"Why would she leave, huh!? *Is* there even a sick aunt!?" Caleb yelled, his body struggling against the strength holding him pinned against the wall.

"No, she's not sick. And honestly, I don't even know if that's where Hilary went. I'm trying to reach her, and I'll keep trying. I won't give up. You have my word. I'll do everything I can to stop her from—"

I inhaled sharply, regretting what little I'd said.

Caleb went still. "Stop her from what?" His eyes went dark. "Answer me!"

"She won't do it. I know her…she won't."

"Ah, Christ, no!" Caleb closed his eyes. His body went slack, and he slid to the floor slowly. Jax let go, but Logan went down on his knees beside him as Caleb continued, his voice distant and shattered.

"No. No, she can't. Fuck! She wouldn't. She knows me! I let her in, God damn it!"

"We'll bring her home," Logan told him.

"I'm so sorry," I said, choking on a sob.

Logan looked up at me, and the disappointment that met my gaze wrenched my gut. This wasn't my fault, but what was I supposed to do? I needed to talk to Hilary. She had to come back home. I'd go find her and bring her back myself if I had to.

Jax moved my way. "You might want to leave now," he whispered.

Leave? Was I being dismissed? One more look at Logan, who was occupied with reassuring Caleb, confirmed just that. Apparently I'd done enough.

Without another word, I trudged up the stairs to Logan's room and packed my bag. It'd been the longest week of my life, and I was due back to school in the morning. Playing house had officially ended.

With my bag full and slung over my shoulder, I looked once more around Logan's room. Would I ever be welcome there again? Would he not trust me now? He had to understand why I couldn't tell him.

The longer I stood there waiting, the more I realized Logan wasn't going to come up and ask me to explain so he could hear my side. Not yet, anyway.

With tears welling up in my eyes, I made my way downstairs and out the front door. It was time to go home.

Chapter Nineteen

SEARCHING

Sadness shadowed me for the rest of the day. I paced, cried, and dialed every member in Hilary's family tree until I finally got the number of her aunt in Ontario.

The woman answered on the second ring, and for the first time that afternoon I breathed easy. I slid down onto my couch, allowing a thread of optimism to peek out only to have it beaten back into the submission of despair as soon as she began talking.

A state of somber wistfulness crept through me as Hilary's aunt dutifully explained she hadn't heard from her in over a week. Whether that was true or not, I was forced to either accept defeat or fly there and search her house myself. I stressed the importance of her calling me if she heard from Hilary, then rattled off my number. After a curt goodbye, the phone fell from my hands and the tears resumed.

Hilary had yet to respond after more than twenty texts and numerous calls. Either her phone was off or she was too ashamed to answer. I hated that she'd left me in such a bad position, but as much as I tried, I couldn't squelch the worry I felt for her. Where was she? Was she safe?

Exhausted, alone, and completely useless, I curled my

knees to my chest and rested my head on the arm of the couch. I sat there motionless until my gloom flowed out and the wave of anger rolled in.

Hilary was the one responsible for her actions. This was about everyone else, not me. I'd gotten the crap end of the stick once again, but this time I was throwing it to the ground and stomping away. I had my own things to worry about—the first being my job, which I was due to return to the next morning.

I dropped my legs to the floor and sat up, allowing my body time to absorb the newfound strength revitalizing my limbs. I smiled to myself, picturing my class of kindergarteners that would be awaiting me in the morning. That was my only focus.

I skipped lunch and spent the evening preparing everything I needed for my class. At sunset, I crawled into bed with a peanut-butter-and-jelly sandwich and glass of milk. I plugged my phone into the charger on the nightstand and checked to confirm there'd been no activity on it. Logan had gone about his day without even sending a text.

I finished my snack, debating sending him a goodnight or 'I love you' text, but decided against it. Instead, I lay there and closed my eyes, allowing my grief to stew.

As if punishing me, sleep evaded me throughout the night. I tossed and turned until finally finding my mind's reprieve through rounds of online solitaire.

I eventually managed to doze off for a few short hours, only to wake with a second wind dragging me out of bed. As dawn approached, I was dressed in jogging clothes and pulling on my boots—the same boots Logan had insisted I not remove when he'd encased my body with his on his front porch a week earlier.

My teeth dug into my bottom lip to cease the trembling.

It was too soon for us to be at odds, and I despised what it did to me. The dull ache was unavoidable when the enormous weight of reality set in and I saw exactly how deeply rooted Logan was in every piece of me. It was downright terrifying.

I wrapped a scarf twice around my neck and walked outside, grateful for the earbuds that sang out tunes of independent women rather than failed love affairs. The sky was clear with no falling snow, but the air was frigid and chilled me to my bones. I welcomed the sun as I set out down the empty road, finding warmth in my long strides.

I hit the shower the moment I returned home, emerging with clear thoughts and enthusiasm to start the day. With a towel around my body and one in my hands, working through strands of hair, I stepped into my bedroom humming a cheerful melody.

"We need to talk."

I jerked back, my breath stolen and eyes wide. Logan was sitting on the edge of my bed, watching me.

Dropping my gaze to calm my traumatized nervous system, I gradually composed myself enough to be able to at least pretend to appear cool. When I did, I was fully able to take in Logan's tight features and stern eyes.

He didn't look happy; in fact, he looked exhausted. He wore a crisp black suit, his tie not yet in place, shirt collar opened. His hair was noticeably tousled and slightly damp, as though his hands had done nothing but run through it since he'd showered.

My heart plummeted, body begging to run to him—to pull him into my arms, where he could bury himself in my warmth and love. Purely instinctual yet wild flames burned furiously to life in my chest, rooting me in place despite my unwavering need to apologize for keeping a secret from him.

My chin rose. "Then you should have come by yesterday," I said bluntly, turning away to open my closet door.

"Why didn't you tell me about Hilary?" His voice was rough and impatient.

My back remained to him as I pulled out a dress, appraising it for longer than necessary. "Seriously, Logan, we need to do this later. After school."

"No, I want this settled now." The anger in his tone sparked my own.

I reared back. "I've been here the last twenty-four hours waiting to talk to you and explain. I didn't sleep at all, actually—spent a lot of last night feeling like crap—and now I need to get ready and go to school. I can't be a mess on my first day back!"

With slow, deliberate movements, he stood and made his way toward me. When he reached out, I stepped aside. I couldn't bear his hands on me. I ached for them too much.

It didn't stop him. He captured my hands, holding them in his despite my every attempt to tug them away. "Cassandra, just tell me why you kept this from me. Do you not trust me?"

My brows shot up. "Are you seriously asking me that after everything we've been through? Screw you!" Fully insulted, I was successful at tearing myself away that time.

"What am I supposed to think? You kept a huge secret from me, which makes me wonder what others there might be."

"It wasn't my secret to tell, Logan!" I all but screamed. "It was between Caleb and Hilary. You think I *liked* not being able to confide in you? I wanted to—God, I've never been more torn. She's my best friend. If I told you she was thinking about running off to hand his child over to strangers, you can't honestly stand there and expect me to believe that you'd have been able to keep that from him."

"For you, I would have."

I snorted and rolled my eyes. "Right, I forgot—you're a saint. Never hidden anything from me, correct?"

His head tipped slightly to the side, eyes locked fiercely on mine. "I'm far from a saint, but I tell you everything you *need* to know."

"*Need* to know?" My voice shot up an octave. "Is that some new rule your arrogant ass created just to piss me off?" My words were explosive as I stepped into him. Despite his towering height, I felt anything but intimidated. "Well, then let me make myself very clear when I say you did not *need to know* Hilary's secret. But me? I *did* deserve to know that you were paying guards to beat the crap out of Kurt—especially considering the reason he attacked me was because of it!"

I blanched the moment the words rolled off my tongue, and his eyes flashed. No longer were they bright blue, but almost black as his pupils dilated.

My body went slack on a heavy sigh, no longer able to hold the pressure of my defensive stance. "I didn't mean you're to blame, just…"

My attempt to backtrack faded as I watched Logan's lips part, his expression shifting to almost impassive. Any spark of concern that'd leaked through his features was now gone, leaving no signs of regret. And the longer he remained silent, the more loudly the truth rang between us. The allegation of the guards was true.

"I didn't pay them," Logan said roughly.

I needed more. "But—"

"Kurt had to be punished for hurting you that night outside Haven. I called in a favor. That was all."

"A favor?" I whispered. "From a *guard*?"

"Yes." He reached for me again, but I scooted around him and across the room, in need of air. "I never considered it a secret from you, Cassandra. He hurt you that night, and—"

"What about the other day?" I interrupted.

"When?"

"You were having lunch with those two guards. Why?" My voice trembled. I was afraid of his reply.

He shook his head. "I didn't ask them to touch Kurt. I swear to you. I just wanted them to help me get on the visitors' list."

"You want to go *see* him!?" I blew out, outraged.

Logan advanced toward me. "I needed him to know, to fully understand, that if he ever comes near you again, I will kill him."

I blinked, tears brimming in my eyes at the wrath radiating off him. "He can't hurt me. He's locked up."

"For now. But one day, he'll get out, and I don't ever want you worried about him coming for you again." His thumb grazed my jaw gently. "I'll always protect you with everything I have, Cassandra. I'll fight dirty if I have to, and I'll never apologize for it."

"Logan…" I murmured, closing my eyes as I sagged against him.

"When it comes to your safety…I may not always be upfront with you if I think it will protect you not to be, but I'll never lie to you."

What did that mean? He'd lie by omission? It wasn't how I preferred communication to work in our relationship, but for the moment, I'd let the subject drop. We'd tackle that issue when I wasn't on a timeline for work, because something told me it wouldn't be an easy battle.

His arms encased me, drawing me in, palms splayed flat against my backside. "You have to trust me."

"Ditto," I whispered, resting my head against his hard chest. He smelled like my Logan: of soap, mint, and virility.

There was a moment of silence before he spoke again. "I'm sorry. Natasha's been under my skin; I want her gone, and adding the Caleb and Hilary shit just overloaded me. I should have never allowed you to walk out yesterday. That was my fuckup, but Caleb and I had some things to finish up before he could leave." He tilted my chin up with his fingertip. "I spent the night regretting not stopping you. Never again. Forgive me."

I smiled, moistening my lips. "You know I do. I love you. Just tell me one thing."

"Anything." He was already pressing his lips to my cheek, peppering kisses down toward my neck.

"Can I bitch slap Natasha the next time I see her?"

He pulled back, his brows lifting in amusement. "Bitch slap?"

"You heard me." I grinned, biting my bottom lip to contain my giggle.

"I love it when your gorgeous mouth surprises me. Such a naughty little angel."

"She was pissed, and you know why," I said, still smiling as I thought about the enormous painting hanging above his fireplace.

"Yes, I imagine I do, but I don't care. I hung that canvas hoping to surprise you when we woke. Never imagined the day would take such a dreadful turn."

My hands slipped up to the collar of his shirt and tugged him forward. "It's beautiful. Massive and extremely unexpected, but by far the best piece of art I've ever seen."

"Just you wait. There will be plenty more." A smirk appeared on his lips.

"When did you paint it?" I asked, intrigued.

"Back in the fall. I was at the window of my office watching you with Oliver and couldn't help myself. I snapped a picture and spent that week working on it after Oliver went to bed. I was afraid if he saw it, he'd tell you, and the last thing I wanted to do was freak you out."

My laughter bubbled up. "Since when did you care about freaking me out, Mr. Invite Me to Join you for a Threesome?"

His hands slipped behind my neck as his mouth slanted over mine.

"Hm, good point."

He took control of the kiss as I parted my lips, feeling his tongue sink inside my mouth, caressing and stroking the contours of my own. My fingers dug into his arms, and I felt addicted to his embrace, savoring the decadent growl he released.

He tasted of lust, sex, love—everything I'd ever need to survive. My fingers sank into his hair and my body fell flush against his, begging for more.

My brain somehow found its way back from the fog, and with one annoying glance at the clock, I was reminded that there was no time.

"I need to get dressed. I can't be late," I said, breaking the kiss before it led to something I knew neither of us would be able to stop.

He released me reluctantly and stared down at his cock, which strained against the designer fabric of his trousers.

I stroked my hand over him and grinned. "If I wasn't in a hurry, I'd surprise you with my mouth again."

His thumb traced my lip. "Tonight, I expect to enjoy just that."

"We'll see how good you are till then," I teased.

He grinned, totally relaxed—the polar opposite from how he'd looked when he'd arrived. "I have to get Oliver ready for school." He stole another nip at my lips as his hands explored down my back and over my ass, squeezing. "You want me to give you a ride there?"

"I do love the rides you take me on," I murmured against his skin, my lips skating over the scruff of his jaw as my arousal began to boil. Someone needed to stop us. He was an addiction.

"Tonight, I'm all yours." He placed one more kiss to my forehead, then strode to the doorway. "And if you hear from Hilary, let Caleb know. The man's a mess. He'd make a damn good father. It's a shame she didn't have more faith in him and their relationship."

"I've been trying to reach her, but she's not answering," I explained, sobering.

The tightness in Logan's features returned when he turned to face me. "Caleb flew to her aunt's house last night. She'll be sorry when he finds her—and trust me, he *will* find her."

The blood drained from my face. "If he hurts her..."

Logan leaned against the doorframe, a wicked smile curving his lips. "Oh, he'll hurt her, but she'll love every minute of it. That is, unless she's done the unthinkable, in which case..." Logan's voice lowered with grief. "She'll break him, and I don't know what he'll do. He loves her. I've never seen him so distraught."

"She would never abort the baby." The words rushed out as though I needed to reassure myself, but I knew they were true. Despite her recent actions, I knew where her heart was. "That was never her plan, and she wouldn't do it now."

"Hilary doesn't strike me as a fool. There's no way she honestly believed she'd have been able to put the child up for adoption without Caleb finding out."

I fell onto my bed, exhausted, not wanting to discuss it

further. Not then, anyway. "I don't know. She was scared and didn't think it all out."

His hand scrubbed through his hair. "She'd need his permission to do such a thing, even in Canada, and I can assure you Caleb would never allow it."

"Can we just talk about this later? Please, I can't be late today."

"Of course. Get dressed and I'll meet you out front in thirty to drop you at school."

"Thanks, but I haven't had a chance to drive my car yet. I just want a little normalcy today. How about you and Oliver come to dinner and I can cook for *you* for once?"

His eyes brightened. "Mmm, you in the kitchen preparing my meal. I do like the image that presents."

"Pig!" I giggled.

"I can't tell you what it did to me when I walked in on you covered in flour the day you watched Oliver after school. I still think about it from all those months ago."

After dragging myself back up, I sauntered toward him, fueled by my unyielding desire to taste him just once more. He watched me, his eyes bright as I dragged my fingers gently up his chest. "You liked that, huh?"

His lips curled up into a smirk. "You have no idea. But you will…very soon."

"All these promises…"

"So many I plan to deliver on." He swathed me in his arms, then swatted my backside. "Now go get that fine ass dressed, and I'll see you later."

As I stood outside my classroom, my life came back into view. Greeting students and parents was exhilarating. I felt useful—needed. Their words were supportive and caring. They were genuinely happy about my return, wishing me well and explaining how they'd kept me in their thoughts and prayers. It was nice to be back in my element.

The crowd in the hall thinned as the clock ticked closer to class time. My students put their coats and book bags in their cubbies and shuffled to their seats while I watched from my door, my smile unwavering.

As I was about to enter the room, I paused when I noticed Logan walking past with Oliver. His eyes locked on mine.

Be professional, I reminded myself, giving him a friendly nod. Oliver waved before entering his classroom, and Logan turned my way as another of my students appeared with her mother.

"Miss Clarke, you're back!" the little girl, Victoria, exclaimed.

"I sure am, and I can't wait to see what you guys have been up to while I was gone."

"We made you a giant picture on the wall."

I'd already seen it when I'd come in, and had taken multiple photos of the masterpiece. A large canvas of paper covered the wall, and the substitute had had all the kids paint flowers and rainbows however they chose. It was the cutest piece of art I'd ever seen, and the perfect start to my day.

"Welcome back," her mother said.

I smiled. "Thank you."

I watched her leave after kissing her daughter's cheek. As I turned to enter the room, I saw Logan standing across the hall, as still and silent as a predator, watching me.

Hi, I mouthed.

His stare was penetrating and primal. *Gorgeous*, he mouthed in reply.

"Hi, Miss Clarke!" another student exclaimed as she entered the room. I smiled at her, then looked back to Logan.

He strode over and dipped his head to my neck, his lips brushing my ear. "Keep that dress on tonight," he whispered before walking away.

The day went better than I'd expected. My students were happy to have me back, and eager to help my day run smoothly. It was nice, but I wasn't naïve enough to believe it would last. I'd just enjoy it until they got comfortable again and made me work to hold their attention.

As I left my class at the end of the day, part of me hoped to see Logan waiting. It wasn't the plan, but I knew he'd be there to pick up Oliver, so there was a chance. But no such luck.

I was heading to my car when my phone pinged to life in my coat pocket. It was the first sound it had made in almost two days. With a rush of hope, I stopped mid-step a few feet from my car to retrieve it.

With one look, my heart jolted. Hilary's name lit my screen. It was a text and not a call, but it was a start.

I rushed to my car, unlocked the door, and shoved my tote in the backseat, taking shelter from the deep chill.

With a nervous hand, I opened the text.

I just need some time to think. Tell Caleb I'll call him soon

No way! I needed more than that. Irritated, I twisted my hair up in a knot, then replied.

He knows! You have to call.

There's no way he hadn't texted her that he'd found out about the baby, but just in case, I felt I should let her know.

My phone lit up with an incoming call. *Thank God.*

"Hilary, where are you?" I blurted out the second I answered.

"How could you tell him, Cassandra!?" she screamed hysterically, sobs dominating her speech.

"I didn't get a chance to. Natasha had that honor. Now where are you?"

"Natasha! That bitch!" she hissed.

"What did she say to you in the bathroom at Haven, exactly?" I cranked on the heat.

"Nothing I didn't already know."

"Don't lie to me, Hilary. You left me in a real crappy position here. Caleb's furious, hurt, and…I don't know what he's going to do when he finds you. So you need to just call him and explain—or, better yet, come home."

"I really screwed up." She sounded dejected.

I blew out a breath, forcing myself to calm down. She needed my support, not a bombardment of demands. "You panicked. He'll forgive you, but you *need* to call him."

"What if I'm a shit mother like Natasha was? What if I forget to feed the baby, or leave it somewhere? Oh God, I can't." Alarm rang through her voice.

"First of all, we're talking about a baby, not an object. You'll feed him or her, and if you forget, they'll cry and remind you. And I'll be there any time you need me, day or night."

She continued as though in a fog, my words lost on her. "Caleb hates me. He has to. I just *left* him, Cassandra—snuck out! What the hell is the matter with me? He's everything I could ever want or need, and I lied to him—betrayed him. Oh my God. Oh my God. I can't breathe."

"Hilary, listen to me: You have to calm down, okay?"

"I love him. I love him so much, Cassandra." Her words were broken between sobs and pants.

I hated not knowing where she was. I needed to find out and go to her. "I know you do. Has he texted?"

"Not since yesterday morning. He stopped and now it's

only been calls, about every hour. I can't answer, though. What is there to say? He's gonna see me—the real me. I'm not good enough for him, and he's finally going to figure that out. I'm not a fighter like you, Cassandra. I'm weak and pathetic, obviously, and now he knows. The only man I've ever loved now sees me for what I've become: a coward."

"Hilary, he—"

"Oh God," she gasped, her words slurred. "What if he takes the baby?"

"Let's worry about that later, all right?"

"You think he will, don't you?"

Obviously, my attempt to pacify her had failed. Hoping the truth would at least knock *some* sense into her, I said, "He has the right to—it's his child. You can't go ahead with an adoption when the father is there waiting in the wings, and honestly I wouldn't be surprised if he does. I mean, if you don't work it out with him, anyway."

"He's calling now," she whispered, as though he could hear.

"Answer it. Be honest with him. He'll understand."

"Yeah, right. I know Caleb, Cassandra. He has a temper."

"Yeah, I saw it," I said, remembering how Caleb's fists had redecorated Logan's living room.

"He'd never lay a hand on me," she added quickly, "but he *would* shut me out...remove me from his life. I can't even imagine it. It hurts too much."

"Listen, whether you answer his call or not, he left for your aunt's house yesterday. He should be there by now."

She sighed into the phone. "I'm not there. I wasn't ready to go...I just needed to think."

"Then where are you?"

"I should go." I could feel her numbness setting in through the phone. "I don't want to put you in the middle of this."

"Too late for that! Hilary, just tell me where you are. I'll come to you. Caleb doesn't have to know, I promise."

"I'm sorry. I'll call you soon. Love you."

She hung up, and there was no stopping the tears that ran down my cheeks. *Damn her!* Why did she have to be so bullheaded? Well, if she wouldn't let me help her, she left me no other choice.

I dialed Caleb.

"Did you find her?" was his rushed greeting.

With the car fully heated now, I tugged the scarf loose from my neck. "No, but she called. I just got off the phone with her."

"Thank Christ," he blew into the phone, sounding relieved.

"She's not at her aunt's."

"Yeah, I know. I was already there and searched the place."

My smile was instant. "Searched it? Her aunt let you?"

"Not at first, but once I explained why I was there, she agreed to help to put my mind at ease. It didn't work and I'm back to square one, so you need to call her back and tell her to pick up the fucking phone when I call!"

I shook my head and leaned my throbbing head back. "She won't. You should try texting her. She's just scared."

"She should be." The dark threat in his voice twisted my gut.

"Okay, that's *not* gonna get her to speak to you!" I snapped.

"She was planning to off my child, Cassie!"

"No, she wasn't. She was looking at adoption."

He let out a low, dark chuckle. "Well, let's give her a medal when she returns, shall we?"

"Are you going to take the baby from her?"

"I'm going to do what needs to be done. Just call me again if you hear from her—and let her know I won't stop looking."

With that, he hung up. I sat there, watching the last of the parents picking up their kids. I was going to kill Hilary when Caleb was finished with her.

Chapter Twenty

PRIORITIES

After a quick detour to the local market to stock my fridge, I was on my way home. Eager to see Logan, I passed by his property with a small smile that fell the moment I saw a squad car parked in his driveway. It wasn't my mother's, either—it was the sheriff's.

Forcing myself to remain calm, I rushed my groceries inside, tossed them on the counter, and called Logan. It rang several times before his voicemail kicked back. It wasn't the norm from Logan's cell, but considering the presence of the vehicle, I wasn't surprised.

I stared out the window, chewing my bottom lip. It was a single squad car and no ambulance. *A good sign.* I needed to relax. It could be anything, and growing up around the sheriff's department, I knew that if they were there without paramedics it meant they were talking. There was no need to rush over, make a scene, or distract anyone from doing their job. The problem with that, though, was that patience had never been a friend of mine.

With an occasional peek out my window, I put the groceries away, then poured myself a glass of juice. The reverberating sound of a car door slamming penetrated my eardrums and I ran back to the window, reaching it just in time to watch the squad car drive away.

Seconds later, my phone was in my hands. I dialed Logan, only to hit his voicemail again. After another peek outside, my curiosity growing, I spotted Jax's car. *He's my next phone call*, I thought, my mind racing with worst-case scenarios. If he didn't answer, I'd go over and check in.

With bated breath, I leaned against the wall and waited until Jax answered.

"What's up, baby?"

I rolled my eyes, but smiled at the surge of relief I felt. He wouldn't be acting playful if something terrible had happened…right?

"First, I'm not your baby." I kicked off from the wall. "Second, is Logan home?"

"He is, but kinda in the middle of something." Jax's voice grew distant as he began speaking to someone in the background. "Okay, set it up and I'll play."

My smile grew, my tension relaxing further. "Tell Oliver I said hi. So is everything okay? Saw that the sheriff was over."

"Probably not, but I don't have specifics yet. I'll let Logan know you called, though. See ya…*baby*."

A strange mix of irritation and relief balanced me enough to placate my nerves for the time being. Turning my focus on something other than waiting for Logan's call, I tossed my phone on the couch and ambled back to the kitchen to prepare a meal for my boys. I'd promised them dinner, after all.

An hour later, one of my finest culinary masterpieces was set out on the table with no one there to enjoy it other than myself. Aggravation reared its ugly head, stomping out the distressing anxiety. I dialed Logan, and was sent straight to voicemail this time.

Something was wrong.

Less than five minutes later, I was ringing Logan's doorbell, a scarf wrapped tight around my neck to battle the endless-winter-air bitterness. Jax finally answered, with Oliver at his side.

"Cassandra!" Oliver leapt forward, his arms wide.

I stumbled back at his sudden embrace, laughing. "Hey, buddy, have you eaten dinner yet?"

"Nope, I'm hungry. Uncle Jax can't cook." He stepped back, looking up at his uncle.

Jax snorted. "I don't need to cook. Plenty of women are willing to do it for me." He cocked a brow at me, his eyes filled with humor.

I shook my head, ignoring the jab. "I made dinner if *you* want to come over," I said directly to Oliver and Oliver alone. "Is your daddy here?"

Jax spoke up before Oliver could. "He's busy, but lucky for you I'm free and have no problem taking his place for a meal."

I stepped farther inside, unwinding my scarf and opening my jacket. "Fine, you're invited, but not in Logan's place. Where is he, anyway? It's after seven." It wasn't like him to not have dinner ready for Oliver by six. Something was definitely up.

"His office, but I'd leave him be for a bit," Jax said, eerily serious.

"Everything okay?" I asked, my body tensing.

"As much as you may think I'm a prick, I'll prove you wrong today and leave things for Logan to tell you."

That didn't sound good, but with Oliver standing between us I didn't press for any further information.

"I'll get Oliver bundled up. Hurry, we're starved. No dilly-dallying upstairs!" Playful Jax was back, grabbing Oliver's coat from the closet.

I made my way up the stairs to Logan's office, worrying myself over the unknown. Was someone hurt? Was it about Caleb, or Hilary? That thought alone was too overwhelming to bear.

The door to Logan's office was open, so I walked in. He stood behind his desk, phone in hand, looking down at nothing.

"Hey," I said, almost in a whisper. The thick air crackled around us.

Logan raised his head, set the phone on his desk, and walked across the room. I met him halfway, where he hauled me into his arms, holding me close. He exhaled, his body wound tightly with tension so tangible I could feel it radiating off him.

"Hey," he finally husked.

I pulled back and cupped his face. His usually vibrant blue eyes were hooded and tired.

"Everything okay? I made dinner. Jax is downstairs getting Oliver ready to come over."

His hands loosened around my waist. "Sorry sweetheart. I'm gonna need a rain check on that one."

I nodded gingerly. "Talk to me."

He held my gaze for a moment before releasing a sigh and stepping backward toward his desk. "Kurt died last night."

My hands flew to my mouth. "Oh my God." I couldn't breathe. I could barely speak, my words shooting out in gasped syllables. "What? How?"

"Waiting on the autopsy. They suspect he was drugged."

My head throbbed. Kurt was dead and never coming back. No trial to suffer through. No fear about his release. He was…dead.

"Did you…?" It came out before I could stop myself. I dropped my head, ashamed I'd even allowed it to slip out.

"No, I had nothing to do with it." His voice was strong—honest. I peered back up, watching him stand there regarding me with a new intensity.

"I don't understand. Then who?" I said, more calmly than I'd expected.

Logan held out his hand and guided me to his colossal leather chair. I sat, despite the rigidity in my limbs.

"They're looking into every possible lead. Your mother came by Saturday night to tell me Kurt was in the infirmary, but she didn't have any facts then—just that they suspected foul play."

My neck craned his way. "Why didn't you tell me this morning?"

"Because I didn't think it was serious. Besides, I had nothing to do with it, so it seemed insignificant." Agitation edged his tone. "Honestly, I figured the fucker would live."

My head bobbed in understanding. "That's why the sheriff was here—to tell you?"

Logan rubbed his jaw and sighed. "Not exactly. Like I said, they're looking into every possible suspect."

"Suspect? They think you—?" My head fell back, eyes slamming shut at the sting of tears. "I can't believe this. They really think you had something to do with murdering someone?"

He moved closer, dropping to his haunches in front of me. He pried my hands free from the arms of the chair and held them in his. "They're just trying to look productive. They don't have any reliable leads right now—only gossip."

"Logan—"

"I didn't do this." His voice was a powerful, definitive growl. "But I'm not sorry he's dead. The only reason the sheriff's looking at me is because of Kurt's cellmate, who gave a statement this morning filled with hearsay and lies."

My tears fell. Why was this happening to us?

"Listen to me, Cassandra: This is all going to go away. You understand me?"

"You don't know that," I mumbled between sobs. "What if they arrest you, Logan? What if—"

His mouth crushed mine, hot and demanding, silencing me with his tongue. His strong fingers skimmed up my neck, capturing my chin.

When he finally broke the kiss, my tears lingered over both our lips. I felt utterly hopeless.

"Trust me. I'm not going anywhere. I promise you that."

The conviction in his words settled my anxiety, and the ferocious look in his eyes demanded I trust him. So I did, letting the subject drop.

"Okay, well then come have dinner with us."

His mouth slanted over my lips once more in a tender, quick peck. "I wish I could, but I need to make a few calls and then go down to Haven and make sure everything's running smoothly. Been having a few problems without Caleb at the helm."

He went to stand, bending back down to press a kiss to the top of my head. "Can you tell Jax to make sure Oliver gets his bath after he eats? I'll be back in time to tuck him in."

"Of course," I said, my voice weak.

"How about, after everything is settled, I sneak over to tuck you in as well?"

And there it was: that ravenous look paired with his throaty timbre, full of delicious possibilities. It had a miraculous way of weakening every worry I held.

My lips curled upward. "I may be hard to rouse. You sure you can find some…new method?"

"I'm always up for a challenge—especially when it involves you."

He was still standing directly in front of me. My fingers danced up his thighs, his erection tenting his slacks inches from my face. I sat up straighter.

"Then stop over." I cupped his bulge. "I won't kick you out."

He reached down, gripped my shoulders, and pulled me up flush against him. His arms snaked around my waist, settling on my ass and grasping it with greedy hands. "I wouldn't let you anyway, and you know it."

"I do."

The phone rang, interrupting our moment. It was probably for the best, since I had two hungry West guys waiting downstairs for me. Logan answered the phone; he'd obviously been expecting the call.

"Hold on a minute," he said into the receiver before covering it with his hand and claiming one final kiss from me.

"I'll see you later tonight," he murmured.

I nodded and strode back to the door. "I'll have Jax bring you a plate over."

He was already too occupied on the call to reply so I turned and left, my thoughts rewinding and planting a heavy weight of anxious fear in my gut.

Kurt was dead.

When I woke the next morning, it wasn't with a satisfied grin but an empty void. Logan had never shown up. Not that I didn't understand—between the newspaper, Haven, and now Kurt, he had a lot on his mind.

I checked my phone, relieved to find a text from him.

Not gonna make it tonight. Dream of me sweetheart. X

Two long nights passed that included said dreams, but with only intermittent texts from Logan. It was frustrating, but I'd always despised girlfriends who clung to their men, unable to go so much as one night alone. That wouldn't be me. I occupied my time by catching up on some housework and doing a little reading. A couple days alone were probably exactly what I needed.

My only issue was that I didn't just have a busy boyfriend, but one who purposely kept me in the dark about something everyone around me couldn't stop discussing. That was a hard pill to swallow. After that day in his home office, he hadn't so much as mentioned Kurt's name to me in any of the messages he sent—even when I asked.

The gossip mill around town spoke volumes to the stress he was dealing with. Rumors swirled like wildfire: *Logan West was responsible for Kurt's death.* The sheriff had yet to name Logan a prime suspect, but had hinted he was a person of interest.

The looks and hushed whispers around the school ran rampant, but never once was I asked point blank for details. Besides seeing Oliver at school, happily unaware of the drama unfolding around him, I hadn't spent any time with him, either. The West house sat quietly beside mine, with no activity and only the occasional flicker of light in the evening.

By Thursday night, I was aching to see Logan. I'd been lying on my couch, flipping through channels filled with reality shows and infomercials, and needed something from him.

I sent him a text, hoping he'd be free.

I miss you.

It took almost an hour before my phone chimed with a reply.

I know. Me too. Hate this. I'm going to kill Caleb.

I'd had no contact from Hilary since Monday after school, which had me even more worried.

Is he home yet? Has he found Hilary?

This time, his reply was instant.

No, but he owes me after this. If it was anyone other than his woman he was blowing shit off for, he'd be a dead man.

Sorry.

Don't be. I'll be at Haven tonight, then have some paperwork to finish. How about dinner tomorrow? Anything you want, I'll make it.

I tugged my bottom lip between my teeth, stifling my grin. I liked the sound of that. I pictured him down at the bar, leaning against the brick wall, looking gorgeous in his suit with the jacket missing and sleeves rolled up, texting me and only me. *How did I get so lucky?*

Anything?

You know it, but be careful. My dick's hard just thinking about you. No teasing tonight.

I want to do more than tease you.

You have no idea how bad I want you right now. Send me a pic.

A pic? Did he mean, like, a nude pic? I looked down at my blue sweats and yellow varsity shirt. Nude would be better than that, but still, I didn't have the nerve.

How about I stop down there and u can show me exactly how much u want me…in the backroom.

This time, his reply took a couple minutes, but it was worth the wait.

Do you need the definition of TEASING!!

I laughed, falling back onto the sofa and tucking a pillow under my head.

Not when I plan to deliver.

!!!! My dick's gonna explode damn you. Get that fine ass down here!

I jumped up. Ignoring the head rush, I was hopping into my boots when an idea sparked. My heart pounded and center wept as I kicked the boots back off and ran into my room. I tore out of my clothes, including underwear and bra. It only took a second to find what I needed in my top drawer. With an eager grin, I pulled on the white nightie I'd worn in his pool all those months ago.

I grabbed my keys and opened the front door, wearing only the nightie, my long trench coat, a red scarf, and boots. It was totally not enough to battle the weather, but I was certain my arousal would keep me warm. Cliché or not, I knew he wouldn't be complaining.

My phone. I jogged back to the couch and went to slip it into my pocket when I saw a new text from Logan. My giddiness went vocal; a wild squeal floated out as I opened it.

Don't hate me but do me a favor, stay warm at home and take a hot bath. No sense u coming down here. The idiots in the kitchen won't give me any quality time with u. Promise I'll make up for this.

The phone fell back to the sofa. Was this really happening? It was as though the universe were determined to keep us apart. I stomped back to the front door and slammed it shut, kicking off my boots yet again.

The scarf was suddenly constricting, the silk of the nightie against my bare skin a cruelty that needed to be shed. I undressed in my living room, exhaustion and aggravation sending my arousal into oblivion.

Damn it!

I made my way back to my bedroom, tucked the nightie back in my drawer, then crawled into bed. A bath was only fun with him in it.

After debating what to message back, I finally replied.

U owe me 4 nights of orgasms! And I expect

payment in full! Soon! XO!

I waited for his response, and was nearly dozing off when it chimed.

Look forward to it baby. If u think Logan won't mind.

I lurched up. *What?*

Who is this?

Who u think?

Jax?

That's my girl. So we gonna start those orgasms tonight? C u in ten.

Ewww! Where did Logan go?

He left his phone on the bar when he dragged a waiter out back to either beat his ass or fire him.

Why?

Shit mood tonight. Now I know why, text kitten

Ewwww x10! Tell Logan I'm going to bed!

'Night baby!

I tossed my phone across the room, hauled my blankets up over my head, and closed my eyes.

Morning couldn't come fast enough after hours of restlessness. With my body begging for a snooze button, I sat up and found two missed calls and three texts from Logan.

So sorry! Jax is a dumb ass that will apologize next time he sees you. Call me.

I'm guessing you're either asleep or too pissed to answer the phone. I love you and will call you in the morning.

The next text was received only a few minutes previous, at barely seven a.m.

I love you Cassandra X
With groggy eyes, I replied.
Love u too XO

I stopped by his house right after school later that day. It was Jax who opened the door again, smug as always.

"Come to claim something? I'm all yours." He leaned in as I entered, walking past him. "Perfect timing, too."

"What part of 'ewww' are you having trouble with, exactly?" I drawled, smiling at the way he chuckled. The guy was harmless. I unbuttoned my coat and opened the closet to hang it up. "Is Logan home? Please say yes."

"Yes."

I sighed with relief. "Great, where is he?"

"Not here."

My brows pinched together. "Wait, but you just said—"

"I said what you told me to say. And in case you're wondering, I don't mind taking orders in the bedroom from time to time either."

I slugged him in the shoulder. "Smart ass."

"Always." He winked.

I reached back into the closet to retrieve my coat. "Is he at Haven?"

"Nah, he picked Oliver up from school and left from there."

"Left?" I reared back, surprised.

Jax shrugged. "You might wanna give him a shout. Kinda shocked he didn't call you. Guess all this murder bullshit is taking up more headspace than your pussy. Sorry."

"Are you ever not crude?" I tugged my coat back on, frustrated.

"Not really, no." I watched him walk away to the kitchen as I dialed Logan, hoping everything was all right.

He answered on the second ring.

"Cassandra." He spoke my name as though he needed it to breathe. "You have no idea how much I miss you."

"Well, I'm standing in your foyer if you want to come home and show me."

He exhaled loudly. He wasn't going to be showing me anything.

"I miss you too," I continued, giving him an out. "Jax said you left. Couldn't at least call me?"

"Long story, but I'm heading to the city. I was going to call, but it's been one thing after another and I'm trying to end it as fast as possible. My lawyer wants to sit down and get started on a better game plan, in case things get pursued."

"Pursued?" I repeated, cutting him off.

"Just want to be prepared, and since my mother's a mess worrying over everything that's happened, I figured a few days with her would help her see everything is okay."

"Okay, so a few days?" I walked over to his steps across from the foyer and sat, silently chanting to myself not to punish him for leaving without so much as a text.

"Yeah, we should be back Sunday. I promise I'm going to make up for this week and last night. You have no idea how disappoi—"

"I know. Don't even think about it. We'll get through this, and then we'll have all the time in the world to spend together. Just focus on what needs to be done. And give Oliver a hug for me, okay?"

"You're too good for me, you know that? I don't know how I got so lucky to convince you to stick around."

"Ditto. Now drive safe, and let me know when you get there so I don't worry."

"I will, and I swear the minute I'm home I'm coming for you and not letting you go till I've had my fill. Which will never happen, so consider yourself warned." He sounded relaxed. That was all I needed to hear.

"Mmm, I look forward to it. " I smiled to myself, closing my legs tightly.

"I gotta go. Try to relax this weekend. Get lots of sleep to prepare that body for me."

"That, I can do. Oh, wait, have you heard from Caleb?" I asked quickly.

"He called a few hours ago to check in. He found her last night."

"What!? Why didn't you tell me?" I shot up from the steps and began to pace. She was safe—or safe enough, depending on how pissed Caleb was.

"Sorry, slipped my mind with everything going on."

How could I complain, given the circumstances? But still, it only added to my brewing irritation. "Is she okay at least? Is he...what did he do?"

"From what he said, she called him but chickened out and hung up when he answered the phone. He used some connections to track the call."

"That's a relief. I mean, he'll bring her home, right?" I suddenly realized I had no clue *what* Caleb would do, but I knew she was better off with him than alone.

"I have no doubt, although she may not be able to walk by the time he's done with her."

"What? Why?" I halted my steps, my eyes wide, voice higher than necessary.

"Sweetheart, that man is gonna—" He lowered his voice, reminding me Oliver was with him. "Put your headphones back on just for a moment longer, okay? Thank you." He must have said the last bit to Oliver, because his voice was muffled.

It made me giggle.

His normal voice finally returned. "Fill her up till she can't stand it."

"Oh." That wasn't the worst punishment in the world—especially since Hilary couldn't get enough of Caleb anyway.

"That's what I'd do to you. I'd remind you exactly why you'd never want to run again."

"That would certainly work." I felt my face flush.

"You have no idea how badly I wish I was…" His voice dropped again. "…filling you up right now."

"Me too. But go take care of this Kurt stuff, and then come home to me."

"I will. Love you," he said, so sincerely the words cocooned my heart and planted themselves deep inside.

"Bye, Cassie!" Oliver yelled in the background. Logan chuckled.

"So much for the headphones, huh?" I teased.

Logan let out a playful grunt in response.

"Love you both. Bye."

I hung up and slid the phone into my coat pocket. A weekend alone…it didn't sound fun at all. No Logan, no Hilary. The thought of calling my mom reminded me of Kurt, so I thought better of that as well. It wasn't fair to be upset, but it was still there, just under the surface. It seemed I wasn't ranking very high on Logan's list of priorities.

"What we drinkin'?"

Jax stood in the kitchen doorway, holding up a bottle of tequila in one hand and vodka in the other.

Looked like I was going to get my chance at deconstructing another West enigma.

"Both."

Chapter Twenty-One

FRENEMIES

"I'm in so much trouble!" I spluttered, knocking back a shot with Jax. "You're not even legal!"

"And your point?" he quipped back, refilling my glass.

"Your brother's gonna kill me."

"Nah, Logan has better things to do with you. Besides, he's never said much about me drinking before—at least, not other than threatening to knock my teeth out if he ever caught me driving under the influence."

"Really? Does he let them serve you at Haven?" I blurted out, appalled.

Jax's forehead wrinkled. "Hell no. Sad, actually—Logan cares more about his businesses than letting me have any fun sometimes." His mouth twisted into an impish pout.

"Aw, you poor baby." I laughed, shaking my head.

It was official: I was drunk—and in Logan's house, without him. It was totally *not* how I'd planned my night, but then again, after the week I'd had trying to pin Logan down, it was the first night I hadn't sulked over his absence.

"You wanna make me feel better?" He wiggled his brows, and my elbow shot into his gut.

"Your loss." He chuckled. "Now lay down and try to stay

still if we're seriously going to do this."

"Yes, we're *seriously* going to do this!" I slurred. "But be gentle."

"Gotta admit, considering the noises I hear you howl from Logan's room, I wouldn't have pegged *gentle* for your style."

My face twisted up. "You're a pig."

"I know. Now, come on—lay down for me."

"I am, jeez!" I giggled, situating myself to rest flat on my back. For the first time all night, Jax became silent, instantly enthralled with the idea I'd given him to sketch. Surprising, considering Oliver could've doodled it.

My eyes closed slowly as I enjoyed the alcohol-induced bliss, completely relaxed in Jax's bedroom: a place I never thought I'd be lying in.

Jax sat beside me on a short stool while I began humming a melody my grandma used to play. He didn't seem to pay me any mind.

"You think Logan misses me?" I mused.

"Oh, hell no! Don't act like a sixteen-year-old bitch on me now. Total buzzkill, baby."

"I'm serious."

He groaned, clearly agitated. I popped one eye open to catch him shaking his head. It was my turn to pout now, and I did without shame. Still, he said nothing, ignoring me as he leaned over the clipboard in his hands to sketch.

It was only a second later when he peeked back up, smiling. It was an annoyingly cute smile—one that made it clear he'd appease me, if only the tiniest bit.

"I like you drunk; you're not as mean. So I'll say one thing, and then we drop you moping about Logan. Deal?"

"Deal!" I grinned, my giddiness returning.

He rolled his eyes, still smiling when he muttered, "Girls."

"Come on," I probed.

"All right, listen up: Besides Oliver, you're the best damn thing that's ever happened to my brother. He adores the hell out of you. Believe me, he misses you. Probably jerking off right now thinking about you."

My face turned up. "Doubtful. He hasn't even texted to tell me he arrived safely." A frown set in. What was wrong with me?

"If he didn't make it there, my mother would be blowing up my phone by now. You're good—he's just got a lot on his mind. I mean, he's dealing with this Kurt bullshit. Gotta cut him some slack."

Kurt. He made my blood boil. Amazing how liquor could send one spiraling from one emotion to another without pause.

"I hate Kurt," I spewed, my face tight, a new fury replacing my blues.

"Good." Jax chuckled. He held up the sketch, and I gave him a thumbs up and giant grin.

"You sure you want it lopsided?" he asked.

My mood shifted yet again and I giggled, unable to help myself given the way his eyes squinted in disapproval. "Hm. Perfect!"

Jax winked. "I sure am. Now let's get you out of those jeans."

He placed his hands on my hips and I bucked them off, springing upright. "What? No way!"

He stood beside me. "Well, how else am I gonna do this?"

"Here." I climbed off the table and turned my back to him, then opened my jeans and folded the waist over twice. The purple thong hiding underneath peeked out, but there was little I could do about that other than grab a towel he had folded beside him and tuck it slightly over the front of my jeans. It hid everything he didn't need to see.

"How's that?" I whirled back around and hopped up on the table, ready to lie back and cease the spinning in my head. *Slow movements next time.*

"Works for me, although it's not as much fun."

I narrowed my eyes at him and he shrugged his shoulders. "Just saying," he said with a snicker.

He set the sketchpad on the tray beside him, pulled on a pair of rubber gloves, then wiped something cool between my bellybutton and hip. He'd explained earlier that the design I wanted was easy to freehand, so I went with it.

This would be my first and probably last tattoo—a live-in-the-moment idea I'd happened upon out of the blue. The liquor was to blame, and Jax wasn't gentleman enough to talk me into waiting until I'd sobered up. On the contrary, he'd practically dragged me up to his room.

I wanted it somewhere special for only Logan to enjoy, and Jax had pointed out the best spot: low enough that no one could ever see it unless I wanted them to. Worked for me.

With my pants open, it hit me that this probably wasn't the most appropriate thing to be doing with my boyfriend's little brother. But again, with alcohol involved, it seemed like a stellar idea. Plus, Jax was all talk. He was a flirt, yes, but I knew he'd never do anything that truly made me uncomfortable. Weirdly, I trusted him.

"Can I tell you a secret?" I asked, my hands fidgeting.

"As long as it's a juicy one." He studied his drawing, then dipped the needle in the tiny bit of ink.

"Promise you won't tell anyone?"

His hand rubbed over the canvas of my flesh. "Yeah yeah, spill it already."

I leaned sideways, which seemed to annoy him, but I didn't stop until I was beside his ear. I attempted to whisper, but in my drunken state, it was probably more of a mild shout.

"I'm glad he's dead."

Jax pulled back, his features lit with amusement. "Baby, that's no secret. And we all feel the same way."

That didn't make *me* feel any better. "But he's a human being. No one deserves to die."

"We all die eventually, and Kurt...he made his own choices. Not smart ones. Horrible ones, actually, that got him what he had coming."

"But that's not—"

"Did you deserve to get attacked?" he interrupted, his voice strained. My mouth snapped shut as he continued. "He was going to rape you, Cassandra! Was that deserved?"

I shook my head, understanding and agreeing. "I know, but still, I feel bad. And now they think Logan did it...because of me." My voice dropped from the weight of the guilt.

"Come on, don't be a sad drunk. Stop worrying so much. My brother didn't kill Kurt—not that he wouldn't have, but this wasn't him. Now sit still so I can get started."

"It's going to hurt, huh?"

"Are you going to start crying on me next? 'Cause I swear to God—"

"More tequila!" I shouted.

"Good call. " He poured me a shot, and I sat up to take it. "Drink up, then lie down and stay there. No more talking unless it's to praise my work or get a little handsy, got it?"

"Got it. But just to be clear: My hands aren't going anywhere near you."

"Yeah yeah, I know." He threw me a playful wink and I smiled, relaxing.

When the needle hit my skin a few seconds later, I bolted upright. Jax muttered a few curses under his breath as he leaned back, glaring at me.

"For Christ's sake, woman! Lie the hell back down or I'm done."

My face pinched, full of an apology that he ignored. The man was serious about his work.

"Sorry. I'm ready now." I fell back and closed my eyes, focusing on my breathing. As he started again, my mind went off to my happy place, fantasizing about Logan's expression when I showed him the tattoo. And I would—the instant he returned home.

"All right, that's it," Jax said, setting the needle down and cracking his knuckles. "She's a beauty, if I do say so myself."

"I wanna see."

I sat up on my elbows and took the handheld mirror he held out for me. "Jax, it's…it's gorgeous. I can't believe you did this."

It was exactly what I'd envisioned: simple, classic, clean, and meaningful to the only people who mattered.

"Still think it looks lopsided, but that's on you," Jax replied with a smile.

After he placed a bandage over his work, I handed the mirror back and swung my legs off the side of the table, grinning so widely my cheeks complained. I didn't care. I felt alive.

Jax's phone pinged beside us. With one glance down at it, he hit the silence button, growling under his breath.

"Avoiding a clinging one-night stand?" I teased.

"I wish." He snapped off his gloves and threw them in the trash. His frown left me curious.

"Who's the buzzkill now, huh?" I giggled, crossing his room to snoop around the books on a small shelf in the corner. I held up a worn copy of Joe Hill's *Heart-Shaped Box*.

"Horror fan, I take it?"

He snatched the book from me. "What, shocked I'm literate?"

"Maybe." My laughter bubbled up.

Jax shook his head, his smile returning. As he pivoted toward the shelf to place the book back in its rightful spot, I sprinted forward and snatched his phone from the desk. He was pressed against my back a second later, reaching to steal the device, but it was too late. The name that highlighted the screen with eight new text messages was loud and clear.

Natasha.

He moved away, and my jaw dropped as I whirled around to face him.

"You hate her! Why is she sending you so many messages?"

Before he could answer, the phone pinged with another. I touched the screen and gasped, reading the newest one.

Call me now or Logan will hear everything!

I peered back up warily to find Jax sitting on his bed with his head in his hands. I scrolled up through the messages.

Seduce her if you have to!
I don't care what it takes!
I mean it Jax, I want her out of his life.

Was she talking about me? I continued skimming until one message glared bright and alarming, sent the evening Hilary and I had gone to Haven with Natasha.

Natasha: I found my leverage. Seems Hilary has been keeping secrets.
Jax: Leave her out of this.
Natasha: What's the fun in that?
Jax: Caleb will kill you if you do anything to hurt her!
Natasha: Caleb will be too distracted to do anything

to me.

My anger was beyond anything I could control, emphasized by the tequila, but I couldn't stop reading. The next message was sent the following day—the morning Caleb had showed up at Logan's looking for Hilary.

Jax: Caleb's here. What did u do?!

Natasha: Wasn't me. I'd planned on visiting him at the bar later. Why is he there? He know about the baby?

Jax: Fuck off!

Natasha: Tell me what's going on over there or I'm coming over for a little chat with Logan about your demanding cock!

I dropped the phone and moved in on Jax, smacking him in the back of the head.

"You son of a bitch!" I screamed, backing away before I went off again. Violence wasn't the answer, but it sure felt good.

"You...you and...oh my God, Jax! You screwed Natasha? When? Was she still with Logan? Is that why she left him?" My own eardrums hurt at my incessant shrieking.

He sprung off the bed, his features hard. "No! Hell, I was still in high school when they dated."

"Okay, then when? Or better yet, *why?*"

He blew out a deep breath and stood in front of me, looking genuinely ashamed.

"Last year, right before Logan moved here. Oliver kept asking about his mother, and one day a friend of mine sent me some pics of himself posing with girls he partied with on the beach down in Miami. One was Natasha. I recognized her right away, and went down there to try and convince her to come see Oliver or at least call him. Shit, he deserved that much." His voice colored with disgrace. "Thought she could explain why she wasn't around. I love that kid more than anything. I'd never hurt him."

I didn't know what to say. "Jax..."

He sat on the bed, his shoulders hunched, and I sat beside him.

"I fucked up. I brought her a bunch of photos of Oliver and tried to tell her how funny and smart he was, but all she wanted to do was party." His hands yanked through his hair. "It's all a blur. I don't even know half the shit I took while I was there, just that when I left she had no interest in coming back for Oliver—at least, none that I saw. I mean, she refused to even *talk* about him! At first I thought it was because she was ashamed she left, but I don't know. I wish I could take it back. You have to believe me on that." He tilted his head my way. His eyes were glazed over. "When she showed up on New Year's, I was as shocked as everyone else."

"Logan doesn't know?" Sympathy tinged my words. He'd thought he was doing the right thing.

"No—not about me finding her, and *definitely* not that I fucked her. I was fresh out of high school, and she was all over me!"

I made a face of disgust. What was the appeal of Natasha other than on a superficial level? I guessed that was enough for some guys.

"I know it was wrong. I'm not trying to justify what I did, but Logan won't care. He'll throw my ass out. He'll never speak to me or let me near Oliver again." He grabbed my hands, panicked. "Please, Cassandra. You can't say anything."

"He'll forgive you," I reasoned.

Jax threw my hands aside and leapt up from the bed, hands balled into fists at his sides. "I'm the reason she's back, which led to you almost dying in a car accident! Don't you get that? You think he's really gonna forgive me? I fucked the first woman he ever loved—and not just once! He's gonna kill me!"

I stood, approaching him like I was cornering an animal, and placed my hands on his shoulders. "He loves you. He's going to see your intentions were good. And as far as the sex, Natasha was the one who took advantage of you. You were still basically a kid. And don't for one second put the blame of my accident on you or even Natasha. I shouldn't have driven home that night. That's on me and nobody else."

He shoved away from me. "Doesn't matter! I *wanted* to screw her! Not at first, but when I got there and she started strutting her half-naked ass all around me, I wanted nothing else than to fuck her, and I did. *That's* on me, and I've been suffering ever since."

How had he hidden all this from Logan? So much for him knowing everything.

"That's why she's blackmailing you."

"Bingo!" He threw up his hands.

"Then why give her grief whenever she's around? You treat her like trash."

"She may think I'm her little bitch, but I refuse to kiss her ass. Besides, if I didn't give her shit, Logan would know something was up. Win-win."

Made sense—at least, as much as any of it could. "We need to explain all this to Logan."

"Hell no!" His eyes grew impossibly wide.

"I won't lie to him, Jax."

"Fine, then at least give me a little time here—at least a week to try and shut her the hell out of our lives for good. She thought you were the weak link—the one to manipulate to gain better access to Logan—but obviously that went to shit. She's desperate now, and it's only a matter of time before she makes a wrong move."

"Jax, we *need* to tell Logan. It will be worse if he finds out on his own."

"You really think he can handle another bomb with everything he has going on? He's under investigation for *murder*, Cassandra. Please, just give me a week, and if I can't get rid of her then I'll tell him myself."

The thought of lying to Logan was crushing, but Jax was right: Now wasn't the best time to add to Logan's stress. He'd have to understand that later.

"One week. That's it. And if Logan suspects anything, then I'm telling him. But don't get it twisted—the only reason I'm agreeing to this is because you're right about him not needing it right now."

"Fuck," he blew out, grabbing the bottle of tequila and pouring us each a shot—one I needed desperately. "I owe you big, woman."

"Yeah, you do."

Somewhere between finishing off the bottle and Jax revealing hidden tattoos he had on his chest, his arms, and even the back of his neck, my eyelids drooped and sleep set in.

"What the fuck!?"

I snapped my groggy eyes open, feeling a warm body resting under my head. I blinked to clear away the sleep, my vision focusing just enough for me to see Logan towering over me.

Which meant his wasn't the hard, naked chest under me.

The pain in my head made my movements slow as a wave of nausea hit hard. I peeked to the side to find Jax lying under me, his eyes wide and staring back at me. I shot up and off the bed, my hands covering my mouth.

"Why the hell are you in bed with my girl!?" Logan bellowed, throwing clothes at Jax.

I doubled over, my dry heaves punishing and relentless.

"Logan—" was all I could manage before my stomach emptied at his feet.

"Get your ass dressed, and get the hell out of my house!" Logan growled.

Debilitating tremors made it nearly impossible to lift my head. I saw enough to know Logan was talking to Jax, who stood, wearing only boxers. When had that happened?

I fought through the haze, remembering him removing his shirt to show me his tattoos. But his pants?

Oh crap.

Another surge of nausea hit as I remembered the tiny kitten tattoo on his upper thigh that he'd supposedly been dared to give himself at a frat party. It was hilarious when he'd showed it to me the previous night, when I was too drunk to realize his pants needed to be removed for me to get a view. But now...now it was a nightmare.

I heard Jax leave as I righted myself, ready to explain. Thankfully, *I* was fully clothed.

"Logan, it's not—"

"I'm going out for a drink. Get cleaned up." He wouldn't even look at me.

"Wait!" I stumbled after him, my head an unbearable anchor. I'd made it to the hallway when Julia stepped in front of me.

"I'd let him go if I were you."

Was she serious? "No, nothing happened." I held my head still in my hands. The room spun faster.

"I believe you, and he will too when he calms down. He's just had a bad week, and you have to admit: You in bed with a practically naked Jax looks pretty bad."

I took a few breaths, choking down the acidic burn. "Why is he home early? Did something happen?"

"I don't know. I just stopped by to do some laundry. Oliver's still with my mom. Logan did mention that it was going to be a busy week, and he wanted to see you."

My stomach sank further. He'd come home for me, and this is what he'd found. I needed to find him and make things right.

Julia walked away and I bolted to the stairs, ignoring my nausea.

"Logan!" I yelled from the top step.

He stopped halfway through the front doorway, about to leave. He didn't even look back.

"Leave me the hell alone, Cassandra." His voice was deadly calm. He walked out, slamming the door behind him.

Sadness wracked my body. I should've fallen down crying, but I didn't. In fact, I felt the urge to do the exact opposite. I was tired of being pushed aside while he dealt with things alone. And after he'd thrown me out over the Hilary incident, this was the final straw.

He thought *he* was the angry one? I was livid.

Chapter Twenty-Two

TRUTH

For the first time in my life, I was thankful for the anger coursing through my veins, ripping through the alcohol-fueled haze. There was no more nausea or spinning rooms—just a pissed-off woman storming home through melting sludge.

I fell into bed the moment my coat hit the floor. My kicked-off shoes flew through the air while I held up my phone and sent a text, but not to Logan. This one was to yet someone else currently responsible for the drama in my life, and frankly, it was time for me to speak up.

I know you're with Caleb! U coulda called so I'd stop worrying but then again u and your man are the same that way! Selfish!

The text to Hilary was followed by one to Jax.

Did u set me up?!

His reply came less than a minute later.

NO! Didn't even know he was comin home. Swear it!

The message I'd read on his phone from Natasha the previous night had set off my internal alarms. *Seduce her, if you have to*, she'd told him—and according to Logan right about now, that was exactly how it looked.

If I check your phone will I see u texted her this

morning with the play by play?

Don't hate me. I need to keep her off my back till I can put a plan together. I had to tell her. She needs to think I'm still on her side.

I was fuming. Jax couldn't be trusted, and after the previous night, that little revelation actually hurt. I wanted to like him; despite his actions involving Natasha, he was a good guy. But it didn't change the fact that I felt used.

Screw u! You didn't have to tell her, she'd have never known you didn't.

What happened last night was innocent. Go talk to Logan. He'll understand.

Oh, I'd be talking to Logan all right.

Consider your week up. Logan's going to hear everything.

Wait!! I was never gonna follow thru w/ anything the bitch wanted. I consider u a friend. Last night wasn't some plan to trick u. Please do me a solid and give me some time here.

If the amount of rage I felt could've been converted into physical strength, my phone would've crumbled in my grip. There were few people I downright hated, but Natasha was now at the top of that short list.

I replied with the only thing my brain had energy to process.

I need sleep.

His response was instant.

Do I still have that week?
IDK g'night

When I woke hours later, the afternoon was fading into

evening and I didn't feel any better. A quick shower and bite to eat only squelched the alcohol-fueled hangover—not the emotional one.

Finished biding my time in an effort to not have to deal with life again, I finally grabbed my phone and confirmed Logan hadn't tried to reach out.

But someone else had: Hilary. One new text awaited me.

Sorry. You're right I shoulda called. What's going on? Caleb took my phone & only gave it back when he saw your message.

I replied, keeping it short.

Everything is falling apart. I miss u! Tell Caleb to bring u home soon.

Who knew when she'd get the message, or when she—my venting ear—would be back.

Pushing it all from my mind, I dropped the phone beside me on the sofa, exchanging it for the TV remote that proved *everything* was pissing me off today: the usually hilarious sitcoms, Ellen, and even the little old woman on QVC selling pearls.

With a discouraged groan and nothing interesting to capture my brooding mind, I got dressed, climbed in my car, and drove. With no destination planned, I ended up in my mother's driveway.

She wasn't home, but her boyfriend, George, was. He shot off the couch when I threw my coat over the back of it, previously oblivious to the fact that I was there.

Our gazes met—his complete with bulging eyes, and mine, for some ungodly reason, dropping to the tighty whities he wore. Those things looked good on very few men, and George was unfortunately not one of them.

As if just realizing he was showing way too much—and sporting what looked unmistakably and disturbingly like morning wood—he snatched the crocheted pillow my grandmother had knit to cover himself.

I spun around, embarrassed for us both. "Sorry. I didn't know you were here." *In fact, I wasn't even aware you were shacking up with my mom at all.*

"No, my fault," George said quickly. "Give me a minute to get dressed."

I nodded, my back still facing him, listening as he shuffled out of the room.

Good God, that did not *just happen.* Could I *not* catch a break? There were some things I'd have liked to be kept in the loop on—like not being able to visit my childhood home without enduring awkward run-ins with half-naked men I hardly knew.

Just as I began thinking up a convincing excuse to leave, George proved to be as much a gentleman as my mother had portrayed him. He strolled back out fully dressed in slacks, a polo, and an easy smile.

"Cassandra, I can't apologize enough."

"It's fine, really." *Can we just pretend it never happened? Is that too much to ask?*

He stopped in front of me, relaxed and friendly. "I'm sorry. This is still your home, and I shouldn't have fallen asleep out here, especially without—"

I threw my hands up, not needing a visual. "No problem. Really—we're good."

He nodded, smiling with a slight chuckle. "Well, how about we just—"

"Already forgotten, seriously," I interrupted.

"I was going to say have a soda, but that's good to hear too."

Unsure how to respond and slightly off balance, I laughed. Surprisingly, it was a real, feel-good kind of laughter.

"Your mom's shift ends soon. Why don't you stick around? She'd love to see you."

"Sure. She got anything to eat in the fridge?" My mom rarely had anything other than snack foods in her kitchen, but it was worth asking about anyway.

"Yeah, I keep it stocked for her," he said with a small smile. "Why don't you have a seat, and I'll whip something up?"

I didn't complain as I watched him disappear into the kitchen. He emerged a few minutes later with turkey sandwiches and sodas.

"You feeling okay?" he asked. "You look tired."

I sipped my cola, rolling the chilly can in my palm. "Yeah, I'm good. Didn't sleep well, that's all. So you're living here now?"

That could've come out a little less blunt, but George took it in stride, smiling as he gave the room a once-over.

"Nah, I just stay over from time to time. Your mom's not a fan of my bachelor pad, so we spend most of our time here—that is, until we get it sold."

Soda almost spattered from my mouth. I swallowed, wincing at the burn as it slid down my throat.

"Sold?"

His jaw dropped, eyes widening. "Oh, darling, I'm sorry. I thought your mom told you."

"Told me what!? She's selling the house!?" I nearly shrieked. *Can this week get any worse?* That house was as much a sanctuary as my grandparents'. Why would she want to sell it?

"We talked about living here together, but thought it best to make a fresh start in our own place—build new memories together, in a place to grow old in."

"Right," was all I could say. A change of subject was needed as the cruel sting of bittersweet tears hit me. Before they could fall, I decided to go for the giant elephant in the room.

"Any word on Kurt's case?"

The look on his stunned face served exactly the purpose I needed, settling my blossoming tears. The man worked at the prison where Kurt had died. He had to know something.

"Ah." He swiped his cheek with his hand, his eyes looking everywhere but at me. "I can't really talk about that."

I sat up straighter in the chair. He did know something.

Flipping to the doe-eyed expression my grandfather could never turn away from, I batted my eyelashes. Sad eyes got a lot out of a man—especially one planning to marry your mother.

George's lips quirked despite his grunt of disapproval at my tactic. "This is strictly off the record, and if you repeat *any* of it, I'll deny ever telling you. Got it?"

My head bobbed, a grin firmly in place. "Got it. Lips sealed."

He took a second before he spoke, worrying me that he was having second thoughts.

"The DA has nothing but the cellmate's statement, which claims Kurt told him that if anything happened to him, Logan West was behind it. A few of his buddies inside corroborated that as well. But those ones won't stick; it's just hearsay. The cellmate's is the focus."

My frown was instant. I already knew all that. But before I could tell him so, he continued.

"I'm sorry, but between that, Logan's priors, and the rumors spreading that Kurt's trip to the infirmary during his last stint was somehow related to Logan, it looks like the DA is moving forward."

"Forward?" I gasped.

George nodded once, his eyes soft. "Not sure when, but they're about to announce your boyfriend as an official suspect and bring him down to the station."

I couldn't breathe. "Priors?"

He nodded again, the movement disturbing me further. How could he sit there so calmly while I was a bundle of kindling, doused dangerously with lighter fluid?

"Logan has a couple arrests on record for assault. One was with a deadly weapon—he beat a man with a baseball bat."

"What?" The word escaped as a soft, unbelieving whisper that hung between us.

"I'm sorry, but I've already told you too much."

He stood and I leapt up, blocking him from leaving the room.

"You love my mother, right?" I demanded, my voice cracking.

He hit me again with that damn nod, although this time it was slow. His features were wary; he was unsure where I was going with my question.

"Going to buy a home together probably means you're planning to marry her, yeah?" I continued.

"Cassandra—"

"That makes you family." I raised my chin, demanding his full attention. "I know we're practically strangers, but family helps each other out and sticks together. And if you're going to be part of mine, that makes you part of Logan's, because he's *my* family—my world. And there's a precious little boy involved that depends on his father. So please tell me everything."

George's posture drooped, and his sigh was troubled. I wasn't sure what his next move would be. He stared at me a moment more, then moved back to his seat, looking conflicted. The relief I felt when he sat back down was overwhelming.

I followed his actions, sitting up straight on the edge of my seat, my watery eyes on him.

"Your mom looked into him when you two got close."

A memory of her mentioning this suddenly usurped my thoughts—or maybe it had been more of a warning. Regardless, I'd brushed it off at the time.

"And?"

"One was just a bar fight—something about Logan hitting on another man's girlfriend. Both of them were drunk, fists flew, cops were called. Simple as that. The other one, though…Logan went after a man for no apparent reason—attacked him outside of a gym, broke his hands. Used a baseball bat and shattered his ribs."

My breath caught. There wasn't a single place in my head where a violent image of Logan could reside. It wasn't possible.

"Why would he do that?"

"That's the thing: Neither Logan nor the victim would explain. Weirder than that, a few days later, the victim dropped all charges. It's still on file, though. Something like that doesn't go away."

"That's everything?" I murmured, almost afraid of the answer.

"Yeah, that's all I got. Again, I'm sorry, Cassandra. Anything I can do to help, I'm here. Your mother went to talk to Logan last Saturday. She wouldn't tell me what he told her—she said it was personal—but whatever it was, she's on his side. And that's all I need to know to trust the man."

Unsure what else there was to say and not wanting to face my mother right then, I stood on wobbly legs. My voice was distant when I spoke.

"Thanks. Tell my mom I stopped by, please."

I never heard his response. Dazed, I walked outside, inhaling gulp after gulp of cool air to stop the sputtering of my errant thoughts.

Operating on autopilot, I drove a few blocks ahead and

pulled off into a small park, then dialed on my phone. There was one person who knew Logan even better than I did.

It rang multiple times before it went to voicemail. I dialed the same number incessantly until Caleb's angry voice shouted back.

"WHAT!?"

"Why did Logan nearly beat a man to death!?" It was a hell of a greeting—not that his was much better. But it was clear I was interrupting something.

"Shit, one sec." I heard rustling, and his voice dissolved into the background. "Don't even *think* about moving that ass, understand? Good. I'll be right back."

Another moment passed before he spoke again—this time to me. "What's going on, Cassie?"

"Logan's in trouble."

"Yeah, I heard. Good news is he's innocent, and your man has more connections than anyone I know. He'll be fine."

"No, he won't. It's not official yet, but…he's going to be named the official suspect."

There was a long pause. "Shit. All right, listen to me: Logan will get through this, okay? Just give him some space to work it out. Now, I gotta go."

"Are you *kidding* me!?" I snapped, no longer able to keep it in. "He's supposed to be your best friend! He's running the paper, raising a son, and dealing with possible murder charges all on top of handling *your* shit at Haven! Real good friend you are!"

"Damn, don't think I've ever heard you swear before. Bet Logan loves that." He sounded impressed, which only sent my rage higher.

"You need to come home, with Hilary, and man up!"

"I don't have time for this. Logan knows where to find me, and if he needed me, he'd call, which he has. As far as

Haven, you're right, but I called in two good buddies the other day to come down and watch over the place. We good?"

Now he just sounded bored, which pissed me off even more.

"No! Tell me about the fight. The Logan I know wouldn't attack an innocent man with a baseball bat."

"That's because he didn't," he snapped.

"Oh, *right*, so someone else did it?"

"Oh, no, that was all Logan. I was there. He wouldn't let me do anything other than watch, and it was a hell of a show. But the guy was far from innocent."

"Keep going."

He blew out an agitated breath. "Look, this isn't my story to tell. Talk to Logan."

"What's wrong? Don't want to spill a friend's *secret*?" I hissed.

"Cassandra." It was a low warning—and one I ignored.

"No, you stormed into my boyfriend's house, screaming and pointing fingers, not to mention scaring a four-year-old all because I kept someone *else's* secret. You owe me!"

Feeling proud for laying it out there, I was hit with a slug to the gut when Caleb had the gall to burst out laughing.

"First of all, Oliver has never and *will* never be afraid of me. Second, you're right, and I owe you an apology. I lost my cool; Hilary does that to me. But I already paid up for that."

"Paid up?" *What the hell does that mean?*

"You really think Logan let me out of that house without adding to my suffering? Bastard left me walking away with a black eye and split lip."

"What? Why?" Logan knew Caleb was hurting, desperate to find Hilary, yet he fought him? Whom exactly was I dating?

Caleb chuckled again. "Cassandra, I know Logan, and I knew before I even arrived that morning that he'd make me regret my decision. But I didn't care. I took both hits and a cheap knee to my gut all while listening to him explain what I already knew: Nobody comes at his woman like I did. It's why I respect the man."

"Because he kicked your ass?"

Caleb snickered. "No, because he protects what's his. And you were doing the same for Hilary: protecting her by keeping that secret. I get it, and I respect you for it. I'm sorry. It's water under the bridge. So we good now? 'Cause I got some things going on here that need my attention."

How the hell could he sound so calm? It didn't matter, but one thing did.

"So you won't tell me about Logan's fight with the baseball bat?"

"No, but I'll help you out." His voice was friendly, yet impatient. "Talk to Julia."

"Julia?" That caught me by surprise.

"She's one of the few people he'd kill for—you should know that. She'll have your answers. I need to go."

"No, you *need* to come home and support your friend when he needs it most, like he's done for you. If you and Hilary are fine now, don't leave the rest of us *un*fine. And tell Hilary to call—*soon*. She doesn't get to throw a tit fit, get me verbally attacked, and run off only to be chased and punished with your penis when I haven't had five minutes with my man in over a week!" I rushed out before he could hang up.

"Not gonna be for a while, but she'll call."

The call disconnected. I sank back against my seat, watching kids laughing as they went down the slide one after another. It was tempting to follow suit as I remembered how much easier life was when I was younger. Even with a single mother who worked too much, I at least knew what to expect on a daily basis. Now, I was at a loss.

My world was rocked once again. But at least I'd gotten a few things off my chest.

Chapter Twenty-Three

Control

I walked around the park for over an hour, circling the grounds and even enjoying a hot chocolate with extra whipped cream from the vendor who passed through.

I'd messaged Julia, asking her to meet me, and by the time the sun was setting I was sitting next to her on a bench outside Haven. I'd refused to meet her inside; I wasn't quite ready to involve Logan, whom I could see sitting at the bar, oblivious to the fact that I was near. I spotted only a broad back covered in a grey T-shirt and short hair with a slight wave, but I recognized him instantly as I stared through the large window in front of the sidewalk.

"So what's up?" Julia asked, too cheerful for the conversation I was about to explore. But that didn't stop me. Without peace of mind, I was practically crippled with 'what if's.

"I need to ask you something. And I know it's not my business, but I just…I just need to understand."

Her smile faltered but didn't drop. "Sure, what is it?"

"I know about Logan being arrested for attacking a man with a bat. Do you know why he'd do that?"

Julia's smile vanished that time, a tight frown its gloomy

replacement. She was no longer relaxed and jovial; her entire posture had changed. From the look of it, I'd struck an unfriendly chord. She didn't speak, staring down at her lap and fidgeting with her gloved hands. She crossed and uncrossed her legs, as though neither position was comfortable, then finally cleared her throat and looked over at me with a slight pink hue to her cheeks that wasn't there before.

"Cassandra, I don't want to go there. The charges were dropped. I just want to move on."

My thoughts ran rampant, straight to my worst fear. The image of Kurt holding me down flashed across my mind, and my heart sank.

She'd been hurt. Attacked, maybe—raped?

"I'm so sorry." Moisture struck my eyes as I spoke, my tone soft and sympathetic. Whatever had happened, Logan was obviously protecting his sister or making the guy pay for hurting her, which were both good-enough reasons for me. "I understand wanting to move on—"

"Wait!" she shrieked, her expression filled with horror. "Stop looking at me like that. I wasn't hurt or anything. It wasn't like that."

"Oh, I just assumed—"

"Logan was pissed because I was sixteen and got a tattoo."

"What?" My entire face scrunched.

She blew out a long, embarrassed groan. "It was in a back room at some lame party, and I ended up getting an infection. The tattoo artist was like fifty and brought everyone beer and pot. He did a bunch of work that night and said there was no charge for girls."

"Sounds like a sleaze," I mumbled.

Her cheeks flushed brighter. "I don't know what I was thinking. Anyway, I had to go on antibiotics…which led to me having to tell my parents, who told Logan, who went apeshit."

She lifted her jacket and shirt to reveal a bright-purple shape of what I guessed was supposed to be a butterfly, with crooked wings.

"Did he do it in the dark?" I blurted without thinking.

She dropped her jacket and puffed out an insulted sigh.

"Sorry," I said, but my apology was too late. I couldn't help it—that was the worst so-called butterfly I'd ever seen, and definitely qualified for some cover-up work.

"So I take it Logan hates tattoos?" My hand shot over my hip, where my own body art was hidden. Oh, I was in trouble.

"It wasn't that. It was more the fact that his underage sister was drinking and smoking weed at a party, and then found herself in a dirty room getting an unsanitary tattoo from a man way too old to be there. It's my own fault. I should have asked to make sure he was using a fresh needle, but I was drunk!"

"I'm understanding your brother's rage a bit more."

"My friend got one right before me and it looked cute. How was I supposed to know it would get infected? Luckily I didn't catch any diseases, but it didn't matter. Logan wouldn't even look at me, he was so mad. It was right after we met Caleb, so they searched the guy out together and Logan broke his hands. The bat belonged to one of the guy's buddies that tried to intervene. Long story short, Logan's unstoppable when he's pissed. Add in the fact that it had to do with his *baby sister*, and I'm sure you can paint your own picture of how things went down."

"I sure can," I muttered.

"You have to understand: Logan's always looked out for me and Jax. And Natasha had just left him, so he wasn't exactly a happy-go-lucky sort of guy."

"Obviously." I was at a loss, which had been happening a

lot lately. I felt like a one-woman episode of *CSI*, but on rewind. Here I was, setting up meetings and questioning everyone about the man I thought I knew as well as he did me, yet I'd barely spoken to him over the past week. And even though he currently sat only thirty feet from me, it still felt worlds away.

"I felt like crap when he was arrested. Oliver was still a baby. It was Caleb that saved him from real jail time. He broke into the tattoo artist's apartment and found some videos of the perv screwing around with some underage girls. One trip to the hospital later and all charges were dropped. As far as the tattoo, I'm waiting for Jax to cover it for me."

"Waiting?"

"Yeah, till he saves up for some equipment. He wants to open his own shop one day. I'll be his first customer." She sounded proud, and her smile returned.

One day? It looked like twins didn't tell each other everything. As much as I wanted to, now wasn't the time to divulge that fact that Jax not only had high-end equipment stashed in his bedroom, but also that half the campus already comprised his clientele.

We sat for a few more minutes chatting about lighter topics, such as Oliver and how he was staying at his grandma's until Monday night. Logan didn't strike me as the type of father to allow his son to miss a day of school, which had me even more worried.

Did he know about the DA's decision? Was that why he'd come home early—to see me? I might've felt better about his police record, but considering everything else happening, it didn't matter.

After a quick goodbye to Julia, I entered Haven, still harboring some resentment for being thrown out of Logan's house but ready to explain and work things through with him.

He needed me now more than ever, and I needed my man.

I stole a quick stop to the ladies' room to pee and check my face, which was in dire need of under-eye concealer. I compromised by swiping on some clear lip gloss, then left the restroom and sneaked up to the bar.

But he wasn't there. After surveying the room, I came up empty on seeing the broad shoulders and charming smirk I missed.

I snared a seat at the bar and flagged the bartender. He walked right over with a bright, welcoming smile in place. Surprisingly, it did wonders for my mood.

"Hey, what can I get you?"

"I'm looking for Logan. Is he still here?"

"Uh, yeah. I'm, ah, not sure where he went though. Give me a sec to check, all right?"

"Sure."

The blaring music surrounding me faded to a dull rumble. I watched the bartender walk away and gaze indiscreetly back in my direction, looking uneasy.

Something happened.

My focus remained on him as he stepped out from behind the bar and walked up to a waitress. He dipped his head and whispered into her ear, throwing a cautious, sidelong glance my way and nudging his head toward the stairs in the corner, which I knew led to the hotel rooms.

My stomach dropped and heart sputtered. I shoved off from the counter and approached them, still huddled and whispering.

"Where is he?" I demanded, my gaze darting between

them.

"I'm sorry, but he went upstairs a few minutes ago," the waitress replied. "You just missed him."

The explanation didn't match the pity written all over her face. Logan kept a room up there, and if he'd been drinking all day, it would make sense that he'd stay there. It was better than driving drunk.

"Okay, so why all the whispers?" I asked.

The bartender sneaked away, not even looking my way in the process while the waitress twirled a dishrag in her hand. She opened her mouth to speak, then closed it again. My pulse pounded, sweat beading at the nape of my neck.

"Just tell me."

"He didn't go up alone."

As though someone had sounded a starting pistol, I was off before she said another word. I raced up the stairs two at a time, experiencing a case of déjà vu. *I did this with Mark.* If Logan was up there with another woman, I wouldn't walk away without my own police record.

I didn't even stop outside his door, busting it open to face the scene behind it.

Logan was lying flat on his back on the bed, his shirt missing but hanging around one arm, pants exactly where they should be: on his body. His eyes were closed, almost peacefully.

Natasha stood beside him, her skanky tube dress resting at her feet. Her cheap black lace panties were almost as repulsive as her fake tits.

She couldn't act any better than she could shop for decent underwear, either. The amusement in her eyes spoke louder than the hand she placed strategically over her supposed-to-look-stunned mouth. She didn't even bother to shield her breasts.

"Cassandra, I'm sorry. It just happened."

Rolling my eyes at the obvious performance, I stormed over to the bed, yelling Logan's name. He didn't even flinch. He was out cold.

"I know this hurts right now, but Logan and I have so much history. You can't be that surprised."

Was she trying to sound sympathetic? Because it wasn't working.

I lowered my ear to Logan's chest. He was breathing. That was a good sign.

"I tried to tell him we should talk to you first—let him break things off before we started up again—but he didn't want to wait. One thing led to another, and we just ended up here in bed together."

Why was she still talking? She tilted her head to the side, watching me smooth back Logan's tousled hair. The incessant urge to knock him around a bit was unbearable. How had he gotten himself into this mess? The man was in for it when he woke up, but I had someone else to deal with first.

I recaptured my senses, preparing myself for a long-awaited battle. I lifted my head slowly, piercing Natasha with a sharp stare, seeing through every tawdry façade she'd ever attempted to parade around.

"You should probably go," she said, having the audacity to speak to me with determination—almost condescension—in her words.

Was she insane, or just stupid? I was ready to find out once and for all.

My laughter was harsh and menacingly brittle when I finally opened my mouth. "You've got some nerve."

"We never meant for you to find us like this," she tried to reason.

"*Find* you like this? Like what, exactly—about to rape my

boyfriend?" I stepped around the bed, moving toward her.

"Are you blind? We just went two rounds in that bed."

More laughter erupted from my throat. "Right, well, considering I was told he's only been up here a few minutes, I call bullshit. Logan isn't a minute man, *and* he prefers to sleep nude when he finishes." I waved my hand over his fully clothed legs, then nudged my head to the shirt around his bicep. "What happened—his unconscious body too heavy to undress?"

"You can believe what you want, Cassandra. I know the truth."

"The only truth I want right now is whether he passed out drunk or you drugged him."

"I don't need to drug a man to—"

"Obviously you do."

I stepped closer until I was only a few feet away from her. It put her on edge; I could see that clearly. *Good. You mess with a woman's man, you should be very afraid of the consequences.*

She snatched her dress from the floor, pulling it back over her hips and up to cover her breasts. *Finally!*

"You and Logan are through. You need to accept that," she said, trying to sound reasonable.

I wanted to laugh, although I didn't find it funny.

"No, we're not. I know Logan. He wouldn't do this to me."

"You know *nothing* about him. I'm the mother of his child! You think just because he moved in next door to you and sweet-talked his way into your panties that he actually *loves* you? What a joke. You're just a passing amusement."

"Here's the thing, Natasha: I couldn't care less what you think about my connection with Logan. It doesn't involve you, and you'll never understand what he and I have. It wasn't some love-at-first-sight, superficial romance. We built this relationship one strong, honest brick at a time, and *nothing* you do will destroy that."

Her sneer deepened. "He'll get bored of you."

Serenely calm, I replied, "Maybe. But it doesn't change the fact that I'm here now. You really think Logan would ever want you back after you abandoned him and your child? And let's not forget about taking advantage of his kid brother, who had only pure intentions that you used against him."

"Jax wanted *me*!" she exclaimed, looking surprised at my knowledge.

I shook my head, folding my arms across my chest. "You used him. And it worked out great for you too, huh? Jax is so ashamed of what he did, so *terrified* of Logan finding out, that he'll do practically anything you want—well, almost, considering he confessed everything to me. I'm guessing you didn't ask him to do that.

"Do you see what's happening here, Natasha? Your desperate plans are falling apart all around you. Logan's going to find out soon enough, and then what? What big scheme are you going to run next before Logan kicks you out of Oliver's life for good?"

"Logan can't do anything," she barked, fury heavy in her tone. "He'll be sitting in prison, and Oliver will be with me, away from all of you."

I felt sick. "What did you do?"

"Nothing. I didn't have to. Seems luck might be on my side for once. Kurt's death was a happy coincidence."

My arms dropped, hands balling into tense fists at my sides. "You won't get custody of Oliver if Logan goes away."

She looked smug, her grin too bright. "Then who will? *You?*" She chuckled darkly. "You're not even family."

I moved forward until I was inches from her face. "Trust me, *nobody* in Logan's family is going to let you take Oliver anywhere."

"Watch me," she spit back.

My palm connected with her cheek, fast and hard. It wasn't planned—it was purely an instinctual act, but not one I regretted. It felt amazing; the sting was totally worth it.

She stumbled back, speechless, her eyes wide.

"Get out—NOW!" I shouted, watching her cradle her red cheek and scurry around for her heels before she ran out, slamming the door behind her.

Chapter Twenty-Four

SPURNED

Battling through a field of cumbersome emotions, I gazed down at Logan. He looked so gorgeous and serene.

I wanted to slap the hell out of him.

But it would do no good, considering he wouldn't even feel it, so I went the opposite route. I removed my shoes, slid out of my jeans, and crawled into bed beside him, resting against the headboard and cradling his head in my lap. He never budged—not even a twitch.

There was no way he'd gotten that drunk. No matter how scary the thought was, I knew Natasha must have slipped him something. *Bitch*.

I fought back my rising fury, needing to deal with her later and take care of Logan first. I stroked his cheek, my heart swelling, eyes brimming with tears. I loved this man more than anything, and would protect him from everything within my power.

That was the reason I stayed awake checking his pulse and watching for any signs of distress. When I felt confident enough that there would be no trips to the ER in our immediate future, my eyes slid shut in the darkness.

It wasn't long before I woke to the feeling of warm breath

caressing my stomach.

"Sweetheart...so perfect."

His almost-tangible words pressed against my chest. My eyes fluttered open, a deliciously familiar mass weighing me down.

Logan's head was lost amongst my breasts; my shirt was pulled up, breast freed from my bra and bathed in the warmth of his soft lips. I melted against the sensual and tender sensation. He lavished one nipple, then the next with his exquisite tongue. My head dipped back, an unstoppable moan clawing its way up from my throat.

It wasn't long until his movements began to slow and I felt his body relax. He was tired—or still reeling from whatever toxin had taken up residence in his system.

My fingers trailed slowly up and down the curve of his bicep, tracing the outline of muscle, soothing him into a slumber. Moments later, he abruptly ceased his swirling tongue over my pebbled peak, his entire body going slack.

He was falling asleep again.

"Logan," I whispered, trying to squelch my concern.

There was a long pause before he slurred, "My angel. Always here."

"I'm not going anywhere," I confessed.

"I know," he said in a somewhat incoherent murmur. "Gonna marry you."

My breath caught and I froze, my hand stiff against his elbow.

Seconds ticked by, and he didn't speak again. My brain sputtered. Was I supposed to respond? I didn't move an inch, listening as his breath began to even out, his body idling.

He was asleep.

I blew out a long-winded stream of air to unload my lungs, forcing myself to unwind. He'd been talking in his sleep—nothing more. *Forget you heard it*, I reasoned to myself.

My fingers weaved through his short wavy hair, relishing the feeling of him sprawled over me. I couldn't imagine waking up without him in my life, but there was no way I was ready for that kind of commitment. But of course I couldn't erase the subject from my mind, instead finding myself focusing solely on what it would be like to be married to Logan West.

There was no denying how much the idea of spending the rest of my life with him lit me from the inside and placed not-so-subtle hints of bliss around my thoughts. I closed my eyes, reprimanding myself for foolishly hoping for something way too early to explore, but just knowing he felt that way, even subconsciously, eased me back into my own sleep with a smile.

The next time I woke, Logan was sitting up beside me. The room was still dark.

My eyes popped opened, instantly shaking me to the here and now when they met Logan's glazed-over pale blue depths staring over at me. The intensity they held was startling.

"Are you all right?" I asked, stifling a yawn as I propped myself up higher against the headboard. He remained silent, his eyes pinning me in place.

"Logan?" Something was wrong. He sat lifeless, his face pained. "What can I do?"

It was then that he spoke, his words blasting through my fatigue.

"Marry me."

My jaw dropped. The heat from his gaze grew warmer in the dark room, searing right through me. This wasn't like earlier—this was very much real.

No. I shook my head; he didn't know what he was saying. He wasn't with me, not really. He was still soaring from the drugs.

"Logan, you need to sleep."

He grasped my arms, pulling me into his lap.

"Marry me. Don't let me fuck things up again."

I sighed, completely drained. "Even husbands screw up," I said, which was completely true but absurd for me to even be reasoning. Why was I entertaining this? We'd barely begun to officially date. *It's been, what—a couple weeks?*

Something in my words struck him. His hands fell away, releasing me to tug through his hair. He looked lost and restless.

I sat back up beside him. "Please sleep. We can talk in the morning." And we would—about a lot of things.

His jaw clenched, the fire in his features reigniting. "Not yet. I want your answer."

I sensed pain behind his tired words and wiped my eyes, reminding myself it wasn't a dream. "Logan, tonight was all kinds of messed up. Please just sleep."

His features hardened. "You love me. I know you do."

I reached out and caressed the stubble of his cheek, desperate to soothe him. "Of course I do, and I always will. I'm not going anywhere. But we need to talk about things…in the morning, not now."

His hand covered mine against his cheek, moving it over so he could kiss my palm. The act was so tender, yet his expression remained bleak.

"Marry me. We can leave tomorrow—go to Vegas and make you mine forever."

My shoulders slumped on a sigh. It wasn't exactly a girl's dream wedding, though it did match the sudden, unromantic proposal.

I maneuvered myself back, needing space to think of a response that would settle his restlessness. But he didn't allow it, snaring my knees to lock me in place.

"I'm sorry. I can't marry you—not right now, amidst

everything going on. And to be honest, I'm pretty sure when that sun rises you won't even remember this conversation. Now lay down," I said, keeping my voice gentle but stern. "You need to rest."

Logan didn't reply, his expression slipping to one of stoic regard. I was about to speak again when he hauled me back into his arms, scooting us down to lie flat. He held me snugly against his chest, my head resting over his beating heart. He didn't push the issue again, and I was thankful.

When my eyes closed, my thoughts flipped between Logan's unexpected proposal and all the drama surrounding us. I was unable to fall asleep but grateful when his grip loosened, knowing he'd been able to.

Moments later, thinking he was fast asleep, I heard him murmur, "I'll remember."

At some point early the next morning, I woke alone in bed. I shot up and threw my feet off the side, relief replacing the growing panic inside me when I picked up the sound of water running in the en suite across the room.

He was awake, and apparently feeling strong enough for a shower. After falling back into bed, I rolled over and stared up at nothing.

Logan had proposed. He'd done it while possibly drugged, but still, he wanted to marry me. And judging by the stampede of butterflies in my gut, I knew he was the one. We'd been through so much together, and there would never be anyone else I could love more.

But I had no idea what I'd say when or if he asked me about it once he reentered the room. It all felt so rushed—not to mention I was still spinning from the last couple days. Last night wasn't the time to show him just how much damage control he had to endure, but today, if he was conscious, he was fair game. There was no way he was walking out of that room without a damn good explanation of what he planned to do about the Natasha problem.

I sat up when I heard the shower shut off. A few moments later, Logan stepped out with a towel around his waist, his hair wet and unruly.

My thighs squeezed together—my body's typical reaction at the sight of him. Yeah, I could marry him. The man was every woman's fantasy, and had one of the kindest hearts I'd ever known. He'd love me and protect me.

Knowing this led me to an overly confident mood, and as I crawled out of the blankets and across the bed, I was sure he'd hear me out.

"How do you feel?" I asked, starting with a little honey before the bees came out.

"Headache. The shower helped some."

He looked distant, like he was contemplating something, and his gaze flickered around the room before settling on me. He didn't say anything else, and regarded me with an inquisitive stare instead of his usual bright look of adoration and lust.

Was he trying to remember what happened the previous night, or wondering what he'd been thinking by asking me to marry him? Either way, I wasn't feeling so hot under his scrutiny.

I sat up on my knees and held out my hands for him to come closer. "We should talk."

He sighed and walked toward me hesitantly, stopping just out of my reach.

My arms dropped. He wasn't going to make this easy. It was hard to yell at someone who looked so miserable.

Before I could start, he sighed. "I know you didn't screw around with Jax. It's been a long week, and seeing you two in bed together was a breaking point. I'm sorry. I was a dick."

"I know. I mean, that you're sorry, not the dick part." I chuckled, but the humor was lost on him.

"I need to call my mother and check on Oliver. Didn't plan on being out all night. He'll be worried that I didn't call to say goodnight."

The air was thick and uncomfortable. "Right. I think Natasha's to blame for that."

"Yeah." He blew out a breath and raked a hand through his wet hair, looking exhausted. "I'll deal with her later. You need a ride home?"

"My car's here, and we'll deal with her now. Do you even know what happened last night?"

Logan didn't reply, instead moving farther away. "I've got to make some calls. We'll talk later."

"That's it?" I scoffed, scooting off the bed.

He didn't bother to look at me as he opened a door to reveal a small chest of drawers and a couple suits on a hanging bar. "I've got things to do right now." He grabbed a suit and shut the door.

"No, we're going talk *right now*. Natasha was all over you last night. I found you in this room, with her, and she was naked. Ring a bell? If I hadn't come up here…"

He pivoted around. His expression was no longer pained—it was all agitation.

"I had a drink and she sat down at the bar beside me. Last thing I expected was for her to slip me something." His phone rang. "Shit, I've got to take this. I'll call you later."

"You were out cold last night. How do you even *know* what she did to you? Do you even care!?" I yelled, irate.

His eyes narrowed dangerously. "I know she didn't get

what she wanted, considering I still had pants on when I woke up and my dick would have been incapable of an erection. You're standing here and she's not, which is the only thing I *care* about. We'll finish this later."

He kissed me quickly on the cheek and, despite my stunned expression, headed back into the bathroom with the phone to his ear.

It was an insult. Did he really believe a kiss would pacify an overlooked-once-again girlfriend? After this week, he was severely wrong.

I saw red. This wasn't a relationship—and definitely not one headed toward wedding bells. I was fed up with him pushing me away.

My rage pushed me out of the room, down the stairs, and past the bar before I heard someone call my name.

I whirled around to see Luke and Julia in a booth together.

"You all right?" Julia asked.

"No, I'm not. And you won't be either if you don't open your eyes and see that you have one of the best guys in this town waiting around for you! Don't ruin it."

Julia gasped, caught off guard by my abrupt and slightly harsh honesty. I shifted my gaze to Luke, and his lips quirked up as he sipped his soda. "Fight for her. You guys belong together."

I started walking again, adding my final words they both needed to hear before I left the building.

"Logan won't do a damn thing to stop you."

Chapter Twenty-Five

COLLIDE

The sky outside may have been clear, but it was a dreary Sunday inside my home. I spent it stewing, switching from rage to sorrow between bags of potato chips. Logan didn't call or text, and his car never appeared in his driveway. I checked more times than I cared to admit.

It was sometime that afternoon when I was hit with a realization that floored me: I was sitting around and wasting a beautiful day for a man too busy to make time for me. He'd kicked me out of his home, put himself in a compromising situation with his ex, and then blown me off without letting me get a word in edgewise.

I wasn't blind, nor was I insensitive. I knew he was in trouble, and that he needed me as a supporter, rallying around him. And I'd always be there for him as one, but I wouldn't be a punching bag. We were either in this relationship together, or he was going to get only one side of me: friend Cassandra.

My phone was in my hand. I knew the perfect distraction was only a call away, and I wasn't going to stop dialing until Hilary answered.

She picked up on the third call.

"Cassie! Hey, Caleb told me about Logan and Kurt. Are

you okay?"

The tension rolled out through my limbs upon hearing her voice. "Not really. Everything turned to crap after you ran off. I need you back home."

I heard her sigh. "I know. I would be there tonight if I could."

"What's stopping you—Caleb?" That ticked me off. I'd never thought of Caleb as the controlling type, but then again, how was I supposed to know how he was in a relationship?

"Yeah, he says he has some plans for us. I'm just relieved he's still here with me, but I have no clue what's going to happen. He won't give me a clear answer when I ask about the baby or our future."

"He wouldn't be there if he didn't want you. Enjoy the time together—you'll miss it after the baby arrives." I wanted Hilary to be happy more than anything. I just wished I was alone with my man, as well. "At least Caleb and you are talking. That must be nice."

Hilary chuckled. It was muffled and short, but I heard it. "Conversation isn't exactly Caleb's top priority. I'm hoping that will change soon."

"Looks like Caleb and Logan have more in common than I realized. Where is he, anyway?" I asked.

"He ran out to grab us some dinner. So has there been any word on who killed Kurt? Caleb's pretty insistent Logan had nothing to do with it," she said, concern crippling her voice.

"Not yet, and no, Logan didn't do this," I told her, my voice rising in candor.

"I know. You got a good man. I miss you, and I'm only a phone call away. Promise you'll call if you need anything." Her tone grew impatient.

"Yeah, I will," I said, unsure what had changed.

"Sorry, I have to go. He's back." Panic riddled her voice.

"Hilary, are you all right?" I sat up straight on the couch.

"We'll talk soon. Love you, and take care," she finished hurriedly, and then the line disconnected before I could respond.

Seemed I wasn't the only one with an unconventional relationship at the moment.

After convincing myself she was safe regardless of whatever was happening between her and Caleb, I finished the day with a good book and a bottle of wine. It wasn't until late that night when my thoughts drifted to Logan once again. And he must've sensed it, because my phone chimed with a new message from him at the same time.

I'm coming over.

I smiled, feeling a burden of weight lift. Finally we could at least talk.

Good. We have a lot to discuss.

Not tonight. Need to touch u. Feel myself lost in every part of that perfect body.

I never thought those words coming from him could repel me in any way, but they did. I would not be his whore. I wanted to be his everything, exactly how he used to make me feel—not just a body to be used at his convenience.

Already in bed. Too sleepy.

Looking heavenward, I sent up silent pleas that he'd see the error of his ways and offer me more. I'd even settle for cuddling as a compromise.

U can just lay there and let me play ;)

My phone was nothing but an evil nemesis waiting to be destroyed for delivering such a cruel blow. I was livid, ready to reply with words I wouldn't be able to take back. But instead, I beat the hell out of a pillow before replying with dignity.

Goodnight Logan

I didn't wait for his reply, but when the phone hadn't pinged again even an hour later, it took everything I had to endure my trampled emotions. He didn't even care enough to text back. He was either busy—the norm these days—or pissed off and ignoring me. Either option hurt.

I drew the blankets up over my head and pulled my knees to my chest, curling up in a ball and closing my eyes. Tears came and went, and before I knew it the sun was illuminating the room. I hadn't slept more than an hour or two; my brain had refused to shut down.

Still, I was out of bed with my hair pulled up in a high ponytail. I dressed in sweats and a T-shirt, threw on my icy-weather necessities, slipped into my running shoes, and was jogging down my driveway by seven a.m. The sun was bright, and the snow that had blown in overnight was already melting.

As I neared the turnaround point on my path, I felt Logan behind me. His scent—a mix of soap and masculinity—smacked me in the face before I even saw him.

The memory I held of the first morning I'd crossed the road to head back and noticed him behind me flashed through my mind. We'd come so far from that day.

I slowed, allowing him to fall in step beside me. His stare was set ahead of him, never once turning to connect with mine.

"Hey. How long have you been back there?" My smile was friendly, my voice tight.

His entire expression was impassive and his pace matched mine, giving nothing away. It was too early to fight. Plus, I missed us jogging together, so I smiled wider and nudged his arm with my elbow.

"Fine, don't talk to—" I started, nearly falling backward when he shot in front of me and stopped abruptly.

His eyes held mine, calculating and alarmingly dark. "Why

didn't you wait for me to join you?"

"I wasn't sure you were running this morning." My hands flew to my hips; I was instantly on the defense. "You haven't for a while." I watched while the white smoke of our breaths mingled.

"Is that so?" he asked, his voice lowering. "Or were you worried I'd just want to fuck you out here?"

I recoiled at how bitter he made the words sound. He stalked toward me, and my body stayed fixed in place.

"I know you're mad at me and I know I've been a shitty boyfriend lately, but I can't do this without you." He caught me off guard when he gripped my forearms and leaned in, whispering, "I won't lose you."

"Then stop pushing me away." My whisper trembled. "Let me be here for you."

"You're here now." His breath tickled across my neck.

"It's not enough. I want you to talk to me—to trust me as much as I trust you." My head lowered, and his finger was right there to lift it back up so our eyes met.

"I know, but right now I need you, sweetheart. Only you." His hands dipped down the back of my sweats, grasping my ass.

Not fair. My entire body quaked as a current shot through me. It felt so right, yet so wrong.

Logan's eyes lit up, the stubble over his jaw scorching against my cheek. "You love me? Then *trust me*. Give me this."

One hand slipped around to the front of my panties, cupping my sex that was already wet and wanting.

I couldn't stop myself when my head lifted, my mouth meeting his. He took full control, gliding his tongue across my lips before parting them and delving in.

His arms encased me in their bulk, hands freeing themselves from my pants so he could seize the backs of my thighs. He hitched up my legs, carrying me a few feet just off the road until my back hit the trunk of a stout old tree.

"Logan," I gasped, needing oxygen—needing him.

His mouth slid over my cheek and up to my ear, his teeth capturing my lobe and biting down. "I love every single thing about you. This isn't just sex for me, and you know it. But right now, I need to feel you."

"Ahhh," I moaned, unable to control it.

His chilly hands were everywhere, ravenous as they caressed under my coat, skimmed up my stomach, then stilled briefly over the bandage hiding my tattoo.

I waited for him to say something, but he continued his ascent, his deft fingers fondling my breast. He obviously knew it was a tattoo, or else he would've been concerned I was injured.

His fingers made their way up under my sports bra, arousing me further and tossing all thoughts from my head. He unzipped my coat just enough to pull my breasts free, growling in approval before taking the peak of one into his mouth.

My hands were around his neck, pulling off my gloves so I could feel him, touch him, experience every sensation. As my nipple slid from his lips, I was all but burrowing against him.

Wet, open-mouthed kisses were placed along my neck until he reached my lips and claimed them once more. My fingers tugged at his light coat and my palms slipped underneath, taking in as much of his broad chest as possible.

Unexpectedly, he released me from the hand that'd been holding me in place and slid it into the waistband of my yoga pants, hooking my panties and drawing them down. He released me long enough to slip one leg out before I was pinned between him and the tree once more.

The hunger that fueled us both threw me deeper into a wanton haze. I shoved his black running pants down and slid my hand between our bodies, wrapping my fingers around his hard, velvety length. With his mouth on mine, he thrust into me.

"So good!" he barked out, plunging harder and faster.

My eyes rolled back, chest heaving, legs wrapped tightly around his hips. His fingers gripped my ass, the pressure divine. Spiraling, I began to shake, thrashing in his arms.

"Stay. Away. From. Jax," he demanded with each thrust.

What? Where the hell did that come from? I could hardly process his demand, but I knew it was ridiculous. He tilted my hips, sending his cock deeper.

I cried out, unable to control my impending orgasm.

"Promise me, Cassandra!"

I couldn't answer. It felt so good—so perfect. My hands were tugging his coat up over his back, desperate to feel his skin.

"Promise me!" he called out again, irritating me that he was using this moment to make demands.

His lips devoured mine as I finally found my word and screamed, "No!"

My nerves were on fire, tightening and ready to explode. I should've pushed him away and proven that I wasn't someone he could manipulate with sex, but I'd spent too much time the past few months doing just that. I was greedy now—taking what was coiling deep in my gut, exploding over him a moment later.

"Logan!" I screamed as my body began pulsating with spasms of ecstasy.

He was continuing to thrust, not yet having reached his own climax, when I yanked my legs free. He fought to hold me close, desperate for his release, but that wasn't happening.

"Let me go!" My words escaped through gritted teeth, and he pulled away so quickly he nearly dropped me. He held his swollen cock, pumping it in his hand.

"I can see whoever the hell I want—including Jax."

"Fuck!" he growled, his gaze shooting toward the sky. His hand slowed, erection softening into an angry red beast. It wasn't fair of me, but then again he was the one who'd brought Jax into the mix.

After righting my bra, I bent down to pull my pants back on. With rough breaths and my head in a fog, I watched his eyes darken. A car passed by, reminding me I hadn't paid any attention whether others *had* during our incredible tryst. Odds weren't on my side.

"I'm going home. You can either come with me and we can talk things through, or you can stand there glaring at my back. Your choice."

"I need to go pick Oliver up from my mother's," he explained more calmly than he appeared. His lips were pressed together in a thin line, jaw clenched tightly.

My brows pinched together. "I thought he was staying till tomorrow night."

"Change of plans." His pants snapped against his taut waist when he pulled them back up. "I'll walk you home."

"Logan, please talk to me. I hate this."

He gazed at me a moment longer, then took my hand, guiding us back to the road.

"Things might go bad with this case, Cassandra. If they do, I want you far away from it."

Tears sprung to my eyes as I took in his defeated expression. He knew about the DA.

"Logan—"

"I won't go down for something I didn't do. That won't happen. But it looks like it may be a hell of a fight." He pressed my hand to his lips. "I love you—nothing will ever change that. I just need time to focus on beating this, all right?"

"Yeah." I wrapped my arms around his neck, needing to feel fully embraced by his strength. "Is that why you came home early?"

He nodded, holding me close as I rested my head against him. "I needed to see you. I don't know when, but they're going to bring me in for more questions. It's getting serious. My lawyer's doing everything he can, and I have a couple PIs looking into other possible leads. I need to focus all my energy on finding out what really happened to Kurt."

My sobs were unrestrained. Logan drew back and reached out to cup my cheeks, wiping away the streaming tears.

"I'm not trying to push you away—I swear it. I spend every day lately talking to lawyers, private investigators, detectives, and my family, all needing to *talk*. I do trust you, Cassandra—more than most of them—but only you can give me what I *need*. Please don't make me have to repeat every night to you what I've spent hours going over with them."

His lips pressed to my own quivering ones before he continued. "When we're together, I want to hold you, love you, and experience the solace I only find there during those fleeting moments in time. I can't lose you."

"You won't. Anything you need—I'm yours." My eyes closed, vulnerability uninhibited. "I don't want to go to bed at night angry with you, or alone. I just need to feel like I'm not forgotten."

He kissed me harder, resting his forehead against mine when he broke the kiss. My eyes closed, and I felt his words soothe every neglected part of me.

"Never. You're with me every second of the day. Every night last week, when I got home, it was after two in the morning. The bar needed me there to close it down even though I had to be up at seven, and knowing I'd see your face before I went to bed every night got me through it."

"Wait, what nights?" My eyes shot open, and I shoved back enough to fully see his growing smirk. "I never saw you. You barely even texted."

"You really thought I wouldn't stop over? I have my own key, you know." He rattled his coat pocket. The sound of keys jingling caused my heart to swell and eased my soul.

"Why didn't you wake me up?" I asked, my grin almost painful. Tears returned to my eyes, but at least they were the happy kind.

"It was your first week back at school. I didn't want you to be tired."

"So, what, you just peeked in on me?"

His gaze dropped to the ground. "Not exactly."

I swallowed, unsure what else he could've done.

"I slept in the chair across from your bed. Set my alarm for an hour before you woke." He sounded almost embarrassed.

"Why didn't—"

"I just needed to be near you—refill my tank before another grueling day."

My arms wove back around his neck. "Next time, climb in that bed with me. Promise?"

"Promise."

I nuzzled his neck, drinking his masculine scent.

"I asked you a question last night," he said, his voice tense.

My mouth ceased its actions, words stalling on my tongue. I was stunned he remembered. I lifted my head slowly, staring at the gentleness of his features.

"Logan, I…"

"Shhh." His finger rested over my parted lips. "I don't need an answer. I hadn't planned on asking yet. But waking up to you there, knowing you believed in me, in what we have, and that I'd never hurt you with anyone—*especially* Natasha—was the most incredible feeling."

He leaned forward, his finger slipping away to allow his lips to brush across mine gently. "I'm going to ask you again after everything's settled, and I'll spend the rest of my life asking you until you're completely mine in every possible way. I'll never take no for an answer."

I had nothing to top that—just my kiss, which I gave freely.

His smile was almost sad when I broke contact. We walked home hand in hand, no words needed. We were together, and wanted the same things. That was enough…for now.

Chapter Twenty-Six

DARE

Monday was the start of a new week that held so many unknown possibilities. I'd seen Logan early that morning; we'd passed each other in the hall as he was on his way to drop Oliver off at his class. I couldn't help myself, subtly reaching my hand out from my side to brush it against his. He clasped it, our eyes speaking their own language before he released me and continued on as if he'd hadn't touched a hidden piece of me accessible to only him. It was just enough to see me through the day without worrying.

By the final bell, I was eager to get out the door, feeling giddy about the surprise I had for Oliver: Scout was coming home.

I'd spoken with Luke the previous night, listening as he explained how he'd taken my advice and demanded Julia go on an official date with him. It seemed to have worked, considering he'd just dropped her off before I'd called. She'd finally given in and confessed how much she liked him, and Luke said that no matter what Logan did, he wouldn't give up. That was all I needed to hear, and I knew Logan would smile when I relayed that little tidbit.

Luke also said Scout was a bundle of nonstop chaos,

which meant he could go home anytime. I inferred that Luke preferred sooner rather than later, based on his rant about Julia's favorite heels that Scout enjoyed playing with a little too roughly.

I cleared off the paint table in the back of my classroom and collected the items I needed from my desk into a large tote. I left the classroom and was closing the door behind me when I noticed Oliver's teacher headed my way, frown lines over her brow.

"You should go to the office," she said, something in her voice not quite right.

"Is everything all right?" I started down the hall with her at my side.

"I oversaw pickup today, and Oliver's ride never came. We called his father at home and work and haven't been able to reach him."

Logan never forgot Oliver. He wouldn't. If he was unable to make it, he would've called someone—would've called me. Anxiety rang through my limbs.

"I'll take care of it, thank you," I told her, pulling out my phone.

"No problem. I know you and Mr. West are...*close*."

My head shot up at the bitterness edging her tone.

"He's my neighbor, and yes, a *close* friend." I held onto my pleasant poise, even smiling at her—an action she mimicked before walking back the way she'd come.

I dialed Logan. Not surprised when it went straight to voicemail, I made a second, gut-wrenching call to my mom.

She answered on the second ring.

"Hi, honey."

I knew where he was just by the tone of her voice.

"Logan?" It was all I needed to say.

"Yeah, I'm sorry. They brought him in about an hour

ago."

My throat sealed, chest constricting. I needed air. "They arrested him?"

"Baby, listen to me: Logan's a fighter. He has some powerful people in his corner. He'll beat this."

She sounded so sure, but it still took every bit of strength I had to keep myself upright. My stomach twisted, temple throbbing.

"You really believe in him," I whispered, turning to face the wall.

"I know he loves my daughter, and he's a good man that will do anything to protect his family. I've seen enough to know he wouldn't destroy his son's future by doing something that would cause him to spend his life in prison."

"Can I talk to him?" I slammed my eyes shut, inhaling deeply to push away the demanding emotions boiling up.

"Sorry, not right now."

"Can you at least tell him I'll take Oliver home if he can call and give the school permission? Oliver's waiting here." Just speaking Oliver's name was all it took to assure myself I was in control. He needed me.

"Of course. Let me go see what I can do. Try to stay positive. I love you."

"Love you too, Mom."

I hung up, straightening myself and sweeping over my eyelids with my fingers, wanting to look like carefree Cassie when Oliver saw me. Determined to give him a full night of so much fun he'd be too distracted to ask where his daddy was, I made my way to the front office.

I spotted him sitting on the hallway bench just outside the door. His tiny body was hunched over as he kicked his feet back and forth.

"Hey there," I said with a broad smile.

"Cassie!" He sat up straighter and stared over at me, looking semi-relieved. "Daddy never showed up outside."

I squatted down in front of him. "I know. He had something really important that came up, and he's so sorry. If you can hang out here for a little while longer, I'll take you over to my house. You can stay there till he gets done working."

"'Kay."

He knew something was up. Kids and their pesky intuitions. More than ever, I wanted to see him smile.

I squeezed his knee, reassuring him. "If you don't mind, we're going to make a stopover at my friend Luke's house."

A small glimpse of a smile peeked out. "I like Luke."

I grinned wider. "Me too. Now hold tight, and we'll get going in a few minutes." I stood, thankful for his nod, and walked across the hall.

"Has Oliver's father called yet?" I asked the secretary.

She responded with a slight frown and shake of the head.

"I live next door to him, so when he calls, he should give permission for me to take Oliver. Did you try any family? His uncle should be around." It didn't matter who picked Oliver up. I'd take him from there.

"We tried him, but it went to voicemail," she said.

It was hard to say what Jax was up to.

"Doesn't his father own the newspaper? Maybe I should try there," she offered, already grabbing the phone book.

"I don't think he's—"

"Oliver! There you are," Natasha's exaggerated drawl rang through the halls.

I rolled my eyes with an irritated sigh when I realized there'd be only one reason she was there. No way was she on the list of acceptable people to entrust Oliver to.

"Can I see Oliver's file for the list of people with

permission to pick him up?"

"Sure." She handed it over, and one glace at it confirmed what I already knew: Natasha's name was nowhere on it.

After squaring my shoulders to face a woman who was grating my final nerve, I stepped out into the hall.

"Natasha, what are you doing here?" I asked, my mouth twisting from the bitterness of speaking her name.

"Came to get my son. Heard he needed a ride." She snatched his book bag from the floor. "Ready to go, baby?"

"Sorry, Oliver, but you'll have to visit your mom another day," I explained, feigning a sympathetic smile before snapping my attention back to Natasha. "Logan will be calling any minute to give permission for Oliver to be released to me," I said coldly. "You can go."

Natasha didn't seem fazed as she glanced between Oliver and me. "Hm, from what I've been told, he might not get a *phone call* right away. Oliver's coming with me."

"Not happening," I nearly growled, stepping forward.

"Let's get going, baby. I have to make a few stops before we go home." She held out her hand, and Oliver jumped down from the bench.

"Where we goin'?" he asked, zipping his jacket before taking her outstretched hand.

"You're not taking him," I warned again, my words monotone yet adamant.

"I'm his mother. Watch me."

I spoke over my shoulder to the secretary. "Call the police. She doesn't have any rights over Oliver, and she's not on the list."

"Police?" Oliver questioned, his gaze bouncing from me to his mother.

"Don't worry about it. Cassie's being silly. She's only pretending. Let's go." When Natasha turned and began to walk away, I shot around her, blocking her path. There was no way Oliver was going anywhere with her.

"Oliver, why don't you go in the office and wait while I speak with your mother a moment?"

He didn't complain as he attempted to tug his hand from her hold, but she wasn't letting go.

"Ouch!" he shrieked. Her grip was noticeably tight.

"Let him go—*now*," I hissed slowly.

"No, we're leaving. Josh is in the car waiting for us." She leered down at her son, who didn't move. "Come on, Oliver."

"My hand hurts." He yanked again and I grabbed Natasha's wrist, squeezing until she released him.

"Go sit in the office, Oliver," I repeated. "Now."

He did so immediately.

Natasha chuckled under her breath, watching him scurry away. "He's too sweet. Logan should have toughened him up." When she looked back, it was to meet my threatening scowl.

She rolled her eyes. "Look, Cassandra, I don't have time for your petty jealousy. Oliver is *mine*, and I'm taking him with me."

"No, you're not." I felt like cracking my knuckles to prepare for the inevitable.

"Because of you, Logan won't let me visit my own son! That's about to change, and you can't stop me. You're nothing but Oliver's neighbor, and the pathetic *girl* fucking his father."

Her lack of common decency in not bothering to watch her mouth or at least lower her voice drove me crazy. How had Logan ever wanted to marry her?

"After the other night, you should be *real* careful what you say to me. I'm done playing your games, Natasha. Oliver deserves so much better than you, and I'm proud that *my* man is smart enough to keep you away."

Natasha's nostrils flared. "You really are a dumb little

girl." She moved toward me, closing the small gap between us. Her body swayed, and her liquored-up breath hit me in the face. "You really think you have what Logan needs? You have no clue what type of man he is."

I stepped back, wiping spit from my face, disgusted but not letting it distract me. I held firm in my stance.

"Your son is in the next room, and police are on their way. I'd suggest we discuss Logan at a more appropriate time."

"You're a moron," she leaned in and whispered. "Logan loves everything about me, including *fucking* me, and you...are nothing...but a distraction—and one that has worn out her welcome."

If we were anywhere other than my place of employment and in front of her son, I would've knocked her on her drunken ass. It took everything in me to keep my fists at my sides.

"Logan won't admit it, but he misses us," she continued in a hissed whisper. "Misses what I do to him, for him...the fun we had, and how hot he'd get watching me with the girls I'd bring home to share our bed." Her menacing laugh caused my blood to boil. "You think he's a man that will settle down and spend a lifetime enduring boring old sex with a schoolteacher? You're in for a rude awakening." She sniffed, wiping her nose with the palm of her hand.

"You need to leave the premises, or you'll be arrested," I informed her, blocking out what she'd said about Logan's previous bedroom preferences. "You're drunk, and an embarrassment to your son. Go home."

"I have rights to Oliver!" she shouted, obviously interested in making a scene. Two teachers who were passing by stopped, exchanged glances, then looked to me. But my focus remained on Natasha.

"No, you don't. You gave them up the day you

abandoned him," I bit back.

"Oliver, let's go, baby!" she called out.

"Stay there, Oliver." I didn't look back to see if he was up or sticking to his seat, not wanting to take my eyes off Natasha. We stood toe to toe, our eyes daring each other to make the first move.

"I'm gonna destroy you," she taunted.

She was the first to look away. Grinning to herself, she tried to step around me toward the office. I moved with her, hindering her every time, my aggressive scowl set deep.

"I will put you on your ass if you go anywhere near him—especially while you're drunk," I threatened in a low, foreboding snarl.

"Drunk?" She cackled. "You're ridiculous. I have a fabulous life that's about to get even better once Logan gets rid of you."

"But that's the thing, isn't it?" My head tilted. "He never will. You know it, and your son is seeing your true colors right now—which aren't exactly *fabulous*, if you ask me."

"Mr. West is on the phone," the secretary said, breaking up our standoff. "He's asked to speak with you, Miss Clarke."

With a contrived smile, I turned on my heel, walked into the office, and grabbed the phone.

"Take Oliver into the nurse's station, and don't let that woman anywhere near him," I rattled off to the secretary, my hand covering the receiver.

She did so instantly as I closed the door to prevent Natasha from entering.

"Logan?" I asked, needing to hear his voice.

"Sweetheart, I only have a minute. I told them to let you take Oliver. Keep him with you. I'm not sure how long this will take or what's going to happen. I called Jax; he knows everything, and will keep you updated."

"Just take care of yourself. Don't worry about Oliver. I got him." The last thing he needed to worry about was Natasha, so I kept that situation quiet. I'd handle her myself.

"My angel…always there." I heard him sigh. "I love you, Cassandra. Tell Oliver I miss him and will be home soon."

Before I could reply, he hung up. I placed the phone back on the hook, burying my concern for Logan. I had to deal with someone else first.

Impatiently, I moved behind the desk and cracked open the door to the nurse's station.

"You ready?" I asked, smiling.

Oliver looked up somewhat reluctantly, his expression conveying a myriad of emotions.

I took his hand—the opposite of the one that was still slightly pink, the victim of Natasha's insecurity-fueled wrath—and walked him out into the hall.

"Say goodbye to your mom," I told him, keeping him close. I held out my hand for his backpack that she still held over her shoulder.

"Bye. Cassie's gonna take me to see Luke." His frown barely lifted.

As though the prior five minutes had never occurred, she drew on what some unknowing fool might call a heartwarming smile. I rolled my eyes, willing myself not to rip the bag from her outstretched hand.

"I'll see you at home, baby doll." She blew him a kiss, unable to get close enough to do more than that. "I love you—and tell your daddy I love him too."

Was she bipolar, or could she really bounce back into faux mother-of-the-year grace that quickly?

"Love you too," Oliver replied, staring after her as she walked away.

Oliver was back to his normal giddy self once he saw Scout waiting behind Luke's door. He dropped to his knees, his arms wide and ready when Scout leapt up into them. The two re-bonded seamlessly, rolling around on the floor while I thanked Luke for all his help. I didn't mention anything about Logan, as I figured Julia would fill him in if she hadn't already. On the ride home, Oliver was all giggles in the backseat, holding Scout on his lap.

Less than an hour after we arrived at my place, ready to eat dinner, Jax showed up looking like death. He slumped down onto my couch, not saying anything after his initial, "I'll kill that bitch if she had anything to do with Kurt." Luckily Oliver didn't seem to notice, as he was distracted by Scout most of the time.

If not for his occasional grunt, I'd have forgotten Jax was there too until Julia showed up with Luke a little while later. She curled up on the floor to play beside Oliver and Scout, forcing smiles until Oliver mentioned wanting to show his daddy that Scout was home.

Julia lost it, running from the room with Luke on her heels. This was a family—a real one, solid and loving, and at the center of it was Logan. He had to come home. We needed him.

By nightfall, Jax had persuaded me to let them take Oliver home for the night. We worked it out so that I'd drive him to school the next morning. It hurt to even think about how Logan wouldn't be there to do so himself.

I'd fought back demanding tears as I'd watched Jax pull Oliver aside to tell him his daddy had to go away for a meeting and would be home soon. I wasn't positive Oliver bought it, though, considering everyone sitting in my living room with somber faces and occasional hushed talk. It was mainly just speculation, though. We had no idea what was really going on.

A while after they left, I was still brokenhearted from Julia's profound hug during which she'd whispered her gratefulness for me watching out for Oliver. I'd said it was nothing, and it was the truth. No matter what happened with Logan, Oliver could always count on me.

That night, I lay in the tub, soaking in the stresses of it all. I imagined Logan behind me, his arms clutching me to his broad, powerful chest. I never wanted to leave the warmth of that fantasy, but my phone had chimed twice since I'd climbed in, and I knew if I didn't get out soon that the pruning of my fingers would be permanent.

I had a feeling it was Hilary. I missed her more than ever; she'd know what to say to make me feel better. There was always the possibility Jax had heard something from Logan, as well, but I wouldn't allow myself such hope.

I climbed out of the tub, wrapped a towel around my hair and another around my body, and trudged to my room. I sank down onto my bed, propped a pillow behind my damp back, and slid my finger across my blank phone screen. Two new messages: one from Jax and the other from my mom.

She'd never texted me before—or anyone, for that matter. I didn't even think she knew how. I was instantly on edge, opening hers first.

It's Logan. I'll be home soon. Sleep well. No tears tonight. X

My entire body sprung up and off the bed, the towel on my head unwrapping and falling down over the phone. I threw it aside, unable to control my growing smile. It was too late for no tears, but at least the ones running down my cheeks were of relief and joy.

I replied, hoping he was still around. The text had been sent only four minutes prior.

Logan? U still there?

I only had to wait a few seconds. My mom must've left her phone with him, which meant he was still at the sheriff's office and not sitting in a cell down at county. That was a good sign.

I'll explain everything tomorrow. Don't want to jinx it.

I smiled, typing so fast I wasn't even sure my words were legible.

Ok. I love u. Miss u

Ditto. U ready for the big house reveal?

Talk about subject change. What house?

What?

Julia's place. It's ready. Meet me there after school.

I wanted to laugh. After the day he'd endured, he cared about Julia's house?

It's ready?

Yes. U worried?

The bet. If Julia loved it—and I was convinced she would—I'd win, and he'd be my slave for a weekend. If she hated it...well, I had no problem spending a few days under his thumb. The thought of spending an entire weekend with him was enough. But because I didn't want him worried about me, I texted back exactly what I knew he needed to hear.

Not at all, slave boy!

Bring it on sweetheart XO

I laughed, feeling euphoric.

C u there at 4. Just got out of tub...fantasized u were in there with me, holding me.

Wish I was. Fyi This is your mother's phone remember. ;)

Oh crap! My fingers ran frantically over the keypad, typing for him to delete the message until I realized that if I had to endure seeing her boyfriend in his undies, she could read how much I adored mine.

Oh well. Lol. R U coming home tonight?

Soon…

Before I could reply, he messaged again.

Have to go. No more worrying. Promise I got this handled.

Always the protector, worrying about everyone else.

:) Goodnight. Love you. XO

Sleep well x

Chapter Twenty-Seven

HUNGER

As I pulled up outside Julia's potential new home, I was even more convinced she'd love it. The exterior was not only stunning and regal, but also held a cool modern edge. I was dying to see how the interior had changed, given all the design ideas Logan and I had gone over shortly after my car accident.

It seemed like forever ago...another world.

Logan appeared through the front door and descended the porch steps as soon as my car came to a stop in the driveway. My smile was broad, and my mood almost giddy.

"There you are," he said, opening my door.

"You said four."

He glanced mockingly at his watch. "It's two after."

I rolled my eyes with a soft giggle, placed my hand in his that was extended to me, and climbed out.

"Is Julia here?" I asked, looking around for her vehicle. I only spotted his.

"Not yet. She has an afternoon class and said she'd be here after." He led me inside, his palm resting over the small of my back.

"Oh." My heart jolted happily as I realized we were alone.

"I needed time to give you a tour before she arrived," he

explained, his eyes bright and features carefree.

As desperate as I was to know what'd happened with his case, there was no way I'd erase that boyish grin by asking about it. I longed to reach out and trace its curves with the tip of my finger, memorizing that perfect shape.

"So this wasn't a scheme to get me alone in a big, beautiful house where you could seduce me?" I asked playfully, batting my eyelashes.

He helped me out of my coat and hung it next to his on a coat rack.

"That may or may not have crossed my mind." We stood in the foyer, his hand sliding around my back to settle on the curve of my hip. His other hand swiped away a tendril of hair that had slid from my loose bun. "I'd do anything for time alone with you…and here you are."

I closed my eyes as his warm, minty breath washed over my lips. I waited for him to kiss me, anticipation set in my stiff shoulders. Instead, I was left disoriented and slightly disappointed when his hand slid down into mine.

"Come. I'm curious to hear what you think of the place now."

The heady need he easily woke within me was hard to stow away, but I managed well enough. I followed him into the living room, shifting my focus to the brilliance of the furniture layout.

Logan wanted me to win—there was no doubt about that. It was breathtaking, and I knew then I'd win the bet hands down. But each room we entered was even better than the last.

The master bedroom with my dream closet had been transformed into a room fit for a queen. I stared at it in wonder. However, it was the kitchen that left me in true awe. It was set up more for a top chef than a college girl, and I couldn't stop myself from running my fingers over the granite countertop that rested above sleek black cabinets—no doubt custom made.

I twirled around on my heel, grinning. "You wanted me to win this."

He raised his shoulders slightly. "Perhaps."

"I'd have thought you'd enjoy having me as a slave at your will for a weekend."

"At one time, yes, but now I'd much rather be at your disposal."

"There's nothing disposable about you, Mr. West."

His eyebrows shot up, a pleased smile playing at his lips. "Is that so?" He was leaning against the counter across from me with his arms crossed over his chest, watching me intently.

"Mm-hmm." I pranced toward him and tugged his arms apart so I could slip in closer, wedging myself between his legs. My head dipped back as I stared up into the blue pools looking down at me with such tenderness it sent a shiver up my spine.

"I'm no longer a suspect in the case," he said so calmly I thought I'd heard him wrong.

"You're not?" I needed to hear it again. Was it really over?

He shook his head as his lips curled upward. "There's a reason I hire the best. Turns out there was a lead the police chose not to follow. Not sure what, and I don't care. It has nothing to do with me, and they know I'm not responsible for Kurt's death. That's all that matters."

I squealed, lifting myself up on my tiptoes and locking my hands behind his neck. I'd begun showering him with kisses over his neck and across his cheeks when he clasped my face with his hands and claimed my mouth with his own.

"I've missed you like crazy," I confessed, basking in the feeling of his wandering hands.

"You have no idea." He swung me around and pulled my back against his chest before his hand plunged down the front of my slacks. It barely fit, but that didn't stop him. The button popped, flying across the counter I was nearly bent over now.

Gyrating against his hand, I cried out when his finger brushed over my clit, lingered at my opening, then slammed up inside me. His other hand curled around my stomach, stopping over my tattoo. It was still covered with a bandage, though it had already healed. I just wasn't ready for him to see it yet.

"Jax do that to you?"

Did he know Jax did tattoos? How? Since when?

"Maybe?"

His finger sank deeper, thumb circling my clit.

"I know what my brother does in that room of his." His voice was grave.

I stiffened as he continued.

"I told you: I know everything that happens in my house."

"You want to see it?" I moaned, my head falling back onto his shoulder.

"Later. Right now I want you—all of you."

Instantly, his fingers were gone and my pants were down around my ankles before being fully removed and thrown aside. Logan's hand rested at the center of my back to hold me in place, the sound of his zipper sending me spiraling. Anticipation had never been sweeter.

"You're coming home with me tonight. Understand?" The head of his cock poked my entrance.

"Yes. Please."

He thrust forward to bury himself deep. My resulting moans were lurid and wanton.

Somehow we ended up on the counter, Logan on his

back with me riding him through my third orgasm.

The doorbell rang right as I finished, driving Logan harder toward his own release. He gripped my hips, rocking me faster.

"Don't you dare stop, Cassandra!" he barked.

Logan began bucking up off the countertop. He pounded into me again and again until his head dropped and eyes slammed shut, an appreciative groan clawing its way up from his throat.

The bell rang two, three, four times in a row.

"Damn it!" Logan complained as I hopped down.

"She's going to kill us!" I pouted.

"She'll get over it." Logan climbed down and handed me my clothes—all of which had been peeled off during our little sexcapade. "Go upstairs to the guestroom and get cleaned up."

The bell rang again, and was followed by Julia's high-pitched screech. "I know you guys are in there! I see your cars!"

I ran naked through the house, ignoring Logan's chuckle.

"Fucking beautiful," I heard him say as I sprinted up the stairs.

Utterly satisfied and deliriously out of sorts, I slipped into my clothes, minus my destroyed panties that I quickly realized were missing. It was one thing to have left my shoes in the kitchen—I could use the excuse of not wanting to ruin the new carpet—but my panties? I could only hope Logan found them first.

My hair, which had been up in a high bun, was now down. The hair tie I'd come in with was also magically gone, so I did the best I could, smoothing my fingers through my unruly locks to tame their recently ravished look.

As I stared in the mirror, it hit me: The drama was over. Logan was cleared, and Natasha had gotten the not-so-subtle hint that I wouldn't take her crap.

I was nearly skipping out of the room to return to my man until I realized Julia was down there with him. She'd take one look at me and undoubtedly know why we'd made her stand on the stoop for so long.

After a deep breath, I sneaked out of the guest bedroom and descended the stairs. I could hear Julia and Logan talking in the living room. I walked in to find her wearing a giant grin as she took in the room.

I stood in the doorway, looking on without them noticing.

"So what do you think?" Logan asked her. His hands were shoved deep in his pockets.

"It's wonderful! I mean, I knew you were working on a house as an investment property, but this…this is stunning. But why decorate it and fill it with all this if you're just renting it out?"

"Because it's more than an investment. I bought it for you."

"What!?" she shrieked, bouncing up and down, her hands clasped.

"That is, as long as you finish school—and for if you decide to stay in Harmony and come work for me at the newspaper when you're ready. If you choose to move back to the city after graduation, you can sell it and use the money for your next place."

I smiled. Julia was lucky to have Logan as a brother. I was lucky to have him, too.

"Logan!" She ran at him, embracing him in an enormous hug. "You're the best! Oh, I can't wait to show it off. And I can have roommates. And Luke…oh, he's going to love it!"

Logan's body tightened; I could see it from across the room. His eyes darkened, lips pulling into a stern line. "I take it you two are no longer just friends?"

The sneer she threw his way rivaled his own. "That's right." She placed her hands on her hips. "And nothing you do will change that. I like him and he likes me, so if you're even *thinking* about running him off, you can take this place and shove it up your—"

"He's a good guy," Logan interrupted, actually looking amused.

Julia swayed, looking somewhat lost before recovering quickly. "Yes, he is."

"I don't want him spending the night here."

"Fine, we can have sex at his place. Then I'll drive home *all* alone on icy roads in the middle of the night. Sure gets dark out there."

My hand shot to my mouth to stifle my bubbling laughter. She was good.

"Fine," Logan blew out. "But he's not moving in. Got it?"

Her bouncing, shrieking self was back. "Thank you!" She was twirling around, doing a ridiculously silly happy dance that even Logan seemed to enjoy, when she spotted me lurking.

"Cassandra! You helped with this?" She ran at me.

I laughed, nodding.

"Thank you! I love it!" She drew me in for an embrace, and I caught the smile on Logan's face as he watched. She pulled back, swung her head from me to do a once-over of the room, then squealed again. "I have to make some calls and finish checking this place out. Oh my God!" she squeaked, then rushed out of the room, bounding up the stairs.

But after one step, she stopped abruptly and craned her neck back toward us. Her gaze darted slowly between Logan and me.

"Please tell me you were *not* in here christening my house!"

I swallowed, dropping my ashamed gaze to the exquisite

marble floor. I felt Logan walk up behind me and slip his arms around my waist.

"I believe Jax has the number of a good cleaning company that specializes in sterilization."

I bit my lip to refrain from laughing, peeking up for her response.

She shook her head, rolling her eyes. "Ewww!" She threw her hands in the air. "I'm going to pretend I never heard that, because I am *way* too excited about this house and hearing that you're not going to prison." Her smile returned as she added, "It's also nice to see you two happy."

He must've told her about his name being cleared. I sneaked my hand into his as Julia pointed her finger at us, her eyes narrowed into slits.

"But the next time you come over, keep your damn clothes on!"

It was Logan who broke first, his snicker sweet music to my ears.

Once she was out of sight, Logan turned me around in his arms.

"Do you have my panties?" I whispered, earning me a roguish laugh.

"Perhaps."

"Logan…" I threatened.

"Let's go. You won the bet, and I'm ready to be at your beck and call for the weekend." He leaned in and nipped my earlobe with his teeth, then murmured, "Anything you desire, I *will* make it possible."

"Anything?" I leaned back, grinning.

"Anything."

Chapter Twenty-Eight

Progress

When Logan showed up at my door Saturday morning, my cheeks ached from the broad grin I couldn't avoid, my eyes taking in every inch of him. My tongue darted out, running across my lips. It was the finest sight I'd ever beheld—delicious in every sense of the word.

"You gonna devour me on the spot or invite me in first?" Logan's brow cocked in a challenge. "I'm good with either."

I stepped aside, sliding my hand across his granite ass as he entered, his body pressing against mine despite the extra room surrounding us. Logan slipped out of his coat to reveal the wardrobe I'd ordered for his weekend as my lapdog.

"I have to admit, Cassandra…when I said 'anything', this wasn't exactly what I had in mind." His fingers threaded through his hair, head dipping as he chuckled.

"You don't say." I fought to control my giggle, remaining as passive as I could and attempting to force my eyes to remain on his face.

It wasn't possible. He was bare-chested, and wearing faded jeans that hung low on his hips. I tugged on their belt loops to bring him closer, and his brow shot up.

"On second thought, maybe this *is* what I had in mind."

His voice grew rough, breath nipping at my neck.

My shoulder shot up, pushing him away. "Not exactly. Come here—let me show you what you'll be doing for me the next two days, *slave*," I said in a seductive purr.

I took his hand and led him to the hallway, where the attic ladder was pulled down.

Oliver was with Julia for the day and Natasha was mysteriously MIA, which gave us some much-needed time alone. I didn't ask where she was; I was too happy to care. Jax's week to devise a plan to battle her craziness was about up, and he'd been sure to steer clear of me.

The week had also surprisingly passed with no drama, and although the sheriff had yet to release the names of any new suspects, Logan was officially cleared.

"Climb, stud!" I ordered, biting my lip to hold back my giggle.

He raised his brows, amusement painting his expression. "Stud, huh?"

My entire body shook with laughter. "You gonna complain or move that ass?"

A giggle broke through, short and awkward. Heat seared my cheeks. The mere thought of me as anything resembling a dominatrix was ludicrous. I'd never come close—and from the humor dancing across Logan's face, I guessed he probably agreed.

"Ladies first."

I knew what that meant: He'd be treated to a face full of my behind, and then we'd get no work done.

I shook my head. "No, you first."

He caught the look on my face and chuckled to himself. "As you wish."

Once he was climbing into the hole of my attic, I followed.

"And now?" he asked, looking around.

I picked up a broom and smiled, holding it out to him. "And now you clean. I expect this place to be spotless, with a fresh coat of paint on the walls by Sunday evening. And then *maybe* I'll treat you to a little reward."

"Hm, I like the sound of that." He stepped closer.

"Work *first*," I said, fighting to keep my façade of control.

"You sure I can't do anything else before I start cleaning?" He stalked closer, and my back hit the wall. He caught my face, brushing his lips over mine. I dropped the broom, snaking my arms up around his neck. "Hm?"

"You *do* have all weekend," I reasoned, giggling again. "Maybe I could go for a massage, or something a bit more...*intimate*."

"Now we're talking." His tone deepened with need as he lifted me in his arms, kissing me harder.

By the time we finished making love—my body glued to the wall, him taking me from behind—I was exhausted and starving.

"You get to work up here, and I'll make lunch," I said, running my fingers through my hair.

He swatted my ass as I shimmied past him, my dress askew.

"Take your time."

I climbed down, made my way to the kitchen, and started preparing us some food. Half an hour later, I called up the ladder for him to join me. I set two taco-laden plates at the kitchen table, with a bowl of chips and another of homemade salsa in the center.

"Looks delicious." Logan stood in the doorway, staring.

"Wasn't sure if you were a taco guy."

He walked over, sweat over his brow, and placed a soft kiss next to my ear before whispering, "I was talking about you, but yes, lunch looks good as well."

I flushed. "Go wash up and come eat."

"Yes, ma'am." He winked and disappeared out of sight for the restroom.

Once he was back, he grabbed his chair and brought it closer to mine at the table—so close our legs were touching—and took a bite of one of his tacos.

"Mmm, yeah. That's good." He closed his eyes as he chewed.

I smiled, loving how it felt to please him.

"So how's it going up there? You think you'll be able to paint today?"

He swallowed and took a big drink of water from his glass. "First, tell me what you plan on using the room for."

"Does that matter?"

"Yes, or else I wouldn't have asked." He popped a chip full of salsa into his mouth.

I leaned over and kissed the corner of his mouth. The man even made eating look sexy.

"I was thinking about turning it into an office or library, or maybe both. I don't know yet, but it's extra space that I would love to take advantage of having."

He thought that over for a few minutes as he finished the taco. "It's going to take more than a coat of paint to turn it into an office."

"I know that," I said, slightly offended.

He smiled. "Do you trust me?"

"Why?"

"Do you?"

I nodded. "Yes."

His smile broadened. "Good. Then give me a few more days to get the attic done right."

"How long? And to do what?" I propped my elbows on the table, my curious eyes on him.

"It needs insulation and new wiring, to start."

I shook my head, not liking where this was going. "No. I just wanted some paint, and was planning on throwing down a giant rug. I can't afford a construction crew, Logan."

"I know," he said too easily.

He is not paying for this.

"Logan," I sighed. "I don't want you to spend money on my house. You've done enough for me."

He pivoted to face me. "You said you trusted me. What if I promise not to spend a dime on construction?"

My eyes narrowed with skepticism. "And how will you do that?"

"Believe it or not, I have a lot of friends—and many that owe me favors. I haven't had a reason to call them in before now."

"Don't waste them on me," I mumbled. How had a weekend of him cleaning my attic and making love to me turned into construction talk?

"Shut up and come here." He tugged me onto his lap. "It's not a waste. Nothing I do for you is, and if you ever say that again, you might just regret it."

"Are you threatening me?" A smile played on my lips.

"Do you want to find out?" Something wicked flashed across his eyes.

I kind of did. Was that wrong? He was gorgeous when he was in charge.

"Another time. Right now, it's *you* that's supposed to be *mine* for the weekend."

"Right, and as such, I believe a massage is in order."

"I can go for that," I said with a smile, "after we eat."

We finished our plates, and Logan began to load the dishwasher. I needed to bet him more often.

"I wanted to ask before I forget," Logan said, still focusing on his task. "My mother's having a party next Saturday, and I'd love for you to come and meet my family."

"Your family? As in…"

"As in my mother and my brother, Lawrence, as well as his wife and their son Charlie."

I took a large gulp of water to give myself time to think it over. Was I ready to meet his mother?

"It would mean a lot to me. I want them to finally meet you—know you. They'll love you as much as I do."

"All right," I answered, not needing any more convincing.

"You'll come?" He turned around, a dirty plate in his hand and still looking gorgeous but also relieved. Had he honestly thought I'd say no?

"Yeah. Of course I will."

"Great." He turned back, finished putting the last plate in, then dried his hands. "We'll drive up Saturday morning. Make sure to pack an extra set of clothes and some modest pajamas."

"Pajamas?" I all but gasped.

"Yes, we're staying overnight. Much like I am here tonight, where I can spend my time with you…" He drew me into his arms and kissed me once. "Hold you…" He kissed me again. "Get lost inside you."

"So I'll be staying…"

"At my mother's townhouse. She's old-fashioned, so you'll have your own room. But she sleeps like a rock, so I'll be sneaking over to visit."

"Okay." That sounded enticing, but still...

Logan clasped my chin and raised my head. "Look at me. It's going to be fine. Now, let's go see about that massage."

"I haven't finished my water," I teased, taking a small sip.

"You need another countdown, sweetheart?"

I raised my brows and brought the glass back to my lips. "Perhaps?"

"You're really asking for it."

"Am I?" I took another sip, heat racing to my groin.

"Time's up!"

He was on me instantly, lifting me onto the table and tugging my dress over my head. He wasted no time unbuttoning his jeans and burying himself inside me.

Lying in bed, wrapped in his arms, I couldn't be happier.

"Ready to show me that tattoo yet?" Logan asked, breaking the silence enveloping our post-sex bliss. I knew he'd gotten glimpses of it, but he'd had yet to ask for a closer look. The bandage had come off a couple days earlier, and I wasn't sure how to explain the meaning behind it.

"Are you mad?" I asked with nervous hesitation.

"About what? My little brother hiding an illegal operation in my house, or him tattooing you in a place I'd prefer he never saw?" He traced Jax's work with his fingertip, his eyes on me.

"How about you just look at it and tell me if you like it?" No way was I getting into a fight today.

I sat up, pulling him with me until he was leaning back against the headboard with me straddling his waist. It was a position we'd been in a lot lately.

"It's an arrow," I said sheepishly.

"I see that. Cute. Any reason for it, or just seemed like a good idea at the time, seeing as you had consumed half your weight in tequila?"

I would've been offended by his tone if I wasn't suddenly embarrassed. "It's you," I whispered, placing my hands on his shoulders and raising myself up to give him a closer look.

"Gonna need a few more details here."

"You came into my life out of nowhere: sharp and deadly, but so unbelievable and beautiful, full of so many possibilities and fears. I felt like I'd been shot the first time I saw you standing out on your porch, but I loved it. And I love you." I curled my arms around his neck and added in a hushed whisper, "And yes, I was also drunk."

Logan didn't laugh along with me. He simply continued to trace the simple arrow with his finger, his eyes focused on the smooth line.

"Why only three nocks?" he asked. "Jax to blame for that? He forget to add a fourth to even it out?"

I shook my head, my cheeks warming. "No," I murmured, staring down at the tattoo. "They represent you, Oliver, and me."

"Leaving room to grow?"

I smiled to myself, unable to meet the penetrating stare I could feel on me.

He continued, letting the question drop. "I know the feeling of being struck—pierced through the soul. You do it to me every single day. It's why it's so important for you to meet my family next week." He kissed me softly.

"So will your father be there?" I asked, changing the subject.

"Yes." His voice was neutral. He rarely spoke of his father, which left me curious.

"That's nice. Your parents are still friendly, I take it?"

I always wondered whether, if my father had divorced my mom and stuck around, they would've eventually become friends. Probably not as long as my babysitter was bearing his children. The thought made me sad.

"Tell me about him," I said, wanting to know as much about Logan as he'd offer up.

With me cradled against his chest, he didn't seem to mind. "He's a hard ass—works a lot, and always provided for us."

"When did they split?" I traced lazy circles on his skin with my fingertips.

"Right before Jax and Julia were born. He had an affair."

I lifted my head to meet his thoughtful gaze. "I'm sorry."

"Don't be. It was a long time ago." His hands skimmed down my spine. "He loved her—my mother. Tried to make it work after she found out. So cliché…he was screwing his secretary." He snorted. "My mother was pregnant, and too good to put up with it. She kicked him out, and Lawrence and I went to stay with some family for a little while until she gave birth."

He grew silent for a moment—reminiscing, I assumed—and I waited patiently, giving him the time he needed.

"I remember hearing her cry at night, sitting in the nursery. It was only in there that she let herself be vulnerable. I always thought she was sad because the twins slept all day and were up all night. I tried to help her out. I was about eight or so, and it made me feel useful. My dad would come around on the weekends, but he wasn't allowed to take the babies with us when Lawrence and I stayed with him."

He cleared his throat, his hand stopping its caress at the center of my back. "You don't want to hear all this. I'm going to bore—"

"No, keep talking," I reprimanded, arching back to demand he keep touching me. It was the closest to him I'd ever felt. "I want to hear more."

His hand began descending down my back, and he continued.

"Lawrence was the one who told me why she was really crying—explained she had a broken heart. It made me want to help even more. By the time the twins were one, the divorce was final. My mother's a strong woman. You remind me of her at times—especially at the ridiculous speed-dating night Caleb still thinks was a hit. I knew then she would like you."

"I know I'm going to like her, too. She raised an amazing son." I felt him press a kiss to my shoulder. "So, do they get along now—your parents?"

Logan chuckled, the rumble in his chest catching me off guard. "That's the other side of the story: my father's. He's always loved my mother, and he never forgave himself. He gave her everything: the house, the vehicles. Still paying her alimony, despite her trying to refuse it after all these years. On top of all that, he bought the house right next to her. Overpaid the owner that refused to sell."

My laughter joined his. "Now I know who you take after. Persistence runs in the family, it seems. So, does your mom date?"

He snorted. "No."

"What, is your mother not allowed to have a life? A boyfriend? A *lover*?"

He sat up, pulling me with him while keeping me nuzzled in his neck.

"No, definitely no lovers for my mother. My father would never allow it."

I was the one snorting now, appalled. I knew how lonely my mother had been until she found George. No one deserved that.

"They're divorced. He hardly has a say."

"Believe me, I know my father. He'd never let someone date my mother."

"Has any guy ever tried?" I felt even deeper sympathy for

the woman now. They'd divorced almost twenty years ago, for crying out loud.

"Not that I know of, but then again, my mother's private life has always been just that: private," he said, either losing interest in the topic or not wanting to discuss whether his mother had had sex in the last couple decades.

"Well, I think your father should want her to be happy." I rolled over to face him.

"He does—with him."

What? My face pinched. "They've been divorced for how long, and he still wants her? Has *he* dated since?"

"Yes," Logan sighed, his hands now slipping lower. I swatted them away, wanting to better understand his parents' dynamic. My business or not, I needed to hear it.

"Okay, let me get this straight: He cheated while she was pregnant, even though he was *so* in love with her, and now even though she's divorced and free to date, he won't allow her to. Am I hearing this correctly?"

"Beauty and brains. God, I'm a lucky son of a bitch." His headed dipped, mouth looking for some company when I flew up, pushing him back.

"Wait, no, that's just...*wrong*. Your dad's an ass."

Logan burst out laughing, nodding his head. "You're adorable when angry, you know that?" A spark of wicked desire lit his eyes. I held him back, my palms flat against his chest.

"Sex *after* you admit your mother deserves to move on and find a man to make her happy."

He shook his head, which stunned me even more. "I can't. I agree with him wanting to hold out hope for her. And even *thinking* about making love to you while we're talking about my mother's sex life is...not okay."

I ignored his last statement, as I was still stuck on the

first. "Hope? Twenty years later? Time for him to give that up." I was so agitated I nearly shouted.

"You don't see it from his side. Over all these years, he's never stopped loving her. He hates himself for what he did, and the women he's dated since were nothing but flings. My mother's the only one for him, and he knows it. It's one of the things I admire about him: He won't give up."

My hands fell away. "I'll admit that would be somewhat disturbingly romantic if not for him continuing these so-called 'flings'. Maybe your mother's confused by the messages he's sending. I mean, if he loves her, then he shouldn't be able to screw around with anyone else."

"Some men aren't like most women, sweetheart. Sex can be meaningless—no attachment necessary." He didn't look at me as he spoke, and I knew why.

"That's how it was for you?" The question barely made it out.

"Yes, just a means to an end. I've told you before. And then I met you. I'll never walk away from what we have, or jeopardize it again. Unlike my father, I know how lucky I am and how extraordinary my woman is."

My entire body rested against his. "I'm just as lucky. My mom hardly dated when I was growing up, but I used to dream that it was because she was waiting for my father," I admitted for some unfathomable reason. It just felt natural.

"You don't ever talk about him," Logan said, his attention focused on my words.

"Or *to* him," I added. "He's no longer a father to me. He walked away and never looked back. He didn't want us."

"Cassandra—"

"It's fine. I accepted it a long time ago. I only brought it up because, despite the ridiculousness between your parents, you're lucky to have them both."

He didn't say anything, and my thoughts turned to another child whose parents' future I was uncertain of.

"Does Caleb want to be a father?"

"More than anything, now that it's happening. And before, yeah, I think he did. He's always been good with kids. Loves the hell out of Oliver."

"They're so good together. I hope she didn't screw things up by running."

"No, he's calmed down. And honestly, I think he enjoyed the chase deep down." Logan chuckled. "Although the day he found out, I was a little worried. Never seen him so angry. Caleb isn't close with his father, and he wouldn't want that for his own kid."

"You think they'll get married?"

"Considering he sent me a photo of the ring he had designed and is on a private jet to my home in Aspen right now, I'd say the odds are good."

"What!?" I choked out. "I want to see it! I can't believe you've been holding out on me!"

He chuckled. "Caleb asked me to keep it to myself. Of all people, *you* should understand that."

"Touché." I rolled my eyes, smiling. "Now let me see!"

"Later. My phone's in the kitchen, and there's no way in hell I'm leaving this bed yet."

I sank down against him, reeling with excitement.

"This is huge! I mean, I know they're having a baby, but—"

"But nothing. He loves her, and he's going to prove it. They'll make great parents."

"Wow, Hilary and Caleb married. She got her wish."

"Her wish?"

"Yeah. Ever since we were kids, her wish was always the same on every shooting star: that one day Caleb would notice her and they'd fall in love, get married, and have beautiful babies together." I couldn't stop smiling.

"And what about you? What did you wish for?"

I shrugged, feeling my face heat slightly. "I don't remember."

"Cassandra, we both know you're a horrible liar."

"I'm serious, I don't remember." My face was in flames.

"Is that your final answer?" He pulled away, his brow cocked.

Oh crap. "Yes, it is." There was no way I was telling him anything.

Suddenly, I was flat on the mattress. Logan's fingers pressed into my stomach, tickling me until I couldn't breathe.

"Stop! Logan, stop!"

He stilled his fingers. "Do you remember what you wished for?"

"Yes: a dog!"

He sat there for a moment, searching my eyes. Then, without warning, he dug his fingers back into my sides.

"You can't lie to me, Cassandra." He chuckled as I kicked, clawed, and laughed hysterically.

Gasping for breath, I panted, "Logan! Stop—please!"

"Tell me."

"Love!" I spit out.

He stopped and stared down at me, waiting for more.

I scooted back to rest against the headboard and took a breath, looking down at the ruffled sheet. "I wished for love from a man who would never leave me like my father left my mother."

Logan lifted my chin. "Good thing I moved next door."

His lips were on me and I didn't fight back, basking in everything he had to give.

Chapter Twenty-Nine

FAMILY

"Grandma!"

Oliver ran into the townhouse the moment the door swung open.

"There's my little doll!"

My view of her was blocked when she bent down to hug Oliver. All I caught were a pair of simple black heels and a head of dark, glossy, short hair.

"Is Charlie here?" he asked impatiently.

"In the back," I heard her say, laughing softly as Oliver flew out of her arms and disappeared.

She righted herself, straightening the black slim-fitted blazer she wore paired with simple-fit jeans. It suited her well: laidback elegance. Her radiant smile greeted us next.

Logan's mother was everything I'd expected. Kind and loving, she opened her arms for her son, who walked into them instantly. They embraced for a long moment before her focus landed on me.

"You must be Cassandra. Come in. It's freezing out here. " She ushered us inside her enormously understated home. Everything was clean and simple, with a traditional yet slightly modern aesthetic. It wasn't what I'd expected, given the classic architecture of the exterior.

"It's such a pleasure to finally meet you. I'm Blythe, Logan's mother." She beamed, hugging me. It was heartfelt, and just like that I felt welcomed.

There was an instant resemblance to Julia in Blythe's features. Both were petite, and fierce in the way they held themselves.

I moved back into Logan's space and his hand found mine immediately, giving it a reassuring squeeze. "Thanks for inviting me," I said with a shy smile.

"Of course! I nearly demanded it, although Logan was one step ahead as always. He made it clear a few months back when I first planned this party that you'd be here." Her smile swept to Logan.

Months back, huh? The arrogant brute.

"I have to admit, I wasn't convinced, what with all the gossip Julia spreads." Blythe hooked her arm through mine, leading me deeper into the house and leaving Logan in the foyer with our bags. "Logan, dear, take the bags up to your room, but leave Oliver's. He'll be sleeping downstairs."

Logan didn't question her, setting Oliver's bag off to the side before starting toward the stairs. "Should I put Cassandra in one of the guest rooms at the end of the hall or downstairs?"

His mother stopped, with me locked at her side feeling curious about the subtle smile she sent his direction. "That won't be necessary. She can stay with you in your room."

The look on Logan's face—a mix of shock and bemusement—had me wishing for a camera. "Are you sure?" he asked, his words careful and slow.

"Positive. Now go—and hurry back down for brunch."

Blythe continued down a shallow hallway decorated with family photos, stopping to point out a few of Logan as a child and even promising to pull out old photo albums later. I was instantly intrigued—especially considering she said it in a hushed whisper as though Logan, even on another floor, might not be thrilled with the idea if he heard.

At the top of a second flight of stairs, which led down, she turned to face me and released my arm.

"I can't tell you enough how happy I am that you came. I've heard so much about you, and I'll say, Julia was right: You are a beautiful young lady."

Julia told her that? Jax, I could see, but not Julia. I couldn't help my smile.

"Thank you. Not going to lie, I was nervous to meet you." My face flushed at my honesty. Something about Blythe and how laidback she appeared made it easy to be open. "It means a lot to me that Logan wanted me here, and that you've been so kind and welcoming."

"My son loves you. I've never heard him speak of *anyone* the way he does you. I knew the moment Jax told me Logan was infatuated with a girl who was happier spending time with Oliver than him that you'd be the one to finally get through."

"Oliver's such a sweet kid. It was love at first sight with him, but with Logan...that took some time." I chuckled, relieved when she grinned in understanding.

"How have you been feeling? I know you've been through a lot lately. I've spent every night worrying about you as much as my own children. Logan doesn't tell me much. Jax and Julia are my eyes and ears, usually."

The sincerity and warmth in her words landed deep. Unsure what to say, I steered the conversation in the opposite direction.

"Jax is a bit of a nut," I chuckled. "Don't believe anything he tells you."

Blythe laughed, nodding her head. "I love that boy dearly,

but he's his father through and through." She glanced at the stairs, then hesitantly back at me. "Everyone's downstairs and eager to meet you."

I took a step forward but she placed her hand on my elbow, stopping me.

"Oliver means the world to me. After his mother left, I filled her role as much as Logan would allow. I don't approve of Natasha—never did—but I respected their relationship. And now I need to respect Oliver's relationship with her."

My gaze held hers and I agreed, but didn't fully understand where she was going.

"I don't want you to be uncomfortable this weekend. When Oliver and I planned the party, he sent an invite to his mother."

"She's here," I stated, not needing an answer.

I guess Logan hasn't updated his mother on Natasha's current repertoire of insanity. What really knocked me off balance was the fact that he'd never mentioned her name when he'd rattled off the guest list. He must've predicted the fire and brimstone he'd encounter—and for good reason. But for now, I held my poise as well as my tongue.

"Yes, and Logan has given his blessing. I will say that she's already on her third drink from what I've been told, and if she steps out of line, she'll be gone. I'm sorry to say this, but until she does, I won't ruin my grandson's birthday." Her features were soft and apologetic.

"Don't be. I get it, I do. And it's wonderful Oliver has you to see the big picture. Natasha isn't my favorite person, but I agree—Oliver should have his mother here if he wants her."

It wasn't a lie. I never wanted Natasha to hurt Oliver, but with all the family around, she'd be a fool to try anything. And if she did, she was just digging her own grave.

"Logan's right. You are a sweetheart."

Downstairs looked similar to the floor we'd just left. It was a lounge area that held a bar, enough white leather chairs to seat my entire class, and a casual dining room.

Around the room were at least twenty faces—and they were all staring at me.

I stiffened, unsure whether I should do a big hello to everyone or make rounds for personal introductions.

Saving me from having to decide, Julia and Luke came straight over. We chatted for a few minutes before Jax joined in with a girl I'd never seen hang out at the house, but judging by his hands on her ass, I guessed she was his date.

"Hi, Cassandra." I turned toward the voice and recognized a woman I'd seen only once before, in Logan's driveway: Katherine. "We're so glad you made it. I've been asking Logan repeatedly to bring you over for dinner. It seems he likes to keep you all to himself."

She pulled me in for a hug and I went with it. She was sweet, beautiful, and matched perfectly to the man around Logan's age who sauntered up beside her, his hands encircling her tiny waist.

"This is Katherine and my brother Lawrence," Logan said to me, appearing out of nowhere. He mimicked Lawrence's movement, clutching me to his side.

"Cassandra. An honor," Lawrence said with an easy smile that matched Logan's. *Brothers for sure.* "I was beginning to think they were making you up just to get us off Logan's back about finding a good woman."

I laughed softly. "No, I'm very much real."

"It appears so." His eyes shifted to Logan and they

exchanged a look I didn't understand, but Logan's smile grew wider. Whatever it was, it was good. "I owe you a drink, Cassandra, for leading my brother back to the land of the living."

"I think Logan and I led each other," I replied, almost embarrassed at how deeply that struck me. It was true: I'd been hiding in the country and keeping to myself when he'd stormed in next door and changed my world.

"Whatever it was, I have my brother back, so thank you. Over the past few years, I was worried he'd become a machine that was only capable of working and raising his son."

"Lawrence," Logan warned, his hand tensing on my hip.

"I'm sorry. Don't blame me for missing you."

"Well, here I am, but where is my son? He seems to have disappeared in search of Charlie."

"They're upstairs with your father. He's helping them set up a tent in the living room," Katherine explained, smiling. "Can I get you a drink, Cassandra?"

My face lit up as I nodded. "Please, but I'll go with you."

After a peek up at Logan, I removed his hand from my hip, squeezed it gently, and followed her to the bar.

As we passed behind Luke and Julia, I nudged his side, smiling when he peeked back.

"You two look happy," I whispered.

His smile grew as he held Julia closer. *Very*, was all he mouthed, and I believed it—I could see it written over his soft features. The guy had it bad. Julia was lucky.

My steps were lighter as I continued to the bar.

"What would you like?" Katherine asked, stepping behind it.

The thing was fully stocked, which was great considering a drink would calm my few buzzing nerves. Though it wasn't exactly the best first impression to make—especially when Jax shouted across the room to declare I was a tequila girl.

"I could go for a glass of wine. Nothing too strong for me." I shot Jax a sharp sneer, who brushed it off with a snicker.

"Smart woman." She laughed and filled two glasses with chardonnay, then handed me one.

"So, Katherine—"

"Katie," she clarified. "Logan can be overly formal."

I smiled, taking a sip. *Delicious.* "Yes, I've noticed. So, Katie, how did you and Lawrence meet?" I sat on a stool as she walked around to sit beside me.

"Through Natasha. I've been told you've met her."

I nodded and took a larger sip, scanning the room but coming up blank of the witch. She was there somewhere, though—probably just not allowed to fly the broom in the house.

"She and I were best friends in high school. One day, she met Logan, fell hard, and convinced me to go on a double date with his brother. Swore he was gorgeous."

She practically drawled the last part, and I caught her eyes dance over to her husband. The West men had some good genes, that was for sure.

"I didn't believe it, of course, and she practically had to bribe me to go down to the restaurant. And then he walked in, looking anything but thrilled to be there until our eyes met and he smiled the sexiest smile I'd ever seen. I was smitten. We've been together ever since."

"That's sweet." The hopeful romantic in me was swooning.

"Sweet and boring. That's always been Lawrence and Katie."

Natasha appeared behind us. Exchanging a look of disdain, we both turned to face her.

"I would hardly call us boring," Katie defended, her smile melting into a scowl. "But then again, you wouldn't know anymore, would you?"

"You were nothing like Logan and me. We were young, wild, and in love—couldn't keep our hands off each other." She slipped between us, leaning over the bar. "Sex, sex, and more sex while you and Lawrence barely kissed till, what, the third date?" She blew out an ugly laugh.

Katie stood, ready to throw back, when Natasha pinned me with her stare, reeking of alcohol. "Did he ever tell you about his twenty-first birthday, Cassandra? You should ask him. I'm sure he's *dying* to replay that memory."

"Leave her alone," Katie threatened, "or we'll replay for everyone here exactly how many old geezers you had to screw to keep your rent paid the last five years."

Natasha swung her glare to Katie. "Maybe I'll see if Lawrence is looking for some *real* fun."

"Who's ready to eat?"

Blythe stood across the room, her eyes on us. It was Oliver's day, and I wouldn't let Natasha rattle me. Katie seemed to brush her off, as well.

"Let's go find *our* men," Katie spouted, a broad grin in place as she looped her arm through mine.

Logan held out a seat directly beside him. Oliver was down a few spots, sitting beside a younger version of himself except for the blonde curls—Charlie had short, caramel locks. They sat closer to the end beside Blythe, who fawned over them both.

I missed my grandmother. Watching them together reminded me of how wonderful mine had been.

"Everything all right? I saw you with Natasha," Logan whispered.

Resting my hand below the table over his thigh, I smiled. "Everything's perfect. She may be miserable and bitter, but I couldn't be happier."

His lips brushed over my neck, and he placed a soft kiss on the tender skin behind my ear. "I love you," Logan murmured.

A throat cleared behind us. "Hate to interrupt, but perhaps you can kiss your girl later and introduce her to your father now."

I looked up to meet a pair of deep blue eyes that were identical to Logan's, just on an older face. So this was the man who'd broken Blythe's heart. He was handsome now—I could only imagine how much more so he'd been twenty years ago. He was also charming, which was obvious in the way he held himself and stared down at me.

"Cassandra, this is my father, Edward," Logan said.

"Hello. It's nice to finally meet you," I said, smiling.

"A pleasure, darling. I hope you're feeling better after the accident."

"Yes, thank you." I sneaked a peek at Logan. It was strange that so many people I'd never met knew so much about me.

"Wonderful. You'll need some energy to keep up this afternoon. Oliver and Charlie are set on going to the aquarium."

"Sounds like fun. I've never been to one."

"Never?" Logan and Edward asked in unison.

I shook my head, smiling.

"Well, Logan's been going since he was little. One of his favorite places," Edward explained.

"Yes, it's where he proposed to me," Natasha cut in, and

then leaned in to give Edward an awkward hug. "How have you been, Dad?"

My eyes dropped, as did my stomach. I turned back to face my plate that Logan had piled high with food while I was speaking with his father.

"Natasha. It's been a long time. Maybe not long enough." With that, Edward pulled away from Natasha, placed his hand on my shoulder, and threw me a wink when I peeked up before he walked away to his seat next to Blythe.

Natasha sat on the other side of Oliver, but it was still too close. Logan had proposed at the aquarium, where we were going in a couple hours.

"I'm sorry. We don't have to go," Logan whispered. "I can ask Oliver to pick somewhere else."

"Don't be silly. It obviously means a lot to you, so I'd love to go."

He gave a nervous smile and turned back to his plate, picking at his food. Katie turned out to be quite the conversationalist. She filled the next hour with a multitude of questions for Logan and some for me, even telling stories about Logan and how much of a hands-on father he was. It was nice to hear, even though I didn't need to. I'd seen it firsthand multiple times. I was in love with Logan, and she didn't need to try and convince me he was a good guy. I could've used her a couple months before, though.

Through it all, I didn't miss the way Natasha glared at Jax, who didn't speak a word to her. I'd be talking to him before the weekend was up.

As everyone finished and stood to go upstairs, Logan was checking his phone beside me when I asked the unthinkable. It was stupid that I allowed Natasha's words to eat at me, and why it chose that moment to pop out, I wasn't sure.

"What did you do for your twenty-first birthday?" I asked

in a hushed voice.

Judging by the blood draining from his face as he lifted his head and his inability to look me in the eyes, I knew it was best left in the past.

I suddenly realized I didn't want to know. I groaned, withdrawing my words instantly. "Never mind. Forget I asked."

He turned in his seat and stared back down at his phone, where he typed something. "We can talk later. Caleb just messaged."

"Are they in Aspen yet?" I knew whatever was happening wasn't good, because Logan looked tense. Dread settled in my gut.

He nodded, his jaw clenching as he held up his phone with the display facing me so I could read what it said.

Got in a few minutes ago. Big problem. Place has been raided.

My hand flew to my mouth as he scrolled down, revealing photos of his Aspen home. It was almost bare, and what little was left had been destroyed.

"Who would—" I started, but he cut me off with a hard shake of his head. His eyes cut to Natasha, who was in earshot, standing from the table.

Valentine's, I remembered. He'd sent her there. I closed my eyes, reeling at her audacity.

Logan took my hand, guiding me up. As he walked me toward the stairs, he whispered, "Don't say a word to anyone."

"Are you going to call the cops?" I asked, my voice drastically low.

Logan glared over to Jax, who was holding his date in his lap. "No. Jax is going to make all my problems go away very soon."

What did that mean?

Chapter Thirty

Played

As it was my first visit to an aquarium, I wasn't sure what to expect. But the underwater tunnel that placed us right in the middle of another species' environment was simply breathtaking. I could see why Oliver had chosen the place for his birthday, and as irritating as it was, why Logan would've proposed to Natasha there.

Oliver walked between Logan and me, each of us holding one of his tiny hands.

"You like it?" Oliver asked, staring up at me with sparkling eyes.

"I love it," I replied with a smile.

Oliver dropped our hands and ran ahead of us to pull Charlie over to look at the hammerhead shark passing by. They pressed their noses to the glass, oohing and ahhing over the terrifying creature.

Brave boys.

Logan's arm snaked around my waist, his lips pressing above my ear in a chaste kiss.

"I love having you here. Feels right."

The coaxing static between us sizzled. *Not the place for a rendezvous.*

"How old were you the first time you came here?" I asked, curious and in need of a distraction from the soft caress of his fingers up the back of my shirt.

"Shortly after we moved here from Harmony. Grew up coming here at least once a month. They built this tunnel a couple years before Oliver was born. I brought him every chance I could," he said, staring at his son.

"I like it here. It's peaceful," I said, my eyes on the boys as we stopped behind them.

They were laughing hysterically at the faces they made at the stingray gliding along the glass in front of them. It was nice not having to suffer through a crowd—the entire tunnel was closed off for the next few hours for Oliver to enjoy. Turns out it was a perk of the Wests being long-standing members and regular financial donors.

"Turn around and smile, Oliver!" Natasha called from somewhere behind us.

My eyes rolled back at the grating sound of her voice. Logan turned us to find her holding a camera in her hands, which was pointed our way. I immediately pulled Logan and me out of the shot.

"Say, 'birthday boy'!" Natasha instructed with a grin.

Oliver threw his arm around his little cousin's neck and they both smiled, repeating her words with more enthusiasm than I'd have thought their pint-sized frames could possess.

As soon as Natasha lowered the camera, they swung back around, fascinated once again with the aquarium.

"Can you believe my little boy is six years old already?" Natasha asked. I didn't know whom the question was directed at, nor did I care—especially considering she didn't even know Oliver was turning five, not six.

She moved in front of us, her eyes remaining on Oliver. I wished for his sake to discover some untapped proud mother hidden within her, but all I saw was the cruel woman who'd abandoned her son and was now making my life hell. He deserved so much better.

Neither Logan nor I acknowledged her, pivoting back toward the glass.

"He's growing up too fast. That's all I meant," Natasha muttered.

"Maybe if you'd stuck around earlier, you'd see he's doing just fine in his development," Jax barked, appearing beside her. "And he's five, not six. Seriously?"

Natasha rolled her eyes, ignoring the last part. "What happened to your date, *Jax*? Did she tire of you already?"

"Decided to cut her loose before she picked up any of your skank tactics."

"I want to see an octopus!" Charlie shouted, halting the words that were about to spill from Natasha's open mouth. She snapped her lips shut and pursed them.

"I'm not sure if there are any in there," Logan explained, completely impassive to the lashing Jax was giving.

"We'll find them," Oliver declared, thus beginning the boys' slow movements back and forth through the tunnel.

"Come sit with me," Logan whispered.

There was a bench in the center of the walkway that wasn't yet occupied, and Logan led me to it. Lawrence and Katie were on the opposite end of the room, while Blythe and Edward followed behind the boys.

For being divorced as long as they had, they seemed to get along well. Edward was affectionate, and nothing but a gentleman. You'd never know they weren't still married.

Where Luke and Julia had run off to, I wasn't sure, but I had a feeling it had to do with setting up a separate room for Oliver's cake and presents.

We sat in silence, enjoying the view, my head resting on

Logan's shoulder. A short while later, I caught him tapping his watch while exchanging a look with Jax. Something was going to go down, judging by the impatient looks Jax kept giving his phone. Whatever they had planned, I wasn't thrilled with the timing or venue.

Minutes ticked by with Logan's hand stroking up and down my back while Jax continued to pace the far end of the tunnel, typing rapidly on his phone. I couldn't stand the suspense any longer, and was about to ask what was going on just as Jax gave Logan a thumbs up.

Logan's hand stilled on my back, and his lips curled slowly into a broad, mysterious grin.

I pulled away when he turned to me. "I need you to go with Katherine and my parents for a little while. Oliver will show you the other side of the aquarium. I'll catch up with you."

"What's going on?" My muscles tensed, eyes darting to Natasha standing in the corner, who was seemingly comfortable just watching the creatures.

Logan cradled my face in his palms. "You still trust me?" There was a weary vulnerability in his voice.

My hand covered one of his and slid it to my lips, where I kissed the center of his palm. "More than ever."

His lips slanted over mine in a short, intense kiss, then he pulled away. "Don't hit me—at least, not in front of the kids," Logan whispered, and then he was up.

Uh...what the hell? Hit him? Why would I—

I watched, thunderstruck, as he strolled over to Natasha, slipped his hand around her waist, and settled it over the back pocket of her jeans, tugging her against him. She leaned fully into his body, and my stomach churned. Yeah, I wanted to hit him all right—especially when she began to giggle at whatever words he was whispering into her ear.

My blood boiled, rage igniting at the sight of her hand skimming up his back, resting there as though it belonged. I knew there was a reason for the atrocity, but it was still hard to watch. I noticed Lawrence escorting Katie out of the tunnel with the boys, and Edward and Blythe following behind as if they knew a lot more than I did.

Typical.

Jax stepped in front of me, staring down at me impatiently. "Why don't you go see the penguins with the boys?" he asked, loudly enough for Natasha to hear. "Give Logan some time alone with his son's mother."

She didn't look my way, but I caught the way her body stiffened. She was listening.

Jax's voice lowered to a hushed murmur, and he threw me a wink. "We got this."

"Got what?" I whispered. My eyes were still glued to Natasha, who was practically draped over Logan's front as he walked with her a few feet farther away. If she tried to leave this tunnel with him, he'd be fearing more than my fist.

"Shit, time's up. Get out of here, now, or you'll ruin this. Got it?" Jax leaned in and whispered, then dragged me up, his features darkening. Logan and Natasha were already at the opposite end of the tunnel.

I had to trust him. Moving quickly to the door Lawrence held open for me that led out of the tunnel and into another section of normal-but-still-extremely-large tanks, I was bombarded with anxiety.

As I passed through the doorway, Lawrence grabbed my arm gently. "This shouldn't take long," he said quietly, his smile easy but giving nothing away.

Unsure what to say in response, I smiled and continued out, stopping only when I heard the door shut behind me. I ran back, peeking inside the tiny window. I couldn't see much, but I sure could hear the loud, gravely roar of Natasha's name echoing through the thin door.

I swung back to see if anyone else had heard it, but the room behind me was empty. Wherever Logan's family had disappeared to, it was out of earshot—likely for Oliver's sake.

When I shifted back to the door, I saw Josh rushing in, winded.

"You slut!" he seethed, stalking toward her.

Lawrence stood a few feet inside the door, focused intently on the scene unfolding in front of him and not me propping the door open just enough to hear and see better.

Natasha attempted to pull away from Logan, but he held her tightly at his side. He even took a strand of her hair and wrapped it around his finger, smiling at Josh.

Is he taunting him? Why? My temple throbbed with unanswered questions.

Josh stared at Logan's arm wrapped around his girl. I wasn't sure what he was about to do, but the expression on his face was manic.

"Josh, baby, what are you doing here?" Natasha asked, attempting to shove Logan away once more.

"Came to see my *girlfriend*." He swept his attention to Logan. "Gonna give her back?"

Logan shrugged smugly. "Depends on whether she wants to go back to you," Logan said, completely at ease. "Maybe I'll keep her a while longer."

Natasha began to panic. I saw it clearly in her movements as she squirmed and shoved at Logan to release her. "Let me go, Logan."

"Why? Afraid he'll get the wrong *impression*?" His voice was dark and coarse. "I think it's time you confess to your little boyfriend here. Tell him what's been going on between us."

Even from across the room, I could see Natasha's eyes

bulge. "Logan, what are—" she started, but he cut her off.

"Like how you fucked me just last night and the night before that and that. Does Josh here not know how you tell me he'll never please you like I do?"

My eyes slammed shut, pain coiling in my gut. This wasn't real—I knew that. He was goading them. Still, nausea hit me at the mere thought of it.

"No fucking way!" Josh growled. "You told me it was me and you. That you loved me—needed me!"

"I do!" Natasha slapped at Logan's hands that still didn't release her.

"Bullshit!" Josh roared. "I did your dirty work! That's all you wanted. You lied to me, used me." Josh's face grew redder with every word he hissed. "Promised me we'd leave this shithole town! And here you are with *him*—the man you say you despise, the man you wanted in prison!" Josh was inches from her face now.

"Baby, calm down, please." Natasha looked frightened, and now, instead of demanding Logan release her, she sought protection in his arms. But Logan didn't offer any, stepping away as he pried her hands from his shirt.

"I killed a man for you and *this* is how you repay me? By sleeping with him? You fucking bitch!" Josh flew at her, but Lawrence and Jax were there instantly to flank each side, holding him back.

"Logan, he's lying. He's crazy!" She stumbled toward Logan. His arms were crossed over his chest, his face hard. "I never told him to touch Kurt. You have to believe me. Why would I do that?"

"Because you knew I'd never want you. Because I told you I was going to marry Cassandra, and you couldn't stand it."

He'd told her that? When? Before Kurt was killed, I didn't

know he'd even thought about marriage.

My thoughts were pulled away as Logan continued.

"So, tell me, how did you think it would play out?" Logan asked, way too calm for the conversation. "I'd go to prison, and you'd take Oliver? Or you'd play the supportive role until I let you get close enough, and then what? You thought I'd take you back?"

He placed his hands on her shoulders, his eyes locking with hers.

"I never loved you. I was too young to see I was nothing more than a boy in lust with an immature, ungrateful slut. The only reason I haven't thrown you out of my life for good these past few months is because I wanted to believe you would do right by my son. But not anymore." He dropped his hands. "I'm done."

"No!" Natasha gasped. "I didn't have anything to do with this, I swear. I would have told you about Josh if I knew."

"You're gonna pay for this!" Josh yelled. "Was it all a lie? Just answer me that. Did you ever love me—even *like* me?"

The hurt tone in Josh's voice was too much. The entire thing was overwhelming, and tears welled up in my eyes— angry, needing-to-kick-her-ass tears.

Jax retrieved his phone without releasing his hold on Josh's right side. "Doubtful. I got some snapshots of your little tramp in some compromising positions with my sister's douchebag ex-boyfriend Mark. Took it right after you two started up. Wanna see? Or maybe the one of her blowing the bartender down at Haven last week? Got some of that too."

I didn't miss the smirk Jax threw Natasha, whose face had gone pale.

After peeling his eyes from Natasha, Josh glanced at the phone.

"I loved you!" he yelled as he looked up from the phone,

his rage snapping even further.

"Calm down." Natasha held up her trembling hands, her legs shaking.

"You bitch! I'm taking you down with me! You hear me?" Josh struggled against the hold of Logan's brothers, unable to break free.

"Logan, please. I'm sorry. I didn't do this. You have to believe me." Natasha's hands went for Logan's chest but he stepped back again, moving to stand in front of Josh.

"I know you killed Kurt," Logan said to Josh. "My PI found you on the visitors list. And while you may have convinced the sheriff you two were old friends, I had it looked into. You'd never even met the guy."

"Screw you!" Josh spat.

Logan brushed it off. "You got proof she asked you to do it?"

"Hell yeah, I do! I keep a stream of video going at my place for the parties. Have the entire thing on my computer."

It was Natasha who propelled forward next, screaming incoherent threats. She beat her fists into nothing but the air as Logan pinned her back against his front. Her legs kicked, aiming for Josh but falling short.

Transfixed on the whole interaction, I didn't notice someone behind me until a hand shot out beside my face, pushing the door fully open. I twisted back, startled to find Edward and Blythe frowning at the scene inside the tunnel.

"You need to call the cops," I blew out, my adrenaline running high.

"On their way," Edward replied, sounding almost bored before walking past me inside. Blythe took my hand and led me in behind him at her side.

Logan held Natasha with her arms pinned behind her back, Jax snickering at the empty threats she rattled off in stifled breaths. The look she sent him was lethal, but seemed only to intensify his laughter.

"You think you won, Jax? Well, why don't you tell Logan that *you're* the reason I came back in the first place?"

Jax's laughter cut off. Natasha grinned, thrashing harder against Logan and adding, "Tell him—"

Blythe slapped Natasha across the face, silencing her.

"You listen to me, you trashy little whore." Blythe took hold of her chin, commanding her full attention. "I've stood back and watched you destroy my son, tearing him down to a dark place only *his* son could reach him. I won't let you hurt any more of my children—and you better prepare for a hell of a fight after the cops are through with you, because you will *never* see my grandson again."

"Your *children*, Blythe?" Natasha cackled. "Is that what you tell yourself when you look at Jax? Or do you see the slut your husband fucked: Jax's *real* mother?"

I gasped, my hand flying to my mouth.

"What the hell is she talking about?" Jax's stunned words fell out, his grip loosening around Josh's arm.

Blythe closed her eyes, took a breath, then turned to face him. "Honey, I'm sorry. We'll talk about it—"

"What's the matter, Jax? Didn't know?" Natasha taunted. My palm was itching for another swing at her. "Just like Logan didn't know how much your cock enjoyed my attention when you convinced me to return home last summer?"

Jax's ashen gaze flew to Logan, who said nothing, gripping Josh so tightly he could barely move. Either Logan already knew or he didn't care, but the terror on Jax's face was heart-wrenching. He was scared—I could see it, mixed with a flurry of hurt and confusion.

He released his hold on Josh, who used it to his advantage, whipping around and slugging Lawrence in the gut.

He doubled over and Logan raced forward, dropping Natasha to grab Josh with the help of his father and Lawrence, who'd recovered instantly.

Natasha made a run for it, sprinting out the door with Jax on her tail. I leaned up against the glass, no longer noticing the sharks at my back. I didn't speak until Blythe walked over shortly after the cops arrived to arrest Josh.

"I'm going to check on my grandsons. You coming?" she asked.

I shook my head. "I'm going to wait for Logan...if you don't mind."

She gave me an almost-relieved, genuine smile. "Not at all. You're good for him." It was all she said before stepping away, with Edward there to meet her as they walked out together.

Logan slumped down on the bench after a while of talking with the police. I sat beside him, my arms encasing him instantly, holding him close. His head was down, and he didn't make a move to look my way.

When I moved to speak, I noticed he was staring at his phone. I could see it clearly: a text from Jax.

I wasn't fast enough. She grabbed a cab. Sorry for everything. Always the fuck up. Tell Oliver I love him. I'm done with this shit.

"Logan, I'm sorry about Jax."

He didn't reply as he pulled me into his arms, burying his face in my hair, where he sighed.

"Is this why you allowed Natasha to come today—to turn Josh against her?" It was all making sense, but why would he do it during such a special event as Oliver's birthday party?

"Yes. Only Jax, Lawrence, and my father knew. Natasha will never be allowed near my son again. I thought it only fitting on his birthday, since she's missed every one before it."

I hugged him closer, my head resting against his shoulder. "Poor Oliver. He'll be heartbroken when he finds out she's gone."

"He'll be hurt but he'll eventually accept it. When he's older, I'll be honest with him." Logan shifted back. His knuckles swept over my cheek, a soft but tight smile on his lips. "Besides, he has me and he has you. Nothing else matters, sweetheart. It's over now. We win."

Always the strong one.

He stood and helped me up.

"Let's go give Oliver the birthday he deserves," he said with a hint of a smile.

I nodded in agreement. Oliver's lively enthusiasm was exactly what we needed. I knew we'd talk about Jax later, but for now we had a birthday boy to entertain.

Logan was right: Nothing else mattered.

Chapter Thirty-One

TOGETHER

There are many moments in time I wished I could undo or rewrite, but with Natasha on the run, I knew everything was playing out the way it was supposed to.

Oliver and Charlie had been oblivious for the hour or so most of us had been missing from the birthday festivities, with Julia and Katie doing a great job of distracting them with every tiny reef in the tanks. When we finally entered the party room, which was filled to the ceiling with balloons and streamers, Oliver was too focused on his gifts and giant cake to notice his mother was missing.

That moment occurred when he opened her present: a giant stuffed dinosaur. It was incredible how instantly Logan was at his side to reassure him that Natasha had to leave, but that she told him to make sure Oliver knew she loved him.

Oliver may have frowned, but it was brief, and after that day it got easier every time he'd ask about her. Logan reiterated patiently that she couldn't stay any longer, and after a couple weeks, Oliver stopped asking. He seemed to understand in his own way. The only person he continued to ask for was Jax, who was still MIA and responding to no one's calls.

Turned out Julia wasn't his twin—a fact Blythe had

hidden when she took him in as a newborn just weeks before Julia was born. Logan remembered her going away to give birth and not meeting Jax until the same time he did Julia. What Blythe did for Jax—for her entire family—left me in awe. It was a completely selfless act. Whether she was Jax's birth mother or not, she was his mom, and she'd raised him well.

It wasn't my place to intrude on the heartbreaking family discussion that had been held after the party, so I'd taken Oliver and Charlie to play in another room while Edward and Blythe sat their children down to explain.

I received a goodbye text from Jax shortly after Oliver's birthday.

Keep Logan from turning the little prince into a geek. He needs freedom. Make Caleb take him to the batting cage. He likes sports. Maybe hunting when older. Gonna miss that kid. Take care of em both. I'll see u around sometime sister.

Sister? I smiled. Yeah, he was exactly what I'd imagined a brother would be like.

I replied instantly.

Come home and take him yourself. We miss u.

Nah, need some space. Got some shit to work out. Can't screw off forever. Time to live a little. Maybe someday I'll come back. He better have u knocked up by then.

Tears streamed down my cheeks. Was he really gone for good? I shook the thought from my head, typing feverishly.

How long does Logan have to fulfill that request?

Not sure. Take care. I mean that. Goodbye.

No! Come back and talk to Logan. Work through things. Don't just run!

He didn't reply after that.

I showed Logan the texts. He read over them, scoffed, then handed the phone back and left the room. He refused to discuss Jax, and I wasn't sure if he was angrier that he'd slept with Natasha or that he'd abandoned Oliver when he needed him most. Whatever it was, I didn't bring it up again. Part of me wondered if Jax was bluffing about leaving—that maybe he'd pop in out of nowhere.

Although that didn't happen, in so many ways, life was bouncing back...only this time it was so much better. I had everything I'd always wanted: love, devotion. I had it all.

About three weeks after Oliver's birthday, Natasha seemed to have fled back to where she'd come from. However, her apartment had been left as though she planned to return aside from a few scattered drawers, or so my mother informed us. She must've stopped by there before skipping town, and was in a hurry—for good reason.

It was for the best, and as long as she didn't try to pop in and out of Oliver's life, he was better with her being gone. She was a loose cannon I'd never trust. Not to mention the sheriff had a few questions for her.

"You going to hang that phone up and come finish this game, or do you forfeit?" Logan called from the living room.

Oliver's voice followed. "She's taking too long. That means she quits and it's my turn."

My smile widened. "Hilary, I have to go. I'm in the middle of Monopoly, and if I know Logan, he'll be helping Oliver rob the bank."

She laughed through the line. "That's fine, I just wanted you to know and couldn't wait until I saw you in person. I'll see you at school Monday. Bye!"

"Bye." I hung up, nearly prancing back to my boys and plopping down in front of the coffee table, where the board game was sprawled.

I raised a questioning brow at Oliver. "Do I need to do a recount in here before we proceed?" I waved my hand over the bank cash.

Oliver's face reddened, and out slipped two five-hundred-dollar bills from his sleeve. "Daddy took some too!"

I held out my hand to collect his loot, then moved it to Logan, demanding he pay up. Logan chuckled. "Just wanted to see if you were still up to snuff as the banker after that call."

"You heard?" A wide grin spread across my lips again.

"You screamed really loud," Oliver deadpanned.

Logan's chuckle grew. "You really did. So I take it they found out the sex."

My head bobbed with unrestrained giddiness. "It's a girl!" I blurted out. "Oh my God, they're having a little girl. Just think of all the dresses and tiny shoes. Oh, and the pink!"

"I don't like girls," Oliver said, waiting impatiently for me to take my turn.

Logan's eyes lit with amusement. "Just you wait."

I shook my head, playing my turn before Oliver's head burst from the way he was glaring at my stationary thimble.

Hilary and Caleb returned a week after the Natasha drama ended, and had been inseparable since. Caleb even purchased a stretch of property a few acres over from Logan. They'd be breaking ground in the spring, and judging by the blueprints Caleb had been designing himself, the house could potentially beat Logan's in size.

Hilary wasn't an open book on what had happened with Caleb, but made no effort to hide the enormous diamond on her finger. She flashed that thing around to every pedestrian on the street. She was happy, in love, and by end of summer would be a mother.

The next morning was the perfect start to any Sunday, and one I'd never forget. Logan and I made love in his bed throughout the night until the sun rose and we crashed from exhaustion.

After we'd slept only a few short hours, Oliver flew into the room and jumped on the mattress. Scout was at his side, barking while Oliver demanded pancakes.

I sat up and tugged Oliver down for a morning hug, giggling as my hand scrubbed through his hair. He hated when I did that.

Logan was on his stomach with eyes closed, but there was no way he'd slept through all the commotion. My suspicions were confirmed when the sheet that pooled around his hips shot up and he hauled it over my head, snagging my waist and dragging me back down.

Oliver began smacking Logan's arm, demanding he let me go, calling out to Scout that he needed help saving the princess trapped by the evil wizard.

My hand flew to my mouth, stifling my giggles as Logan pinned me under him, slowly opening his deep blue eyes.

"You better let me up. I've got pancakes to make the little prince," I said, stretching my arm down and swatting Logan's perfect ass.

His head dipped, mouth forceful against mine in a searing kiss. Then he drew back, taking the blanket with him as he sat up on his knees.

"She's all yours," Logan told Oliver, who was on the end of the bed, ready to attack.

"That's no fun," Oliver said, climbing down and frowning at the lack of a battle.

"You can help me make the pancakes," I offered, my feet hitting the floor before Logan could snatch me back.

That was all Oliver needed to hear. He took my hand and led me from the room in pursuit of the kitchen.

After breakfast, Logan and I took showers—separately. It was the only way we ever got out before all the hot water was gone.

When I stepped out of the bathroom into Logan's room, I found him there. His hair was damp and he was dressed in only casual jeans, staring down at the phone in his hands.

"Everything all right?" I asked, drying my hair.

"Yeah," he said, his voice monotone as he typed something then set the phone on the dresser. "That was Julia. Said she needed me to come over…an emergency at the house…and wants Oliver to come, too. Probably a mouse, knowing her."

Instantly worried despite his cool demeanor, I grabbed a grey T-shirt from his drawer and handed it to him.

He tugged it on and took the socks I held out next, kissing my hand in the process.

"I love having you here," he said, sitting to put them on.

"I know." My lips quirked as I slipped into my robe.

Logan smirked at my cockiness then stood, fully dressed. "I'll be back soon."

I followed him downstairs, finding Oliver reading in the living room.

"We're going to go see Aunt Julia," Logan told him while I collected their coats.

"I saw her yesterday," Oliver complained, tossing the book down on the chair.

"And you'll get to see her again today." Logan slid on his coat and grabbed his keys, waiting for Oliver, who wasn't moving.

"Can I stay with Cassie?" he asked.

"I don't mind," I told Logan. "We'll go over to my place and make some lunch for when you get back."

"I want to work in the attic!" Oliver flew off the couch and snatched his coat from my hands.

I laughed at his enthusiasm. Logan had hired a crew of men to turn my dank old space into a full-blown office, with a corner library and ping-pong table in the center. He made me proud when the big reveal came earlier than expected, portraying ten times what I'd pictured.

"All right, stay with Cassandra." Logan walked over and gave his son a hug, then moved back to the door. My arms snaked around his neck, and I kissed him so deeply I knew he'd want to hurry home.

"I'll come back and get him if Julia really needs him there. I hate to drag him out if it's for some silly reason."

"I doubt it's silly if she said it was an emergency."

His head dipped as a chuckle escaped from his mouth. He looked back up, meeting my scowl, and his thumb stroked over the crease on my forehead. "Julia doesn't know the meaning of a true emergency. I'll be back soon. You want me to walk you guys over to your place?"

"No, get going, we'll be fine." I handed him his cell phone.

He nodded, and with one more kiss was out the door.

"Go get Scout, and we'll head over," I told Oliver as I went back upstairs to get dressed.

With Scout in tow, Oliver raced inside my house the moment I opened the door, making a beeline straight for the back stairs Logan had installed.

It was still surreal. I had an upstairs—a gorgeous one. The furniture in the room comprised items I'd marked in the catalogs we'd looked at while decorating Julia's home.

I was shocked Logan had even noticed. I'd marked dozens of items through the various magazines, and placed dreamy little smileys beside the ones I liked for myself. I swore sometimes he could read my mind.

Oliver grabbed a paddle and a ball, situating himself in front of the ping-pong table while I set up the board in the center that allowed him to play solo.

"I'll be in the kitchen if you need me," I told him, climbing back downstairs.

Oliver was already too enthralled in the game to respond, which was fine with me. I headed to the kitchen, and was debating between chicken and dumplings or beef stew when I smelled something.

I whirled around from the sink, where I stood washing my hands, and froze at the smell of gasoline that seemed to be growing stronger by the second.

With deliberate, cautious steps, I ambled to the pantry, where the scent was most pungent. As I reached for the handle, I felt in my gut that something was terribly wrong.

I flung the door open, meeting a wild roar of angry flames shooting around the inside. Smoked rolled in across the ceiling, fire crawling up the walls.

Oliver!

My adrenaline kicked in at the sight, my feet carrying me so fast up the stairs I barely touched the ground. Oliver's stricken face met mine, and I caught the way his nostrils flared.

"It smells funny," he said, his eyes growing wide as they caught the smoke billowing up behind me. He dropped the paddle.

"We need to go." I grabbed him in a rush, lifting him up

and pressing his head against my shoulder to shield his face.

Starting back down, I pulled my shirt over my nose and mouth. Forcing myself to ignore the heat spreading around us, I took precise steps through the darkening clouds of smoke.

I'd never been more terrified in my life. Oliver gripped me more tightly, his sobs cutting through the crackle of the flames, pushing me to move faster.

Once I was out of the hall, I jerked back at the sight of the flames that devastated my grandmother's kitchen, now beginning their destruction to the edges of the living room.

Oliver began to cough and his body rustled in my arms, driving me faster through the chaos. I was determined to get him out safely.

Time stopped with every dreaded step until my hand finally hit the door. I yanked it open and raced outside, nearly stumbling from my speed. Once across the lawn, I placed Oliver down and bent over, gripping my knees, replenishing my dry lungs with clean air. I coughed, clearing out the smoke that had managed to sneak in, and wiped the sweat from my forehead.

Oliver sank down onto the grass, staring at the house. Smoke was billowing out the side where my kitchen had been.

And that was when I saw it: a slight movement in the trees not far away, and then a flash of dark hair getting caught on a tree. I knew exactly what I was chasing when I took off, calling back to Oliver to stay there and not stopping until my body was pouncing on a wide-eyed Natasha, who reeked of gasoline and liquor.

"You bitch!" I slammed her down, my hands clutching her shoulders as I straddled her frame, pressing her deeper into the snow.

"Get off!" she screeched, throwing her arms up, ready to attack.

My adrenaline was at full throttle, which made grabbing her arms and pinning her in place easy.

"How could you do this?" I screamed back, squeezing her wrists. "You could have killed—"

"This is *your* fault!" Natasha spat, rolling wildly from side to side, trying to buck me off. "You took everything from me! Always in the way! Always so sweet! So fucking perfect!" Her laughter was bitter and cruel. "Well, look at your home sweet home now. How's it feel to have shit *stolen* from you?"

Shaking with rage, I pushed off from her arms and leapt back to my feet, staring down at a pitiful excuse for a woman—for a mother.

She was a mess. Her clothes were dirty and disheveled and her hair knotted. Dark bags hung under her eyes. She looked like death, and it only made me pity her.

"I never stole from you. *You* left Logan and Oliver," I said, seething.

Inhaling rapidly as my heart pounded against my ribcage, I shook my head slowly and stared past her into the forest. She was clinically mad—in need of a straightjacket and daily tranquilizers. I peered back at her after catching my breath, my nerves traumatized.

"You wanted to put Logan in *prison*, Natasha. Do you understand that alone *proves* you don't love him?"

"No." She sat up on her elbows. "I just wanted him to need me—to show him I could be there for him and take care of Oliver." Her words blew out frantically, jumbled together in one massive breath. She pulled herself to stand, narrowed eyes sparking with rage and cast on me.

"I would have set Josh up...made sure he took the fall for it. I wanted him to just slip Kurt a few pills to make him sick, because I knew everyone would accuse Logan. I never told him to kill the guy. He must have given him too much." Her head shook violently. "Josh did this—not me! I just wanted Logan to see he could count on me when he needed someone. But he wouldn't let me in—wouldn't let anyone in but you! So *yes*, I'd rather take my son and leave Logan rotting in prison than let you have him!"

My mouth hung open. I was stunned at how little regard she had for the people I loved, as well as what was best for her son.

"But you did this!" I waved my hand toward my house in the background, fighting to control my lip that trembled at the sight of the home my grandfather built going up in flames. "And how would you take Oliver anywhere if you'd killed him?"

"What?" Natasha gasped. Her head shook again, her hands tugging her hair out of the way so she could see me. "No, he's with Logan. I made sure of it."

"No, he's right there."

I pointed to the snowbank he'd been sitting on moments earlier only to find the spot empty. Suddenly, I felt my world crumble around me .

My gaze shot to the house, and I watched as his tiny body disappeared inside. And then I heard his faint words, calling out for Scout.

Chapter Thirty-Two

BRAVERY

"OLIVER!" I screamed. My feet sprinted toward the house, pulse racing.

Natasha was beside me, her sobs hysterical. We reached the porch just as the first beam crashed at our feet. It was still connected to the roof, rendering us unable to go under or over it.

"Oh, God!" Natasha bellowed, tears pouring from her eyes. "No! NO!"

"Shut up!" I pushed her back, needing to think. The charred beam blocked the entrance, but with a little maneuvering using the railing of the porch and Natasha's help, I'd be able to jump over it. It was my only option; the back door would probably be destroyed by now, and there was no time to go check.

I climbed onto the railing, bracing myself against the hot beams overhead.

"What are you doing?" Natasha sobbed, panic-stricken.

"Saving our boy." I kicked the beam, needing to shift it so it would fall away and unblock the doorway enough for me to slip inside. "Help me!" I ordered, seething at her uselessness.

Natasha took my cue and looked around. She grabbed a

small metal patio table and used it to push against the beam until it began to move and finally fell, clearing the way.

Before I could even jump down, Natasha bolted inside frantically, calling out for Oliver.

I ran in after her, screaming over the roar of the flames, explaining that he'd be upstairs. Scout was afraid of the steep steps leading to the attic, and would only come down if Oliver carried him—which meant he'd still be up there.

The smoke was growing denser and blacker with every passing second. Even though I knew my way, I reached my hand out to feel around, my shirt over my face. I stumbled through the living room and down the hall, where the steps were situated at the end, but found myself hindered by a wall of flames.

I couldn't see anything but red heat and black clouds. My eyes burned and my throat was rough. The only sound was that of a crackling hiss.

"Natasha!" I screamed, taking in a mouthful of smoke through the cotton fabric. I choked on it, coughing, but continued. "Oliver! OLIVER!"

Tears rolled down my cheeks in defeated cascades. I couldn't get to the stairs. A loud crash sounded behind me. I jerked back, whipping around to find the ceiling was caving in.

The hardest thing I ever did was move myself farther away from that hall. My entire body shook, the fire nothing compared to the pain ripping through my heart. I couldn't save him—it was up to Natasha now, and Oliver was trapped and alone. Was he even still conscious?

I ran out, unable to face the dire emotions but not willing to give up. Bumping against walls and stumbling over debris, I pushed hard and moved faster.

After I reached the porch, I flew out into the yard. I suddenly noticed my right pant leg was covered in flames; I hadn't even felt it.

I dropped down and rolled, putting the flames out in the snow before bolting back up and running to the side of the house, where there was an attic window.

There, staring back at me, was the frightened face of Oliver, who was clutching Scout in his arms. I could see his tears glistening in the sunlight, even through the substantial smoke surrounding him.

He beat his little fists on the window, his mouth open. His words screamed out, unheard.

I raced to the tree line leading into the forest, found a handful of rocks, and sprinted back.

"Move aside!" I shouted, my throat scorching. He couldn't hear me. I held up the rock and made a throwing motion then waved my other hand, directing him to step out of the way. He understood and vanished from view.

Using all my strength, I hurled the first rock, howling when it beat against the bricks. I threw another, which hit but wasn't strong enough to puncture the glass. With fierce tears and exhausted limbs, I continued chucking rocks over and over until one finally blasted through.

My relief never had a chance as wild flames shot out from the open space.

"NO!" I screamed, my hands gripping my head. "Oliver! OLIVER!"

The fire receded, and smoke billowed out of the window.

"OLIVER!" I screamed more loudly. "ANSWER ME!"

Then I saw it: something large and dark surrounding the window. I waited, but there was nothing.

"Oliver!" I cried, sobbing. "Please!"

Natasha's head suddenly poked out. "Catch him!" she yelled down.

I sobered instantly, my head nodding frantically. She

threw a blanket over the edge of the window, and I watched her help Oliver crawl out.

His little body hung down the side of the house, his hands wrapped around his mother's. She was speaking to him, tears raging down her blackened face, but I couldn't hear what she was saying.

"I'm right here, Oliver!" I shouted up in a way I hoped was reassuring. I stood under him, and when Natasha's eyes moved from her son's to mine, I prepared my stance.

She let go, and Oliver cried out. He fell until he was on me, knocking me down to the ground, breaking his fall.

He rolled over, cradling his arm and rolling into a ball. I didn't need to be a doctor to see that the bone wasn't in the right spot. He'd definitely broken it.

I dropped down beside him, wiping the soot from his face. "It's okay now. It's over." I hugged him tightly, my emotions unhinged.

"It hurts," he wailed.

"I know, honey. I need you to stay strong while I help your mom get out, and then we'll get you to a doctor. Just stay right here, okay?" My words were rushed. I was desperate to get Natasha out.

He nodded, his eyes hooded. "My mommy and Scout."

"They're coming." I stood, looking back up for Natasha.

She was there with Scout in her arms, surprising me when she held him out and dropped him. I caught him with ease and set him beside Oliver quickly.

Another loud commotion filled the air. I watched in horror as the roof began to pop and one side collapsed in.

"Natasha!" I cupped my mouth, shouting as loudly as I could.

"I won't fit!" she hollered, attempting to squeeze her shoulders through.

The window wasn't exactly the largest, but she had to make it work. There was no other option.

"Yes, you will!"

In the distance, I heard the faint sound of sirens. Help was coming.

"I can't!" she screeched, eyes locking down on mine. "Take care of my baby! Please!"

"No! You will *not* do this to him!" Anger fueled my roars. "You don't get to give up today—not in front of your son, and not in *my* house! Try harder—for him, damn it!"

I saw the resolve the instant it flashed across her quivering face. She was in pain, and an agonized scream ripped from her as I saw fire beat against her back. But for the first time, I also saw in her a mother fighting for what needed to be done.

She stepped out of sight for only a second before her legs shot out, her hips tearing over the jagged glass.

Blood streamed down and her cries grew louder, echoing around us. I dropped down beside Oliver and cradled his head in my lap, covering his exposed ear and shielding his eyes as Natasha squeezed herself out before falling to the ground in a motionless heap.

I lifted Oliver's head and cupped his cheek, forcing him to understand the gravity of my words. "Stay here, and keep your eyes closed. Promise me."

He nodded and snapped his eyes shut.

I ran to Natasha and rolled her unconscious form over in the snow, putting out the flames that clung to her skin. She had burns over most of her body. I couldn't see how bad they were, but from what I could gather, it was gruesome. Her hips were shredded from the glass; deep, jagged tears in her flesh bled profusely.

The sirens were directly behind me now. When I turned

to look, an entire crew of firefighters was rushing my way, rattling off commands to battle the flames.

Paramedics surrounded Natasha while I lifted Oliver, careful of his arm, and carried him away toward the next ambulance that arrived. Scout was at our side, lethargic and covered in ash but seemingly generally okay otherwise. That poor dog had been through so much lately.

Paramedics opened the back of the ambulance, guiding me inside to set Oliver down on the gurney.

His eyes were still closed. I rested my forehead against his. We'd made it—all of us.

"Can I open my eyes now?" he asked, his voice raw and barely a whisper. A paramedic placed an oxygen mask over his mouth.

"Yeah, buddy." I inhaled through my nose, tension dissipating from my muscles. "Open your eyes."

"My mommy?" he croaked, looking up at me.

I squeezed his tiny hand. "They're helping her right now. How's your arm feel?" It was a ridiculous question, as the sight alone answered my question. Not only was it broken, with small abrasions, but I could see burns. They were nothing compared to Natasha's, but definitely still in need of care.

He shook his head, then tugged at the mask to speak. "Heroes don't complain."

Hero? *That's* what he thought he was?

I adjusted the mask back over his face and gave him a stern look.

"You're the bravest boy I know, Oliver. I don't even understand how you made it back up those stairs for Scout, but what you did wasn't heroic. You could have been killed in there." I fought through demanding tears. "I love you so much, and I need you to promise me right now that you will *never* again do something so dangerous."

My tears flowed out with the adrenaline in a heavy stream of anguish.

"Promise," he said, his voice tiny.

I cast my gaze to his, so bright and innocent. Then he added, "I crawled."

"What?" I sniffled, rubbing my hands across my eyes.

He moved the mask once more. "Fireman at school said to crawl. It was scary and dark, and Scout was barking so I could find him. He needed me."

Those pesky tears began their assault again as I cradled him close and kissed his forehead. "You scared me to death and back, but all that matters is that you're safe now."

"You won't tell Daddy, right?" His brows creased with worry. "He'll be mad at me."

Sitting back up, I smiled. "Keep this mask on. And your daddy's not the only one upset with you. He's just going to be the loudest."

"Cassandra!"

That voice comforted parts of me that were still traumatized by the day's events.

"Logan." I pulled off my oxygen mask to speak. Where was he?

"You need to keep this on, miss," the paramedic instructed, but the only thing I needed was out there, looking for me.

"No, I need *him*." I choked on the words, coughing harder. "Logan!"

"Miss, please."

As the mask was forced back over my face, I saw him. He rushed around the ambulance, stopping short when he spotted me.

As if in slow motion, he stared at me for a long moment, then moved his gaze to Oliver. I saw the tension disappear from his shoulders, and then he was coming toward me. I was up and throwing the mask aside instantly, desperate for his arms around me.

Logan's entire body cocooned me in the safety and warmth only it could provide. He held me tightly, his fear shrouding his hard features.

"I'm sorry! I shouldn't have left. I knew something was wrong when I got to Julia's and she wasn't there. I found her at Luke's; her phone was missing. Fuck, I just saw Natasha. She's all…Christ." He shoved back, placing his hands on my face and looking me over. "This is my fault. I should—"

I lunged forward, pressing my lips to his. The kiss was slow and gentle. Tears glistened in his eyes.

When I broke the kiss, I said, "Natasha…is she…"

I couldn't say it aloud. The image of her body burned and mangled flashed in my mind.

He slowed his breathing, inhaling deeply before answering. "She'll survive. I went mad trying to find you. And then I saw them load her into the ambulance…I thought…I thought it was you." His first tear slipped out. "I felt my entire body shut down. I couldn't find Oliver, and the thought of him trapped in that house and you…"

On my tip toes, I kissed both his cheeks, collecting saltwater on my lips. Logan wasn't one to cry, which was a shame given how beautiful he looked in that moment—so open and vulnerable, with no walls separating us.

He continued, inhaling deeply again as his tears ceased. "When I got close enough, I saw one of her wrists handcuffed to the gurney. I knew then it wasn't you…that I still had a chance. They told me Oliver was in this ambulance and I took off, pleading with the universe that you were with him. I couldn't lose—"

"Shhh," I murmured. "It's over. We're safe."

Logan's forehead rested against mine. "Marry me."

The most awkward bubble of a laugh burst from me, despite the scene surrounding us. *He did not just ask me that right now.*

With a heavy-hearted sigh, I closed my eyes and answered, "Call me crazy, but is it too much to ask for a little romance?"

"Romance, huh?"

My tired eyes opened to find his glittering with a love deeper than I'd ever thought possible.

I lifted my head, a smile on my lips. "You need the definition?" I raised a brow.

He gripped my arms and drew me back in, kissing me harder. "No, I think I got it covered," he murmured against my lips before releasing me, his hand scrubbing across his jaw.

"Thank you."

My brows pinched together. "For what?"

"Saving my son's life," he replied, staring over at Oliver lying just behind us.

Swallowing hard, I said, "You need to thank Natasha too. If she hadn't gone in first…" I shook the thought away. "She saved his life."

"She was also the one who put his life in danger to begin with," Logan rebuffed as quickly as the words had flown from my mouth. Anger colored his tight voice. "She'll spend the rest of her pitiful life locked away for what she's done today. I'll make sure of it."

Slowly, I nodded. The woman was dangerous, and the farther away from Oliver she was, the better.

"Good," was all I had to say.

Logan placed one more lingering kiss to the top of my head, then moved around me to climb inside the ambulance with his son.

I watched as Logan hugged Oliver close, speaking quietly to him. Logan peeked up at me and waved his hand for me to climb in as well. When I did, he slid the oxygen mask over my face and held my hand in his while his other held Oliver's.

We made it—all of us. A family.

Oliver lifted his mask just enough to whisper a single sentence to Logan.

"She's my angel too, Daddy."

Epilogue

"How much longer?" I pouted. A shiver surged through me, my body unable to resist shuddering. "It's getting chilly in here."

"I can tell." Logan's eyes landed on my pert nipples, his lips curling up into a wicked smirk. "Just stay still a while longer, sweetheart. "

A while *longer?* It'd been over three hours, and as sexy as the first two were, I was ready to climb either under some blankets or him. Either would work, though I preferred the latter.

"Come on, you have to be close to finished by now," I sulked after a few more minutes.

Logan stared at the canvas before him, entranced by his work, each brush stroke deliberate and thoughtful. It was one of the most gorgeous sights I'd ever witnessed.

I lay sprawled on the couch in his studio. The silk nightie I'd worn in his pool months ago was bunched around my hips, my legs spread just enough to barely reveal what was already his. The strap on one shoulder was down, and my breast peeked out just the slightest. Logan had taken great care to pose me exactly as his vision entailed.

The moment Oliver was out the door and in Julia's car, heading to Blythe's, Logan had been there with something behind his back and smugness in his grin. The last thing I'd expected him to surprise me with was the nightie I'd worn in his pool all those months ago. How he'd come into possession of it when the rest of my house was ash, I didn't know. But that was the thing about Logan: He always kept me guessing.

Since I was waiting for construction to start on my house rebuild, I was staying with Logan for the time being. And when he led me up the stairs and opened the door to his studio, I knew exactly what he had in mind for our weekend alone.

Logan couldn't be happier, but the longer I sat, the stiffer my neck became. Even my legs were weak from my stationary position.

Unable to hold the pose for much longer, I was relieved when Logan set his brush down and slipped out from around his canvas.

"We done?" I asked, reluctant to move until I knew for sure. Recreating the pose wasn't exactly easy the last time I'd gotten up for a bathroom break.

His head shook with one slow movement.

"Oh." I frowned, my composure dwindling.

He moved toward me with easy grace, his face as classically handsome as the first day I'd seen it. Paint streaked his hands, his chest bare and smooth with only a tiny bit of hair.

"Need to reposition me?" I asked, my voice weak as I caught the predatory spark in his bright eyes.

Logan shook his head again, his lips parting in a dazzling smile.

My stomach lit up with only the greediest, most ravenous butterflies that had been dormant with anticipation until that moment.

My tongue skimmed my lips. I peered up at those powerful shoulders I spent every night clinging to, then down to the massive bulge restrained beneath soft white cotton lounge pants.

He stopped at the edge of the couch, his strong thighs inches from my face.

"Thought you could use a break," he said. His voice was low and gravelly, filled with countless innuendos.

I reached my hand out, stroking his length through the fabric. "I could use a little rest," I purred, peeking up to meet his searing gaze.

"You can sleep later." His fingers traced my cheek. "Right now, I'm going to show you every last fantasy that has played through my mind over the past couple hours."

I sat up on my elbows, untying the drawstring at his waist.

"Is that so?" I murmured, freeing his granite cock and caressing him in my hand.

"You lying here like this, allowing me to celebrate every part of you? I don't think it gets much better."

I cupped my hands under the warm weight of him. "I'd beg to differ," I said, sliding my tongue down the length of him.

His mouth fell open with a low growl, hands cradling my head as I bobbed my mouth up and down. My joy at the groans he released was short-lived when Logan grasped my arms abruptly and pulled me up against his chest.

He kissed me hard, his hands weaving through my hair that was down, loose, and wavy—just how he preferred it.

"I'm gonna make love to you over and over again tonight, but first, I want you to see." There was a hint of vulnerability in his words; he didn't sound as confident as I was used to, but he was quick to add, with an assertive tone, "This will be the first of many portraits."

I didn't complain, excited at the thought of posing again for him.

Logan released my hand, still feet away from his work, allowing me to finish the walk toward it on my own. Before I stepped around for the view, I looked back at him.

"I know I'm going to love it," I said, feeling the need to reassure him.

He looked suddenly worried, and almost shy—an expression I rarely saw on Logan. His head tilted to the side, eyes hooded. "I hope so," he said softly.

Unexpectedly nervous, I moved closer. As I stood in front of the masterpiece, a gasp caught in my throat. My hand rose to my lips, and tears welled up in my eyes.

The painting wasn't finished, but what he'd captured thus far was magnificent.

I saw a confident, beautiful woman—nothing like the girl I saw myself as when Logan had first entered my life. Her body was lean and fit, with a subtle curve to the thighs. Her breasts were small but full, matching her proportions.

And then there was her face. It was so relaxed. She was undeniably comfortable in her skin, and only I knew why.

It was because of him—because of his love. For the strength he gave me, and the protection so tangible it bundled me in a warm, cozy shelter where I could be myself, let go, and fly with the man I loved and cherished more than anything else in the world. He saw me like no one else ever could, and he was mine.

I shed a scalding tear. A second was following close behind as I caught the silver band sparkling from her ring finger.

The tears streamed heavier as I lowered my head for a closer look at the delicate band of tiny stones, with a large princess-cut diamond framed in the center. It was simple and classic, but nothing short of exquisite.

When I lifted my head back up, the impact of the painting

having wakened buried emotions within me, I found Logan on one knee with a black box in his hands, open and revealing the exact ring from the painting.

"I told you I'd keep asking, and I will. I'll propose to you every day for the rest of my life if I have to." Tears glistened in his bright eyes. "You're it for me, Cassandra. I'll never want or need for anyone else. You're my angel, sent from above to resurrect the man I no longer believed was inside me. You saved me, and brought joy and love to both me and my son. I told you before, and I'll say it again: I'll never take for granted how incredible you are. And I want to spend the rest of my life proving that to you."

With heavy steps and a pounding heart, I moved around the canvas, my eyes locking on his. He continued, his voice growing stronger and deeper with each word he spoke.

"Cassandra Clarke, will you do me the honor of making me the luckiest man alive by becoming my wife?"

My lip quivered, my sobs unrestrained as my feet skittered across the floor, sending me straight into Logan's open arms. He caught me when I fell into him, his mouth colliding with mine.

Breathless, I broke the kiss, weeping with nothing but exhilaration.

"Yes. Yes, I'll marry you!"

Logan nearly gasped. Was he that worried I'd say no?

"Does that mean you'll make love to me now?" I teased, placing my hands on his shoulders so I could pull back and see the gorgeous face of my future husband.

His lips quirked up in a wicked smirk. "I'm going to make love to you every chance I have until this sexy little body of yours is carrying my child—our child."

My cheeks erupted in flames. A baby? I couldn't deny that even just the thought of it felt right, but I still had a lot of growing up of my own to do before that happened.

"I say we wait on the babies—spend some time with it being just us. Let Oliver adjust to me being around."

He stared at me thoughtfully.

"Why rush? You have all of me now," I murmured, kissing the corner of his mouth.

"And you have me—completely."

"Maybe next year." I leaned forward and placed kisses along his jaw.

"'Next year'," he mimicked, smiling. "Oliver would love a brother…maybe a couple sisters to drive him insane like mine does."

I froze mid-kiss and swallowed, biting down on my bottom lip. Logan's fingers cradled my chin, lifting my gaze to his.

"What is it?" he asked.

Fighting back my laughter, I confessed, "That reminds me: So Julia and I had this bet…"

The End

Not quite ready to say goodbye to Logan and Cassandra just yet? You don't have to.

Angela's currently working on a spin-off series featuring the characters of Harmony.

Questions will be answered and happily-ever-afters will be granted.

Each story is set to be a standalone book, no cliffhangers for those wondering, and both Logan and Cassandra will be secondary characters throughout.

Stay connected by signing up to receive monthly newsletters.

These include New Releases, Sales, Excerpts, Teasers, & more...

Sign-Up Link: http://eepurl.com/WrIKX

About the Author

Angela Graham resides in Tipp City, Ohio with her three beautiful children. She is a *USA Today* bestselling author of the Harmony series, *Inevitable*, *Irreplaceable* and *Indestructible*, as well as a novella, *Indulge*. Collaborating with S.E. Hall, she released two erotic short stories and is currently working on the next.

Connect with the Author

Visit Angela's website at:
www.loveangelagraham.com

Follow Angela on Facebook at:
https://www.facebook.com/angelagraham.author?focus_composer=true&ref_type=bookmark

Find Angela's books at:
http:/www.amazon.com/Angela-Graham/e/B00D3RZ5U2/ref=ntt_athr_dp_pel_1

Find Angela on Twitter at:
https://twitter.com/angelagraham01

Acknowledgments

This journey I've taken over the past year has been nothing short of incredible. I've met so many wonderful and kind people whom I can't imagine not having in my life. To create a story and bring it to life for readers is something I couldn't do without the amazing team surrounding and supporting me.

This book wouldn't be the same without S.E. Hall, my CP. You'll always be the top dog on my team—my favorite quickie partner!

Whitney Baer, where do I start? Over the past year, you've become a close and trusted friend. Nothing will ever change that. Thank you for bringing sanity to my life and allowing me the time to write without worry. I love you for that and much more. I hope you're at my side for many more books and vacations.

To my talented and patient editor, Jen Juneau, who comes in behind me and polishes my words like no one else can. Thank you! It was great to meet you in person, and I hope we can go out for drinks again soon to celebrate another book together.

I am in love with my books' covers, and *Indestructible*'s is one of my favorites thanks to the incredible Sommer Stein. You rock it every time! Thank you for always being only a message away. You truly blow my mind each and every time we work together. There's no way I could've done this without you.

To Kristi Pelton, who pulled me out of a writing funk. Thank you for the honesty and feedback. Can't wait to read your next one!

A huge thank you to Amber Warne for making me smile every time I click open a message from her! Keep those teasers coming...and feel free to share more goodies from your private file anytime.

Vanessa Wallace and Brittney Mears: two unbelievable and kind women I have the honor of knowing and calling friends. I adore you both.

To Jennifer Alumbaugh, Lynne Christie, and Natasha Giagnacovo Rochon: When I open your messages, I know I'll be either grinning, laughing, or crying. You dolls make my days brighter. Thank you for the love and support!

A shout-out to some amazing ladies whom I absolutely adore: Michelle Santos, Chantal Davis, Nikki Costello, Teri Fantastic, Danielle Sanchez, Renee Entress. I can't say thank you enough! I'll be forever grateful for everything you do to support me.

An enormous thank you to my betas and street teamers, and anyone who has every shared a post about or tweeted a link to my books. I appreciate each and every one of you. I may not be around as much to tell you every day, but know that I see what you do for me, and appreciate it more than I can say.

To the entire blogger community...there are not enough words to describe how grateful I am to you all. Without your hard work and dedication to spread the word about my books, I would not be living my dream. Thank you.

The most essential support team I have is my family. To Tommy, I'll always love you and without your support I wouldn't have been able to do this. Thank you for all the long weekends you picked up my slack around the house, and with the kids.

And last but far from the least, to my little darlings William, James, and Tinsley. I love you so much. Every word I write is for you.

While You're Waiting

While you're waiting for more from Angela, be sure to check out S.E. Hall

Facebook—
https://www.facebook.com/S.E.HallAuthorEmerge

Blog—http://www.mysehallauthor.com/

Amazon—http://www.amazon.com/S.E.-Hall/e/B00D0AB9TI

Chapter Three Excerpt from *Pretty Instinct*

By S.E. Hall

After the longest two hours of any of our lives, with suffocating amounts of tension in the air, we finally make it to the rest stop Cami designated. Lucky for her, we'd still been in our homeland of Ohio when she'd lost her shit, so she was able to call someone to meet her a small jaunt down the road. Otherwise, I *would* have offloaded her randomly. At least, I think I would have.

Throwing down his cards in the middle of our four man game of Uno, Conner's up and ready as soon as we stop and he sees a park out the window.

"You didn't say Uno," Rhett teases him as he picks up the scattered cards. "I win."

"Move," Cami barks at Conner, trying to shove past him and knocking her case into his hip as she does so.

"I'm not playing with her," I warn Jarrett in a menacingly low snarl. "Get her the fuck off my bus before you have to alibi my whereabouts at the time of the murder." I'm truly floored, no idea of the deep-rooted venom she'd hidden. And maybe she's just having a *categorically* bad day…but I won't risk her having another one on my bus.

Jarrett hurries to the door, throwing an arm around Conner's shoulders. "Let's scoot back, buddy, give Cami room to get off the bus."

"Where's Cami going?" He looks around, confused. "Cami, where are you going?"

"The fuck away from you!"

Instinctually, Jarrett has Conner moved back already, thank goodness, 'cause I'm done, up with a fist full of her hair and my arm reared back as Rhett chuckles from behind me, his arm squeezing around my waist.

"Almost over," he whispers, his lips brushing the shell of my ear. "Hold it together long enough for her to get off the bus and you never have to worry about her again. Come on." He untangles my fingers from her greasy strands and walks backwards, dragging me with him. "Come sit down with me until she's gone."

I only do so under duress. He holds me down forcefully on his lap, my head falling against his chest. As relieved as I am that the debacle's seconds from being over, it's created a whole new problem. "We have a gig in a few days and no fucking bassist. What're we gonna do?"

"I can play!" Conner raises his hand, eavesdropping from way over there.

Jarrett nudges him with a shoulder and heads to sit down by us, Cami completely unloaded now. Time for our little family to have a meeting, minus Bruce. He'll stay put in his captain's chair, steering clear of any drama.

"You play great, Con." And he did. He was talented, even wrote some songs way back when. "But we need you on tambourine, remember?" Jarrett lovingly reminds him.

Every show, Uncle Bruce watches over Conner, right off

stage, shaking his tambourine like a champ. I feel awful that all he can do now is shake the noisy thing from the wings, but it's too unpredictable to let him on stage, some crowds nicer than others, venues ranging from large and rowdy to small and accommodating. We adjust accordingly.

"That is right." His brow wrinkles. *Sweetness.*

"Don't worry, we'll think of something." I stand, moving to the door, figuring Cami's long gone. "You wanna stretch your legs in the fresh air a minute, Bubs?"

A jaunt in the sun is as much to clear my mind as his. I have no idea what we'll think of, and I'd dragged them all on this misadventure, only to have it now collapsing. Although originally my idea, it's become all Rhett and Jarrett have. Even if we call it quits today, I have Conner and a fallback nest egg, but the boys were ostracized socially and financially from their shitty "family" the minute they'd stepped onboard. Well, officially, anyway; the groundwork of such was laid *long* before. They'd finally given their parents the excuse they needed to justify their douchery at tea parties and such: *"It's okay to shit on our kids because they..."*

So I can't just cancel the gig. It may be no big deal to me—this was never about being discovered or getting signed as the next "big thing" in my eyes—but I suspect it's become exactly that to Rhett and Jarrett.

I need a miracle...preferably one that has some empathy, or at least fakes it with their mouth closed, and can pluck a mean bass.

What started as stretching our legs for a minute turned into an afternoon picnic and a game of Frisbee golf. I'm heading to hole five, a par two (the trash can), cleaning up what's left of our lunch when something, or some*one* rather, catches my eye.

Hello, miracle.

The glint of the sun reflecting off the guitar slung across his back is what first snags my attention, but the favors he's doing that pair of Levis is what's keeping it.

Hell yes, I noticed. How could I not? I am, after all, a healthy twenty-three-year-old woman.

"You thinking what I'm thinking?" Jarrett creeps up behind me, scheming in my ear.

Positive he's not thinking "*I wish I had an hour all my own to let that guy fuck the legs off me,*" I turn my head back to him and attempt undeterred sarcasm. "If my answer to that question is ever yes, feed me lots of fish. Brain food. Not any from Conner's tank, though."

*Which reminds me…*eh, we'll wait for Bubs to mention it.

"Seriously smartass, we gonna stand here and pant 'til he notices us or we gonna go ask him?"

"Ask him *what?*" We both know I'm full of shit—I know exactly what he means. And yes, in a perfect world, this would appear to be divine intervention…guy with guitar conveniently located at same rest stop as band coincidentally in need of a guitar player, but I far from believe in a perfect world. I do, however, let my head fall back for just a moment to take in the clear, endless blue sky and wonder, filled with warmth at the thought. *Good lookin' out, Mom.*

"I can't let a stranger on the bus with Bubs. What if he's a mass murderer?" *What if he's not as pretty on the inside as he is on the outside?*

"Ah, Mama Bear, run him through all the tests. You're careful. And he might say we're crazy and tell us to fuck off. Let's ask before we worry about it."

Biding my time, I chew on the inside of my cheek and

look back, confirming Conner's still tossing the Frisbee happily, Rhett watching him. "You asking or am I?" I sigh, hopefully masking the foreign tingle of anticipation working its way up my battered spine.

"He's hetero, I can tell from here. I say we send in," he flicks a finger back and forth between my boobs, "the big guns."

"Don't lick your lips!" I shove him, mouth agape. "You're like my brother. That's illegal in at least forty states, *and gross*."

"You didn't think it was gross when—"

"Enough." I slap my hand over his mouth hastily. "I'll go, but you stay right here and watch, closely. He makes a move for a weapon, dial 911 *as* you run to rescue me."

"On it." He grins at me, full of victory, a hint of his earlier teasing still lingering in his expression.

Girding my loins, I think, *do women have loins and can they be girded or is that only a guy thing?* Summoning my courage, I move with slow, hesitant steps in the miraculous unknown's direction, reminding myself with each one that it's for the boys, the band, the overall goal of staying the hell out of Sutton. And it is, but I'm kidding myself if I don't admit I wouldn't be this anxious if I was walking up to an ugly man. Or even a kinda good-looking man. *Shallow much, Liz?* Nah, I have no control over biological response.

Almost there now, his head lifts and turns at my approach, connecting eyes as sable brown as thick molasses to my own. He was tummy-turning enough far away. Up close, he's better than photoshopped, a clear-cut case for Guinness Genetics. His lips are full, much plumper than my own, and he has a strong nose and jawline, both very masculine, the latter covered in a dark scruff. His hair is the same rich chestnut as his eyes, not too short, but definitely not too long. "Just fucked" hair (isn't that what they call it?) be damned. He's got "just fucked her and she had to hold on" locks, unruly in the most intricate fashion. The black boots at the end of long, thick legs are scuffed, faded jeans worn, *well*, and the long sleeved black thermal he's wearing? Oh, he *wears* it, or rather, every muscle in his torso holds it up flawlessly.

Bottom line—he's easy to look at.

"Are you a deranged serial killer and/or rapist?"

I like to open subtly.

"No, are you?" His timbre is deep and gravely, sending my vagina subliminal messages. Something along the lines of "yup, you want it." With a voice like that, I'm praying he isn't a chain smoker. To fuzz this perfect picture with the stench of an ever-present cloud of smoke would be one helluva slap in the face of the Almighty creator.

"No," I answer too defensively, this instant, highly unusual attraction frying my staple "too cool to care" attitude that, up until right now, I'd like to think I pull off fabulously. "You any good?" I lean and point to the instrument on his back, brows bowed in questioning antagonism.

"Define good," he deadpans, head down as he pulls the guitar off his back and puts it back in its case.

"Hendrix."

"Not left-handed." He shrugs as he straightens back up and captures my gaze.

"Page."

He laughs, treating me to one seriously enlightening sound, accompanied by the sexiest blindingly white smile. "Then no, not even close to good."

Damn, I should've gone with a mediocre guitarist! Now I've backed myself into a corner, Stranger Danger not giving me anything in the form of segue. Struggling, I shove my hands in my back pockets and rock nervously back and forth on my heels, forced to come up with another revealing yet seemingly aloof question.

"Why do you ask?" he rescues me.

"Our band." I toss my head back toward the bus. "We need a bassist. And since you're hitchhiking, I thought maybe—"

He drops down from his perch on the top edge of the bench and stands, well over six feet of sinister sex appeal stretching out before my eager eyes. "Do you *know* what a hitchhiker is?"

"What?" I shake my head to clear it and take a step back. "Yes, of course."

"You sure about that?" He eats up the steps I'd retreated, placing his body close enough to mine that I can literally *feel* the battle of push and pull between us. "'Cause where I come from, hitchhikers stand *at* the road, where you can see them. It increases their chances of actually landing a ride." His left eyebrow curves up at one end and that same eye, I swear it, twinkles at me. "Seeing as how I'm sitting at the back of a desolate rest stop, I'm either the worst hitchhiker in history," another step closer, "or you're labeling me with the wrong tag."

Some weird sensation creeps up my neck, then my face, ending with a tingle all over my scalp. Confused, I reach up to feel my cheek. *What the hell? Am I blushing?* I had no idea my body was capable of such an act.

Am I a delicate, femininely light blusher or one of those hideous, red as a beet, blotchy kinds? Also, and *most importantly*, what is it with this guy? I don't blush, I certainly don't notice what brand of jeans a guy wears, and…I don't usually enjoy challenging yet intriguing conversations with strangers. In the blip of time I've spent with him, I've morphed into a completely unrecognizable version of myself, one I really don't like…*and I wasn't overly thrilled with the original.* Nothing, no one, ever surprises me in a good way or brings to curious life parts of me I thought were long since dead or didn't exist at all.

Seriously, girls in high school? Complete anomalies. Gushing, blushing, obnoxious freaks of nature. I was never one of those girls and won't allow myself to become one.

"I don't play bass anyway, just dabble on that thing some." He casts a fleeting glance at his case. Close enough that his breath grazes my already heated cheeks, I can clearly see that his pupils have dilated, a sure sign he's fibbing and being modest. *He can play.*

I step back again, beginning to resent him, this may be *vagabond*, for daring to stir my damn *Kool-Aid*. Nine out of ten receptors in my brain, although I have no clue how many a human brain actually has, are screaming at me to tuck and run far, far away. My heartbeat is thumping against its own cage like I just freebased crack and I haven't turned to look for Conner in at least a full five minutes, neglectful and careless.

Yeah, not good. Time to regroup.

I need to come up with a solution that doesn't make my nipples wanna cut glass.

And yet...I shift my eyes right, seeing that Conner is fine, and find myself speaking again as though I didn't just have a back-out plan damn near planned. "Jarrett does. Play bass, I mean. He plays almost anything, and well." My chin juts up and out, pride in my boy not to be tamed as I give him a curt nod. "So if you can hang on guitar, he can switch to bass no problem."

He rubs his chin between thumb and forefinger and considers me, but in a classy, eyes above the neck kinda way. This time the *right* brow lifts in contemplation as he slides his tongue back and forth across that enchanting bottom lip. Women worldwide would pay top dollar for the chance to watch this guy do *anything*, algebra even; *trust me*. I'm cataloguing his habits *strictly* in case he does end up on the bus—left eyebrow up is playful and joking, right brow means serious and analyzing.

"Why don't you let me try this, since you suck at it? Cannon Blackwell, *not* a hitchhiker." He offers his right hand. "And you are?"

"Liz."

A frown line mars his forehead as he awkwardly draws back the hand I didn't shake—no way I'm actually going to risk touching him, as in, his skin, my skin. I'm becoming even more confused about the array of rabid, conflicting emotions stirring within me as the moments pass.

"Do you have a last name, *Liz*?"

Evading his question, I take a deep breath, and let 'er rip. "Here's the deal. I pegged you for a wandering musician, and we need one. You'll have to pass a background check, body search, and piss in a cup for a drug test before you step one foot on my bus. We're not a die-hard, international sensation, just a small band having fun. You split all the money from the gigs with Jarrett and Rhett, less a small cut for Bruce and Conner, and I pay for everything else. In return, you agree not to do drugs, on or off my bus, *ever*. You can do whores, not any of my business, but also, not on the bus. You *can* drink onboard, but never so much that you get sloppy in front of my brother." After a long, loud exhale, I let my shoulders drop, done with the winded, practiced speech I've given before, and take another step back.

"What's the name of the band?" *That's* what he got out of that spiel? Definitely not the usual initial response I get. Most people start asking exactly what shows up on a background check, or what drugs the test picks up, things like that.

"See You Next Tuesday."

His head cocks to the side, a few brown locks falling near

his eye, and he smirks. "Your band is called cu—the uh, c-word?"

"Now did you hear me say the word cunt?" I challenge, twisting my lip in jest.

"Do *you* play, Liz?"

"Why?" I ask, a hint of defiance.

"Well, you're as feisty as you are cute. Not sure I can handle a triple threat. You play too and I may be in trouble." He smiles; well, his mouth does some upturning, mind-fuckery type thing. I'm not exactly sure it'd be considered a smile.

"Sister!" blares through the peaceful afternoon air, and then again, more desperately. "Bethy! Come find me!"

I hold up one finger, silently requesting a minute, and turn, smiling at Conner running toward me, Jarrett right behind him. "Come 'ere, Bubs! I want you to meet someone."

Tell me he's not a genius with super powers—his timing is spot on. I'm on the fence with this guy. No kill us in our sleep vibes or so much as a flinch at my gamut of requirements, he should be an automatic yes. Yet I'm torn, all my hesitancies resting on the scary *good* vibrations he's giving me. I need to continue focusing on what's important, my ace "people reader," who's joining us now, and *not* the ass on the new guy. I find Cannon Blackwell disarming…and quite frankly, it's pissing me off.

"I thought you got lost," Conner pants, habitually throwing his body on and around me, igniting a reminder twinge in my back. "Jarrett! I FOUND HER!"

I wince, dislodging my arm from his deadlock to stick a finger in my ear, wiggling it around to stop the ringing.

"Right behind ya, buddy," Jarrett chuckles in a normal volume. "Good job, though."

"Bethy needs a Bubcuff," Conner states, holding up his wrist.

Jarrett grins at me sideways. "I think you may be right there, Con Man. Liz, do you need a Bubcuff?"

Ever since I was granted custody of Conner, almost a full two years of red tape after I turned eighteen, I'd made him wear what came to be known as the "Bubcuff" any time he's not right beside me. It's nothing more than a thick, brown leather wristband, but Conner thinks it's magic and sends me a signal if he gets too far from whomever I've entrusted him with.

I do what I have to do. You lose your brother, who faces certain challenges, in the middle of a carnival and then come talk to me. And in my defense, Bubs is actually the one who first suggested I was able to find him because of the bracelet. I just didn't correct him.

"I wasn't lost, Bubs. Jarrett knew where I was the whole time, but thanks for finding me. I should have told you where I was going too. Can I have a *soft* hug?" I reach my arms out, hoping he caught my specific request.

Thankfully, he did, wrapping him arms around me half as tight as normal, kissing my forehead as he pulls back. "Soft enough, Bethy?"

Eaten up with happy and the goofy grin to match, I nod my head. "Perfect. Now, there's someone I want you to meet."

When I turn Conner by the arm, Cannon's watching us with, hmmm, I don't know him well enough yet to say with what exactly. But none of my intuitive hackles go up, so it's not anything offensive, nothing I'm usually braced for when introducing someone to my brother for the first time.

"Conner, this is Cannon Blackwell. He plays—"

"He almost has my same name!" I'm interrupted with a shout.

"You're right, they do sound a lot alike, but I wasn't done, bud."

He ducks his head. "Sorry, Sister."

I tilt his chin with my finger, not specifically acknowledging the pouting as the doctors advised me, and continue on. "He plays the guitar and I was talking to him about maybe giving the band a try. Cannon," I shift my body, opening my stance to include them both, "this is my big brother, Conner. He plays the tambourine for us."

"I'm the second other boss of the band." Con steps forward, puffing out his chest.

What Cannon does next, reflexively, not only casts away any doubts that may have still been lingering in the back of my head, but also testifies largely toward my preliminary sizing up of his character. "It's nice to meet you, Conner." His hand's already extended. "What kind of music does your band play?"

I sneak a glance at Jarrett to find he's already looking at me, wearing a "told ya so" smile on his lips. *Cannon's in with him.*

"Not my sister's music. She won't let us. We play Rhett's songs, and other people's. It's called Al, At—"

I place a hand on Conner's back, helping out a little. "Think Evanescence has a baby with City & Colour. We call it Alternatwang. Jarrett and I wanna rock, but Rhett writes the songs and *should* have been born the gritty Everly Brother, so we compromise."

He nods, surprisingly not needing further explanation on our genre. "So, Conner, I'm sittin' here, minding my own business, when your sassy sister comes over and asks me to jump on a bus full of strangers. Sounds crazy to me. I'm hoping maybe you can tell me why I should join your band?"

"Where are you going?" Conner asks him.

He bounces his shoulders and looks off in the distance. "No idea," he barely wisps out.

"Do you like Pez?"

Cannon turns back to him slowly, an amused spark of interest lifting *both* brows, which I note to mean "you've pleasantly surprised me." "Sure, who doesn't like Pez?"

"I got a bunch on the bus, let's go!" Conner yells, grabbing Jarrett's and my hands, dragging us back the way we came. "Come on, Cannon Blackwell, we're heading out! Woo woo!" His train noise carries off on the breeze.

Made in the USA
Charleston, SC
09 November 2014